Into the Darkness

by brandon spacey

Into the Darkness

by brandon spacey

Second Edition

Cover art by brandon spacey.
Thank you to Kiera, the cover model.

Novels by brandon spacey

Callie Simmons Novels

book 1: Midnight's Park
book 2: Resurrecting Mars
book 3: Into the Darkness
book 4: Red Bell

Shawn Stedwin Novels

book 1: A Flutter in the Window
book 2: Hello, World

Standalone Novels

Shedding Sadness
Chasing Comets

For Laynie, who never feared the darkness.

CHAPTER 1

Thevi Watson sat staring into the mirror. Her pale green eyes twitched as she studied the mascara she had just applied. She furled her lips and tried some faces, opening her eyes wide, smiling wildly, then frowning. She then spun on the squeaky stool and leaned forward, her hands gripping the seat between her legs. "I don't know. What do you think?"

Callie shook her head. "You know what I think, darling. I think it looks gorgeous." She pronounced it 'garjus'. "It makes you look dark and mysterious."

Thevi twisted her mouth and shook her head, then spun back to face the mirror again. "Yeah, but I'm not mysterious. And I'm sure as shit not dark."

Callie shrugged and leaned forward, putting her elbows on her knees, and rested her chin on her hand, nails clicking against her perfect white teeth. "You need to try something new, TJ. Open your mind and the world will follow!" The J in her pet name came from her maiden name, Jackson. Callie had introduced her to Walter several years before, and he had swept her up, making her a Watson after two years of courtship. The J stuck around though.

Thevi sighed again, then began removing the dark raccoon's eyes with a mineral-oil-soaked cotton ball. "Nope. I can't get there. I'll just go plain like always."

Callie made a face, then sighed herself. "Fine. You know that works too. You're naturally beautiful."

Thevi spun around to face Callie again, one eye still darkened with the thick makeup. "You really think so? I mean, I know you've told me so many times before," she said, looking up to illustrate the depth of the statement, "But I just see plain. When I look at myself, I see plain."

"When you look at yourself you see a plane?" Callie joked, frowning.

"Yeah. Exactly," Thevi said, missing it entirely.

"Well, plain works for you. Plain and simple. But you know what?" Callie said, standing up and crossing the rug to meet Thevi on the stool. She ran her finger across Thevi's forehead, pulling her hair off her face and back behind her ear. "Your facial structure, and – well, just you in general – are nowhere close to plain. You're so far from being *plain* it's ridiculous. Look at me."

Callie leaned into the mirror, holding onto Thevi's shoulder. She began making faces like Thevi had made a minute before. "*This* is plain."

Thevi laughed out loud. "Yeah, whatever. You're stunning, Callie Simmons."

Callie didn't respond. She just kept making silly faces in the mirror. "Does it look good when I do this?" she said. She made a face like a monkey, stretching her mouth as low on her face as she could get it.

Thevi laughed again and stood up, leaning against the vanity table to join Callie in the mirror. "Yeah. Go like that!"

Callie stood up straight and met Thevi's eyes in the mirror. "Seriously. Before I met Chris, I hadn't had a date in three years. How stunning can I really be?"

Thevi looked at her again. "Baby, you have that Chinese porcelain doll thing going on. You're exotic!" Thevi now ran her fingers behind Callie's ears, pulling her hair back, standing very close to her.

"I look Chinese?

"Ha. Ha. You know what I mean."

"Whatever. I'm just a simple, plain-faced bimbo. I'm not unhappy with the way I look. I just... I just think..." she frowned again.

Thevi ran her thumbs across Callie's cheeks, looking deep into her eyes. "If I were a man I would kiss you so hard right now."

Callie laughed out loud. "If I were a man, I'd let you!" she said, then stopped short, twisting her mouth. "Wait. No, because you'd be a man too. Never mind..." She laughed again. But Thevi did not. Thevi was still gently brushing her cheeks and lips with soft fingers, staring at Callie's thick lips as if she were seriously entertaining the thought of kissing her. Callie's smile finally faded and she stood still, letting Thevi fondle her face. It was very sensual, yet at the same time, secure. Callie did not feel threatened by it at all. She had known Thevi for almost fifteen years, and had come to trust her in everything. They were remarkably close, and if Thevi felt like she needed to molest Callie, Callie knew there was probably some pragmatic reason for it.

Several years ago, Callie had introduced Thevi to Walter, her best guy-friend, and almost before she knew what happened, Thevi and Walter were married. Callie was still waiting for hers though. Chris Bennett had proposed, but they had not yet waited their standard year before marriage.

Thevi's mouth was slightly open as she watched her own fingers running over Callie's face. She closed Callie's eyes and began running her fingers down the sides of her cheeks very lightly, just barely touching Callie's skin with her fingernails. Callie's mouth opened slightly and she breathed in deeply. Then Thevi ran her thumbs over Callie's top lip again, and then touched her tongue. Callie opened her mouth a little wider, but kept her eyes closed, as Thevi's hands had instructed her to.

Thevi's thumb tasted weakly like rubbing alcohol. Callie found herself flooding with chills, all down her spine and legs. She was consumed by this seemingly very conspicuously erotic experience, but believed there was still some exterior reason for Thevi's actions. She did not think Thevi wanted to have sex with her. Neither of them had ever had any interest in experimenting, or finding out about their own side.

Thevi finally pulled her thumb out of Callie's mouth and put it in her own, then back into Callie's again. Callie closed her mouth around it and tasted it fervently.

"Uh, do I have time to grab the video camera before you get started?"

They both jumped and stepped back, hurriedly trying to hide their intimate encounter.

"Darn it, Walter!" Callie said, feeling her face flood. "Shouldn't you knock?"

"Whoa, Calstar! Such language!"

Thevi stood staring at him, arms crossed, leaning back against the vanity. A faint smile threatened her lips.

"Seriously, dude," Callie said. She turned and tried to busy herself with some objects on the counter. Walter shook his head, smiling.

"Well if you gals are going to get after it, I want to be a part of it."

"Of course you would, Walt."

Thevi smiled. "We haven't quite gotten there, babe. Callie here was just telling me I need to get used to makeup."

"Well I'm liking the black-eye look," Walter said, approaching her.

Thevi frowned, then spun back to the mirror. "Oh shit!" He grabbed her hips from behind and stood there staring at her in the mirror. Callie slapped his shoulder.

"You're such a pig."

"No, I'm such a man," he corrected, then assessed Callie from neck to waist and back.

She glanced down and noticed two very vivid bumps in her shirt where her body had responded obviously to Thevi's earlier gesture. She crossed her arms to cover up the evidence.

"It's okay, I already saw 'em, Callie," Walter said, returning his gaze to the mirror. "You have beautiful tits."

Callie blushed at that. "Uggh! Will you stop it!" she said, and stormed out of the room.

Thevi eyed him in the mirror. "You two just need to screw and get it over with."

"Nope. All yours, babe. Besides, if it were going to happen with Cal, it would have happened many eons ago." He leaned over and kissed her on the back.

"So are you almost ready, or what?"

Thevi sighed. "Well I have a decision to make. Either remove the makeup from this eye, or re-apply it to the other." She stood up and turned to face him, turning easily in his arms. She rested her hands on his hips, mirroring his posture. She was now nose-to-nose with him. She pushed forward and kissed his lips lightly, staring wild-eyed at him through the half-finished makeup.

"What do you think, Dub Dub?" she said, trying a sexy face.

"I don't know. I've never seen you wear makeup out of the house." He shrugged. "Surprise me." He kissed her again, then turned to leave the room. "But hurry the fuck up. The band starts in an hour."

With Walter out of the room, Callie had returned. As they dressed, Callie continued trying to talk Thevi into wearing some makeup. Since tonight was a special night, Callie thought it would be a good time to shock Walter with it. Like a stun gun, she had said. In the end, Thevi had finally given in and put the mascara back on. She looked like a movie star to Callie, but was fidgety and nervous about it for some reason.

⌘   ⌘   ⌘

The phone was ringing, but Codi could not hear it. She had her ear buds in. Her phone, tucked into her back pocket, was running a music app from which she blasted One Last Orbit into her head like musical shrapnel, while dutifully pulling her belongings from the cardboard boxes and placing them on shelves where they belonged.

Codi was legally blind, so she did most of it by feel, though she could see blurred shapes and colors through her powerful glasses. She'd had lasik and ocular surgery several times in the last few years in an effort to correct the deterioration of her worsening eyesight. Soon, she knew, she would be completely blind, and left to the devices of her other four senses, feeling and listening her way around a dark world. But at least she could hear her music. She had tried to take solace in that sentiment when the opticians had told her that blindness was eventually inevitable. Macular degeneration was what they had called it. And typically it did not happen until someone's fifties. Codi was twenty-four.

As she emptied a box, she flipped it over and sliced the tape on the bottom with a pocket razor, then broke it down and stacked it neatly in the corner, where the pile was growing slowly but steadily. She had been working all morning and it was time for a break. Codi stood with her hands in her pockets, peering around the room at the stacks of boxes remaining. At one time she had been able to see perfectly, and all this stuff seemed meaningful. What would she do with collections and trinkets and photo albums when she could no longer see them?   What purpose were photographic memories if the only eyes they meant something to could no longer gaze upon them? It saddened her, but she maintained. If the best surgeons could not fix her, she had to accept it as fate – something she had once not believed in.

Codi reached into her back pocket and fingered the pause button on her music player, then popped the buds out of her ears and made her way to the kitchen. She sat on the hard wooden chair beside the tiny nook table and looked out the window at the bright, confusing day outside. A tall glass of tea stood sweating on the table, balanced precariously on a small silver coaster she could not see well. Shiny objects played special tricks with her vision, and were almost indiscernible against the monotonous backgrounds of other blurred things. Shiny objects to her looked like bright spots of light with no hard edges and no definition within.

She sipped from her tea and carefully returned it to the coaster, using her free hand to ensure they lined up when she set the glass down. Curling her mouth and biting her lip, Codi stared out the window, wondering what it would be like when she couldn't see at all. It was a wonder she found herself fondling more and more often, trying to prepare herself for the ultimate, untimely darkness. Would she be able to live alone, or would she need a caretaker to move in with her? She had just moved in with her boyfriend, Tim, but he could not be there all the time. He had his own job. Not to mention his mood swings and temper outbursts. Codi was taking it on good faith that he would be better to her. He had been attending anger-management therapy, but – against the advice of her friends back home – Codi had made the huge step of faith moving to another town and into his apartment. What if that turned out not to be permanent? What if his mood finally went violent? Where would she go? She had no real source of income anymore. She had been relying on Tim as he promised that she wouldn't need to work. Codi knew other blind people made it on their own, but would she be one of them? She did not feel like she had a very good grasp on the lifestyle yet, and reckoned she wouldn't know until well after it had finally happened. She would have to get used to it. She had been studying Braille in preparation for the coming darkness, but was having a hard time with it.

The phone rang again and she turned in her chair, feeling around the counter behind her until she knocked it off the base, where it clunked down and bounced against the ceramic tile floor with a plastic racket. She traced the cord down with her fingers and picked the receiver up, then spoke into it in a soft, tired voice.

"Hello, good afternoon," she said.

"Hello, is this Codi?" the voice said.

"Mm hmm, it sure is," she said.

"Hi Codi. This is Phyllis at the optometry clinic. Do you have a moment?"

"Certainly!" Codi said. Any call from the clinic was potentially good news, and excited her. She took another sip of her tea, then set it awkwardly back on the coaster, where she missed by half. The tea glass tipped and clunked down onto the table, pouring sixteen ounces of cold liquid right onto her lap. She squinted and breathed in sharply, but kept quiet.

"Good. I see you have an appointment Friday with Doctor Steadman, but I was calling to reschedule it with you."

"Ah, okay, sure, that would be fine, Phyllis. Can you tell me why? I've been waiting for this appointment for quite a while..." she said and stood up, trying to escape the burning cold against her thighs. Her jeans were soaked as if she had wet herself.

"Well, there's been an unfortunate tragedy. Doctor Steadman passed away last week."

Codi stopped and covered her mouth with her hand, inhaling sharply. "Oh my God! How did that happen? I thought she was in perfect health!"

Phyllis held the air for a moment before she finally spoke again, a slight tinge of sadness in her words. "We're not sure what the cause of death is yet. For now, we are moving all her appointments to Dr. Goff, but he's booked out for a couple of months due to the workload. There may come an opening if we find a replacement soon, and we will certainly let you know if that happens."

"Oh no! Okay. Well, do what you need to do," Codi said. She stood wide-eyed and shocked, frozen in her position with soaked jeans cooling her legs.

"Thank you for your patience. I'm very sorry for the inconvenience, and the extra wait. Anyway, I know you were scheduled for a procedure Friday morning, but we're going to have to push that back to next month. Can you come in sometime around the 20th of February or so?" Phyllis said.

"That should be fine. I can't check my schedule right now because I haven't unpacked my computer, but if you could pencil me in on that date, that would be great." Codi pulled at her lip and stared at nothing several feet in front of her. Her range was terribly short, so she could not see anything with any kind of clarity unless it was directly in front of her face.

"Okay, I'll do that. Thank you again for your patience, Ms. Cohl. We'll see you Monday morning, February 20th then."

Codi rang off and hung up the phone, then crept through the new apartment to her bedroom to find some dry jeans.

⌘   ⌘   ⌘

Chris Bennett and Walter Watson sat on the couch, watching the last episode of the *Western Wagons* marathon, drinking Red Stripe beer and waiting for the women to finish getting ready. They had missed most of the other episodes, but were able to tune in to catch the last one, vowing not to miss the second season marathon, which would be showing next weekend. It was late January, and network television had not yet started their regular seasons – all to Chris's and Walter's benefit.

"So are they always like this when they're together?" Chris asked Walter, turning to look at him.

Walter met his gaze with a tired look and nodded his head, rolling his eyes. "Thevi continually thinks she needs to try to start wearing makeup, then changes her mind at the last minute. Then she changes it again several more times before we're ever able to leave the house. It's ridiculous."

Chris laughed. "Always late then, huh?"

Walter nodded again. "Callie only compounds the problem. She tries to talk her into it every time she takes it off."

"Oh, so Thevi actually puts it on then takes it back off?"

"Dude, she's gone through several tubes of mascara this month. And she has yet to leave the house wearing any," Walter said.

Chris and Callie had been dating for a year or so, but had just recently moved in together. He had been working a night shift and only just recently moved to days. He had, therefore, not gotten to be part of Callie's ring of friends very much yet. Now that he was working the hours of a normal person, they had begun going out as couples, double-dates and having company over. It was a definite change for him.

Chris stood up, pulling his jeans up, and took the last swig of his beer. "Want another one?"

Walter looked at his bottle, then drained it. "Yeah, man."

Chris went into the kitchen to get two more bottles, and the phone rang. "Hello?" he said, picking up the receiver over the bar.

"Callie Simmons, please."

"Sure. Wait." Chris put the mouthpiece against his chest. "Honey! Phone!" After waiting a few seconds, he set the phone down and headed back to the master bedroom, where the girls were getting ready. He knocked and waited for an answer. After a moment, Callie poked her head out.

"What. Do not tell me to hurry up."

Chris reached up and pinched her nose. "I wouldn't dare. The phone's for you." Callie was about to close the door, but Chris stopped it. "Hey, is Thev almost ready, though?"

Callie gave him a mean glare, then shut the door in his face.

After fetching two fresh beers from the kitchen, Chris returned to his seat on the couch. "It's too fuckin' bad this is the last episode of the day," he said to Walter.

"Still not ready, huh?"

Chris rolled his eyes and shook his head this time. "Hey, it ain't my woman."

"Oh, you don't know the half of it," Walter replied.

After ten more minutes, Callie came out of the bedroom and stood directly in front of Chris, her knees mingling with his between the coffee table and the couch. She took one of his hands as she stood there, but looked at Walter.

"Do you know anything about some underwater project, Walt?" Callie asked.

He looked up at her. "No."

"You'll never guess who that was on the phone just now," she said, throwing a thumb over her shoulder.

"Matt Minus?"

"Uh, okay. Well, yeah. Okay, so yeah… You guessed it, but, um, do you know what he wanted? How the heck did you know?"

"Well you said I would never guess. Every time you've ever said that, it's been Minus."

Callie rolled her eyes up and began twirling her hair with her finger. "Okay. Whatever. So can you guess what he wanted?"

"Uh, some underwater project?" Walter said, staring levelly at her.

"Okay, stop it! You're scaring me!"

Walter looked at Chris, then back up at Callie. "You know, Callie, that's why I like you. I'm never quite sure if you're faking it or not." Walter sighed, then said, "So what did he want?"

"Well he wants to meet me for lunch tomorrow. Apparently he's seeking my help with some new underwater project or something."

Walter shook his head, then returned his gaze to the television.

Chris squeezed her hand, so she looked down at him. "What underwater project? And who the hell is Minus?"

"We used to work for him at Royal," Walter said sideways.

"What is he calling you for then?" Chris said.

"Because, dummy, I get shoot done!"

"Callie, Goddammit! You can't use shoot in place of shit," Walter said loudly, pointing all the fingers of his right hand at her. "Shoot is a verb, or an interjection by itself. It's not a noun, not ever."

Callie dived onto Walter, slapping at him and trying to pinch his earlobes. Walter had her by the hands though, and quickly wrestled her to a seat between the two men and started tickling her on the sides of her waist. She laughed and kicked like a maniac, almost knocking the beers off the table.

"You better get your bitch under control, Chris!" Walter said.

"Get over here, gangsta," Chris said, grabbing her by the waist and pulling her up on top of him, caging her in with his arms.

"Yeah, that's what I thought!" Callie shouted at Walter. "I knew you were too scared to take me on, chicken butt."

"I quiver with fear at the very sight of you, blond waif."

Callie sat staring at Walter for a moment, a frown crossing her brow. "Chris, what does that mean? A waif is a skinny girl, right?"

"Yes."

"Oh, well, thank you, dahling," she said, flipping her hair back.

"Uh, it's not really a desirable moniker, Cal. It's someone so skinny she looks needy and undernourished."

Callie stuck her tongue out and blew at Walter, spitting all over Chris's arm in the process. "Let me up. I need to get up."

Chris grabbed her by the rump and pushed her to a stand in front of him, then wiped his arm on his t-shirt. Callie straightened her skirt and turned around. "So anyway, you want to roll with me up there tomorrow, Walt?" she said, acting like she was turning a steering wheel.

"Yeah, sure. I haven't seen Minus in a couple of years."

"Can I come, too?" Chris said, feeling left out.

"No," Walter and Callie said simultaneously.

"No offense, dude. He's not a people person. You think you feel left out by not going, you have no idea. It's worse in person if you don't know him," Walter said. He then looked up at Callie again. "Is he up here for good now?"

Callie shrugged and furled her lips. *I don't care enough to have asked.* "He's lived here for a couple of years. You never see him at work, Walter?"

"Callie, that office building is thirty-three stories. A couple thousand people work there." He took a sip of his beer, then added, "So is my wife ready yet or not? Good God. You two have been in there for almost three hours."

"Hey, Walt, you know where you can stick it?" she said, then turned on her heel and tried to strut out of the room. However, the coffee table got in the way, so she tripped and stumbled, gracefully swinging through the room like a drunken sailor on his first port of call.

CHAPTER 2

As Codi finished unpacking the last of the boxes, she stood and stretched her back, looking around the small apartment. She heard the key turn in the front door, then it swung open. Shortly, a blurry figure appeared in the doorway.

"Hey, babe," it said.

"Hi!" Codi said, making her way quickly across the room, hands on the walls, until she found herself in Tim's embrace.

"You finished unpacking yet?" he said.

"Yup. Just got done this very minute," she said, leaning her head against his chest. Tim was a foot taller than Codi, standing at six-two, but thin as a rail. He rubbed her back for a moment, then kissed her on the top of the head.

"Good, good. So you hungry?" he said.

Codi looked up at him, trying to discern his structured face in the low light of the hallway. "Yes sir. I am."

"How about seafood?" Tim said.

"You had me at hello, babe," she said.

Tim led Codi to the car, holding her arm as she fumbled down the stairs and into the parking lot. As he helped her into the car, her vision blinked out briefly, scaring her before it returned.

"It happened again, Tim," she said as he slipped into the driver seat.

"What, it went dark again?" he said.

"Uh huh. It's so scary when it happens. Sometimes it lasts a minute or so, and I always wonder if that will be it. If this will be the time it doesn't come back."

"Yeah, I know, babe. Don't you have an appointment with the doctor this week?"

Tim started the car and pulled out of the parking space.

"It got canceled. The office lady called me this morning and said Dr. Steadman passed away Tuesday."

"What the hell? Are you serious?"

Codi nodded. "Yeah. It was going to be the appointment where she did more shock therapy on my nerve. It got pushed back to February 20th."

"Well, do we need to find you another doctor?"

"No, then I would have to start all over. She's scheduling me with Dr. Goff in the same office, but I'm just crestfallen. At least Dr. Steadman knew everything that was going on with me."

Tim shook his head. "I'm sorry, babe," he said, stroking the back of her head.

"I'm just so scared, Tim," Codi said, leaning over to lay her head on his lap as he drove.

"I know. I am too. I'm scared too, Codi."

Callie pulled to the curb in front of Walter's house to pick him up. It was an hour before they were supposed to meet Minus for lunch. As she skipped up to the front door, a small dog ran around from the side of the house, yipping and yapping at her, wagging its tail. "Hey, Fotchie! Come here, gorgeous," Callie said, squatting down to pick up the Jack Russell. The dog jumped up into her arms and licked her face with reckless fervor, and Callie knocked on the front door.

After a few moments, Thevi swung it open, wearing nothing but a flimsy tank top and a pair of Walter's boxer shorts. "Good morning, my lady," she said, swinging her hand into the entry hall as if to offer Callie the house.

"Hello, love. Did I catch you guys playing?" Callie said, stopping to kiss Thevi on the cheek. She then stooped to set the dog down on the tile, where it clicked away excitedly.

"No, no, I'm just about to get dressed. We just got up."

"What in the world? How can you sleep this late? It's almost eleven!" Callie said, raising her shades to the top of her head.

"Oh, honey, when we got home last night, Dub Dub wouldn't stay off of me," Thevi said, pushing the heavy door closed. Callie could hear the sound of Ray Charles playing loudly from the turntable in the living room.

"You two are like newlyweds," Callie said. "So is he ready? We have to leave pretty quick."

"Yeah. He's in the game room playing with his trains."

"Okay, cool" Callie said. Thevi disappeared down the hall towards the bedroom. Callie stepped down onto the wooden floor of the game room. At the back of the house, this room was large and spacious but well decorated. The walls were covered with posters of pretty rock stars like Gwen Stefani, and Tanis of One Last Orbit. There were also movie posters and tin signs. This is where the dart board was. This was where Walter's life was, as he liked to say. He had built a bar in one end of the room, at the end of which stood a beer fridge with band and beer brewery stickers all over it. In one corner of the room was a bookshelf loaded with board and table top games, right next to a shelf wall that contained all iterations of twisty puzzles from Rubik's Cubes to every other shape and size imaginable. On this shelf wall also stood a small treasure chest full of metal pirate coins and fake jewels. Walter, ever against growing up, kept all his toys and life passions in this room. Callie approached him from behind as he stood bending over a large table filled with miniature buildings and trees, railroad tracks and roads. He was fiddling with a piece of the track, and concentrating very intently on it.

As she sneaked up behind him, he said, "Hello, Callie."

She snapped her fingers and joined him beside the table, squatting to his level. "What's up, sugar?"

"Nothin." He turned his head to give her a quick kiss on the lips, then returned his attention to the track. "Damn thing keeps derailing right here. But only," he said, turning to her and raising one finger in the air, "when there are more than five cars behind the engine."

"Well run it with five cars then, dorky goof."

"Callie. You don't understand. The whole model train experience is based upon realism." He stood and walked around to the other side of the table, spreading his hands as he spoke. "If you run it with five cars, it's not real. No train would ever pull such a small load in real life. The cost would outweigh the benefits."

Callie rolled her eyes. "Oh yeah. I forgot this was real."

"Honey. Just stick with your clowns and physics books, okay?" Walter said, picking up the controller.

She stuck her tongue out at him and crossed her arms. Walter turned on the train and watched tentatively as the long train circled the track, and once again derailed at the bad piece of track. Callie laughed out loud.

"Man, you really don't know how to appreciate a hobby, do you?"

"Nope. Not wired for it," she said, looking up at him. "You know I have to be doing something productive, Walt. Why don't you just replace that one piece of track?"

Walter frowned at her. "Look at it! It runs underneath that mountain. It's a long section, and I'd have to rip up half the table just to get to it." He turned the power off and set the controller back on the table, then came back around to stand next to Callie. "What time do we have to be there?"

Callie looked at her wrist, where there was no watch, and said, "About forty-five minutes."

"All right. Let me grab my coat and pinch the wife's boobies."

"Men," Callie said, and bent to scratch Fotchie again, who was licking at her ankles. "Yeah, sugar, you're not really a man, so you don't count. You know I'll always wuv woo, yes I will."

After a few minutes, Walter reemerged from the bedroom and slung his coat on. "Let's go."

As they drove, Walter talked endlessly about model trains, and how selecting the right hobby could take one's mind off the stresses and grinds of life in the daily mill of work. Callie mostly said, "Hmm" and "Is that right?" and nodded her head a lot. When they finally pulled into the parking lot of the Broken Anchor and she shut the car off, she turned to look at Walter, who was staring at her.

"You didn't hear a word I said, did you?"

"Of course I did, donkey butt. I just didn't care," she said, patting his leg, then getting out of the car.

"Women."

The Broken Anchor, despite its relaxed name, served the best lobster in Neptune City. Some people claimed it was the best in all of New Jersey. The Anchor also belied its name in that it catered an almost formal atmosphere. The wait staff wore formal wear and served wine against an elegant backdrop of light rock and occasional live bands playing everything from Elton John to the Commodores, and Ray Charles to Frank Sinatra. Patrons were free to dress as they pleased, and often came in wearing sandals and swimsuits, but the class of the establishment was never in doubt. The Anchor sat on the bay overlooking the cove, and was almost constantly packed with people.

As they entered the dark foyer of the restaurant, Callie smiled at the maitre d' and said, "Hi. We have a reservation under Minus, please?"

The man raised his eyebrows and smiled, then grabbed two menus and led them back to a table by a large window where they could see the water. "Thank you," Callie said as she pulled a seat out. "Oh my gosh, it's too early for a view this gorgeous, Walter," she said before setting her purse on the table and shaking hands with Minus.

"Walter Watson. How the hell are you?" said Minus.

Walter shook his small hand and took a seat. "Not bad, Matt. I've only one complaint, and you'd probably rather not hear it."

"Right you probably are." Matt Minus leaned back in his chair and set a curious smile on his face. "So Walter, you went and got married. And Callie, you're engaged, right? But not married – or engaged – to each other."

Callie shook her head and furled her mouth. "Nope. Chris and I are planning to be married next fall."

"Nice. So why the hell didn't you just marry each other?" he said.

Walter looked over at Callie, then back at Matt. "Excuse me, have you fucking met her?"

"Walter!" she said, slapping his shoulder. She then leaned into the table and spoke in a low voice. "Minus, he married my friend, Thevi. He had to have a redhead."

Walter furled his lips and nodded. "Yeah, it's that simple. That truly is all there is to it, dude."

Minus snorted, then pulled a cigarette out of his shirt pocket. He wore an appropriate Hawaiian shirt, having skipped the top two buttons and allowing his dark chest hair to make an appearance. A large gold chain hung round his neck and his receding, wiry black hair was cropped close to his head. He wore thick-rimmed Costello specs and had two days' worth of beard on his face. He looked to Callie like he had been sitting on a beach for the last week.

"Can I get one of them from you, chief?" Walter said.

"Ummm, I'm gonna tell Thevi!" Callie said, widening her eyes.

Walter looked over at her and said, "You tell Thevi, and I'll buy Chris a case of Old Lantern." Minus smirked at the mention of the stout beer and handed him the pack of Bald Eagles and his Zippo. Walter pulled one out of the pack and lit it, breathing in deeply, leaning his head back. "Oh, so good."

"Okay, you win," Callie said. "But you're going to stink like smoky cigarettes when you get home." Callie knew if Walter bought Chris a case of Old Lantern, Chris would drink them. Probably several nights in a row. And the nights after he had drunk Lantern, she was the one who suffered. He would pass gas the whole time they were together. And though Callie and Chris did not sleep together, it would almost be intolerable for her to be around him at all.

"Well, we'll just have to take the top down then, won't we?"

Callie shrugged. She was losing this battle from all angles. A waiter approached and set two long-stemmed glasses of ice water on the table, then asked if they wanted any of the Chianti.

Walter turned to Minus and said, "You haven't told him to leave the bottle yet?"

Minus nodded at the waiter and waved him away.

"Well you're quiet today, mister Matt," Callie said, pulling her hair back.

"Just watching you two act like a married couple is enough entertainment to keep me from needing to talk."

Walter ignored the comment, looking instead out the window and concentrating on his smoke. Callie shook her head though. She loved being with Walter, and people always assumed they were married because they got on so well. But they had never been intimate. She had always loved him like a brother. "Well maybe we're married in a different universe," she finally said.

"Yeah, maybe one where you have a little bit bigger boobs," Walter said, looking over at her.

"Uh! Or maybe one where you actually have balls, Walter."

"Oooh, sassy. I like it when you talk dirty, little lady," he said. Minus just looked on, a bemused smile on his face.

"Okay," Callie said, slapping her hand lightly on the table. "Why are we here?"

The server set down two more long-stemmed glasses and filled them with the dry red. He then set the bottle on the table and took their orders. After they had finished ordering, the waiter walked away, and Callie slapped the table again.

"Okay. So *now* tell us why we're here."

Minus shrugged. "I don't know why the hell he's here. You invited him."

"No. Me and you. Why are me and you here? Smarty pants."

Minus leaned forward and clasped his hands on the table. He was suddenly serious.

"Callie, have you ever heard of the Bloop?"

"The bloop?" she said, frowning. "No."

"Walter?"

Walter shook his head, staring at the ash on his cigarette. Callie thought he was enjoying it a little too much, and suddenly worried that he would start smoking again, breaking his vow to Thevi.

"In the mid-nineties, the National Oceanic and Atmospheric Administration picked up some sounds in the ocean," Matt said, tapping his smoke on the rim of the ashtray. Callie watched him, only partly interested so far.

"Some sounds?" Walter said, looking up.

"Yeah. Back in the seventies, the U.S. set up some microphones about three miles deep in the sea in several different locations. They used multiple microphones so they could track the location and movement of Soviet submarines during the Cold War."

"Got ya," Callie said, nodding.

"Three miles deep?" Walter said.

Matt looked at him. "Yeah. So NOAA picks up some sounds in the mid-nineties. They triangulated the location of them with these mikes. When the sound is sped up sixteen times, it sounds, literally, like *bloop*."

"Bloop!" Callie said, smiling. "That's cute!"

Minus looked at her with a raised eyebrow.

"Hang on a second," Walter said, waving his cigarette over the table. "You had to speed it up sixteen times to hear it?"

"Well I didn't. But yeah. For it to sound like anything recognizable, they sped it up. At normal speed, it's just a long, drawn out vibration that increases in pitch over the span of a minute or so."

Walter leaned back, shaking his head. "What the fuck was it?"

Callie looked at him sharply. "Walt, watch your language!"

He looked at her for a moment, and blinked several times before looking back at Minus.

"Something gigantic," said Minus.

"Yeah, no shit. Probably one of them cruise liners." Walter took the last pull from his cigarette, then crushed it out and took a sip of the Chianti.

"That's the thing. It's organic."

"Ah. Whale or something?" Walter said.

Matt ignored the question. "The thing is, these mikes said it was somewhere around the southwestern coast of South America."

"So?" Callie said, beginning to take interest.

Matt looked her in the eyes for a moment, blowing smoke out the corner of his mouth. "The microphones were over three thousand miles away."

Walter choked on his wine and had to sit up straight. "Three thousand miles? What in the horrible sweaty shit?"

Matt Minus was now nodding, a smirk on his face. "Yeah. That's the point. No ship can make a sound that big that travels that far. And the largest living organism we know of is the Blue Whale. Their sounds can travel a few hundred miles at most."

"Three thousand miles?" Callie said, screwing up her face. "How big does that make it?"

Matt held his palms up and made a face. "Who knows. They never found it. And it went silent in the summer of ninety-seven. No one's heard from it since."

"Man, that's pretty creepy," Walter said. "Like Cthulu or some shit."

"Exactly," Matt said, pointing at him. Matt had a wild look in his eyes now.

"What's Cthulu?" Callie said, frowning at Walter.

"You never read Lovecraft?"

She shrugged, screwing up her mouth. "Guess not." She tasted the wine and made a sour face. "You drink mine, Walter. I have to drive anyway."

"Okay, so why are we here?" Walter said, lifting his chin as he spoke to Minus.

"The Bloop has begun to stir again. And we want to find it this time."

They did not discuss the details of Callie's involvement in the Bloop project, but decided to meet the following Monday in Minus's office so they could discuss it in private. As they finished their plates of lobster and snow crab, Callie set her napkin down and watched as a tall man guided a woman to a seat at a table beside them. The woman looked as though she could not see very well, but her eyes looked alive – darting around and trying to find focus on things in the dimly lit restaurant.

Callie grabbed Walter's leg under the table. "Look, Walt, that girl is blind."

Walter looked over at the woman, then back at Callie. "So?"

"Uh, Walter, show some respect! She can't see well!"

"Well that sucks, because she looks good," he said. Minus shook his head, stifling a laugh.

"You are so tacky. You know, our bionics department has been looking for a young candidate for a study. I'm going to go over and talk to her." Callie stood up and brushed her skirt off, then walked over to the other table.

"Excuse me," Callie said, squatting beside the woman's chair. "Hi, my name is Callie. What's yours?"

"Hi, Callie, I'm Codi," Codi said, extending her hand in the general direction of Callie. "This is my boyfriend, Tim," she added.

"Hi, Tim," Callie said, smiling widely at him.

"Are you visually impaired, Codi?" Callie said.

She saw Codi's eyes trying to focus on her. "Almost. I have macular degeneration. I will probably be blind by July."

Callie placed her soothing hand on Codi's forearm, which rested upon the arm of the chair. "I'm so sorry. I couldn't help but notice you coming in." Callie looked about the restaurant, then back to Codi. "Well I noticed you weren't carrying a cane, so I thought maybe you could see a little bit."

"Yes, just a little. Everything is blurry and crazy looking," Codi said.

Callie nodded. "Well, Codi, the reason I came over here is because I work for Bohr Enterprises," Callie started. Codi interrupted her quickly.

"You work for Bohr?" she said, then looked over towards Tim.

Tim raised his eyebrows and nodded.

"Yes. Second time, actually. I tried something else for a few years, but I'm back at Bohr. So I guess you've heard of them then?"

"Uh huh. I've heard they do research on stuff like what I have," Codi said, now adjusting in her seat so she could face Callie. "Would you like to sit down?"

"Oh, no thank you. We're about to leave. I just wanted to come say hello and introduce myself." She looked back over her shoulder at Walter and Matt, who were smoking again, engaged in some deep conversation.

"Well," Callie said, holding up her fingertips, then pausing while she stared at them. "Okay, we have a department that is looking for people who have what you have. So they can experiment with the new technologies and whatnot. I actually heard something about it in the break room a couple of weeks ago." She tilted her head back and forth momentarily then jerked it back toward Walter and said, "Walter over there knows the lady who runs the department." She chewed her lip and frowned, then continued. "Funny, I work there but haven't even met her. Anyway," she smiled, "would you be interested in coming in?"

"Oh, absolutely, I would," Codi said, nodding excessively.

Callie smiled a friendly smile at her and squeezed her arm. "Okay. Well let me get your phone number and I'll call you in a week or so. They may be able to help you."

"Oh my God, that would be so fantastic," Codi said. "Thank you so much, Callie."

Callie got her number and shook her hand again, then put her hand on her shoulder. She then leaned in close to her and said, "I really hope they can help you, Codi. You're too young to go through this."

Codi tried to smile, but tears were forming in her eyes. "Thank you, Callie. You're very kind."

On the way back to Walter's house, Callie and he spoke more of the mysterious Bloop, and wondered what part she would play in finding it. Obviously, Walter had pointed out, she would be involved in the physics behind the craft they would use to explore the ocean floor. Callie was not certain though, because she had no experience with building anything, nor did she know anything exceptional about the ocean.

"I'm glad I met Codi, Walt," she finally said.

"Yeah? That's a pretty noble step you took there," Walter replied.

"Well, yeah. I feel sorry for her. She's younger than I am, Walt! She deserves to be able to see!"

Walter shrugged. "If you say so. Either way, yeah, I'll give Beck a shout Monday morning and see if we can get her in there."

"Excellent. Thank you, Walt. I knew you were a good person underneath it all," Callie said, patting his leg.

CHAPTER 3

Rebecca Judas stood in the kitchen, her hands covered with flour, rolling dough. Her long brown hair hung in a tight braid, halfway down her back. She swayed her hips and danced across the kitchen to the music of One Last Orbit on her radio as she cooked.

As she plunged her fingers back into the dough, the phone rang. With the deft move of a professional, she knocked the phone off the cradle on the wall and grabbed it between her cheek and shoulder. "Uh huh?" she said, glancing up at the clock.

"Where are you right now?" the voice asked.

"I'm in the kitchen. I'm making dough."

"What are you wearing?"

"Oh, you know, I'm wearing a thong and a really sexy wife-beater. It's got holes all in the front."

"I dig it. Any mirrors around?"

"Just the two I set up on my counter so I can stare at myself as I cook."

"That's hot. And no bra, right?"

"A bra? What's that? Look, I have flour all over my hands, can I call you back in a while?" she said.

"No, I'll make it quick. I need you to see someone."

"Who? What, right now?" Rebecca asked. She was frowning now, and making pained expressions, shifting the phone around for a better position against her neck.

"Which one of those questions do you want me to answer?"

"Knock it off, Walter. Tell me what you want."

"Callie met a girl the other day. She's going blind. I want you to see her."

"Callie's going blind?"

Walter sighed. "You're only prolonging it yourself now. Will you bring her in?"

"Walter, I don't know what her problem even is. Do you? Do you know why she's going blind even?"

"Uh, well I guess not. I think it has something to do with her eyes though. Does that matter? Callie thought you would be able to check on her though."

"Call me back in ten minutes, okay?"

"Fine."

Rebecca turned and leaned over the counter, letting the phone slide onto the granite counter top. She picked up the large slab of dough and exercised her adroit hands against it, forming it into a disk.

After ten minutes, Rebecca's phone rang again. She was sitting in her recliner, smoking a cigarette, scribbling notes on a small pad on the table beside her. "Uh huh?" she answered.

"It's me. How's your dough?"

"It died a sad death on my kitchen floor."

"Uh oh," Walter snickered. "You're about as graceful as an epileptic on ice skates."

"It is my middle name. So tell me about this blind girl, Walter," she said, squinting her eyes as she took a drag from the long filter of the Curio Delight between her fingers.

"Well she's really cute. She's got a great little set of-…"

"Knock it off, Walter. Why do I need to see her?"

"Well, she's going blind. Like I said, I don't know why. Why aren't you at work, by the way?"

"It's National Hat Day, Walter."

"What the shit? And what will it be tomorrow?" he asked.

"Well tomorrow is National Nothing Day. But on the eighteenth we've got Thesaurus Day coming up. So we all get to use hefty surrogates for the diminutive words typically found in our drab diction."

"How do you keep up with all that shit?"

"It's what I do, chap." She took another drag of her cigarette.

"Well look at you. Just full of useless, trivial knowledge."

"Yeah, I'm celebrated on January tenth for Peculiar People Day." Rebecca crushed her cigarette out and pulled her braid out from behind her, leaning back in the recliner and curling her legs up under her. "So when do you want me to meet this girl?"

"Just whenever you get time. I was hoping you could put her in your research thing. Make her a lab rat. Callie says she deserves to see," Walter said.

"Don't we all. Okay, fuck it. Tell her to come see me tomorrow if she can. I'll have a chat with her at least. See if she's special."

"Well, I'm telling you, once you get a look at her tits, you'll see that she is," Walter said.

"Sorry, honey. I'm happily tied down already. You don't get to live out your fantasy of watching me seduce this girl."

"Okay, so you're honestly telling me that you lesbians don't just get together with whoever you want and have cheap, sloppy sex?"

Rebecca sighed. "You're such a moron. Commitment is genderless. Besides, I doubt I could find someone with better tits than my current love."

"Fair enough."

"I'll see you tomorrow, Walter," said Rebecca, and hung up.

⌘   ⌘   ⌘

Callie pushed closed the door to Matt Minus's office and stood there with her hands on the handle behind her while he finished up a phone call. He then directed her to sit. "You're early."

"I'm always early, Matt. That's why you hired me once upon a time."

"Once upon a time, we all made twice as much money in half the time, too, didn't we?"

Callie shrugged and dropped into a chair, straightening her skirt as she sat, crossing her legs. "I'm making good money at Bohr though. I can't complain."

Matt looked at her through the tops of his glasses. "You make more than you did at Royal?"

Callie nodded, raising her eyebrows. "Yeah, actually, I make more than I did at Royal and Oliver Company."

"Combined?"

"Heck no. Don't get ridiculous. No one makes that much money."

Matt cleared his throat. "Right. So check this out. Read over it and tell me what you think," he said, sliding a document across the desk to her. Callie pulled her glasses out of her purse and picked up the three-page set as she sat down. As her eyes scanned it and she turned the first page, she started nodding. By the end of the second page, she looked up at Matt.

"Is this real? Are you serious?"

Minus just nodded, almost imperceptibly.

Callie returned to the document, and turned to the third page, finishing within a couple of minutes. She set the papers back on the desk and raised one eyebrow at Matt. "This can't be real. This is too sci-fi."

"No more than a trip to Mars on a shuttle powered by a propulsion system you designed, am I right?"

Callie widened her eyes and grunted. Then she sighed and moved her glasses to the top of her head, and began playing with her hair. "Yeah. But no. Yeah, this is pretty fantastic."

"Tell me why," Minus said, leaning back in his chair. He scratched the top of his almost bald head, then pointed at the document. "What's incredible about it?"

Callie looked at the document on the desk and clasped her hands on her knee. "You want me to design a force shield."

"That's it?"

"What more do you need? That's ridiculous sounding," she said, shaking her head.

"Okay," he said, nodding. "But can you do it?"

"Oh, good Lord, I don't know."

"You know, you've never said that before."

"Come on, Matt. I don't know anything about the ocean. I mean, this looks exciting, and I like the thought of what you're doing, but you want me to build a force field? Isn't that a little hokey? I mean, this isn't Star Track."

Minus giggled. "Trek. It's Trek. Have you ever seen the show?"

"Whatever. Beside the point."

"Okay. So can you do it?" Minus said, looking hard at her.

"I don't know. Is this even realistic?" she said.

"That's what you're supposed to tell me. You're the physicist. You know, yours was the first name that came to mind when the project came up."

"I appreciate that you hold me in such high regard, Minus. But I don't know. I just…" she held up her hands, then dropped them to her lap again. "And forget all that! What's it for?" Callie asked, holding a hand up.

"Well, let's say we actually run into this beast. I'm thinking it's a high-powered, shock-the-shit-outta-something field that might help us escape in case of emergency," Minus said, looking proud of himself.

Callie shook her head. "So it's more of a weapon."

"No. Completely defensive."

"Either way," Callie said.

"Take your time. But let me tell you our vision." Matt stood up and walked over to a large pad of paper set on an easel. It was two feet wide and three feet tall. He turned the page and found a blank, then popped the cap off of a red marker and began drawing.

"We build a ship. Like this. Then we build some sort of-…"

Callie cut him off. "Wrong shape."

He turned to look at her, holding the marker between both hands. "Go on."

"Well first of all, it needs to be like a sphere," Callie said.

"*Like* a sphere?"

"A sphere."

"See, Callie? That's why I thought of you. In the first ten seconds you've already corrected something," he said, pointing the marker at her. "Now tell me why."

"Hang on a second, Minus," she said, waving her hands in front of her. "I haven't agreed to do this yet."

Matt stared at her for a long moment, then walked over to his desk and opened the top drawer, removing an envelope, then handed it to her.

Callie frowned at it, then flipped the top open and peaked inside. It was a check for a ridiculous amount of money. "That's a lot of zeros, Minus."

"That's your first paycheck. So are you on board or not?"

She sighed and set the check on the desk, then looked at him again. "It's not about the money, Minus. I just don't know if I can do this right now. I have a lot going on at work right now."

"Well, do you need more money?" Matt Minus said, returning to the board.

"No! I told you, it's not about the money. It would take me almost three years to make this much money at Bohr. But I can't just quit! I'm in the middle of some research projects! You know how I love my research!"

"Callie, I'm not hearing words I want to hear. Tell me bottom line, what it would take to get you over here."

Callie sighed again, then looked at her fingernails. "I don't know. I think it's about time. I don't think I have enough of it."

"You need another time machine, Cal?" he said, grinning.

She looked up at him sharply, but did not smile. "Yeah, let's just pretend that whole train wreck never happened."

"But it was you who saved the day, Callie. Amalie screwed everything up, but you fixed it! That's why you're the best!" said Minus.

Callie rolled her eyes. "Okay, look. I can put my projects on hold for about a month. Maybe six weeks. I can give you that long, but I'm serious, I really can't stay here, Matt."

"Six weeks is great. By that time, you can have a schematic drawn up and we can start building it." Minus stared at her with the marker in both hands again, then finally said, "And at the end of the six weeks, I'll give you another paycheck just as heavy as this one."

Some faraway part of Callie lit up with excitement at the thought of such a great windfall of money. She made really good money at Bohr, but to receive a check this large all in one lump sum meant entirely different things. And though she was not driven by money alone, it did not turn her off, either. This check, plus the other half she would get in six weeks, would put her in an entirely different league.

"Well?" Minus said.

Callie breathed in deeply. "A sphere is the most perfect and efficient shape something can attain. Energy preservation, distribution of stress and harmonious replication of power over the entire shape."

Matt Minus was nodding slowly.

"Every square inch is exactly like every other square inch of surface area in a sphere. There are no corners and no unique angles to interrupt the consonance of perfection," she said. She then stuck her bottom lip out and squinted. "It's going deep, right?"

"Mariana Trench."

"Where's that, off the coast of Japan?" Callie asked.

"Yeah. Between New Guinea and Japan. Right there in that fold. That's where we think he is."

"Yeah, yeah, yeah, I remember now. That movie director already tried this a few years ago, didn't he?"

Minus shrugged. "Yeah. But we're doing it better. And it wasn't a failure, anyway."

"Yeah, but I remember reading about it at the time. His craft was fine, but stuff started messing up at depth. Nothing worked like it was supposed to," Callie said.

"Well that's why I was hoping you could build this repulsion system. Maybe it could help repel some of the water pressure as well," Minus tried.

"Doubt that," Callie replied.

"Well, if nothing else, could it not help knock off any monsters and just get us back up to the surface?"

"So, like an anti-gravity force field," Callie said, holding her hands out again. "Piece of cake."

Callie came through the front door like a stiff wind and jumped on Chris as he sat on the couch. "Oh my gosh, honey, honey, honey, guess what?" Callie shouted, bouncing up and down on him like a little girl on a rocking horse.

"Whoa, calm down, tiger! You're gonna crush me. What's up?" Chris grabbed her by the waist and tried to get her to stop bouncing. Her face was a blur and her hair bounced wildly around.

"Look at this!" she said, and whipped the check out, holding it a few inches in front of his eyes. Chris frowned and leaned back as far as he could, trying to read it.

Suddenly he snatched it from her and pushed her off of him, moving forward on the couch.

"Is this real?"

Callie made a grand show of her nodding, widening her eyes and tightening her mouth.

"Holy shit, Callie. Is this yours?"

"Well if I'm still 'Callie Simmons' then yeah." She suddenly leaned in real close, almost touching his nose with her own, and made a mean face. "But I'll split it with ya!"

Chris grabbed her and pulled her back onto him, wrapping his hands around her head, pulling her in as he kissed her. "You are too awesome, Callie Simmons. I can't wait to make you a Bennett."

Callie's face got serious as she pulled back and looked at him. "Me neither, baby."

"So what are you going to do with all this money?" Chris said.

"I don't know. Buy a house? Buy a boat?" She looked over at him. She felt like she had not stopped smiling in thirty minutes. "Buy a houseboat?"

"Maybe all three. Shit. This is a serious, stupid ass amount of money." Chris shook his head.

"Uh, I forgot to tell you something, Chris." Chris looked at her, his smile falling fast.

"What?"

"That's only half of it. I get the other half in six weeks," said Callie.

This time, Chris's face got serious. His eyes widened and his jaw dropped. He stared dumbly at Callie. She kissed him.

⌘   ⌘   ⌘

Tuesday morning, Callie sat waiting on the bench at the bus stop outside the Bohr Enterprises campus. She watched as Tim dropped Codi off at the curb, then stood to meet her at the car. Callie helped Codi get out, then closed the door, waving at Tim. She looped her arm through Codi's and led her up the sidewalk to the research building.

"How are you feeling this morning?" Callie asked.

"Oh I'm fine. I just thank you so much for doing this for me," Codi said, holding onto Callie's guiding arm with both of her hands.

"It's not a problem, really. My friend Walter called someone in the department and got her to agree to see you. I can't promise you anything, but at least she'll talk to you for a bit and maybe see if you could be a candidate for one of their studies."

"Oh wow, your friend works here too?" Codi asked.

"No, he's just friends with Rebecca over here. He works for the bad guys."

Codi laughed out loud. "Who are the bad guys?" she asked. She almost sounded serious to Callie.

"Royal Research. I used to work there, too. Until I decided to become a good guy."

Callie guided Codi into the revolving door and scooted in right behind her. As they emerged on the other side, Codi looked up, trying to focus on something. Callie once again offered Codi her arm and led the way. After a short ride up in the elevator, Callie led her to the end of the hall, where presumably, Rebecca would be waiting for her.

Callie knocked on the door. After a moment, it popped open and there stood Rebecca, smiling and welcoming them in.

"Hi Rebecca, I'm Callie. I don't think we've met," Callie said, extending her hand. Rebecca shook it. "And this is Codi Cohl," she added.

"Hi Codi. Rebecca Judas. It's good to meet you."

"Rebecca, I'm at extension 6838 if you just want to call me when you're done. I'll come get her."

"Sounds great, Callie. Thanks," Rebecca said. Callie excused herself.

"If you'd like to sit down over here, I'll get my notepad." Rebecca guided Codi to a chair, then fetched her pad and pen from the desk. She then sat facing Codi and crossed her legs, setting the pad on her knees.

"Can you tell me a little about your condition, Codi?" she said.

"My optician said I have macular degeneration, and I've only got about six months left to see," Codi said, rubbing her left eye.

"Hmm. That's odd. That would be pretty remote. Typically people don't suffer MD until their seventies. Sometimes it's earlier, but it's pretty rare."

"Yeah I thought so too. It's pretty scary."

Rebecca nodded slowly. "Can you tell me what you see on that wall?" she asked, pointing her pen toward a poster behind her. The poster pictured a woman holding a bouquet of flowers against her chest. She was standing in the middle of a street with cars around her.

Codi squinted at the poster, then shook her head. "Is it a picture?"

"Mm hmm. Go ahead and get closer. See what you can make out."

Codi rose and crept up to the poster, until she was about two feet away. "I think it's a picture of someone."

"Staring straight at the person's face, can you tell me the gender?"

"No," Codi said.

"What about if you look at the bottom of the poster. Can you make out the face peripherally?"

"No," Codi said.

"And from each side?" said Rebecca, making small notations on the paper.

"No. It's all blurry." She stepped closer and looked again. "I think it's a woman. I can see her if I get really close like this."

Rebecca nodded again, squinting. "Honey, this doesn't sound like macular degeneration. Go ahead and sit down." She wheeled back in her chair to the desk and picked up a book from the corner, then shuffled through the pages. She found what she was looking for and handed the book to Codi. There were two pictures on one page. The top picture illustrated normal vision, and the bottom picture was the same on the edges, but the centered was blurred out beyond recognition, and resembled the view someone would see if he or she suffered macular degeneration.

"Can you make out those two pictures if you get up close? The bottom one is what the top one looks like through the eyes of someone with MD. It's typically a loss of central vision. It sounds like to me your vision loss is pretty evenly distributed."

"Yeah, that's right. The bottom picture doesn't look like what I normally see. So what does that mean?"

"Well, assuming your optic nerve isn't damaged, you could be a candidate for eye replacement. But that would require some extensive testing to be able to determine." Rebecca took the book back from Codi and tossed it back on the desk. "That doesn't completely rule out MD either. Exudative macular degeneration can explain a rapid loss of vision."

"Oh," Codi simply said. What little hope she had when she had walked into this office was quickly fading. Back to square one. Whatever medical term they wanted to use to describe it, she was going blind. And soon, there would be no turning back. "So what is eye replacement?"

Rebecca shrugged. "It's just what it sounds like. We replace part of the eye with a bionic lens. Older technologies meant you had to wear a sort of sunglass that had in it two tiny cameras. They would relay vision to a small chip near your cornea. We've now modeled some implants that basically put the cameras and chips in your eyeball itself. It's pretty spectacular science."

"Wow, that is fascinating. Would it restore my vision completely?"

"It's something the patient has to get used to. You interpret things differently, but you're able to learn pretty quickly, and you can tell objects you're already familiar with, apart from each other. It's better by far than being blind." Rebecca stood up and walked around to the other side of her desk, taking her seat behind the computer keyboard. "The new models allow for facial recognition too, which is exciting."

Codi did not know what to say. The thought that there were robot eyes available was something she had never dreamed of. She hoped she could be considered for the replacement if it came down to that. "How much does it cost?"

Rebecca popped her bubble gum and said, "The bionic eyes? They're quite expensive. But we don't really sell them. We're manufacturing the science and technology behind them. There are some on the market already. We hope to release these new models by the end of the year though."

"How much are the current models?" Codi asked. She was trembling.

"I think they're about thirty thousand dollars apiece."

And there went that hope again. Any chance she had believed she might have just evaporated with the figure Rebecca had just told her. There was no way she could afford sixty grand. She sighed, showing perhaps a little of her disappointment.

"Don't worry about it, sweetie," Rebecca said. "If we believe you're a good candidate for the surgery, we'll fit you with them as part of a study. It wouldn't cost you anything."

"Oh, really? Well that would be great," Codi said with a sigh of relief.

"Yeah. We'll just have to see. Can you come back here next week so we can run some tests? It would be an all-day thing. Like start at six o'clock in the morning, and we'd get done sometime after three, probably."

"That's just the testing though?" Codi asked.

"Yep.   The surgery takes about ninety minutes." Rebecca tapped the keys on the keyboard as she spoke, and popped her gum loudly. It was almost annoying to Codi, but Codi was of the opinion that Rebecca Judas could be her savior here in the coming weeks. Her mind briefly made the connection with Rebecca's last name to the story of Judas, the great betrayer of Jesus. How ironic that would be if Judas became her savior. She wondered what it would take to be part of the study. What would have to be wrong with her? Rebecca had mentioned something about optic nerve damage. Codi hoped she didn't have that.

"Well I can definitely come back next week. I'm always free!" she said, perhaps a little too excitedly.

"Wow. Well, that must be nice. How'd you get that gig?" Rebecca asked.

"Well I just moved in with my boyfriend. We moved up here from Detroit together, but we were living separately out there. He told me if I moved in with him, I wouldn't have to worry about working," Codi said.

"Well that's nice. Lucky you! So, how about next Monday morning, six o'clock?" Rebecca said.

"Perfect.   Thank you so much, Rebecca.   I really appreciate you doing this."

"Well, we'll see what we can do for you, Codi. I hope we're able to help." She stood up and pulled her khakis up, then rounded the desk again.   "Do you remember the extension Callie said to call her on?"

"6838," Codi blurted with no hesitation.   Rebecca stopped in her tracks momentarily, staring hard at Codi. "Okay, wow. Good memory." She then dialed the digits on the phone and told Callie they were finished.

CHAPTER 5

operation

Codi Cohl was back in Rebecca's office by five-fifty the next Monday morning, trembling with excitement and worry simultaneously. Part of her was afraid something would be wrong, or would go wrong, that would prevent her from being a candidate for the procedure. But the other parts were so excited to have someone taking her case so seriously that they were even willing to consider her for such a thing. Her experiences with the opticians previously had made her feel almost like a number. She was just the next girl in line, waiting to go blind. Here, there seemed to be a sense of humanity, and Rebecca, though hard to read, seemed like she genuinely cared about Codi. Even if she did not get the treatment she wanted, she felt like Rebecca might continue to help her in some way.

As she sat with her face against the binocular autorefractor, she felt a new hope. Maybe Rebecca would see something the other doctors had not seen. Maybe with that humanity Rebecca exuded, she would *want* to look deeper, to find something more. When Rebecca finally wheeled up to the other side of the desk, Codi's heart began to beat faster. She was now worried she was too excited and she might screw something up.

"I'm sorry if I'm shaking, Rebecca. I'm a little anxious, I think."

"It's okay. There's nothing to be afraid of. I'm just going to have a look inside your eyes. You won't feel a thing."

"Okay. I'm trying so hard to be still!"

"You're doing just fine, sugar," Rebecca said. "Take a few deep breaths."

Codi did as she was told, and began to relax a little. "Okay, you ready? Open your eyes nice and wide for me," Rebecca said. Then she leaned up to the refractor and looked deep into Codi's eyes through the powerful machine.

Codi sat still for a long time, trying not to even blink. After what seemed like an eternity, Rebecca finally leaned back, frowning. "You know what, Codi?"

"Huh?"

"Hang on. Let me look again." She leaned back up to the device and took another long look. After several more minutes, she adjusted the settings on the refractor and then scratched something on a notepad.

"Okay," she said, shutting it off. "You can relax. Your eyes don't look abnormal. What it looks like to me, and I'd like to get Doctor Jeffers to take a second look, but it looks to me like your retina has begun to deteriorate." Rebecca took a seat directly in front of Codi and scooted up real close, so Codi could see her well. "Basically your photoreceptors start shutting down, and you're unable to capture light from the environment. Do you have trouble seeing at night?"

"More so than in the day, yes."

"You remember walking into a dark house after being outside on a sunny day? Is it kind of like that at night, all the time?"

"Yes, yes!" Codi said. "It's always like that at night. It's like my eyes never adjust and I have to turn lights on just to get around."

Rebecca nodded. "It sounds like to me you have retinitis pigmentosa. But not macular degeneration. Your rod and cone cells deteriorate and you begin to lose vision progressively."

"Oh no," Codi said. "Is that worse than macular degeneration then?"

Rebecca shrugged and leaned back, folding her hands on her knee. "Who can say? But retinitis pigmentosa isn't treatable. There is no known cure for it currently."

"Oh no. I was so worried you would say that." Codi felt tears stinging her eyes. She had already experienced so many letdowns that she figured she should be getting used to it by now. It still knocked her back every time she got more bad news about her eyesight though. She wiped her eyes.

"Well, don't give up, Codi. We're not done yet."

"Okay. What else can we do?" she asked.

"Well if Dr. Jeffers agrees with my assessment, he may decide he wants to use your eyes in the bionic eye study."

"Oh my God, really?"

Rebecca nodded thoughtfully. "We haven't begun the next round yet, but you look – at least to me – like you'd be a good candidate for it."

"Oh thank God," Codi said.

Rebecca smiled. "Well let's not get ahead of ourselves, okay? He will still need to look at you, and we still have a whole bunch of tests to run on your eyes, okay?"

"Okay," Codi said, trying to smile. Rebecca handed her a tissue and she wiped her eyes and blew her nose. "Thank you, Rebecca."

Rebecca patted her knee. "Well you're welcome. I hope we can do something for you."

Rebecca then took Codi into another room and took x-rays of her eyes, then had her wait in a dark room for half an hour while she prepared some other tests. Rebecca looked in her eyes with a pen light in the dark room, then ran a laser test before bringing her out into a lighted therapy room, where she had Codi lie on her back on a table. She told Codi to stare straight up at the ceiling as she swung a tennis ball on a string above the bed. It moved all around in circles and back and forth, and Rebecca recorded all the little twitches and movements Codi's irises made. After several hours of these strenuous, tiring tests, Codi finally got a break. Rebecca had her sit in the front office and told her she could relax.

And there she waited for almost an hour before Rebecca came back. There were thousands of thoughts running through her head. It was like a circus of thought. Would they find some way to repair her eyesight? Would they give her a different diagnosis entirely? Would it all be for nothing? She found herself trembling and nervous again when Rebecca finally came back into the room.

"Codi, you okay?" she said.

"Yes, I am. Just nervous, you know?"

"Good. It's good to be nervous. You're human," Rebecca said, and put her hand on Codi's shoulder. She squeezed gently, massaging it for a moment, just helping Codi to relax. "You ready to go see Dr. Jeffers?"

"Oh, he's here?"

"Uh huh. He's ready to look at your big gorgeous brown eyes!"

"Goody goody!"

Rebecca led her into Dr. Jeffers's office, where he rose from a chair behind the desk and immediately approached her. "Hello, Codi," he said in a deep, friendly voice. "Tom Jeffers," he said and shook her hand.

"Hi doctor. Good to meet you."

"Let me look at those eyes," he said, and put his fingers on her chin and cheeks. He tilted her head back and looked into her eyes over the tops of his glasses. Codi thought it odd that anyone who worked here would even require glasses. She felt a sudden tinge of fear and despair.

"Those are some gorgeous eyes, Codi!" he said. He was silent for a moment, just moving her head around and looking at her from different angles. "I wear these glasses so that people can see me better," he said, showing no emotion on his old face.

Codi smiled. It was a smile of relief. Had he just read her mind? She had the silly thought that he had looked into her eyes and seen all the fears and questions waiting in there to be asked.

"Okay, let's get you over here so I can take a deeper look."

She put her chin up on the chin pad of another binocular autorefractor and he turned it on. After less than thirty seconds, he clicked it off and stood up. "It was good to meet you, Codi. Thanks for coming to see us."

Was that a pun? "Um, thank you doctor."

Rebecca took her by the arm and led her out of the office. When they got back to the front office, she told Codi she could sit down again.

Codi looked up at the blurry vision of Rebecca, wondering what she really looked like. "Did I do something wrong, Rebecca?"

"What do you mean?"

"Well he sort of got me out of there in a hurry. I thought he would run more tests or something. Like you did."

"Oh no, sweetie, I ran all the tests we needed. He just needed to take a quick look. You're in."

"I'm sorry?"

"You're in. He wants you in the program. You're gonna get new peepers, Codi!"

"Oh my God! I'm so excited! Thank you so much!" she said, darting up out of her chair to hug Rebecca.

Callie and Walter were solids. Chris had put the thirteen ball in the corner pocket on the break, and Thevi cleaned up the twelve and the fourteen. She was now rechalking her cue, and Callie was beginning to get worried. She was not very good at the game, and needed a big head start to have any shot at winning. Walter was better, but Chris and Thevi were pros. "Who picked these teams?" Callie asked, shaking her head.

"What do you mean?" Walter asked. "You don't think I'm good enough to handle this deficit?"

Callie looked at him, but didn't say anything. She returned her gaze to the table, where Thevi now bent over, stretching to reach the cue ball for a long shot on the ten.

"Don't sweat it, babe. I'll leave you a good shot," Chris said.

"Uh huh. Sure you will."

"I'll set you up," Walter said, nodding.

"Uh huh. Sure you will. Just like you used to in our absentee games."

"Hey, I always played fair!"

"Uh huh. You're a cheater dork and you know it," Callie returned.

Thevi missed the ten, so Callie lined up, looking for a clean shot.

"What the hell is an absentee game?" Chris said.

Walter took Thevi's cue and began chalking it. "We used to play pool over the phone back when I lived in Manhattan and she lived in Dallas. I'd break, then take a picture of the results with my phone camera. I'd send her the picture and she'd arrange them exactly like that on her side and make her shot. Rinse, repeat."

"You took pictures of every shot?" Chris said.

"Well, yeah. You have to. How did you play?" Walter said.

"Yeah, but Walter was a cheater dork. Sometimes he would send me a picture where all his balls were sunk except for the eight. And he'd say, 'Oh what's wrong, Callie, you didn't get my in-between pictures?'" She stuck her tongue out at him.

"That's ridiculous. That had to take hours just to play one game," Thevi said.

"It did. But what else did we have to do? It was how we spent time together when we couldn't hang out."

"You two are crazy," Thevi said, her face blank.

"So is that why you married me?" Walter asked her.

She shook her head, rolling her eyes. Callie shot for the four, but scratched.

Walter stood with the cue stick under his chin, watching the table as Thevi made three shots in a row, then called the side pocket for the eight. "So what ever happened to that blind chick?"

"She got new eyes!" Callie said.

"Oh that's damn cool," Thevi said, sinking the eight. She dropped the cue on the table and popped her knuckles.

"Nice shot, red," Chris said, high-fiving her.

"She already got 'em?" Walter asked.

"This morning. She'll spend a couple of months in therapy, learning how to interpret the new vision, then she'll be ready for the world."

"Wasn't that the name of a band?" Chris said.

"Yes," Walter said, shaking his head. "I'd prefer you not have reminded me though."

"Well that's just bad ass. Robot eyes!" Thevi said.

Chris laughed out loud, then said, "Ah, hell do they light up all red like the Terminator?"

Callie shook her head, an embarrassed sort of condescension painting her features. "You guys are dorks."

⌘　　　⌘　　　⌘

The world, according to Codi, was now all reds and blues. Dr. Jeffers had assured her things would become a little clearer in the coming days. More colors and shapes would become evident, until she could finally get used to her new vision and it would feel normal. Of course, she still had on her eye patches, and would until the sutures on her eyes were healed. Then she would start to see some real color, granted it would never be like it was before.

Gone were her normal visions – the ones every normal person saw. She now had a sort of computer-generated vision where everything looked like blocks and pixelated shapes. After the surgery, in low light, the doctor had tested her vision to see if the surgery had been a success or not, only letting her look around the room. The initial impression to Codi had been terrifying, and a sort of claustrophobia had settled in as she realized she would never see through human eyes again.

Of course, the second-guessing and doubt had immediately set in. Had she done the right thing? What if they had all been wrong before, and her vision would actually have eventually healed? She had given up her natural lenses for these simulacrums. She had not yet been fully blind, which made the decision that much more difficult. And second-guessing was perpetuated by this computer-vision. It was downright scary to think this was as good as it would ever get.

When Tim had come to visit her the morning after her surgery was complete, even through the thick black patches on her eyes, she had felt as though she could see some evidence of him standing there – a shadow of a ghost in a dream. Was this what he looked like now – a blocky, pixelated low-resolution version of the real thing done in dark blues and maroons? And who's to say, she thought, but what if that was how he really looked? If vision was the brain's interpretation of electrical signals sent from a human organ, then what if it had always been wrong? What if this four-bit Atari-age graphic was the real Tim? Had she had it wrong the whole time? This would definitely take some getting used to. She knew that instantly. And the dread and fear of it all weighed heavily in her stomach. And if this was Tim, what did she look like? She shivered.

CHAPTER 6

Callie sat cross-legged in Matt Minus's office with a legal pad on a clipboard in her lap, taking notes. Minus was pacing in front of his desk, a mug of coffee in his hands that Callie suspected he had emptied a long time before.

"I'm going to have to dive, Minus."

He stopped in his tracks and stared at her, then looked down at the empty mug, frowned, and set it on the desk. "Dive?"

"Dive. SCUBA dive. I will need to get certified to dive for this," she said.

He shook his head quickly, as if trying to set free a flock of angry gnats in his eye sockets. "No. You're not going down in the vessel. You just design it."

"Matt, I will have to test it. I have to build prototypes. I have to experiment. I will need to dive to do all of this."

He stopped again. "Oh. That. Yeah. Well, okay, that sounds right." He started pacing again, then stopped suddenly, frowning. "Wait. So what? Just get training and expense it."

Callie shook her head. "Fine. That's not what I'm worried about."

"Well, then what is it that you're worried about?" Minus said.

Callie breathed in deeply and tilted her head. "I think I'm hydrophobic."

Minus stared dumbly at her for a long moment before answering. "You're serious."

Callie nodded somberly.

"Well, do you really need to dive then? Can you not run your tests in a pool or something? I mean," Minus said, scratching his thinning hair, "it doesn't seem like you'd have to go all that deep." He held his hands out in a questioning manner.

"Ha!" Callie almost shouted. "This whole thing is about deep! The Trench is almost seven miles deep! How the heck am I supposed to test anything if I can't stand in two feet of water without crumbling into a nervous wreck? Well, at least in the ocean. I can stand in a pool."

Minus held his hands up now in defense. "Okay, calm down, Callie." He stood staring at her for a moment, hands behind his back. He looked to Callie like a military general waiting for a report on the war from one of his majors. "What do you want me to do? How can I help you?"

Callie took a deep breath, staring at nothing, and finally began to calm. "I'm sorry. I guess I'm just a little scared by this whole thing, Minus. I know absolutely bullcocky about the ocean, this trench, this... this," she trailed off, waving her hands around. She looked as though she were trying to find a word that would come if she could get her hands to mimic the right motion in the air between them. "What the heck is it called? This goop?"

Matt nodded, a smile on his thin lips. "Bloop."

"Bloop. Thank you." She returned her hands to her lap, fingers still holding her ink pen. "I know nothing about the ocean or the bloop or about building a stupid dumb ship that will withstand that kind of pressure. It's a whole lot of, well, pressure."

Matt nodded slowly, patiently. "It's okay, Callie. Leave the ship building to the experts. You concentrate on the field. And take your time!" he said, extending his hand. "No one is saying you have to rush through this. But I know you're capable. You've designed things no one ever imagined. You're very, very good at what you do. I know you can do this."

Callie chewed her lip, staring at the floor. "I'm glad you're confident, Minus. Because I feel like someone who's been given nothing but a pad and a pen and told I have to come up with a flippin' force field."

Minus chuckled, then walked over to the window and twisted open the blinds, looking out onto the street below. "Yeah, well if anyone can do it, Callie, you'd be the most likely candidate."

⌘   ⌘   ⌘

Therapy was slow and laborious for Codi Cohl, who was not only learning to use her new eyes, but how to adapt to an entirely new way of seeing. There was no textbook one could read – nor could she read it if there were – that told someone how to replace everything she had ever learned about what she sees with completely new information. It was like being thrown into a new universe where nothing was familiar. Nothing made sense. Every shape, every color, every shade was completely foreign. An entire new language for the eyes. A table no longer looked like the hard, wooden, brown flattop she was used to. It now looked like a red, fuzzy semi-rectangle with no tangible hold in reality. And to focus on the legs of that table, she had to change direction with her mind entirely. Now she was staring at something less red, less rectangular, less horizontal – less real. The translations that took place between her eyes and her brain she used to take for granted were now lessons in patience and frustration. An entirely new study of definition and perception. She was an infant in an adult's world of vision. And worse than a child learning to construct her reality from what she saw, she was having to reconstruct. Rebuild. Relearn. She had to forget what she had learned before and replace it with new perspective and observation.

Therapy, therefore, also seemed hopeless. But she was learning. Codi knew she would never read again. She would never see flowers or tablecloths or storefronts or faces again the same way. But she would see them. Sometimes she felt an overwhelming sense of depression knowing her old way of seeing was gone. She would never curl up by a fire and read a novel again. Never stare into the eyes of her lover and bask in his handsome visage again. She would never again drive a car. It was during these times that Codi would have to remind herself that at least she wasn't fully blind. This was leaps and bounds better than being blind. Or was it? It seemed to her that it might take less time to adapt to a world with no sight – especially with heightened senses otherwise – than to learn this new, confusing version of vision. The world was now a colorless blend of puzzling shapes and contours, but in time she tried to believe she could learn to interpret them. In time, she would make her way. And maybe someday, she reminded herself, she would get so good at it that perhaps she would forget the old way of seeing things. All she had now of her lover's face was a fast-fading memory. And in time, that too would vanish. Like the ink on a purchase receipt, it would wash away with the ticking of the clock until all that was left was a vague recollection of reality.

Rebecca was the definition of patience. During the frustrating outbursts Codi would suffer, Rebecca was always there holding her hand, reminding her she could do it. Codi's therapy was long and tiresome, ritualistic and repetitive. Rebecca would start in the mornings by showing Codi cards with high-contrast images on them: a black box on a white card, a red star on blue. The goal was not yet to have Codi decipher the exact shape on the page, but rather to recognize that contrast – to discern not only the shape on the card but the card from the background of the low-lighted room beyond.

She would then move to solid objects on the table, working with Codi to define the shape, the size, the color – the name of the object. *A cube no longer looks like a cube to you. What does it look like now? This is what you have to start thinking of a cube as being. And though it might no longer look like what a cube used to look like, there is nothing else that looks exactly like it. It's safe to assign a new shape in your memory to the nomenclature.*

And it was more difficult than just that. For, what if Rebecca turned the cube on the table by forty degrees? Codi had to not only discern that it was the same cube, but that it had rotated on one of its three axes and was now facing a different direction.

There were many times Codi would get so flustered and frustrated that she would break down into fits of crying and exhaustion. It was indeed very taxing and tiresome work and it often defeated her, leaving her sobbing and banging her fists on the table when she couldn't make something connect with reality. But Rebecca was ever patient, stroking her hair or holding her hand, reminding her that it would eventually make sense. Codi would finally get used to this new version of sight. It would eventually get to the point where it made sense, and she would have some semblance of sanity about her vision.

Codi abandoned her appointment with Dr. Goff, seeing as how the opportunity had arisen for her to participate in the study under the direction of Dr. Jeffers and Rebecca Judas. But sometimes she wondered if she had done the right thing. What if – just *what if* – Dr. Goff had been able to help her in some other way? She tried to shake these thoughts from her head, but it was hard to get away from the thought that she had jumped into this without a whole lot of consideration. When offered the bionic lenses, Codi had been so excited that she had scarcely considered how scary the reality of it really was. She had not fully considered the fact that it would be a totally different type of vision.

⌘   ⌘   ⌘

Callie and Thevi stood in the accessories section of Randall's department store, trying on sunglasses. Slightly drunk and excited about getting to spend the day shopping together, they stood laughing, purses hung on elbows, trying on the most outlandish shades they could find. Callie found a pair of large white frames with window-blind-like strips across them and put them on, lifting her chin to Thevi.

"What about these? The sun only bothers if I hold my chin too high."

Thevi laughed aloud, adjusting the frames on Callie's nose. "Oh, then they'll never do for you, my dear. You're far too plush to benefit from such impecunious fashion!"

"Oh my grief! You did not!" Callie said, slapping at Thevi and simultaneously removing the plastic accoutrement.

"Oh no, you need something a lot more arrogant, darling," Thevi replied, handing Callie another pair from the rack. "These are far more your style."

Callie looked in the mirror at the gigantic frames now on her face. They covered not only her eyes, but her eyebrows and most of her upper cheeks as well. "I look like a bug!" she shouted. She quickly removed them, tossing them onto the counter beneath the racks. She grabbed a square shade and handed them to Thevi. "These have your name written all over them. They're as square as you!"

Thevi put them on and posed for Callie, and they both burst out laughing. "Apropos."

"Totally," Callie agreed.

"Okay, we should totally buy the worst, ugliest, biggest ones we can find and wear them out," Thevi said after removing them and tossing them aside.

"Yes!" Callie insisted. "And let's get hats to match!"

As they waltzed out of the Randall's in their ridiculous new garb, arm in arm, they skipped and laughed, singing *Blue Bayou* and waving at everyone they passed. One man they approached stood with hands in his pockets, smoking a cigarette. Callie didn't at first recognize him because he, too, was wearing dark shades. They were almost past him when she stopped and looked at him, realizing he had just called her by name.

"Excuse me?" said Callie.

"I was under the impression that big check I wrote you would last a lot longer. I can tell by the shades you've already spent most of it," said Minus.

Callie, suddenly embarrassed, whipped them off quickly and tried to make them disappear. She finally turned to him and tilted her head. "What are you doing here, Minus?"

"I'm looking for you," Minus said, tamping his cigarette out on the trashcan he was leaning on. "I called the house. Chris told me you guys were coming out to see the Western Wagons movie."

"Well he was bullshooting you, Minus," Callie said, rolling her eyes. "Seriously? You believed him? Only guys watch that crap."

Minus chuckled. He shrugged, then tossed the cigarette butt in the trashcan. He nodded, then looked at Thevi. "How you doing, Thevi?"

Thevi just shrugged, crossing her arms.

"So what are you guys seeing, if not *Paradise Trail*?" Minus said, looking around at the crowd. Callie followed his gaze for a moment before looking back at him.

"We're not seeing a movie. We're just out shopping. Being girls. So what's with the smalltalk? Why did you call the house?"

Minus stuffed his hands in his pockets. "Callie, something's come up. We need to talk."

Callie chewed her lip for a moment, then sighed and turned to Thevi. "Can you give us just a few minutes, babe?"

Thevi nodded somberly and started digging in her purse. "Yeah. I'll go grab a coffee."

Callie smiled wanly at her and patted her on the shoulder. "Thanks, darling. I'll meet you in there in a few minutes." Then she turned to Minus. He was watching Thevi walk away.

"What's her problem?" he asked.

Callie made a face. "Seriously? What's this all about, Minus? Did something happen?"

"Not as such," he said, taking her elbow and guiding her out of the middle of the sidewalk to a bench at the edge of the grass. "We're getting a lot of action over there. A lot."

"Over where? The trench?"

Minus nodded. "Yeah. Big stuff. Whatever the hell is down there is making a helluva lot of noise. It sounds angry, in fact." He shook another cigarette out of the package, and lit it, staring Callie in the eyes.

"That's spooky, dude. I'd like to hear some of it. What do you think is going on?"

"Who can say?" Minus blew smoke out his nose and cracked his neck, then took a deep breath. "There's just really nothing to compare the sound to. No one could have any idea what's going on. It's actually kind of scary."

"So you needed to come find me on my day off and tell me you're scared of the big sea monster?" Callie teased, pushing his shoulder. "Are you changing your mind?"

"Hell no," he said, frowning. "I'm just getting worried that shit's about to start happening."

"I'm not following," said Callie. "Would you get to the point, please? I'm supposed to be spending girl time."

"*Paradise Trail*? You'd be better off missing that, anyway."

"We're not seeing a movie, Minus!" Callie looked around, shuffling her stance, trying her best to maintain her patience. Matt Minus showed no signs of catching her sense of urgency though, even though he had proposed to have an emergency.

"That's actually comforting. I can't believe anyone watches that horse shit. You know how low-budget that show was? Clayton West forgot his lines almost constantly. Dawndy was kind of cute, though."

"Knock it off, Minus. Are we here to talk about *Western Wagons* or do you have something to tell me about our project?"

He shrugged. "Listen, Cal. I think the Japs are going to try to get in on this."

"The Japs? What are you talking about, Minus?"

"The Japs. Those little people that live on that island called Japan? You might have heard of it."

"Yes, Minus, I know who the *Japs* are! Just no one with any couth actually calls them that. Jeez!" Callie almost shouted.

"What I'm telling you, Callie, is that I think they're getting interested." Minus took a long pull from his cigarette and watched two women walk by holding hands. He stared at their rumps, fully formed, thick flesh behind shiny stretch pants that showed no panty lines. Callie rolled her eyes.

"They've started noticing. They published something in the Japan Herald about it. And the science community over there is getting real forward about it."

"So what are you saying?" Callie said, cocking her head at him and frowning. "You think they're going down there too?"

Minus nodded, furling his lips. He took another drag and flicked his cigarette toward the trashcan, missing wildly. "It's beginning to look that way."

"Well who cares? Is there not room enough for all of us to go have a look?"

"And let them have the discovery? Hell no! There's never room for seconds in science, Cal." He shook his head. "I thought you knew this."

"I know about competitive enterprise, but I'm not a showboat, Minus. I've never cared for the limelight. I just want the science," Callie said. Her gaze followed a child walking down the sidewalk dragging a popped balloon on a dirty ribbon. She finally met Minus's eyes again and said, "Look, Minus. Can we talk about this Monday morning? I don't think anything is going to change over the weekend."

"Oh, but it is," Minus said, a mischievous grin falling over his face.

Callie bit her lip hard and breathed in, crossing her arms. "Boy I just want to punch you in your face sometimes, Minus. Will you please tell me what the turkey is going on? All of it!"

Minus laughed out loud and reached for another cigarette. Callie knocked his hand down when he went to light it. "Seriously, Minus. You have about thirty seconds and then I'm walking away."

"Callie, I took your initial calculations. Your schematic for the shield? I ran that to the dev department the other day when you left."

Callie frowned hard, feeling a kind of anger pour into her chest. She could feel her face and neck getting red. "What? You did what? Minus, I wasn't even finished with them! They were..."

Minus closed his eyes and held his hands up. "I know, Cal. I know all that. I just wanted to see if what you had already would hold up so far." She tried to interrupt but he kept going. "Just to see if what you had so far was stable." Minus waited for her to object, then seeing that she wasn't going to, finally finished. "I know it wasn't done, Callie. I just wanted to test it. You know, sort of a baseline. Just for shits and giggles."

She continued chewing her lip, and was about to stare a hole through him. But she remained quiet. Then after an uncomfortable silence, she raised her eyebrows.

Minus smiled and nodded. "It's good."

Callie cocked her head again, looking hard at his eyes, trying to read what he wasn't saying.

"Callie, it's good. It works. As is."

"You're kidding me," she said. "Are you stinking kidding me, Minus? I hadn't even proofed it!"

"Yeah. I know, Callie! I know all that! But it works! Phillips said everything checks out. They've been working on a scale model for three days now."

"What is a scale model?" Callie asked carefully.

"Scaled down. About this big," he said, making a circle with his fingers, no bigger than a golf ball.

"And it works?" she said, her eyes widening.

He laughed. "That's what I'm telling you, Callie! Your fucking genius prevails! Well," he said, changing his face suddenly, "we haven't tested it at depth or anything yet. But it's powering on."

"Oh my gosh, Minus! This is insane!" Callie pushed him hard on the shoulder. Minus had to take a step back to keep his balance. "What are you telling me?"

"We're go for testing. I think you need to miss your movie, Callie. We need to get to work."

"We're not seeing the stupid movie!"

CHAPTER 7

As Callie Simmons breezed into the Royal building, which felt all too familiar – but at the same time very foreign – she approached the welcome desk and asked for her temporary badge. She was already on a first-name basis with Roy, the day guard who monitored the front desk, but protocol was tight. The small square of paper that had her name and photograph on it hung from a lapel clip inside a clear plastic sheath. It was always the same. But they always printed a new one. And the one she wore would always be turned in when she left for the day.

January's cold blew through the vast, empty room, and she found herself dreading the impending SCUBA training. The thought of it made her shiver, as if she were already descending into the murky depths. As Roy handed her the badge, she thanked him and shook the thought from her head.

The elevator dinged.

Callie stepped on and pressed fourteen, and as the doors slid silently closed and replaced her view of the vast vestibule with her own reflection, she stood up straight and tidied her hair behind her ears. Her cell phone chirped in her pocket.

"Minus, I'm in the elevator. You have got to be the most impatient guy I know."

"Relax, Callie. That's not why I'm calling. I was calling to tell you to meet me in the workroom. It's down the hall from my office. You know it?"

"Yeah, I'll find it," she said and ended the call just as the elevator drew to a stop.

Callie ducked into a refreshment alcove on her way to the workroom and poured herself a tall paper cup of hot coffee, then blew on it as she made her way down the hall, purse beating a steady rhythm against her hip. Most of the offices were closed and dark behind the frosted windows. She had no problem finding the brightly lit doorway of the workroom just down at the end of the hall.

Minus did not look up as she entered the room and slung her purse over the back of a chair by the door. He was leaning on his fists over a desk, looking at a large steel bearing that sat atop an overturned plastic cup.

"Thanks for making coffee, Minus. You almost seem human sometimes," Callie said, approaching the table.

He finally met her eyes. "You think I want to be here on a Saturday any more than you do?" He stood and cracked his back. "Pull up a seat."

Callie sighed and did as she was told, straightening her dress and crossing her legs. "Is that it?"

He nodded. "Yep. It's an amazing little piece of technology, this here." Minus picked up the bearing and held it between his thumb and ring finger, elegantly displaying its dull luster for Callie.

"That's it?" she said.

Minus looked around then frowned at her. "Didn't you just ask me that? Yes, this is it."

"No, tomato head. Is that all of it? Where is the force field?"

"Okay, listen," Minus said, setting the bearing back on the cup. "We're gonna have to stop calling it a force field, okay?"

Callie shook her head as if to try to throw the frown off her face. "What? Why? Who gives a toot what we call it?"

"That term throws off the wrong interpretation. It's been used in way too many sci-fi movies. Besides, that's not really what it is."

Callie rolled her eyes and looked at the ceiling, exasperated. "Okay, then what is it?"

Matt Minus shrugged his shoulders and made a face. "I don't know. Call it a molecular repellant. A molecular shield. Anything."

Callie chuckled. "Okay, dude. Whatever you say." She sat staring at him for a moment, a smile still hung across her lips. Then she tilted her head. "Well? I wanna see it work."

Minus nodded. He then took a deep breath and seemed to tense up.

"What, Minus? What is it now?" Callie asked. Her patience was slowly morphing into something akin to five-pound fishing line.

"Callie, you're going to have to sign an NDA," he finally replied.

"Are you kidding me?" she almost shouted. She leaned forward in her chair, grasping the handles tightly; the backs of her hands formed sharp white daggers. "I created the stupid thing, did I not?"

He shrugged again. "Yeah, I know. I'm sorry, Callie. But you know how strict Royal is with its projects."

Callie sighed and stood up. "Whatever, Matt. Just show me the science, please. I'll sign the stupid crap later."

He looked levelly at her and slid a sheet of paper across the table with three fingertips. "This is how it's got to be."

Callie was not unfamiliar with non-disclosure agreements. She wasn't even offended by having to sign one in this case. It just seemed there was something else going on here that wasn't being spoken. Minus had never been this protective of a project in which she was under his employ. Sure, there was always paperwork, but it was typically an afterthought. Besides, since she had contracted with Royal to attend this creative endeavor, Callie had already signed a mortgage-worth of paperwork. Patent applications, design schematics, EYES ONLY pamphlets concerning the technical details of its makeup. Minus was treating her like an outsider.

She stared at the paper for a moment, knowing she would sign it – she would have to, lest she forfeit the balance of her earnings – but suddenly feeling hesitant with regard to his approach. The wheels of suspicion clicked into motion, and she started filing through her thoughts on the management hierarchy of Royal Research. Those linked to conspiratorial tones and darkroom tactics began to tickle her senses. After what seemed like a very long time, she finally lifted her squinted eyes to Minus.

"Who do you work for, Minus?"

He stood up straight and ran his hand through his thinning hair, then placed his hands on the back of a chair. Then, finally, resignedly, he sat down in it.

"Look, Cal. They're tightening up around here and I'm just trying to cover my bases. I noticed that when we filled out the finance requests, we didn't have an NDA. That's all."

"Matt, you're nervous as a long-tailed cat in a room full of rocking chairs. You're not hiding it well."

He looked up at her sharply. "You get that from Walter?" he said.

"Probably. What's got you so frazzled?"

"You're the one who's trying to avoid signing it!" he retorted.

"I'm not avoiding it, Minus. I'll sign it. It's just the way you presented it to me. You look like you're scared of the new boss."

Minus stared at her for a moment. Then he leaned back in his chair. His fidgeting was getting worse. Callie knew that if she waited patiently, he would break like an egg on pavement. She had always known how to break down his defenses and get whatever information she was looking for. It was all about waiting. Her strategy seemed to be working. She dusted imaginary lint from her dress.

Minus finally broke the silence with two words. "Brian Bradley."

⌘   ⌘   ⌘

Codi stood barefoot in her kitchen turning slowly in place, trying to reorient herself in what should be familiar territory. She reckoned it was serendipitous timing that her surgery had coincided with the move into her new apartment. Or perhaps the worst timing in the world. On one hand, she could not take for granted familiar territory. No bad habits to break. If she had to learn to live in a terrifyingly alien place, she might as well learn it with her new vision. But on the other hand, a little recollection from actual visual perception would probably make worlds of difference.

Since she didn't remember what the counter configuration looked like, she would have to learn it in this new ridiculous code. But that also meant she would not take it too lightly, thinking she knew exactly where everything was, either. Damned if she did, damned if she didn't. Tim was a patient helper when it came to her orientation of the new place. Codi would break down at the slightest mistake and suddenly begin feeling the overwhelming closure of walls all around her dark world. And that, above all, was how she felt most of the time. She felt claustrophobic. She was trapped in a coffin where kinetic freedom was more a curse than a blessing. And during these times, she would burst into tears, beating her small fists against Tim's strong chest, crying into his shoulder as he held her close, weeping, cursing and terrified.

"Why did I do it, Tim! Why did I have to rush into this and forfeit what little vision I had left! I could have lived like that! I could have lived blind! I would have been better off being entirely blind!" she would scream. Tim would hold her and stroke her and speak softly into her ears that calm would come. He would remind her that peace and calm would finally return, and she'd find a way to deal with things the way they were now.

And it was working. It was taking less and less time for him to restore her, and she was having her frightful outbursts less and less often. But they were still a daily ritual, at least for now.

Tim was at work now, though. And though he had instructed her – she had agreed, even – to stay away from the kitchen while he was gone, here she was. The kitchen was dangerous. The kitchen was home to all kinds of killing devices. For that was where the knives lived. The knives and the toaster and the stove, and all other utilities that were designed to make our lives easier – they all became deadly pits. Perhaps she could get the stove-top turned on. But to what end? What if she wandered away and could not get back to it from a safe direction? She could inadvertently sear her palm reaching for the control knob. And though she was well-versed in cooking and doing other such things as a nearly blind woman, she had not been blind. Codi had trained well with a cutting knife as a seeing-impaired woman. She knew where to place her fingers as she cut carrots and squash and onions so as to avoid adding her flesh to the vegetable medley. But now that the lights were out, she would have to take a step back and consider how much that training meant. For this was not total darkness. This was a *new* darkness. The thought had occurred to her that she could benefit from doing everything with her eyes closed. Just remove the stress and pressure of dealing with the weird visual replacements for things she knew so well, in favor of muscle memory in the dark. Trusting her instincts to guide her fingers and hands and feet the way she always did in the dark before. The way someone walks to the bathroom in the middle of the night.

Codi tried to rely on those senses – her mind's recollection of her environment – as she turned slowly between the counters. She reached out and touched the edges of the Formica with her fingertips, making tiny connections in her brain. This *looks* like this, and *feels* like that. This is my new life. This is the new shape of a counter top. This is the new visual representation of a fridge door handle. She continually had to remind herself to break the old connections. The thought that the fridge door handle felt the same was distracting. Because it now looked like something completely different. But she was practicing. Even if Tim came home and saw her in the kitchen and got mad, at least she was practicing. And her will was strong. She wanted to succeed rather than giving up and closing her eyes forever.

The doorbell rang, and Codi suddenly had a new mission in which to garner practice and efficiency. She tasked herself with finding the safest, most expedient path from the hard corners of the kitchen to the soft light of the front door. And she began to scoot her feet.

⌘   ⌘   ⌘

Callie sat silently for a long moment, racking her brain. She knew that she knew the name, but she could not immediately place it. Finally, she shook her head.

"Minus, I know that name is supposed to mean something to me, but I'm not getting it."

"He was with the Oliver crew, Callie," Minus said, almost coldly.

Callie remembered sharply her stint with the Olivers. And the memory of Brian Bradley came flooding back on her with a swift clarity that made her eyes pop open wide.

Bradley had been the mastermind behind the demise of the Olivers' trip to Mars a few years back. The first manned mission to Mars had been by a private company called The Oliver Company – a company that typically produced satellites – and Brian Bradley had been on the crew. But in the end, he had a ship out there near the Red Planet waiting to pick him up. After he had disabled the Olivers' ship, he had blown across to the safety of a deep space rescue. And the rest of the Oliver crew perished.

But worst of all, Callie had been the one to make the initial discovery. When parts had started burning out halfway to Mars, she, earthbound, had figured out Bradley's motivation. He had been siphoning the difference money from the cheap parts into a Royal account. The difference between the cost of those parts and their preferred name-brand parts had been tens of millions of dollars all said and done. And worse, the cheaper parts themselves were designed for airliners and other earthbound conveyances. Not spaceships. Spaceships needed parts that were made for the taxing environment of deep space, where there weren't such luxuries as atmospheric protection from the sun's radiation, and gravity. The parts all failed according to Bradley's – or his company's – master plan. And that had doomed the mission for the Olivers. But why?

Callie searched her mind, trying to recall the details of the event. She had naturally assumed that Brian Bradley had perished with the rest of the Atlas crew. Since neither Donnie Oliver nor Mike Thurman – the two co-captains of the ship – had made it back to report, she had no reason to think anyone did. Yet Minus had just said he was now working for Brian Bradley. Callie did not know, of course, that he had literally jumped ship and been brought back on another vessel. But at this point it seemed obvious to her that that's precisely what must have happened.

"I thought he died with the Oliver crew. What are you telling me, Minus?"

"No. He came back with the Royal bunch."

Like a firecracker popping in a quiet forest clearing, it all came rushing back to Callie. She suddenly remembered that the bank account Bradley had been siphoning his profits into was an account owned by the Royal Research Corporation. And now here she was working for them again. Sleeping with the very enemy she had been fighting in order to try to save the Olivers.

Callie felt sick at her stomach.

"Listen, Callie. All that is behind us."

"I don't know how you can say that, Minus! I lost a whole shipload of close friends!" Matt Minus tried to interrupt, but Callie stood up, knocking her chair over in the process, waving her finger in his face. "Oh no, no, no! You listen to me, Minus! That man is evil! He destroyed that ship on purpose!"

Callie still stood there fuming, trembling as she stood over him, even though she had temporarily run out of things to say. Minus looked at her thoughtfully, and finally dared to take his turn.

"Callie, how do you know that? What makes you think he did it on purpose?"

Her lips were quivering as she fought back tears of rage. And she spoke with a tightness in her chest. "Because, you idiot! He put his profits into a Royal account! Because he didn't know he was going to be on the mission! Someone else was supposed to go but he got cancer, so Brian Bradley was a shoe-in! And right before the mission left, he ordered the real parts he was supposed to have put on that ship in the first place! He was hoping they would get there in time for him to replace all the cheap junk he had installed on the ship!"

Minus was frowning, trying to keep up with her. He raised his hands defensively, and said, "You're losing me, Callie. I don't know about all this. I didn't work there."

"Well I did!" she shouted.

"Yes, I know that," he said, nodding patiently. "But I don't know what you're talking about. What parts?"

"He ordered non spaceworthy equipment for the Atlas ship! And when he finally learned he was actually going to have to fly, he tried to upgrade them to the real stuff! You know why?" she said, jabbing her finger into Minus's chest. She was standing right over him now. He only shook his head. He looked intimidated. The thought that Callie Simmons could intimidate anyone should have made him laugh, but he apparently could not find any humor if the thought did cross his mind.

"Because he got scared! He got scared because he knew those parts would fail and leave them stranded, and he had doubts about whether Royal would actually come pick him up!"

Minus sighed, staring straight into her eyes, and waiting to see if she had any more. For the time, she didn't, so once again, he proceeded cautiously forward. "That doesn't mean he did it on purpose, Callie."

"Oh, bullshoot!" she said, turning away and grabbing her purse from the back of her chair. "Of course it does! If he wouldn't have been on that mission, he would never have tried to replace those parts. It would have failed and no one would have known why."

Minus stared at her, apparently unable to answer. Obviously, Callie had the upper hand in an argument for which he was totally unprepared. He obviously knew very little about Brian Bradley's true character. But then obviously he had known enough to withhold his name at the beginning of the conversation. He had known that Callie would resent some part of the fact that his direct superior was the man she now spoke about with the tongue of a snake.

As Callie slung her purse over her shoulder, she took a deep breath and tried to bring herself back into a calmer place. At the rate she had been proceeding, she was likely on the verge of a stroke. Or at the very least a complete rage.

"What I want to know is what was Royal doing out there. If they were out there waiting to pick him up, why go to the trouble of even letting him go in the first place?" she finally said. "Care to answer that, hotshot?"

Minus shrugged. "Callie, I don't know anything about Royal's involvement out there. All I know is that when I told him I was bringing you on for consultation, he got real nervous. He asked a lot of questions about you. He's real intent on avoiding you at all costs."

"I bet he is. Did he tell you why?"

Minus tilted his head, then shook it. "No, Callie. He doesn't exactly confide in me. He's a ghost around here. Never shows up. He doesn't even have an office in the building."

As Callie turned for the door, she looked back over her shoulder and paused. Then she said, "I'm going to think about things for a while, Minus. Try to get my head around all this. But I'm thinking that if he's back, he's going to face criminal prosecution for the conspiracy against the Olivers." She grabbed the door handle, which still stood wide open.

"You've got some answering to do, bub. You might want to get your ducks in order." And with that, she pulled the door closed on her way out.

CHAPTER 8

As Codi opened the door, she realized that even such a simple event as door-answerings would have to be taken much more seriously. She had not even opened it against the chain, and had left herself completely open and defenseless. Alas, she was safe. It was a familiar voice.

"Hello, Codi," said Rebecca.

"Rebecca? Is that you?"

"The very one, darling. How are you?" she said, bending in to hug Codi.

Codi sighed heavily, dropping her arms to her side, not returning the hug. "I'm defeated, Becca. But I'm trying. I'm trying so hard to be positive."

"Oh, you sweet thing. Come here." Rebecca pulled her in tighter and rested her chin on Codi's shoulder. "I know it's so scary right now. A whole new world. But you are going to get used to it. You will learn to live like this."

Finally, Codi lifted her hands and draped them from Rebecca's shoulders. "I know. I just have to keep telling myself to believe."

They stood for a moment, just swaying in silence, then Codi finally took a deep breath and stepped back. "Come in, friend. I'll make some coffee."

"That sounds superior, Codi Cohl. I shall supervise the excursion myself!"

Rebecca followed her to the kitchen, patiently letting Codi lead the way. Codi expected at any minute to feel Rebecca's hands on her shoulders, guiding her. Part of her was forming a polite statement that told Rebecca to back off and let her do it on her own, while the other part resented the thought. She did not want the help, but still, part of her was perfectly willing to fall back on a motherly figure who could take all this confusion away from her and just guide her everywhere she wanted to go. The hands did not come though, and Codi began to understand that she would get no such help from Rebecca. For as much as Rebecca was there to help her, she was not there to coddle her. Not only would this hands-off distance quicken her return to a sense of normality, but it would toughen Codi's spirit. She would more quickly realize her own self-dependence. And that was precisely what she would need to survive in this sight-tilted world.

"I hope you don't mind my coming to see you, Codi."

"Oh, no problem at all," Codi said, feeling her way around the coffee maker. "I'm glad to have the company, actually." Her hands met the carafe and began drawing water from the tap.

"So I thought you might be interested in this," Rebecca said as she pulled a pamphlet from her purse. "You can have Tim read over it with you."

Codi looked up, though it was only a gesture to let Rebecca know she was listening. She stared at the blank wall directly behind the coffee maker.

Rebecca noticed and continued. "It's a catalog of sorts. There's all these neat things in here to assist the blind. Like one is a doorbell transmitter that plays a message to the person who rings it."

"Oh, telling them to be patient while I waddle my slow ass to the door?"

"Precisely, sister. Though it's not nearly as succinct as that." Rebecca smiled for a moment, then said, "There's more, too. A lot of cool stuff. Sonic replacements for your typically visual aids. Like talking calculators, tactile keyboards, that kind of stuff."

"That sounds awesome, Rebecca. Thanks for bringing it," Codi said. She felt as though she were only trying to be polite though. At the moment, Codi couldn't find the depth to care about such devices. It was, though, she gathered, the thought that counted. As she switched on the coffee pot, she turned to make her way toward the table where Rebecca sat. Without knowing it, she was heading directly for Rebecca's seat.

"Chair on the left, sweetheart," Rebecca called out.

She made the course adjustment and found the empty chair. "Thank you. So what's new?"

"Oh. I also brought you something else," Rebecca said. She pulled a plastic-wrapped placard from her bag and set it on the table, sliding it toward Codi. "This is a placard that reads 'TAXI' on it. You take a lot of cabs, right?"

Codi shrugged. "Sometimes, yeah."

"Well you'll probably be taking a lot more. If you ever want to get around on your own." Codi reached for it, and felt the smooth plastic with her fingertips, but felt no raised lettering. "You can get the same thing with a piece of paper, but this is hard to confuse with papers in your purse or bag," Rebecca added."

"Which way is up?"

Rebecca guided her hand to the top of the placard, where there was a single small hole. The placard itself was about five inches tall and just a little wider. Then she said, "It says it on both sides, too."

"Great. Thanks a bunch, Rebecca. You've been so good to me."

Rebecca smiled and squeezed her wrist.

"Say, Codi. I saw an ashtray over there on the counter. Would that perhaps mean I can smoke here?"

"Oh, sure," Codi said, rising.

Quickly, Rebecca reached out and put her hand on Codi's knee. "No, no, dear. I'll get it myself. Just wanted to check." As she stood up to retrieve the ashtray, she continued. "Listen, Codi. In my line of work, I meet a lot of people who are blind. Or going blind." She paused to light a cigarette, then returned to her seat, blowing smoke out the side of her mouth as she added, "As you might imagine."

"So, um, you think I could get one of those?" Codi interrupted.

"Ah, of course." Rebecca shook one out for her and guided Codi's fingers to the butt. She then slid the ashtray to the center of the glass table and pulled Codi's hand down, touching her wrist to the edge of the thick marble tray.

"So go on," Codi said after the cigarette was lit. She lifted her chin high and expelled blue smoke into the dim light of the breakfast nook. "God, that's good," she said.

Rebecca smiled. "Yeah. I wish it wasn't so good. So anyway, there's someone I want you to meet."

"Is she blind?" Codi asked, taking another drag from the long cigarette.

Rebecca tilted her head and shrugged. "That's the thing, Codi. Yes. Blind. But no, not a she." She paused a moment while Codi seemed to accept this.

"His name is Sam," she finally said.

"Okay. That's the thing?" Codi said, frowning.

"Well, I didn't know how cool it was for you to have guy friends. What with Tim and all."

"What do you mean, 'what with Tim and all'? Tim's not a bad guy."

Rebecca reached out and took Codi's wrist and said, "No, honey, that's not what I meant. I just know you're attached, and I don't know how cool he is about your having male friends."

"I don't think he cares," Codi said. She put the cigarette up to her lips, but pulled away. "Wait. Why do you want me to meet him? Are you trying to hook me up, Becca?" she said, a mischievous smile finding her thick lips.

"Haha, no, sugar. Not at all. But..." Rebecca said, and then smoked.

"But what?" Codi said, getting excited. The suspense of her presentation seemed almost scripted. It was too good.

"Well, to answer your question, I want you to meet him because he's blind. And he's been blind a long time. In fact, he was born that way. Someone who has never seen a thing can sometimes be a great benefit to a newly typhlotic person." Rebecca took another pull from her cigarette then tapped Codi's wrist again. "Honey, I think the coffee is ready. Would you like me to serve?"

"Nope. I'll get it. Go on," she said, getting up from the table.

"Well, he can help you interpret things the way he has learned over the years to interpret. Now obviously his case is a little different than yours in that he has no sight at all. But I think it could be a great help to you, regardless."

Codi found the mugs hanging from brass hooks beneath the upper cabinet and lifted two of them. She set them on the counter and poured steaming coffee into them one at a time, using her thumb as a guide for their fill. She then returned to the table, counting steps.

"Okay, so I'm still unclear why you think this would be a problem for Tim," Codi said.

Rebecca sounded like she smirked, but Codi wasn't sure. "Well, let's just say this: when two people with the same disability find themselves helping one another at great lengths, you can see where romance has a tendency to betide."

Codi laughed out loud with the coffee mug up to her lips. She had been blowing on it. Now part of it ran down her wrist and she cried out. Rebecca grabbed a napkin and wiped the coffee from Codi's arm.

"Well that's true in any situation, Becca."

"I give you that. But there'd not be much reason for you to meet under any other circumstances."

"Okay. So what's your worry? Is he drop-dead gorgeous or something?"

Rebecca took a sip of the coffee and blew smoke out her nose. "There's your advantage, darling. He can look like whatever you want him to."

"Oooh, I like the mystery!" Codi said. She could hear Rebecca smile genuinely.

"Good. I'm glad you're not offended by the thought."

"Of course not," Codi said. She took a sip herself. "But I have to know. Is he beautiful?"

"What do you want me to say, Codi? Do you want him to be beautiful? Or would you prefer him be a total dog?"

"Stop it!" Codi said, laughing through her shout. "I have to know. Tell me what you think of him."

"Wow, you're more interested than I thought!" Rebecca said.

Codi sat still a moment, then let the smile drift away as she considered the proposition – the whole proposition. The mystery appealed to her in a very profane and carnal way. The thought that she could meet someone new – anyone, really; it didn't necessarily have to be Sam – and never know what he looked like with human eyes. Her imagination would never be satiated. Or would it? She would have no recollection of his beauty – or lack thereof. No illusions toward an attraction based solely on his physical appearance.

Of course, this would be true for anyone new she met. But the thought that she could face this new world holding hands with someone in a similar situation was esoterically attractive. It was also perhaps a little frightful. What if they were together? What if they were *together* and neither of them could see? What would life be like with no light bulbs and televisions in their house? No magazines on the coffee table. Only books full of bumps. But to share those books with someone else... Someone who could feel her pain from the inside... She caught a flutter in her lower places where she scarcely felt anything at all anymore.

"What are you thinking behind those beautiful blue eyes, Codi Cohl? I see a smile in there."

"Oh there's a smile in there. You knew I would want to meet him didn't you?"

Rebecca didn't answer. But she allowed Codi to take her hand on the table. The silence went on for a long moment before Codi finally spoke again.

"Yeah, there's a smile in there."

Rebecca squeezed her hand. "That's what I thought."

⌘　　　⌘　　　⌘

Walter and Chris were sitting on the couch when Callie came barging in the front door. She marched directly for the television and slapped at the power sensor several times before it finally read her and turned off.

"Dude, what the fuck?" Walter said.

She turned with hands on her hips and faced the two men, breathing heavily. "Shut it, Walter," she said. Chris raised his eyebrows and looked over at Walter.

"What'd he do this time, Princess Cal?" said Chris.

Walter sat with the remote pointed at the TV, but obviously wasn't going to press anything until he was cleared by the queen. "Callie, dude, we're in the middle of Western Wagons. This is the season two finale."

"Flip your wagons, Walter!" she said, pointing at him. He now raised his eyebrows and nodded slowly, looking back at Chris.

"Not bad," he conceded.

"Guess who's alive, Walter Watson." she said with contempt.

Walter took a deep breath and lowered the remote. She was making it clear this would not just be a short interruption. When he didn't answer, she grabbed the remote from his hand and tossed it on the coffee table. The remote bounced off an ashtray and fell to the floor with a clack that sent the batteries rolling in separate directions.

She was still fuming mad about having to drive all the way back across town when she had gotten home to find no one was home. There was only one other place Chris and Walter would be on a Saturday afternoon, so she had driven back to Walter's house.

"Okay, I don't know what you're talking about, Callie. But I haven't seen the movie. And if you ruin it for me, I'm going to punch you in the neck."

"Okay," Callie said, putting her hands on the sides of her head, exasperated. "Why does everyone keep thinking I saw that stupid movie?"

"Stupid? Dude. Come on," he said, raising his hands. "What the hell is going on here? Was it bad or something?"

"I didn't go see the stupid Wagons, Chris! I ran into Minus!"

Walter lowered his head, rubbing his temples with one hand while he held the other up in a posture of defeat.

"Okay, so tell me who's alive, Callie. I'm guessing you're not talking about Minus."

"We were walking around the mall, just spending girl time. We ran into Minus. He said he called here and you told him where we were. He said I needed to report to work because the Japs are about to go down there."

Walter snickered. "What the hell?"

"I need to sit down," she said. She looked around, and finding no desirable place to set her rump, she opted for knocking Chris's boot-clad feet off the coffee table and took her spot there. She bent her head in much the same way Walter had, rubbing her eyes with trembling fingers.

"Okay. I'm sorry I shouted at you, Walter. Let me start over."

"Okay, apology accepted. What's this about Japs going down somewhere?"

She looked up and stretched her neck, then turned her eyes on Chris. "Chris, sweetie, will you go make me a drink please?"

He rose without answering and squeezed her shoulder on the way by.

"He said the Japanese were already planning to dive the Mariana Trench. Apparently the news has gotten out. And Minus thinks someone's going to beat him to the punch bowl."

"So he called you in to get to work? Like this is some simple book report?"

"What the spit are you talking about?" she said, frowning. "What book report?"

Walter leaned forward, taking her trembling hands. "Calm down, Cal. I'm just saying, I know this project isn't some simple assignment that can be completed in one afternoon. Why would he expect you to report to work on a Saturday?"

"He wants to put a rush on it." Callie held her hand up above her shoulder, and took the drink from Chris as he passed behind her, as if accepting a baton from a relay runner, with perfect grace. She took a sip as he found his seat again. "Thanks, hon."

"If the Japs are really ready to go diving, working on a Saturday isn't going to get you ahead. There's no way you'll beat them," Walter said, leaning back.

"Please, stop calling them Japs, Walter." Before he could object, she held up her empty hand and shushed him. "Anyway, he said I have to sign an NDA, and I could tell he was acting weird about it." She took a bigger sip this time, more of a gulp, then crunched ice in her closed mouth before continuing. The calm was reclaiming its place in her bloodstream now.

"So I asked him who he was working for now."

"Okay, I'm not going to bother asking how you made that leap," Walter said. Chris just sat staring between them. Callie had trained him well when it came to being present during one of their conversations.

"I know I'm not making a heck of a lot of sense right now because my mind is blowing in twenty different directions. But I could tell something was amiss when he asked me to sign an NDA."

Walter took a deep breath and leaned back. "So what, Callie? You have to sign an NDA before you can use the water fountain at Royal. You know that. You've probably signed a thousand of them there."

"Think about it, Walt. Think about what I'm saying. If Minus – this far into the project – is just now asking me to sign one, then I know he's trying to cover his butt for something." Before he could interrupt, she closed her eyes as if blocking him out and continued. "I know, rightfully so. But it's Minus we're talking about. He's the most laxadaisical person we know. Just follow me on this."

"Not when you use words like that," Walter said and Chris smirked.

This bought him a blank look from Callie. "Anyway, work with me here. I get these vibes sometimes. And I'm usually right. The whole point though is that I got a hunch about something being off, so I called him on it. The first thought I had was that he must be reporting to someone more strict than he's used to working for." She stared at him for a moment. "And think about this, Walter. Why did I have to sign one and you didn't? You were there when he told us all about it. He knows you know everything I know about it. Don't you think it's a little weird that he's so open about the project, yet at the same time wants an NDA from the person who's actually building the plans?"

Walter was nodding now. "Yeah, that is a little strange." Callie took a sip of her drink and looked over at Chris and tried to smile. It didn't come off well, so Chris pretended to be distracted by something else.

"So you know, when Jim Kite was in charge over there, Minus had free reign to do anything he wanted. Now he's working for someone else."

"Okay. And this person is alive, right?"

"Yes!" she said, pointing at him and sloshing some of her drink onto the carpet.

"Who's alive, Callie?"

"I thought you would never ask."

"I thought you would never get to the point."

"So I took the long way around. Brian Bradley."

Walter stared at her for a moment. "What? Who? Is that who's alive?"

"Yes!" Callie almost shouted.

"Okay. Great. Who the hell is Brian Bradley?"

Callie rolled her eyes. "Come on, Walter!"

"Sorry, dude. Am I supposed to know who he is?"

"Yes!" she shouted again, reaching to kick him in the leg. She missed and more of her drink sloshed out the side of her glass. She wiped the wet off her leg and licked her finger.

"You told me not to threaten you with physical violence. Can you stop taking your drink out on me please?"

"Brian Bradley is the butt hole who sabotaged the Atlas mission to Mars, Walter!"

He suddenly frowned. "Okay, I thought everyone on the Atlas was dead."

"Walter, we need to talk," said Callie.

"We are talking, Callie," Walter said, leaning forward and suddenly getting interested. "Okay I knew that mission was a failure. They never made it to Mars, right? But..." he leaned back, exasperated, and threw up his hands. "Okay, I thought I had it. Tell me what happened."

"He ordered a bunch of cut-rate parts over the years and funneled the difference in price into a British bank account owned by Royal. So they effectively bought that satellite with the Olivers' own money."

"What satellite?" Walter said, leaning forward again. He was beginning to make Callie dizzy with his swinging posture. She was nearing the bottom of her glass though, and reckoned that could as easily be the reason. Forget that a reasonable share of it was on the floor by now.

"Not the point. Anyway, the week before the mission left, he ordered all the parts again, this time from the proper manufacturer, and with the Olivers' money this time. You with me so far?" Walter nodded. She continued, setting her glass down and waving off Chris when he raised his eyebrows at her, asking if she wanted a refill.

"What this told me was that he was hoping the parts would get there in time for the mission so they wouldn't be stranded. Which basically tells me he knew it would be stranded because of the cheap parts."

"Okay, so he wasn't originally supposed to be on the plane?" Walter said.

Callie shook her head thoughtfully. "Nope." She ran her hair behind her ears with a fingernail devoid of polish. "See, I investigated all this for Donnie way back then. But they were already halfway to Mars when I figured out something needed to be investigated at all."

"So this guy did all this and stranded them in space. So how'd he get home?"

"Apparently Royal had a ship out there too. And they rescued him."

"Why didn't they rescue the whole crew?" Walter said, frowning hard and shaking his head. Clearly this wasn't making sense to him either.

"I don't know. That's what I want to find out. But he's back. And Minus obviously knew I would react because of the way he was stalling when I asked him who he worked for."

"God, babe, you put all this together because he asked you to sign a DNR?" Chris said. He looked amazed.

"NDA. Basically, yeah, I guess," she replied, nodding. Pride never entered her mind though.

"That's what I meant. Brilliant, babe," Chris said, grabbing her ankle and giving it a loving squeeze. "Just brilliant." Then he sat back, looking proud himself.

She smiled a conceited little number at him, then returned her gaze to Walter. "We need to find out how he made it back. And what they were doing out there." She looked at him for a long moment before continuing. "You didn't know about any of this, Walter?"

He shook his head. "No. Well, yeah, I mean I knew about the flubbed mission, but I didn't know Royal had any involvement in it."

"You weren't part of that?" Callie asked, staring holes through him.

"What? Hell no! Why would I have been a part of that? What the Christ are you talking about, Callie?"

"Well, you went to 'Fiji', right about that time, remember?"

He chuffed. "I told you where I was, Callie. I was in Manhattan. And frankly I'm offended you would think I had anything to do with the demise of an entire ship full of human beings."

"That's not what I accused you of. I just asked if you had anything to do with sending Royal out that direction," she said calmly. "And besides, when I met you at the airport that day, you seemed like you were hiding something."

"Callie, we've been over this. You didn't work for Royal at the time. You worked for the Olivers. And I wasn't supposed to talk about what I was working on. You know, non-disclosure agreement? Come on!" Walter looked truly offended now. "Besides, I told you what I was working on anyway. The aphotic camera project."

She stared at him and pursed her lips. "Okay. I'm sorry. I meant no offense by it. I was just trying to break through to you that if you *were* on the Royal Mars project, then now would be the time to break that NDA and talk to me about it."

CHAPTER 9

Lunch was served just after one o'clock on Sunday afternoon. Rebecca had invited Sam and Codi to her place, and had prepared a spicy Italian dish with thick meaty red gravy and lots of garlic, and red wine. In retrospect, she suspected garlic was probably not her best idea. For two people who depended largely on their other senses where sight was non-existent, she reckoned neither one of them would make a great first impression, and considered her folly in not setting out a dish full of Altoids.

But the meal went well and both patrons went on and on about how remarkable it had tasted. They sat on her back balcony at a small table set with nothing more than a tablecloth. The fancy decorations were completely absent and unnecessary. Rebecca had opted instead for mood music and spending her time on the main course. It was a complete success.

She spent her time inside, insisting that Sam and Codi should knock on the glass door if they needed anything. She insisted that she would cater to their every need, but otherwise stay completely out of the way – detached. She was not nosy and did not try to listen in on their conversation, though she did take pleasure in standing just inside the glass door and watching them occasionally in the name of judging the success of her playing Cupid.

Based on the body language Codi was displaying and the amount of time she spent smiling as she spoke, Rebecca gathered that the two really hit it off well, and liked each other almost instantly. Sam's body language was a lot more conservative, but she figured that had to do with the fact that he had never seen anything at all.

Codi was also doing a lot of leaning forward as she spoke, subconsciously trying to get closer to Sam. And though Rebecca had stepped out onto the porch twice, both times announcing her presence loudly, she had only gone out to refill their wine glasses. But they had never knocked on the glass to ask her for anything else.

After a while, Rebecca collected their dishes and checked on them, then settled into the comfortable leather couch in front of the television, but did not turn it on. She slipped her cell phone out from her jeans pocket instead, and slid her finger down the screen running through the contacts until she got to the Ws.

He answered on the first ring.

"Your love bird is fascinating, Walter."

"Who the hell is my love bird?" he said. He sounded distracted.

"Codi Cohl. She's absolutely fabulous."

"Who the hell is Codi Cohl?" he asked.

"Remember the cutie pie you begged me to meet for you? The blind girl?"

"Oh! Yeah! That girl. So now she's my love bird, eh?"

"Well, you spoke highly of her. At least the physical parts," Rebecca said smartly.

"Yeah? And you're finally on board? I told you you'd end up wanting to sleep with her."

"I don't want to sleep with her, Walter. Though I am really beginning to like her."

"I don't see the difference."

"Of course you don't. You're a man," answered Rebecca.

"Well, technically, so are you, Judas."

"Fair point. Is that how you justify my categorical alignment in your People I Can't Talk Into Sleeping With Me group, Walter?"

"It's a small but exclusive group," he said.

"The few, the proud."

"So why are you calling me, Rebecca? Can't you see I'm busy?"

"You working on a puzzle, Walter?"

"I'm wo- what? What the hell gave you that idea?" he said.

"Well it's National Puzzle Day. Just figured maybe I'd rubbed off on you."

"You can rub off on me any time you like, Judas. But right now I'm trying to get this fucking train to stop jumping the track."

"Okay, I'm not following your metaphor," Rebecca said, frowning. She knew Walter was prone to throwing out grand and sometimes long-winded analogies, but she wasn't catching this one.

"I'm being literal, Judas. What do you need if you're not calling to ask me to bed?"

"Ah, I see. You're playing with your toy trains again. Why does there have to be an agenda? I was just calling to chat. To tell you how well your friend is doing and everything."

"She's not really my friend. I don't know her. Only saw her the once, at the restaurant," Walter said. He was clearly agitated.

"Okay, Mr. Grumpy. I'll let you get back to your train set." Rebecca disconnected and curled her legs up under her on the couch, smirking. *So glad I'm gay.*

⌘   ⌘   ⌘

Callie was beginning to grow agitated too, but she maintained her patience by biting her lip a lot and pacing. For now, she sat on a bar stool overlooking Walter's miniature city as he ran the train back and forth over a bad spot of track. Tiny cows in a tiny pasture dotted with tiny trees stared back at her as she gazed disconnectedly at the diminutive landscape.

"Why are you such a butthead, Walter?"

He stood with his hands on his knees, staring at the N-scale replica of an old-fashioned steam engine on shiny gold rails. After frowning at the train for a moment, he finally stood up and looked at Callie.

"What?" he said, spreading his hands wide. "She calls to bullshit while I'm in the middle of tedious tasks. I get short. Big deal."

"She didn't know you were working on tedious tasks, Walter. Besides, why is it so tedious? I thought this was supposed to be a relaxing hobby."

"Who the hell said that? Running an empire is not relaxing."

Callie laughed out loud. "Empires don't feature cow-spotted pastures, dorkas. There should be more castles and trebuchets, don't you think?"

Walter shook his head. "You'll never understand, sugar tits. This is my empire. This is where I come to think. Some of the most complex problems of the universe have been solved over this train table."

"That's great, Walter. But I really wish you would concentrate a little more on the problem at hand."

"Okay, okay, I get it," he said, stuffing his hands in his pockets and walking to the other side of the table to get a better vantage. He then scratched his head and shrugged at her. "Listen. If this shit really bothers you, why don't you take all your evidence to the police and let them handle it?" He held the question out to her on his open hand, like an offering.

"Because, number one, I don't have it anymore. I didn't keep all those receipts or anything. I think I gave them all to Samson Oliver. Regardless, we need to talk to him first. We need to figure out what they were doing out there."

Walter frowned again, then stared her dead in the eyes. "Why, Callie? Why do we care what happened halfway between here and Mars?" He held up a hand to silence her before she spoke, then said, "I mean, I know you care about why those people died. That's not what I'm saying. I'm just saying, why the urgency? What's this got to do with the bloop thing you're working on?"

"Because idiot butt! I'll be working almost directly for the guy who brought down the Oliver mission! Don't you get it?!" she shouted.

He nodded concession. "Okay, fair point. So why not just surprise him then? Walk into his office and put your thing down."

"Put my thing down?" Callie said with a sour look on her face.

"Yeah. Show him your rage. Let him know you caught his ass."

"I don't even know if I want to go forward with this," Callie answered.

Thevi came into the room in her slippers and bathrobe, her long red hair a disheveled mess. "Morning, love birds."

"Hey babe," Walter said, turning to kiss her cheek.

Callie smiled warmly at her – as warmly as her mood would allow. "Good morning, sleepy head. Get enough sleep?"

Thevi yawned widely. "No. There's never enough sleep to be had."

Callie smiled and smirked. "Isn't that the troof."

"I'm gonna make some pancakes. You guys want some?" Thevi said.

Walter shrugged. "I already ate. I will take another cup of coffee though," he said.

"Okay. The pot's in the kitchen," Thevi said as she exited the room.

He stood staring at her for a moment, then turned to find Callie trying very hard to suppress hard laughter. "I guess she told you," she said.

"Shut it, blondie. So what are you talking about?" he said, finally coming back around to her side of the table and forgetting about the train set. At least for the moment. Callie felt a small victory in finally winning his complete attention, if only for a brief instant.

"I'm talking about the whole thing. Like dropping out of the project."

"You're serious," Walter said. He leaned against the table with his arms crossed. "That's a lot of money, isn't it?"

She shrugged and waved a hand in the air. "Who cares? I mean what's the point of it all? He wants to go down to see some legendary sea monster? And do what? Catch it? Try to talk to it? Take pictures of it?"

"Too dark to take pictures. That shit is seven miles deep."

"Beside the point. What *is* the point?"

He shrugged again. "I don't know. I think it's fascinating though. I'd love to go down and see that shit."

"You won't be able to see anything, Walter."

"Well, no. I mean, I..." he trailed off. "Wait. What are you talking about?"

Callie put her hands between her legs on the stool and leaned forward on them. "There won't be any windows on the pod. Can't be."

"Of course there can! Glass can be thick, and just as strong as..." he waved his hand around.

"We can put little bitty ones in. But I'm thinking we are going to avoid them. Remember that movie director?"

"What movie director?" Walter asked.

"The one who went down in the trench a few years ago. He built a sub and went down there to check it out. All kinds of stuff went wrong for him."

"You mean James Cameron?" Walter said.

"Yeah," Callie said, then frowned. "I think so. Anyway, the more stuff you put on there, the more you risk having something go wrong. So I'm thinking we'll slap a bunch of high-pressure cameras on there and call it a day."

"Too dark to take pictures," Walter said again.

"Infrared cameras. Whatever," Callie said, waving a hand dismissively. "But high-pressure ones. At that depth, the pressure is over sixteen thousand pounds per square inch."

"Okay, so right back at ya. What *is* the point of the mission then?" Walter parroted. He was nodding his head and shaking it at the same time.

"My point exactly."

"I guess you could send that Codi chick down there then, for that matter."

Callie had been rocking forward and backward on the bar stool, staring at the floor. She suddenly stopped. After a brief pause full of thought, her eyes shot up to meet Walter's. She tilted her head and squinted at him. "That's not a bad idea, Walter."

"Okay so we have to have a plan of attack. We can't just walk in there and expect to get everything we ask for," Walter said. He was pacing furiously, staring at the floor as he wore treads in the outdoor carpet between the table and the bar. He and Callie had moved to the back porch where he wouldn't be distracted by his train set, or anything else. The wind whipped leaves up against the screen that separated them from the back yard.

Callie sat with her chair turned sideways so she could warm her bare legs with the heat of the gas fire pit. She wasn't entirely comfortable with the cool environment Walter had opted for, but the air was fresh and it got her mind working. Besides, she had his pure, undivided attention now. They were both finally on the same page.

She no longer wondered whether or not she would go back to work for Minus and finish the submersible project. That simply wasn't the subject. The subject had now turned into how to dig into the mystery of what had happened with the Atlas mission, what had gone wrong, and how best to attack it. The problem had sat too long with no one knowing what to do about it – if they even knew there was something that could be done about it.

One of Callie's first objectives and ideas to Walter was to call Samson Oliver and ask him what he knew. He would no doubt take a call from her – they were old colleagues and friends and she still carried a lot of weight with him. But, like she and Walter, she doubted he even knew much. Like the fact that Brian Bradley had somehow managed to stay below the radar ever since the mission had ended. Certain people seemed to know certain things, but no one knew them all. No one knew all the things there were to know, or even that there was more to know at all. How much was there to know?

Quick searches on the Internet revealed that no one had even known Royal had a ship out there at all. Callie reckoned that was how they had avoided litigation in that respect. It had been a completely private – top secret – mission for them. They had publicized no details of their trip. Walter had brought up the point that if they wanted the Atlas crew dead so badly, they could have just had Bradley smuggle a pistol onto the ship, and he could have methodically eliminated them all one by one, in their sleep. Why did Royal spend potentially millions of dollars to follow Atlas out there to rescue him? What was so important about keeping Atlas from reaching Mars that they were willing to go to such great lengths to prevent it? Were they hiding something?

Every question they asked only led to more questions – but never answers. Not yet. That was when Callie had stood up from the bar stool and said, "Okay, we need to officially have a sit-down on this. Right now." And Walter had agreed. Somehow she had talked him into seeing the urgency of the situation – regardless of if she were destined to carry on the deep sea project or not.

But Walter's proposition – putting Codi in that ship – had got her thinking. And her thinking mind sometimes thought sideways. Sometimes thinking of one thing would peripherally lead to thoughts – and answers – on another. Like patients who suffered from macular degeneration – everything in the middle of their field of view was black, and they had to rely on seeing what they weren't looking directly at. But they both knew there was something sinister going on. Going on still, indeed. If Bradley was still alive, and Minus had the good sense to protect his identity from Callie, Bradley had obviously told Minus something about his need for privacy. For anonymity. He was obviously hiding something. And Callie reckoned she knew most of it.

"You're right," she finally agreed. "We need a battle plan. I still say we call Samson first. Get as much as we can straight from the top. He's a safe contact anyway. He trusts me implicitly."

Walter was shaking his finger at her – pointing at her as if to say 'good point'. He stopped and looked out at the swimming pool which lay dormant – covered for the winter. Small pools of dirty brown water lay in various places on the pool cover creating mesas in the negative space. Dirty leaves and frogs gathered in the pools of forty-degree water.

"Let's say he doesn't know anything though."

"Why would we say that?" Callie inquired.

"Because. He's a business man. He would have filed charges if he did." He stood still a minute, then returned to his pacing. "If he knew Bradley was still alive, he would have gone after him."

Callie was nodding, looking at the carpet upon which Walter trod. "That's probably true. I was wondering why no one had filed charges on him. Or Royal, at the very least."

"Yeah, no one knows he's back."

Callie looked up at him. "Minus does. And he's protecting him."

"So we go after Minus?" Walter said.

"I don't know. I doubt it. You know him. If he fears his job is in danger, he'll lock up like a... like a..."

Walter stopped again and turned to look at her. "Like a rusted Master lock in an ice storm?"

She pointed at him. "Yeah. That."

"Yeah but Bradley can't fire him. If he fires Minus, Minus could talk. That's the last thing Bradley wants." He rubbed his chin. "What surprises me is that he's using his real name still."

"He might not be."

"How so?" Walter asked, frowning.

"Well, if Minus knew I would eventually meet him, or see him or something, he would have just gone ahead and told me his real name so as not to look deceptive when I found out."

Walter shrugged. "Weak. But not impossible."

"There's something else, Walt. And it may not be connected, but something deep down tells me it is."

"What's that?" he said, tilting his head. "God, I wish I had a smoke."

Callie rolled her eyes, but didn't acknowledge the comment. "When Oliver was still in the prep phase of the Mars trip, they had a quick trip scheduled to go out to the space station to drop off a load of crates or something. Well, it got canceled, literally at the last minute because someone realized they were going to have room on the mission proper after all."

"Okay, that's pretty vague. I don't follow," Walter said. He now stood at the screen door looking out at the pool, hands on his hips. His untouched coffee mug stood chilling on the table next to Callie.

"They scheduled this spur-of-the-moment trip to take up these two or three crates of something Donnie had determined got left behind. This was before the mission. And when he got down to Houston to mission control, someone figured out there would be room after all on the main trip."

Walter looked over his shoulder at her, but did not speak.

"So Donnie flies back and sets about investigating why these were left off the manifest. I don't know all the details, but I think I remember something about a couple of forgotten crates and a big deal was made about it at the time."

"So what's that got to do with Bradley?"

"Well someone had forged Donnie's name on a contract with ETIS to take some urn shells out to Mars."

"ETIS? What the hell? Could this get any more complex?"

"I think it will, Walter. Anyway I think those two forgotten crates had something to do with someone leaving room on the ship for these crates of urn shells."

Walter turned fully to face her. "What are you saying? They sacrificed space on the ship for dead people? Instead of shit they were supposed to take?"

"Yeah. Something like that," Callie said, nodding. "Someone ended up dead. Not sure if that was related. But Donnie and Mike went out one night to go ask the loadmaster about it, and the guy was dead."

"Okay, dude. You're all over the place. What the hell are you getting at here, Callie?"

"Bear with me. I'm still trying to connect all the pieces. At the time, I didn't make much of any of it, because I knew other people were handling it all. But there was some pretty major conspiracy stuff going on. And every time, the sum of the equation ended up being two crates."

"Two crates."

"Yes. Two crates. So I think that's one of the answers," Callie said. She took a sip of Walter's coffee and made a face. "Now we have to find the questions."

CHAPTER 10

The call to Samson Oliver was over almost before it began. Callie hung up the phone and set it lightly on the glass table beside the two empty coffee mugs, then brushed her hair back behind her ears before turning to Walter. "Well, there goes that lead," said Callie.

Walter looked solidly at her, his hands hanging limply by his sides. "What? What did he say?"

"He passed away last year. Aneurism," Callie said soberly. She sighed heavily, then twisted the phone on the table with a fingertip.

"Damn," was all Walter said.

"That really breaks my heart. Such a good guy." Callie bit her lip; she was beginning to lose the light at the end of the proverbial tunnel.

"Who else can we call? He have a secretary?"

"Everyone else is dead, Walter. Everyone who knew anything about that trip is dead."

He took a deep breath and stuffed his hands in his pockets. "Really wish I had a smoke." He looked out at the pool again, then met eyes with Callie. "Okay, so what next then?"

"We go. Let's you and me go talk to Minus."

"Wait. What? What happened to having a game plan?" Walter asked. He was shaking his head.

"We catch him by surprise. Alone. That's our game plan."

Walter laughed out loud, but it wasn't a real laugh. It was the frustrated output of a man who was on the edge of his last idea. "Have you ever played a game, Callie? That's not really how it works!"

"Look, Walter," she said, standing up. "I have buying power! He needs me on this thing! He cannot let me walk away!"

"He let you walk away once already! Yesterday! Or did you forget?"

"Just grab your keys, okay?"

Walter stood staring at her for a moment, then finally nodded, seeing the seriousness in her eyes. "Okay. Fine. Okay."

As they got into the car, Callie rubbed her hands together and looked at the frosted corners of the windshield. She thought of all the things she wanted to say to Minus, and wondered how she would handle the part of her job that Minus did not want her to pursue. And that was the job that she was not being paid for. She wanted to find the answers to all the questions she had about Royal's mission to Mars. Part of it filled her with dread, while the other part – the part that involved her confronting Minus filled her with sickness.

She decided to put that off for now. She needed to make sure Walter was going to be her wingman on the unpaid job.

"Walter, are you in this with me, all the way?"

"In what, Callie?" Walter said.

"This investigation! I'm not giving this up, no matter what. I have to know what happened out there for – for... Well, not only the sake of my conscience, but to give the Atlas crew a fair shot at redemption."

Walter was sighing and shaking his head. "Sure, Callie. But I don't really know exactly what you're asking."

"I'm asking, Walter, for you to get in with both feet here. I need you to make some calls. Make some trips. Go visit The Olivers or something. Do something to help me, while I'm building this stupid submarine."

"So you're back on the job?" he said, looking at her with a frown.

"I don't know yet. I think I want to stay on as a spy for now. I really want to find out what happened out there, and find some way to bring Brian Bradley down. But I need to know that you're running around in the background helping me tie up the loose ends. Just like the old days," Callie said. She glared at him and pursed her lips.

Walter smirked. "Okay. Fine. I'll help you."

Callie knew that Walter's job in the research department gave him carte blanche to go where he pleased on the company dime. He could fly to France for a week, if he thought he had a lead into some good research there. He had absolute power and a no-ceiling company credit card. And she needed to use it. But she also knew that if she used him like this, he would never let her live it down. Walter would hold it over her every chance he got. He'd rub her nose in it.

The afternoon sun was bright and crisp, though it provided no heat. It came from somewhere far south of them, and only gave them the illusion of warmth. Inside the car, sitting in the leather seats of Walter's Bentley, the warmth was real. Callie knew that outside the tinted safety glass, it was colder than her soul felt.

She had never interrogated someone. She was not built for it. For one, she was not intimidating in the least. Her hundred-pound frame carried no authority on its own. People who knew her knew when to shut up, only because her passion for excellence begged an audience. They knew that if she spoke with anger and aggression, it was backed by a justified passion she had hidden within the walls of her thin chest. Rarely did someone counter her argument with an argument that had any real intellectual merit. She was usually right. In this case, it was not an intellectual pursuit, of course, so she would be fighting on the basis of passion rather than knowledge. She loathed it. It made her quake like the unsteady plates beneath the California coastline. As a child, when confrontation was on the horizon, Callie would turn to cold sweats and nervous stomach that gave her bowel problems and made her stop eating. An impending argument would squash her hunger for days. She would fast and fret, crying and shivering, talking to herself, trying to reason her way out of a situation that saw no reason. Even as an adult, she had not improved much. The thought of a fight made her uneasy and sweaty. Being called to the carpet by an angry manager would send her first to the bathroom to look in the mirror, where she would stare at herself, wondering what she had done wrong. She would talk herself down as best she could, splashing water on her face and walking out of the restroom with damp armpits and a knot in her belly. She was not built for confrontation. But when her fuse finally reached the powder, she would explode with reason and logic on her side – a confidence that would belie her inner feelings. And she usually won.

By tradition alone, they both knew that Matt Minus would be at home because it was Sunday, and football season was not yet over. Even if the day's programming contained no actual football games, there would be press conferences, strategy talk, predictions, and hours upon hours of replays of the season's highlights and follies. The coverage was akin to the endless political dribble that clouded the networks during the weeks preceding a presidential election.

As they pulled up in front of his humble manor on Mayfair Lane, the sun was beginning to seek refuge from the day, creeping below the houses on the left side of the street. Walter killed the engine and sat staring at the house, as if staking out a potential crime scene. Callie stared at the road in front of the car taking deep breaths.

"Callie, he's not going to hurt you."

She looked sharply at him, funneling her anger and insecurity directly at his eyes. Easiest target. "You don't understand, Walt. You'll never understand." She grabbed the door handle and flooded the car with the cold, late-January wind.

It took nearly a full minute before Minus answered the door. It was clear he was not expecting company. His pajama pants and stained t-shirt suggested he had been comfortable and stagnant for most of the weekend. And he was surprised by their unannounced visit.

"Callie! Walter! What the fuck!"

"That's kind of what we came to ask you, Minus. May we come in?" Callie said with a shaky voice.

He stood there for a long minute, looking back and forth between Callie and Walter before finally admitting them with a resigned sigh. He walked away from the door, leaving it hanging open as he scooted into the living room in his house shoes, clearly not happy with the intrusion.

A sweating can of beer stood on a table at the end of the couch, amidst a stack of empties just like it. A giant ashtray sat in their shadow, overflowing with the butts of his used up Bald Eagles. The room smelled dank and musty, like a locker room after a football game. Callie wondered how much beer sweat Minus had poured into the soft suede cushions of the discoloring sofa. And confirming their suspicions, the television that took up most of one wall opposing the couch was displaying several football games in squares the size of clipboards. The sound was mercifully muted.

Callie and Walter had been to Minus's house a time or two before, and had never been impressed. The house itself was certainly nothing special – a small, one-storey brick with a dark grey roof and a chimney that had probably never seen a fire – but the inside was filled with money. Minus obviously spent most of his paychecks on technology and gadgets. Several pairs of 3D adaptive glasses were strewn about the magazine-littered coffee table, and Callie absently wondered why he had so many pairs of them if he never took company. And wondered who would want to come watch a movie in Minus's house. Every time she had seen it, it had been in much the same condition. He made no effort to hide his sloth when it came to cleanliness. The magazines that covered most of the real estate the table had to offer were of the top-shelf variety, and they made her embarrassed to even acknowledge. Callie knew Minus would never marry though. He was the kind of guy who considered the cost-benefit analysis of marriage, and opted for the cheaper and more pragmatic version he practiced by bringing paid lovers in once a month or so.

She tried to find a place on the sofa that didn't totally repulse her, and sat on the very edge, her rump hanging off the front of the overstuffed but worn cushion. Smoke lingered lazily in the air, and defined for her the stagnation she and Walter could smell. For there was no cigarette currently burning. Either Minus's house had poor circulation, or he simply didn't use his central air. The ceiling fan stood still, the blades coated with thick gray dust that clung to it like cat fur on a cardigan.

Walter did not sit. He stood staring at the television, acting like he was interested in tracking the score of a particular game. Clearly, he was only here for backup. Callie would have to do most of the talking. So she began.

"Minus, why were you nervous about telling me you worked for Brian Bradley?"

"I wasn't. Why would I be nervous? It's no more your business who I report to than it is for you to be coming to my house on a Sunday to ask me about it."

"You don't have to be that way, Matt. I come in peace."

"I don't see it that way."

"See it however you want. I have come here seeking knowledge," she said, folding her hands across her knees.

"Okay, Sting. What do you want to know?"

"You were very reticent to tell me you worked for Bradley. Why was that? Surely you knew I would find out."

"Of course you would," Minus said, sighing loudly. "What makes you think I cared?"

"Okay, forget it. But you were acting funny about it. What do you know about the Mars mission he was a part of?" she tried.

"Nothing. He went to Mars?"

"Come on, dude," Callie said. "Cut the crap, Minus. Just talk to me. I didn't have to come here today..."

"Damn right you didn't! And frankly, I'm a little put off by the fact that you did."

"Well I'm sorry to disturb your all-important football game. But this is serious. If I'm going to work for you then I need to feel comfortable in the environment."

Walter still stood staring at the TV, not even looking back at them. His arms were crossed and he was defiantly staying out of it. Callie looked over at him and pursed her lips, then returned her gaze to Minus. Minus reached over the high arm of the couch and grabbed his package of Bald Eagles without looking. Clearly it was a practiced maneuver. His hand, by muscle memory or the odd laws of kinesiology alone guided his hand perfectly to the exact spot where he knew they would be awaiting his stubby fingers.

"So? What does Bradley have to do with your comfort within the environment?" He lit his cigarette with an old brass Zippo that was once probably shiny and golden, but now had taken the color of old Mexican pesos, green and lusterless. He readjusted on the sofa and propped his elbow up on a cushion, his smoke curling thick into the still air.

"Listen, Callie. I like you. I respect you a lot. That's why I asked you to join me on this project. But if you think for a moment that you can't be replaced, then you should consider a different sport."

"Ha!" Callie shouted, throwing her head back. And maybe that was Walter's cue, because he finally turned around.

"Yeah, seriously? That was probably the most retarded thing I've ever heard anyone say, Minus," Walter confirmed.

Callie glanced at him, a smile still lightening her face.

"Why are you even here, Watson?" Minus said, taking a pull from his cigarette. "Don't you have a train to catch?"

Walter chuckled at that, nodding slowly. "Look man, we're not here to fight. We just want to know what you know about Bradley. He's a criminal, dude. A felon, in fact. You know that, right?"

"Then why are you talking to me? Why aren't you standing in his living room today?"

"Because we trust you, Minus," Callie said.

He looked sharply at her. "That's not at all what this feels like. You know my impression of you two has suffered greatly today."

"That's fine. Just help me understand something," she said. The smile had left, but a smirk still remained on her mouth. Here be confidence. Just like a singer after his first song on stage, the stage fright had vacated the premises and left her with a bold sense of perspective.

"What?" Minus said, raising his eyebrows and shrugging. "I don't know anything about that mission to Mars. I didn't even know Royal was involved."

"Then how did you know Royal was involved?" Walter said. Callie looked at him thoughtfully. *Good point,* she thought. It had almost slipped right by her.

Minus stared at Walter for a long moment, obviously knowing he was caught. Then he finally looked down and breathed in deeply. He reached over and grabbed the sweating can and took the last of the beer from it in one gulp, then crushed it and tossed the can aside thoughtlessly.

"All right. Fine. Here's what I know. Bradley approached me when I first put in for you to come to work with me on this. He was concerned that you would corner him."

"Me? That *I* would corner him?" Callie said, putting her hands against her breasts for emphasis.

"Yes, you, Callie. You may not weigh a gnat's ass in a parka, but you can be intimidating in your own way."

She laughed out loud again. She had never considered that. Not in the way that the thought crossed her mind and she categorically scratched it off as impossible – it had simply never crossed her mind at all. It was too outlandish to even be broached.

"That is too funny."

He shrugged again. "Think about who you're talking about, Cal. That guy is a pansy with a capital S. If you sneeze too loudly, you'll put him off his gear."

Callie was shaking her head. Walter's face was unreadable. He made eye contact with her briefly, then he reached down and tossed aside a copy of Hustler and propped his foot up on the coffee table. He leaned over and rested his crossed arms on his knee.

"Okay, so he was afraid I'd ask questions? Is that it?" Callie said.

"Basically, yeah," Minus answered, nodding. He took another drag of the smoke and blew it out sideways. "He told me he was on that crew that went to Mars with the Olivers. He said you made radio contact about halfway into the trip and started feeding Ronnie full of a bunch of shit to make it look like he had sabotaged the trip."

"Donnie," Callie corrected.

"Whatever. He said you had some..." he took another drag and swished the thought around in his mind for a moment before continuing. "Some skewed perceptions about what really happened."

Callie closed her eyes and shook her head.

"He said he was afraid you would come talking all that trash about him and get him in trouble. He wanted me to know the truth before it ever happened."

"What do you believe, Minus?" Callie said.

"I don't know. I'm not paid to know. It's not my business."

"Don't you care? Does it not concern you in the least?"

"Honestly, Callie, I never really thought about it. If he hadn't come to me about it, I would have never known he was even on that trip."

"Well he was."

"So I hear." Minus stared at her for a moment, then finished his cigarette and dropped it into one of the empty cans on the table. "So are you going to tell me your side of the story?"

"Are you going to believe it?" Callie asked.

"Of course I am, Callie. You strike me about as much a liar as Mother Teresa."

"Well thank you." She ran a finger through her hair, pulling it behind her ear, looking at the space between them. "Thank you, Minus."

Callie spent the next twenty minutes filling Minus in on everything she knew about the trip – from the stack of papers she had found beneath Bradley's filing cabinet in the warehouse to the pictures she had found on his hard drive that only Callie and Donnie should have known existed.

Minus seemed very receptive, though he did not talk much during the deluge of information she poured on him. Walter finally moved to the chair that formed a right angle with the couch, and settled into the conversation like he was a part of it.

When she had finished telling him everything she knew, she finally spread her hands as if to say 'that's it' and then waited patiently for him to respond.

Minus sat there for a long moment, staring at the TV, but clearly not following it, scratching his chin slowly.

Considering. When he finally spoke, it was only three words.

"That's a problem," he said.

"Yeah. I thought so, too."

"Well what do you want to do about it? Do you still have the evidence?"

"No," Callie said, looking at her feet. "I left everything in the hands of Samson Oliver when I left the company. I didn't know Bradley was still alive, or I might would have kept it."

"Well you might need to let this one go, then. I don't know that any of this would stand up in court."

Walter cleared his throat, then said, "Wouldn't Oliver still have a copy of the passenger manifest?"

"I don't know. I would assume so," Callie said. "But he might not even be on it, since he wasn't supposed to go."

Minus was rubbing his three-day stubble as he added, "That's the problem with all these private space companies that are popping up. None of them are regulated to any kind of strict protocol."

Callie looked at him pleadingly, as if she could wish the answers from him.

"I can't just let this go. He single-handedly killed off an entire crew."

Minus sighed. "Then you need to consult an attorney. Meanwhile, you stormed out of my office yesterday hurling threats at me and making me believe you were abandoning your position on the project."

Callie lifted her shoulders, trying to hide inside herself. "Sorry, Minus. I was mad."

He waved a hand dismissively at her, and turned it gracefully into a fluid motion that retrieved his cigarettes once again. Callie knew she would be leaving here smelling like a saloon after a Friday-night boot scoot. The thought made her queasy. A long shower was in her very near future.

"Forgiven," he said. "But I need to know if you're with me or not."

"I'm on if she's not," Walter said. Callie felt a jolt of pain like he had just turned on her, and shot him a glance. "What? I think it's bad as hell. I would love to go look for a sea monster."

Minus looked at him steadily, then smirked. "Sorry, Walt. I had to beg to get Callie. I'm not authorized any help if she backs out, because I've already had to pay her a ridiculous sum of money."

She rolled her eyes. "I don't care about the money, Minus."

"Then how's about giving it back?" he shot back.

Her eyes widened and Walter laughed out loud.

"Shut it, butt face," Callie said. She picked lint off her pant leg and straightened her posture, then said, "Well I don't know if I'm on board or not. I can't in good conscience work for that man."

"Oh, Callie, you need to get over *that man*. You're working for me. Not him. You'll never even see him. I can almost guarantee that."

"I said conscience, Minus. That's in place whether or not he's present."

"Well, that's certainly your choice. But this is a really big deal. And I'd really like to have you on my team."

"Well that was the other thing I was going to ask you, Minus. What's this really all about?"

"Come again?" Minus said, coughing on his smoke.

"Callie wants to know why you're playing Lovecraft. She has no real sense of adventure for the sake of the word," Walter said, leaning forward.

"What the hell does that mean?" Minus asked. He was frowning at Walter, but directing his posture at Callie. "You aren't actually going down in the ship anyway. The adventure for you is to design something that's never been done before."

The ridiculousness of that simplicity had failed her entirely when last she spoke about it with Walter. Of course, she knew she wouldn't be going down on the submarine, but the reasons for the mission shouldn't have meant anything to her at all. It didn't matter why Minus wanted to dive. The science of the build was the only thing that had ever attracted her to any of the projects she had been on. Why had she got caught up in the emotion of whether or not it was a viable mission at all? Now she couldn't remember. After all, she had never participated in any of the projects she had worked on beyond just the design and theory phases. She had not been the one to step back in time when she had her hands on a computer that could send her back in time. She had not taken a ride in the shuttle whose powerhouse she had designed. She had never held the yoke in any of those endeavors. She had only held the marker. And here she had been questioning his motives.

"You know, you make a good point. But I'm still interested in knowing why you're after this, Minus." She looked over at Walter, as if for confirmation. "Are you going to try to communicate with this monster? Or catch it?"

Minus laughed out loud. "Hell no! I just want to see it." He dropped the cigarette butt in the can where probably many others lay cooling. "Of course the higher-ups probably have motives of their own. But they've funded me almost without ceiling."

Walter brightened. "Then why the hell can't I be a part of it? I'm already on company salary anyway. You don't have to pay me directly."

Minus shook his head. "What the hell do you know about oceanic exploration that would make you an attractive candidate, cowboy?"

"Well, nothing! But..." Walter saw he was fighting a losing argument, so leaned back and shook his head. "Whatever."

"Well there is only one small problem with your motive, Minus," Callie finally said.

"What's that?"

"You won't be able to see anything."

"What the fuck you talking about? I can put thousand-watt halogens on the outside of that son of a bitch. Light up that trench like Hiroshima on a cold August morning."

Callie was shaking her head, even before he had finished speaking. "Okay, here's the thing. I don't think we should put windows on it. That's just more things to go wrong. Plus, it's not like people can stand there and look out them, right? I mean, I was thinking," she said, and turned toward Walter, "that we just put a bunch of high-pressure cameras on it."

He sat with his mouth hung open, looking suddenly defeated. "What? I thought that's what the force field was for!"

Callie shook her head. "Oh my God! Are you serious? How does this thing keep getting more and more utilities? It started out only being a defense mechanism!"

"Well, yeah. But maybe it could… I don't know."

"No. That thing takes up way too much energy anyway. If we used it for anything *but* emergencies, the batteries would deplete themselves in under an hour! The sub wouldn't have the power to get back to the surface."

He leaned back mouth agape and grunted. "What the hell are we wasting our time for then?"

Callie smiled smugly at him. "It's okay, Minus. I have a pretty good idea how we get around all that." She straightened her posture and took a deep breath. "I want to have some cameras on it behind some pressure-resistant glass. Instead of windows. Windows are stupid. Useless. Let's do cameras with a feed into some monitors on-board, as well as a feed up to the ship above. Then you can see your monster."

⌘   ⌘   ⌘

The next morning, Callie stood in Minus's office again, hands in her coat pockets, waiting for him to get off the phone. As he talked, he searched through the array of papers and stacks of folders on his messy desk with both hands, phone cradled tightly between his shoulder and head. He finally found what he was looking for, and slid a paper across the desk. Callie noticed immediately it was the same NDA she had walked out on two days previous. She stood staring at him, but he leaned back in his chair, now holding the phone and running his other hand through sparse hair, ignoring her pointedly.

When he finally got off the phone, he hung it up and leaned forward, looking at her without speaking. She stared at him for a moment, then finally pulled a chair out from the desk and sat down, crumpling a Sports Illustrated magazine in the process. She rolled her eyes and fetched it from under her behind, then tossed it on the desk, disturbing an untidy mass of pens.

"I'll sign it, Minus. But I want you to know, I will be pursuing Brian Bradley. Completely separate and apart from my work with you, I will be making him a personal project of mine. And I will not stop until something is done about him."

"I don't give a shit what you do in your spare time, Cal. I just want your full devotion to me while we're together."

She raised her eyebrows.

Minus smirked and huffed. "You know what I mean."

"Of course I know what you mean. But the thought that you would even..." she started, but he interrupted.

"You stormed out on me, Callie. Just remember that. It wasn't the other way around." He leaned back and put his hands on the armrests, staring her down in a mental game of chess that seemed to take minutes.

Callie bit back her pride and took a deep breath, then grabbed one of his pens and signed the form.

"What we've got here," Minus was saying, "is an electronic probe with sensors for heat, proximity and atmospheric pressure, accurate to a tenth of a degree." They were standing at the bench in the work room, admiring the prototype sphere that looked so plain to the unknowing eye.

Callie felt the knot in her stomach tighten as the reality of scuba diving edged ever closer to reality. She breathed in heavily and looked up at Minus. "Okay. And how do we see it?"

"Right here," he said, holding up a handheld device no bigger than a smart phone. "This reads everything in real time, via a peer-to-peer partnership."

"Is it..."

"Waterproof? Of course. To a hundred feet or so." Matt Minus set the device down carefully then turned to her. "Look, Callie. There's no reason why you have to be the one to go down with this thing to test it."

"Bull shoot, Minus. There's every reason. If you want this thing tested right, I'm your guy."

Callie straightened and took another deep breath. "I want to know every part of it and I want to know how personal it is."

"Personal?"

"Yeah. I want to know what kind of readings it's taking. I want to feel it myself."

"That makes no sense, Callie. We can get a team of professionals to go down there and vet this thing until there's a stack of stats on it tall enough to make you look short."

"Ha, ha." She crossed her arms and looked him in the eyes. "You know how serious I take my science, Minus."

He nodded slowly. "Suit yourself."

"I plan to. Chris and I are actually going out this afternoon to buy wetsuits and sign me up for scuba training."

⌘   ⌘   ⌘

Codi Cohl had butterflies in her stomach as she hung up the phone. She had agreed to meet Sam and have coffee in the city. Not in the comfort and safety and accessible places she usually confined herself to. She would actually get to use her white cane. This filled her with apprehension and nervousness, but also a certain thrill she could not quite place. Codi had spent weeks training with it at the Center for the Blind, but that was before she had been completely sightless. She had closed her eyes during that training, and reckoned she would probably fair a lot better now doing the same. She was afraid that the sights of the city streets would assail her eyes as her mind tried to make sense of the shapes and colors.

But the butterflies were an aggregate of more than just the dread she felt by venturing out and the coffee date with Sam. There was something else looming there in the recesses of her mind, something she couldn't put her finger on. Perhaps it was her suddenly growing feelings for Sam, and the lackluster relationship she had with Tim that were finally coming to a head. If not a head, then a pre-head. She knew she would have to face up to it at some point in the near future. And there would be confrontation. What would she tell Tim? *I'm falling for a man I've never even seen – and never will. You're not good enough anymore. The two years I've spent with you aren't enough. The six weeks I've known Sam are much better.* Surely she wouldn't fall in love with Sam though, would she? She had, after all, only known him for a couple of weeks. Even still, there was something there. And Rebecca had known it. She had known there would be.

But Rebecca was not to blame for Codi's nature. Perhaps Codi was too romantic for her own good, feeling puppy love for every man who paid her the slightest amount of attention. But she didn't think it would always be that way. She knew deep down inside that once she found the right man, her heart would no longer wander.

She pushed the butterflies down, trying to settle herself. Tim would be home any minute, and she wanted to be gone before he got home. She reckoned it would be best to act in front of him as if nothing were going on, if he were to show up before she left. And in fact, nothing was going on at this point. It was a coffee date. Sam was going to be with her in the city, teaching her hand at the white cane, showing her the tricks of the trade, as it were. She didn't even know if Sam felt the same way for her as she did for him. For now, she was on safe ground. She just didn't feel like it.

The wind whipped her scarf about as she descended the stairs of the apartment, carefully counting her steps. As she got to the edge of the sidewalk, she pulled the taxi placard from her purse and felt for the top hole. After a minute of standing there, she heard the engine and brakes of a vehicle close by. Then the door, followed by a man approaching her. He guided her to his arm and opened the back door for her. "Need a hand?" he asked.

"Yes, please, just show me the corner of the door," she replied.

The man did so, then closed it after she got in. She thought he said something else, but the window was closed so she couldn't make it out. When the driver got in and confirmed her destination, she began to feel a little better about her rendezvous with the blind man named Sam. The drive itself took twenty minutes, and then she was fumbling in her billfold for the proper fare amount. Codi kept her tens folded in half, while her fives were folded with an angle, and twenties were quartered. In this way she could quickly tell them apart. Her ones were flat in the fold, and she always used exact change when possible. This prevented the potential stiffing from someone trying to claim a ten in place of a single.

As she stepped out of the cab, she asked the driver which direction the coffee shop was from her door, then thanked him and began her trek toward the front door where she would again seek the help of a perfect stranger. Trust, it seemed, was something with which she would have to become intensely familiar.

"Hello, my name is Codi. I'm here to meet a..." she began when the host welcomed her inside.

"Hi, Codi. Your party is waiting for you. May I guide you?"

"Yes, please," she said, and pulled her cane close to her chest, a foot or so off the ground. She put her hand on his inner elbow and followed as he led her through the confusing mess of tables to a corner. She thanked him as he pulled a chair out for her and moved her hand to its back.

"Hello, Codi," said Sam.

Her face instantly lit up. Uh oh.

"Hi, Sam. Well, that was an adventure!"

"I imagine so. Good to see you," he said.

"And you as well, Sam," Codi said, tilting her head. "You look nice today."

"Thank you. I wasn't sure whether to go with the blank sweater, or the less attractive but altogether more practical blank one. I'm glad you approve."

She laughed out loud.

They talked for several minutes while they sipped hot coffee, before Codi could finally no longer contain her curiosity. "So since we're getting closer, and since it's *totally* not important, can I ask you something, Sam?" she said.

"Blonde hair. I'm about six feet tall. I think my eyes were supposed to be blue. I have a remarkable smile, my mother tells me all the time. I'm supposedly very good looking."

Codi giggled. "Sounds like it!" She took a sip of the coffee, still smiling, then set it down. "So, do you want to know what I look like?"

"Well, I think I can picture it. Tell me if I miss something. You have short black hair and powerful blue eyes. You have a very soft jawline and gorgeous white teeth. A thin nose and a perfect smile. That about right?"

"See, she wouldn't tell me when I asked her what you looked like," Codi said, still giggling.

"Rebecca is a special kind of knot. You have to twist her just the right way to get her to tell you things."

"I'm beginning to gather. But I really like her," Codi said.

"What's not to like? She's awesome. But you know, none of that really means much to me."

"What, that she's awesome?"

"No. That you're beautiful. See, I still have to make my own decision."

"Oh. Is that right?" Codi said. She found herself giggling yet again, and was instantly reminded of the puppy love that had begun to wash over her.

"Absolutely. And though your physical appearance will have no bearing on whether or not I will like you, I will still have to know what you look like with my own eyes."

"So you want to feel my face up?"

She heard him shrug in his leather coat. "I hope it's not offensive."

Codi blew wind through her lips. "What, are you crazy? I think it's the sweetest thing in the world. To allow a blind person to know what you look like?"

"Good. And of course I'll reciprocate. So shall we proceed with the ballyhoo?"

CHAPTER 11

Codi took a deep breath as she pushed the door closed behind her, waiting for the sound to settle before taking the thirteen steps it took to get to the living room. Her hands were trembling, and her stomach had butterflies in it again, though this time she could easily place them and define the reason for their presence. She knew Tim would be on the sofa, poised for interrogation. Codi did not often leave the apartment by herself, especially not for several hours at a time. But if this was the time for her confrontation, she would be ready. She had steeled herself in the cab ride back home. Some of that steel had rusted on the long walk up the stairs to the second floor, but she still felt strong.

"Hi, honey!" Tim said brightly. She stopped in her tracks, finding the back of the sofa with her right hand. Turning to the sound of his voice, which was not coming from the sofa, she put a smile on her face and answered.

"Hey!" she said, trying to sound cheerful. It felt fake and forced without the pet name attached to the end.

"Over here. In the kitchen. Want some coffee?"

The lump in her stomach dropped and relief flooded over her. Her face felt cool and loose now – having been in a tight forced smile. Had she gotten it all wrong? Would Tim really let her get away with being gone for this long? Would he let her off the hook this easily? She dropped her handbag over the back of the couch and turned to walk into the kitchen.

"No, thanks. I'm pretty beat."

"Yeah, I guess you probably had enough coffee already. How about some Sprite?" Tim said, and the knot instantly returned, full force.

"What does that mean?" she asked. Her hands found the back of the chair and stood staring in the direction she thought he was standing. Given his mood swings, she felt safer behind something solid, but the chair would have to do. She was beginning to tremble visibly, and her head began to swim with thick fear that made her ears burn. She could hear the blood flowing between them.

"Oh, nothing. I'm just guessing the coffee you had with the blind man probably topped you off."

Suddenly, the sound of the cab driver's voice outside the closed door of the taxi came tingling back into her thoughts. He had been addressing someone. Had Tim followed her all the way from the front walk of the apartments? Had he been there for the whole encounter? Had he, more specifically, seen the way Sam ran his fingers over her face, her lips, her brows, learning her physiognomy?

"Why were you following me, Tim?" She felt her hands tightening on the back of the wooden chair, burning her forearms with the strain. Her heart slammed in her chest, pulsing red clouds into her twisted vision. What if this was the time he finally cracked and decided to attack her? What if infidelity was the final straw? She felt wholly unprepared for a physical confrontation against a strong man who had perfect vision and a will against her.

"Why *wouldn't I* follow you, Codi? You're my love. My love. Not someone else's. Does it not make sense that I would want to protect you from someone who would take advantage of you in your handicapped state?"

"I'm not fucking handicapped! You're a stalker!" she shouted, spit wetting her lips as she hurled the words at him like daggers. Codi tried to back up and make a move for the door, not knowing where she would go, or to whom she would turn, but didn't get get any further than one step before his strong hands gripped her shoulders, keeping her square with him. She instantly went into defense mode and started swinging her fists wildly, assaulting him with her anger and fear. She finally connected with one and felt the soft flesh of his mouth mash against the hard bone of the teeth and jaw behind, and he yelled out in pain. And Codi began to panic. She continued to swing, but his hands had instantly come off of her shoulders, and now she was reeling, trying to find something to prevent her fall – to orient her against the uncertainty of her weak sight. She opened her eyes and took in the odd colors and shapes of the strange landscape that made up her dining area, but it was no help. It resembled the alien landscape of an ancient alien city – cubes and curves upon dark ground that made no sense, and rays of red light streaming in from the hard bulb above the sink. She was not fast enough, and in no time, he had her by the shoulders again, this time from behind. And she could not pull away from him. Instead, he pulled her right up against him, his thick, meaty arms wrapping round her like a bear protecting its cub. *The irony,* she thought, *that these arms should make me feel loved...*

"Oh no you don't, sweetheart. You ain't going nowhere," he said in her ear. His chin was pressed right up against her jaw now, and he was grabbing handfuls of her chest, squeezing and kneading like a baker testing his dough.

"Let go of me, you fucking creep! I hate you!" she screamed. She flailed and squirmed in his embrace, but was too weak to overpower his larger frame. His right arm slid down to her waist where he grabbed her hip and hoisted her bodily into the air, then slammed her over the back of the couch. She cried out in agony as her pelvis connected with the hard support of the sofa's frame.

"You like that blind boy, do you?" he said. She could smell the sweet, bitter scent of vodka on his breath. He pushed her forward and began tugging at her jeans, pulling them down over the thick flesh of her hips, but she fought and tried to stand up, so his fingernails dug deep into her skin. "I think you're forgetting what we have here, Codi! Why do you want to go elsewhere for something you already have at home?"

"Get off me you fucking prick!" she screamed. "NO! Let me GO!" She leaned back again, this time with more force, and felt the back of her head slam into his face, sending stars through her brain as he cried out once more in anger and pain.

"Goddammit, Codi! Why are you fighting me! I love you!"

"If you love me then let me fucking go!" she commanded, turning in his failing grasp and pushing him with all her might. He grabbed her hands and held them tightly against his chest, causing her elbows to flail like flopping fish on a wharf, starved for oxygen and crazed with fear.

And suddenly, it was over. He let go.

"Fine," he said. He stepped back and she was free. "Fine. If you want to go, then go. I thought we had something special, Codi. I thought you loved me!"

She was reaching backward over the couch, whipping her hand from side to side in search of her bag. "Yeah? I thought you loved me too, Tim. Thank you for not fucking *raping me*!" she said, shouting the last two words. Her hand found the leather strap of her handbag and she swung it up onto her shoulder, inadvertently hitting herself in the face with it. She heard something hard and plastic hit the wooden floor of the entry hall and knew it was the taxi placard escaping the side pocket of the purse.

"Rape? How can you rape the willing, Codi? We are lovers! Or have you forgotten that?" he shouted back at her.

"Lovers don't take love by force, you fucking pig!" she spat, and turned toward the front door. On her way into the entry hall, she kicked the placard, then scrambled to the ground in search of it, fanning the floor with trembling hands.

"Pig? Pig? Seriously? Codi, you hurt me! I would never take you by force! I thought you wanted it!" he said. After a moment of standing idly by while she searched in perfect darkness for her tool, he added, "Look at you now. You say you're not handicapped? Look at you!"

"Fuck off!" she screamed, tears now entering her voice. "You once swore you would be my eyesight for me when it was gone! Now here you stand mocking me for it!"

Her fingers found the placard; she stood and shoved it into the side pocket, then reached for the doorknob. Finding it quickly, she moved her hand ten inches to the left, where she knew her white cane awaited its calling. It was not there. It was never *not there*. But now, it was perfectly absent. "Oh, that's fucking mature! Give it back, Tim."

"Give what back? You're not handicapped, remember?" he said, the childish wax of sarcasm over-exaggerated in his voice. She then heard the splintering sound of fibers splitting as he cracked it in half behind her.

"Oh, no, Tim. Oh my god. You are the worst piece of shit I can even imagine. You say you loved me? You never loved me!" she cried. Tears were now pouring forth with no reserve down her reddened, angry cheeks. "Goodbye, Tim. Asshole!"

She turned the doorknob and stepped out into the landing, slamming the door behind her. She heard the bolt turn in the door, then shouting and banging as Tim took out his anger on the solid wood that stood between them. Her heart was still beating triple-time as she scooted toward the stairwell and slammed head-on into another person. Codi yelped in surprise, suddenly thinking Tim had somehow gotten out without her knowing, and was putting up his final fence. And this one, she knew, she would not get past. He would make sure of that.

⌘   ⌘   ⌘

Callie bounced comically, her head swinging back and forth like a rag doll as she pulled up on the skin-tight shorty wetsuit that had managed to hang on the thickest part of her thighs. Chris stood with his arms crossed, watching her fight the suit, laughing out loud at her futile gestures. Her face was a jack-o-lantern, wide eyes and an exaggerated wide grin that expressed her comedic outlook of the ridiculous insinuation that her thighs were too fat to don a shorty. Her small breasts bounced freely beneath her loose t-shirt and she noticed Chris's attention being drawn to them like a magnet to an iron barrel.

"God, this is awful!" she said, gasping between the words. "Are they always this hard to put on?"

Chris shrugged. "That's kind of the point, Calgirl. They're supposed to be tight. Keeps a thin layer of water against your skin so your body stays warm," Chris said.

"I know the theory, Chris Butt, but I don't understand why it has to feel like I'm wrestling a monkey!"

"Callie, if you're going to call me a bad name at least say Chris Ass. You sound like a dork."

"Shut up, Chris Butt. Are you going to give me a hand with this, or stand there like a scarecrow?"

He stepped forward and grabbed both of her breasts with his soft hands, looking her dead in the eyes. She immediately stopped the bouncing and looked up at him, taking a deep breath. "What are you doing?"

"I'm helping you. You asked me to help," he replied levelly. "I'm keeping them from bouncing for you."

"I don't need you to support my tits, Chris."

"Oh. Sorry," he said, and bent to help her pull up the tenacious neoprene. "I think your thighs are too big, Callie."

"Do you want me to sock you in the mouth, you flipping freak?"

"I'm just sayin'!" He stood up straight, stepping away from her and looking at the progress he hadn't made.

She reached down and grabbed the inside of the legs and started kneading them upwards, rolling the thick rubber like Silly Putty between her fingers. The fabric began to work its way up her legs until she could finally gain purchase on the rest of the suit.

"God, it feels like my legs are being constricted by a snake," she sighed as she pulled it up over her belly. When she finally got it up to her armpits, she frowned past Chris in the mirror at the ridiculous shape her body was beginning to take. "I look like a cow!"

Chris turned to observe the image in the mirror, clearly measuring any difference between the reflection and the actual image before making a comment. "No. You look nothing like a cow. You actually look kinda hot," he said.

"Kinda hot? What the heck does that mean?" she said. She was staring at her reflection, flattening out tiny wrinkles in the belly of the wetsuit. It smelled strongly of rubber and chemical, and assaulted her nostrils like gasoline spilled on a boot at the filling station.

"It means I would love to rip that thing off of you and take you right now. But I know it would take so long to get the damn thing off, I would lose my hard-on."

Callie laughed out loud. She finally let go the fabric and put her arms around Chris's neck, standing on tip-toes to rub her nose against his. "I'm sorry you have to wait, Chris." She pulled her head back and looked him in the eyes for a long moment, the smile never leaving her face. "I hope you still love me."

"Of course I still love you, Callie. You're worth waiting for."

She stared at him another long moment before she kissed him, then spoke again. "Good. I'm glad. That's the true test of a man's love. If he's willing to wait 'til marriage, you know he's not after sex."

Chris's smile slowly slid off his face, then he said, "Uh, no, it doesn't mean that at all. I'm still after the sex. It just takes me longer to get to it."

She slapped his face lightly, then kissed him again. "Well, maybe we can fool around tonight." She smiled what she thought was her best seductive number and pinched his earlobe.

He frowned again, then said, "Oh, really? Is it March already?" He looked around as if in search of a clock, or – more appropriately – a calendar.

She shook her head and breathed in deeply. "You really do want to prolong the wait, don't you?"

They checked out just as the sun was disappearing beneath the buildings to the west. The windows of the dive shop were cloaked in black screen that kept the worst parts of the sun out of the patrons' eyes, but in the sunset, it dimmed the light to a dark crimson that confused the eyes. Callie had picked out a short-legged wetsuit that had a pink stripe running down the right side, and flippers that matched. Her snorkel and mask were rimmed in the same pink. Chris was already scuba certified, and had his own gear in a bag that sat in the back of his closet at home.

As they walked out to the car, Callie got goosebumps, realizing that she had just solidified her commitment to the project with Matt Minus. Regardless of what happened with Brian Bradley – if anything ever did happen – she was now fully committed to helping Minus find the bloop. Even armed with the knowledge that she would not be confined within the oppressive shell of the ship she was designing, she knew she would be a part of it. Sitting in some dark, cramped control room aboard a ship in the western Pacific would be almost as claustrophobic as being inside the submersible itself. She would presumably be staring at a series of monitors, concentrating fully on the limited sights the infrared cameras themselves were able to pick up.

She was still battling with Minus about putting actual glass windows on the submersible. It could be done, but she was voting for leaving them off, since no one inside would presumably spend much time standing there looking out of them. And without the luxury of glass windows, the occupants would have to get used to the fact that they would not see true sights outside the capsule until they returned to the surface.

"So tell me more, Chris. Is it scary down there at a hundred feet below the surface?" Callie said as they pulled out of the parking lot. She stared at him in the low light of the car's interior. The glow from the instrument panel lit his face in a pale blue and made his eyes look black.

"How many times are you going to ask me that, Cal?" he said, obviously trying to force a smile. She was thankful that he had maintained his patience with her, but she knew she would probably ask him the same question a hundred more times, up until the time they fell backward off the edge of the dive boat holding their masks to their faces.

She took a deep breath and returned her gaze out the front windshield. The highway was a sea of red brake lights ahead of them and the lights of the city stood on the close horizon like Friday-night beacons, reminding her that there was life outside of the home. They almost never got out for dates or dancing anymore, having fallen into the comfort of a monogamous – albeit abstinent – long-term relationship. Callie felt the sting of that thought, suddenly missing the platonic nights out she used to spend with Walter so frequently. She also reckoned that the dive classes and subsequent underwater studies would be good for her. If nothing else, it would be a fun and exciting way to spend some time with Chris.

"I don't know. Just bear with me, okay? Remember, I'm terribly afraid of the water, okay?"

"Yeah I know, but when you're diving, there's very little to do with water."

She looked at him blankly.

"I don't mean that. I mean it feels like that. There's really nothing watery about it. You're underwater and you're weightless, but it's not like swimming. You're not sitting there paddling and trying to stay above it. You're just flowing and moving through it like a fish. It's absolutely wonderful."

"What if I freak out down there though, Chris?"

He shrugged and adjusted the air. "Then you surface. It's not like you're trapped down there. You can come up whenever you want. And get this: even if your tank is out of air, you can still make it to the surface. You breathe out the entire time you're coming up, and you never run out of air."

"Ah. Expansion," she said, nodding very slowly.

He looked at her sharply. "Yeah. Yeah, that's it. Hence why you're exhaling all the way up. You hold your breath and you'll pop your lungs."

"That makes perfect sense." She sat chewing her lip for a long moment, before finally turning sideways in her seat, looking at him in the low light. "Even still. It still seems like it'd be scary being surrounded by all that water."

"You'll never even notice it. Water is the last thing on your mind when you're down there. And furthermore, it's actually safer than swimming for someone like you."

"How is that?" she said, frowning.

"Think about it. You have an air tank for one, and secondly, you're not out there flailing around trying to swim."

She nodded again. "Okay. So tell me, Chris. One more time. Do you think I'll be able to do it?"

He smiled at her. "Of course. You're gonna do fine."

⌘   ⌘   ⌘

Codi screamed and instantly started flailing and swinging her fists, trying to break away from her captor. Very quickly, she realized it was not Tim she'd run into. It was a woman's voice who was now shouting above Codi's own screams, trying to calm her down. She had grabbed Codi's wrists, and was now pulling her close, trying to guide her back to sanity and tranquility.

"Shhh, it's okay, Codi, it's me, Maria!" the woman was saying. "It's okay, honey, you're safe! What's wrong, sweetie? Shhh! It's okay!"

Codi finally stopped thrashing about, and stumbled forward, letting the woman embrace her. She was trembling like electricity and tears flowed freely down her cheeks. "Maria!" she cried between sobs. "You have to help me, Maria! That man is a monster!" she said in almost a scream.

"Okay, honey, come with me. Come on! Shhh!" Maria said, guiding Codi by the shoulders, turning toward her own apartment. "Where's your walking stick, honey?"

"Tim snapped it in half! That bastard! I hate him! He's a sick fuck and I hate him! You have to help me get out of there!"

"Okay," Maria said. "It's okay, Codi. You're okay now. Here. Let's go inside and calm down."

Codi heard her opening the creaking wooden door to her apartment, and was immediately aware of the warmth and the smell of Mexican food. The authentic kind. She was trying her best to stifle her sobbing now, and came off sucking her bottom lip. Maria stayed with her, kneeling in front of her as she guided Codi onto a soft sofa. She continued her motherly cooing and calm reassurances, softly rubbing Codi's wrists with her thumbs as she held her hands.

"There, there. That's better," she said. After a few minutes of letting Codi cry and calm down, she finally asked, "Is there someone you can call? Somewhere you can go?"

Codi was nodding quickly, closing her eyes, trying to let go the final remnants of fear that seemed to want to cling. She noticed she had been closing her eyes a lot more lately, not wanting to use her new vision at all. It was too scary and unfamiliar. The regret she felt for going through with the bionic implants was palatable.

"Yes. Yes, I think so. I have a friend I think I can stay with. Can you call for me?" Codi finally said.

"Sure! Sure I can!" Codi heard her grab the phone off its cradle from somewhere very near. Maria didn't have to move to reach it. "Do you know the number, sweetie?"

She nodded again. "Yes! It's 848-"

"Hang on, hang on. Let's see..." Maria said. This thing..."

After a moment of Maria's fumbling with the device, Codi finally said, "I can dial it. It's okay."

"Okay, here you go," Maria said, placing the receiver into Codi's hand. She found the three distinctive bumps on the five button and centered her hand around the keypad, then dialed the number she had memorized the first time she had heard it.

"Uh huh?" came the voice from the other end. Codi could hear the exhalation of smoke behind the familiar, comforting husk of Rebecca's voice.

"Becca, it's Codi," she said.

"Oh, hey, sugar. How are you?"

"Not good. I'm so sorry to bother you. I hate to call, but..."

"Stop it. What's up, Codi?"

"Well, something bad has happened with Tim, and I was wondering if I could maybe stay with you for a night or two."

"Oh my God! Is he okay? What's wrong?" Rebecca said.

"No, it's me. Can we talk about it later though?" Codi said.

"Of course! Absolutely. Where are you? I'm on my way."

Codi filled Rebecca in on everything that had happened as they made their way across town in the comfortable leather seats of Rebecca's Range Rover. When Rebecca had arrived and taken custody of her, she had guided Codi out into the cold, immediately trying to assess the situation. She helped Codi tuck her breasts back into her bra, where it had been pulled up to the top of her chest. Codi hadn't even noticed it before Rebecca had stopped her and said, "Honey hang on. We have to fix this. Your tits are hanging out." Codi had laughed through her tears at that, and immediately felt the comfort of Rebecca's aura.

Now, here in the warm vehicle, she felt the last vestiges of fear and tears finally begin to slip away. Rebecca held her hand, resting it on Codi's thigh, squeezing at just the right times and letting Codi know she wasn't going anywhere. She listened to everything Codi had to say before she finally spoke.

"Honey, you did the right thing. I would recommend not going back to get your stuff alone. Either go with someone, or have someone get it for you. But I don't think you should ever go back, Codi. You feel me, sister?"

Codi nodded. "Yeah. Yeah. I won't. Trust me. I'm so scared of him. It feels so good to finally be away!" She felt a sudden surge of excitement rise in her that made her want to exclaim her happiness. And thoughts of Sam slipped into her mind at that exact instant, bringing the warmth to an all-time high.

"Bec, I think I'm falling in love with Sam."

"Oooh!" Rebecca screamed. "Ooh, I'm so happy for you! Eeee!" She was literally squealing with delight. "I'm so excited!"

"Yeah, me too!" Codi said, smiling wide. Rebecca's excitement was infectious, and she had caught it quickly. "It's all happening so fast. But I'm so ready!"

"That is so great, Codi! I'm so happy for you!" she said, squeezing her hand again.

"Thank you so much for letting me stay with you. I promise it won't be long."

"Oh hush, Codi. I'm honored to have you in my humble little apartment for as long as you'll stay."

CHAPTER 12

allie lay awake long into the night, excited and anxious about the dive training. She completed the classroom parts of the training with Chris sitting in for a refresher beside her. Now all that was left was to dive. Her first dive would be at seven o'clock in the morning, in the Olympic-size swimming pool at the YMCA. She reckoned that this would be a good gauge to determine whether or not she would freak out when it came to open water. If she could handle the submersion in a pool, maybe she had a better shot at the ocean. Her mind raced with scenarios and situations. The 'what-ifs' were ever-present, and consumed a large portion of her thoughts about the matter. And they weren't all positive.

What if her mask fogged up and she was too afraid to clear it? What if her mask came off? What if something worse happened? Her mind covered just about every angle of every dangerous scenario that could possibly happen, and by the time she finally drifted off to sleep, she had worried herself into a nervous frenzy. She just happened to be more tired than nervous, and dropped off into slumber even though she might have fought it. It was three o'clock. Her alarm would be going off in two hours.

As she sat with Chris at the small table in the breakfast nook in front of an untouched bowl of cereal, she tried to remind herself that he was not a terrible person, so there was no reason for her to be grouchy with him. But her mood was sour and she snapped at everything he offered. After staring at the bowl of raisin bran for several minutes she finally resolved to stick with the coffee and maybe eat a big lunch. By lunch time, she would be well out of the pool and the nervousness of anticipation would be in her rearview mirror. Succeed or fail, she'd know by then what her future in diving looked like.

Chris finally took a deep breath and walked away from the table, hopefully understanding that she did not really hate him. Two hours of sleep was an unkind mentor for anyone's attitude, she thought.

When she emerged from the house and slid into the passenger seat of Chris's warming Cherokee, she turned and looked at him, her lips trembling in the cold morning air. "I'm sorry, baby. I know I've been a complete B this morning. I was up all night."

He nodded. "I know. I heard you tossing and turning. It's okay, Callie." He ran his fingers through her hair, tucking it back behind her ear. "You really are scared aren't you?"

"Have you ever faced a phobia? If it were rational, it wouldn't be a problem."

He nodded and shrugged. "It's okay, babe. I know. But I'll be right there with you. Danny said I could be in the pool with you as long as I don't get in the way."

Callie looked up sharply, her eyes wide. "Really?"

He nodded again. "Yup."

She sighed relief and tried to smile. "Well that makes me feel a little better." In fact, it filled her with excitement. Danny was a certified professional trainer, so she was already in good hands if anything happened. But having Chris there gave her a different peace of mind. And perhaps on a spiritual level she knew that if something did go wrong, it would be better to be with people she loved.

Her stomach was growling with hunger as well as nervous tension, and she reckoned the coffee would start making it worse pretty soon. As they pulled into the parking lot of the YMCA, she said a quick prayer in her head and opened the door with a solid resolve.

The actual diving part of the exercise was made easier by the fact that they spent the first two hours in the pool getting acclimated to the equipment, and practicing non-diving techniques. Callie was reticent to take the stairs into the pool at first, but she strengthened her will and descended trembling into the water, her right hand gripping the stainless steel handrail with an intensity so strong her knuckles looked as though they would break through her pale skin. Standing in the four-foot water, she breathed deeply, her hands atop the water as if to will it down, while Danny stood beside her with his hand on her shoulder, offering comforting words.

The tanks and buoyancy control vests floated nearby with an eerie grace. Only Chris wore his, and he floated lazily by the edge of the pool several yards away, watching silently. The calm he exuded was slowly rubbing off on Callie. He smiled and winked at her occasionally, reminding her that it was only water.

Danny showed her how to snorkel and clear her mask and kick with her flippers, and by the time she remembered to think about her fear, it had nearly abated entirely. If her fear of the water were to be conquered this easily, she would have fought it long ago, she told herself.

When she had finally gone under to practice clearing the mask, she felt the fear trying to return full force, but she fought it off, partially with the help of Danny's hand on her arm, and she was able to finish the task with very little effort. She knew a lot of people washed out at this stage, being blind under water for a considerably long moment.

So when they finally donned the scuba gear, Callie had already done things she had never before accomplished. It was an energizing experience for her, breathing underwater and being completely in control of her buoyancy. During some exercises, Danny had her keep her toes on the floor and pivot her body up and down, or hover a foot above the floor using only the BC vest. She mastered these things pretty quickly, and between each exercise, they would surface and discuss her progress. These little breaks built into the training, and the fact that they were in a pool to start made the whole process a lot more approachable for the hydrophobic Callie. By the end of the afternoon, she felt comfortable in the swimming pool, and was almost looking forward to her first dive in the ocean. Almost.

In the car after training, Callie was all smiles. Her smiles rubbed off on Chris, too, who had not stopped praising her since she got out of the pool and stood dripping on the red concrete shivering and teeth chattering. "I'm so proud of you baby! It was like your phobia disappeared entirely."

"Yeah!" Callie said, shaking her head in wonder. "I don't even get it. I guess the only thing that makes sense is that I didn't really have a phobia."

"Huh? How the hell do you explain your fear of the water?"

"I've never had much problem getting into a pool where I can stand on the bottom. I just refuse to go under. And the ocean, or a lake? No way. But it seems like maybe I've been running scared from it all these years, thinking I was afraid when I really wasn't." She giggled and rubbed her hands together. "Like maybe I talked myself into believing that I had a phobia of water, when I never really did all along."

"That's just weird," Chris said. "Well I'm excited for you. And I'm excited about the ocean! Should be a piece of cake for you now!"

The smile slid off her face and her eyes found a spot on the dash to lose her focus. Then she took a deep breath. "Yeah. Should be. We'll see, Chris."

⌘   ⌘   ⌘

Codi woke to the smell of coffee and bacon, and the sounds of grease popping in the pan. She had slept on Rebecca's over-stuffed sofa, having fallen asleep with one hand behind her head, and apparently not waking up once. Her entire arm was asleep and completely useless. When she sat up, she began rubbing it briskly, trying to restore the blood flow. "Ugh!" she said to herself.

From the kitchen, Rebecca called to her. "You up, sugar?"

"Barely. I'm not sure if you can call this 'up'," Codi said. "Wow, your couch is comfortable."

"Oh, I know, sweetie. I've crashed on it many times when I was either too drunk or tired to make it all the way down the hall to the bedroom."

Codi managed her way into the kitchen and found a chair, then pulled her hair back into a sloppy pony tail, wrapped with a band she kept around her wrist. "So, does the privilege of staying here include a hot shower as well?"

"Babe, it comes with anything you want. Mi casa es su casa."

"You're so wonderful, Bec. If I were gay..."

"Don't speak so soon. You may be by the time I get through with you."

"Ha!" Codi said, laughing hard. "It's nice to have somewhere safe to stay. But isn't it funny the little things that happen that bring people together?"

"Absolutely. But can I ask you to expound upon that a little?" Rebecca asked.

"What do you mean?" Codi asked, wiping her chin with a screwed-up napkin.

"You said it's nice to have somewhere safe to stay," Rebecca said, then took a drink of her coffee. "Do you not have any friends around these parts?"

"Nah," Codi said, shaking her head. She stared at the shapes in front of her that she knew were salt and pepper shakers. She felt comfort in the concentration. "I just moved here. You were actually one of the first people I met here."

"Well that's nice to know. By the way, how do you like your eggs?" Rebecca said.

"Forgotten and unfertilized, please."

"That makes two of us. Is runny okay?"

"Any way you serve them, I will vacuum them up like a Kirby."

"All right! My kind of girl." Rebecca slid a hot plate in front of Codi, then sat down herself. "Yeah, those funny little things all have to line up perfectly. Some crazy butterfly effect brings about the oddest combinations of people sometimes."

"Butterfly effect? Thank you for the food, by the way, Bec. You're fabulous."

"If you don't stop complimenting me, I'm going to assume that you're making a pass."

Codi giggled and felt a warmth in her stomach. Regardless of the attention-giver's gender, she adored the doting.

Rebecca took a bite of her food, then said, "Yeah, butterfly effect. You never heard of it?"

"No. What is it?" Codi said.

"There's orange juice about six inches in front of your left hand," Rebecca said. Codi grunted. "It's a theory in chaos math that suggests that a butterfly flapping its wings in China can affect the weather in California."

"What the hell?" Codi said, swallowing the juice, then popping a piece of bacon in her mouth.

"Not specifically. But that's the fashionable example. It's a premise that suggests that something so tiny and insignificant, through so many orders of magnitude of change, can make great changes in the world. Or in history. Whatever."

Eating for Codi was a messy affair, but she gathered that if anyone was immune to it, Rebecca would probably be the perfect candidate. She felt completely comfortable sopping up the runny eggs with toast, wiping her chin with a napkin between every bite.

"It's pretty cool. But you know, that same weird butterfly effect that brought you and me together, was also responsible for bringing you and Tim together."

"And tearing us apart, I assume."

Rebecca swallowed some juice, then said, "No, not really. His asshole battery treatment of women is responsible for all that."

"So how does that work? I mean your example. How would something that small make a big change somewhere else?"

"Well," Rebecca said, "it's sort of a domino effect on a macro scale. Think about it. Let's take that very example, because it's there. A butterfly flaps its wings in a cage. A boy sees it. Let's say the boy was beginning to think the fly was dead. He sees its wings flap, gets excited. He stands up too fast, knocks his chair over, and it hits a lamp. The light bulb busts on the floor. Maybe he steps on it and slices his foot open. Has to go to the hospital. On the way to the hospital, a car runs a red light and slams into his car. Kills his mother and him instantly. And so on. You get the point."

"Yeah, that's rather morbid. But I see," Codi said.

"Exactly. So it goes. You can keep going with that. But all those tiny changes effect greater and greater changes, to the point where it has global impact. And who knows, that boy might have grown up to be prime minister of Russia." She shrugged.

"That is crazy," Codi agreed. She scooped the last piece of bacon into her mouth and dropped her napkin on her plate. "Ah, that was so yummy delicious. Thank you so much, Bec."

"Any time, sweetie." After a moment, Rebecca took her wrist on the table and gave it a light squeeze. "So will you tell me about Tim, Codi?"

She sighed and took a deep breath. "He used to be so good to me. But he slowly started getting this angry attitude. Like he gets filled with rage sometimes so fast. And it's just uncontrollable. But he usually blows it off as fast as it came on. And like when he gets physical, he'll just stop suddenly in the middle of abusing me. Like he's ADD or something and just changed his mind."

"That's weird. Is that what happened last night?" She was still holding Codi's wrist. Codi did not want her to let go. She liked this closeness. It made her feel safe. She reckoned that with Rebecca's experience in working with the blind, she probably knew all these little tricks. Holding her wrist while Codi talked let her know that she was listening, and not going anywhere. The little things she did were so refreshing.

"Yeah. He – oh, get this!" Codi said suddenly. "He followed me. I guess when I left the house for my coffee date with Sam, he was just getting home. He must have followed my taxi. And then he sat outside at a table close enough to us to hear and see us. And of course, we didn't have any idea. So he was spying on me the whole time. He saw Sam and I touching each other's faces and all that."

"Dear God," Rebecca said. "What an asshole."

"So when I got home, he just laid into me. And now that I can't see at all, I'm really afraid of his mood swings. I'm not used to this vision yet."

"Oh, I'll bet. The world is a scary place for you already. Being in the same room with someone who means to inflict violence on you while you can't see anything must be absolutely terrifying."

Codi nodded. "Yes. It is. And he was about to rape me. He had me bent over the back of the couch and was squeezing my breasts and hurting me." She stopped and took another deep breath, trying to calm herself. Rebecca squeezed her wrist again. "I was screaming at him to stop... and then... well, he finally just did. He just stopped so suddenly. So I got out as fast as I could."

"Well I'm glad you did. It takes a lot of guts to do that. And a lot of women don't have it."

"I guess. I was so scared." Codi wiped a tear from her cheek – a tear that had somehow sneaked past her defenses.

"I know. It's okay. You're safe now," Rebecca said.

"Look at me. I'm crying again. I thought I was done with all that."

"Oh, sister, we never are. We're never done crying."

They were now sitting on the sofa in the living room. Codi's hair was sleek and shiny, and her skin felt soft and smelled like fresh Dove soap and lotion. She had used Rebecca's garden tub to lather and soak herself while Rebecca sat on a stool and kept her company. Codi wondered how much Rebecca had enjoyed the show, and if that had been her intention all along. But for all Bec's inappropriate and come-on talk, she had not said a single untoward word in the bathroom. The level of respect she had shown for Codi's privacy had been clear and present during the entire bath. Part of Codi deep down had enjoyed it too, though. The thought that another woman had been looking upon her naked flesh with a bit of lesbian fervor made her tingle and warm. She had never thought of another woman sexually, and doubted she ever would. But the thought of being looked on did not repulse her in the slightest way.

"So, Bec, can I ask you a question?"

"You mean another one?"

Codi frowned for a second, and then chuckled. "Yes, another one in addition to that one. That one didn't count."

"Okay, shoot."

"What do blind girls do for fun?"

"Well, that's going to have a lot to do with whomever you end up sharing a place with. Your hobbies will form together. You will create and embellish."

"What if we're both blind?" Codi said.

Rebecca giggled. "That's why I said create. I'm not going to lie, it's not an easy lifestyle for two blind people to live together, alone. But you find ways to make do. And Sam has been doing it for a long time. So I'm sure you could learn a lot from him."

"Yeah, I think so too," Codi said. She felt that dreamy feeling slipping over her again.

"But with friends? As a single gal? Opera. Have you ever been to the opera?" Rebecca asked.

"No, but I've kind of always wanted to. That sounds nice!" Codi said.

"Yeah, and just remember, you can do anything anyone can do; you'll just experience it differently. With different senses. I know a girl who likes to water ski. Can you imagine that? Some people get into pottery. It's a very tactile hobby."

"Ooh, yuck. I can't stand getting my hands dirty," Codi said.

"Yeah, then probably not for you. You could take up piano. Or guitar."

"The piano? Are you crazy?" Codi said, slapping at Rebecca's shoulder. She missed.

"I don't know," Rebecca said, lighting a cigarette. "Was Ray Charles?"

"Ooh, okay. Your point. I've always loved the sound of a piano. Maybe I will check that out."

"Want one?" Rebecca said, offering the cigarettes to Codi.

"Sure. Why not? No one's going to punish me for it anymore."

The surface water was cold as it sprayed and misted into their faces, but Callie had been assured that at depth, the water was no colder in January than in June. The Atlantic, Danny had said, is very moderate in climate. No easy outs for Callie. She was committed. And now as they skated across the water toward their dive spot, she was beginning to get butterflies in her stomach again. The gigantic vastness of the ocean was not only intimidating, but foreign. She had never been on it, or in it. And as of a month ago, she had never planned to.

They would be descending to about sixty feet where she would run through some training exercises, and then they'd drift along until they were down to 1500 pounds of air. From there, they would ascend to fifteen feet and stay there for fifteen minutes before popping up to get back on the boat. They would take an hour break, then they'd do it all again. Danny had called it 'drift diving'. He would be dragging a flag along behind them. The flag floated on the surface and followed along behind them, attached to a cord around his wrist. The boat followed the flag, so they didn't have to do any swimming when they returned to the surface.

When the boat finally reached a part of the ocean just like every other part of the ocean as far as Callie's untrained eyes were concerned, the motor shut off and they sat in silence. The water was calm and still. But Callie's stomach was not. There were two other couples on the boat with Chris and Callie, plus Danny the instructor. They were all in training except for Chris. He would be hovering around at a respectful distance while they performed their exercises, and then join them for the drift. Danny stood up and started assisting the couples as they all buddied up to don their BC vests and air tanks. Once everyone was setup, they began dropping backward over the edge of the boat and falling into the water. Each man and woman in turn gave the OK sign as they popped back up, and they all waited in a rough circle for Callie to take the dunk. She steeled herself and pinched her nose through the mask, but could not make herself fall backward into the dark ocean behind her.

"Chris, I can't do it!" she said, pulling the regulator out of her mouth with a shivering hand.

"Yes you can, honey! You can! Trust me! You're falling back less than four feet, and your BC will not let you sink! You'll take a quick dunk and pop right back up just like everyone else did!" Chris said. He was stroking her hair, but she wasn't paying attention. Whether or not it brought her any comfort, she couldn't say.

She looked around the boat as if trying to find a rescue. Danny called to them from the water, asking if everyone was okay up there. "Yeah, she's fine," Chris called over his shoulder. "She's just having a little trouble dropping." Callie knew everyone in the water was already breathing through their regulators, using precious air. And she was wasting it for them. But she could not make herself lean back.

"Isn't there another way I can get in?" she said. "We did that giant stride thing at the pool!"

"Honey, you have to practice all three methods to become certified! You have to drop off backward this time! The giant stride is for stable platforms and large boats." He squeezed her hand, then tilted her chin so she was facing him. "Come on, Callie, you can do this!"

She took long shaky breaths, trying to steady her nerves. "Give me the kick, Chris. That's the only way I'm gonna be able to do this."

"Come again?"

"The kick!" she said, trying to keep her voice down. "Like in that Inception movie."

Chris looked back at the people in the water, then nodded. "Okay. Put your reg in." Then he put his arm on the side of the boat for leverage, and slipped his right leg in behind her legs, which were against the seat. "See you in the water, babe." He swept his leg out, and she toppled over backward, gracelessly plunging into the water, yelping like a shot dog as she splashed in kicking and flailing. Chris came quickly after. When Callie finally got her bearings and spit the saltwater out of her mouth, and replaced the regulator, she turned to notice Danny giving her the I-wish-you'd-have-tried-harder smile. But he remained silent. And the others were smiling and cheering her on.

"Okay guys, we're going to descend to sixty feet. Then we're going to take turns taking our masks off and clearing them. Then we practice our neutral buoyancy and then we swim. Everyone ready?"

Everyone gave the OK sign. Callie gave a thumbs-up.

"Callie, that means return to the surface. Give me the okay, please," Danny said patiently.

She corrected her gesture and grunted a silent apology behind her regulator, feeling foolish and dejected. And then they all held up the pressure release valves on their BCs and started descending. Callie took another deep breath and said a quick prayer, then let the air out of her vest.

Darkness. The darkness was brown and noisy, unlike anything she ever expected. She could see Chris in the left side of her periphery, and the others were murky, cloudy smudges on the outskirts of her visibility. But other than that, there was nothing to see but the occasional tiny white particulate that made up the entire ocean. Chills ran down her spine as the cool temperature of the surface water began to sink in. She was running over a silent prayer in her head, repeating, repeating. *Please, God, get me through this. Bring me calm!*

As they descended below ten feet, the darkness became darker. The noise of the ocean rounded out, thickened. It seemed to close in on her from every direction. She instinctively reached out for Chris's hand, but he held it away from her, shaking his head. She was on her own. To pass the training course, she had to be on her own. The descent was slow, and terrifying. Her heart was slamming in her chest, but she noticed Chris was still looking at her, paddling the water slowly and calmly as he dropped. She knew she was okay. Why didn't she feel that way? Her lungs began to feel full, even though she was still breathing heavily. She looked at Chris again and he gave her the OK sign with his thumb and index finger, nodding his head. She repeated the sign quickly, but immediately went back to flailing. The dull shapes of her peers were disappearing slowly but surely, farther away and deeper down than she. They were pulling ahead and she was fighting to stay up. A sickness rose in her stomach, and she closed her eyes against it. The captivated sound of her own breathing filled her head, and she began to feel very hot between her ears. The ocean was closing in around her and it was growing darker and more and more terrifying. She could not see more than five or ten feet in front of her, and there was nothing at all to see. If she looked left, she could see the dull, fading colors of Chris's wetsuit turning to darker hues of colors she could not reproduce with paints. Everything was losing its color and she wondered how deep they were. She did not have a dive computer, but she remembered that her gauges told her not only how much air she had remaining, but how deep they were. She glanced at the gauges, but suddenly could not read them. She could no longer make sense of the white dials that once seemed so simple and basic. A horrifying sense of claustrophobia began to set in. It crept in like a subtle wind and made Callie's forehead tingle with bright fear and panic. She found herself breathing very heavily – a cardinal sin in diving – and the worry of running out of air too quickly joined the other fears now pounding around in her head. There was nothing at all to see, and it was getting darker with every foot they traveled downward. Was this what diving was all about? Being surrounded by benign brownness that never ended, stretching away in every direction? The bubbles escaping her regulator and flowing up in front of her mask were almost a constant stream now, and the terror that had nearly frozen her now called her to evacuate. *Abort mission!* it screamed, calling her to the surface. She could not go through with this after all. It was too scary, too much to bear for a hydrophobe. The pool was trickery! The pool was a safe haven. She could see the bottom, the sides. She could see everything in the pool. If she were to hit the bottom, someone could see her from the surface. One could not get lost in a pool, even one as large as the lap pools in the YMCA. But here in the ocean... This was completely different. She could barely even see Chris now, and he was only a few feet away from her. But this was not what she had signed up for! What was she thinking? Why did she think she could do this? This was not a game she could just sit down and play for a while, then stand up when she got bored. This was super dangerous, super involved science. She knew she had the smarts to overcome it – to understand it. But not the mind. She didn't have the will, or the strength. *That's it! I can't do this!* she thought. Then she screamed it aloud to Chris. It came out as grunting and humming, and had no sense of language about it at all. He reached an arm out to her, but she knocked it away, screaming again, then started kicking to stop her descent. This wasn't working. This was not for her. Callie needed to surface right now, to sit on the safety and comfort of the boat. She would wait for the others to finish their little fun scuba class, then they'd all skim happily back across the pond to the dock, where dry land awaited her. And she would never again set foot upon the ocean. Chris was motioning with his hand, a slow waving of his hand up and down telling her to slow her breathing. To take it easy. She read his sign easily enough, but refused to comply. She could not comply! Her breathing was so rapid now she felt like she was about to hyperventilate. Suddenly, she felt hands on her wrists – just as her vision was beginning to go black. She shook herself back to consciousness enough to see Danny floating there in front of her with a wide smile on his face. He let go of one of her wrists and gave her an OK sign and nodded his head. She shook her head wildly. *NO! NO! NO!* she was screaming, but he pointed down and nodded his head, telling her it was all okay. *Just look down, Callie!* She finally did. She looked down. And there lay the bottom of the ocean. In all her panic and fear, the bottom had finally risen up to meet them. And now she could see everything. The world had opened up.

CHAPTER 13

Walter Watson stood in the waiting room at the PSS headquarters building in Houston, Texas. Privatized Spacial Services was the company the Olivers used exclusively to run mission control for all their trips. He had an appointment with Julia Callahan, and he was twenty minutes early. He stood looking at the remarkable high-resolution displays on the walls that educated the viewer on everything from space travel to astrophysics. The lobby itself looked like a million dollars'-worth of gadgets and technology. Walter thought he was in the wrong business.

He had been making eyes at the pretty receptionist for a few minutes, until she had finally rolled her own eyes and disappeared into the back, abandoning her station for the relative safety of escape from the forty-something creepy man who still thought he was a movie star. He reckoned he had lost some of his game since he had gotten married. After a few minutes, he heard footsteps coming from the doorway beneath the large silver letters that boasted the company name, and he stood up anticipating the receptionist's reappearance. Walter was prepared to make small talk – something to change the subject and try to make her think he hadn't really been hitting on her. But the woman who walked through the doorway was much shorter, and looked nothing like the previous woman.

"Hi, Mr. Watson?" the woman said.

"Uh, no. Actually I'm Walter. I don't think anyone has ever called me that," he said.

The woman giggled and came around the counter with her hand extended. "Hi, Walter, I'm Julia. Nice to meet you."

He widened his eyes and shook her hand. "Hi. I'm Walter."

"Yeah, I think we covered that," she said, smiling, not without a touch of condescension. "Come on back."

He followed her through a different doorway, and down a hallway, wondering if PSS had ever *seen* an unattractive woman – much less hired one. The hallways were lined with stereoscopic displays that showed moving videos of footage captured in deep space, presumably by telescopes under PSS command. There were some breathtaking images of galaxies he recognized, and some he had never seen before.

"Man, these pictures are stellar!" he said.

She turned to look over her shoulder at him as she walked, smiling. "Did you script your jokes out before you came?"

He realized his pun and started to apologize, but she stopped and offered him into the doorway on her left, which was presumably her office. It was simple by comparison to the hallways. A long L-shaped oak desk stood in the middle of the small room, and a small couch sat under a window, but aside from that, there wasn't much else to look at. Maybe Julia didn't like distractions. The blinds were drawn, blocking out all but thick blinding silver lines of sunlight that illuminated motes in the air just inside the window. She held her hand out again, offering him the wine-colored chair that opposed her desk, and he sat heavily, letting his jacket fall open around his waist.

As Julia took her own seat, she pulled her red hair back behind her ears and gave him a smile, then straightened some papers and moved them out of the way on the desk. "So what can I do for you, Walter Watson?" She picked up a pen and began to twirl it in her fingers. He wondered absently if she were a drummer for an 80s hair-metal band.

"Uh, okay. Well, I just had a few questions for you," he said, trying to compose himself. He was trying not to make it too obvious that he was knocked off his feet by her ridiculous beauty. And it didn't seem to be working.

"What happened to them?" she said, frowning.

"Excuse me?" he said, cocking his head forward.

"The questions. You said you had some."

"Ah. Yeah. Sorry. Have. I have some questions for you." Clearly she was enjoying toying with him in his dumbstruck state.

"Okay, shoot," she said, dropping her pen and patting her desk.

Walter cleared his throat. "You worked with the Oliver Company, right?"

"What would you like to know, Walter? I can't really disclose anything specifically about my clients."

"No, no," he said, waving his hands. He shifted in his seat. "I'm not wanting anything about the company, specifically. I just, ah..."

She took a deep breath and looked down at her desk, then spread her hands on it, clearing the slate. "Okay, look. Why don't you tell me why you're here, and we'll try to go from there."

Walter sat still for a long moment, nodding his head, then cracked his neck and tried to start over mentally. Then he leaned forward, elbows on his knees, and began to level with her. "Okay. Sorry. Look. I'm close personal friends with Callie Simmons."

She smiled again, but it was condescending at best. "Oh? Where is she?"

"At the moment, she's at the bottom of the ocean," he said. Julia bit her lip and looked him directly in the eyes. She was clearly losing her patience. "Sorry. I'm just trying to establish that I'm... Okay, look. That mission was a total failure."

"What mission?" she said. She did not widen her eyes as she said it. This told Walter that he need not elaborate. She knew exactly what he was talking about. But he had to play her game.

"The Olivers' mission to Mars. And we know a lot of what happened. Brian Bradley, a crew member on that flight, was actually working for Royal at the time of the mission. He sabotaged the mission and killed the crew."

The slight smirk Julia had been wearing slowly slid from her face as she made eye contact with Walter again. This time for real. Now she was serious. Now he had her attention.

"Do you remember how parts kept going out on the ship? Callie said she had trouble communicating with Donnie at some points, and that you told her to keep broadcasting blind, because his computer just might not be translating the messages."

Julia was nodding her head slowly, staring at her hand on the desk – the hand that was once again twirling the pen in her fingers. He was taking her back several years, and he could see the gears turning in her head. "Yes. I remember."

"Okay. Good," Walter said. He clapped his hands together once, and scooted forward on his chair. "Shit was – sorry, stuff was going out on that ship left and right. I don't know how much of this you already know, but Bradley had been ordering cheap parts and making receipts for the actual parts he was supposed to be ordering. He was siphoning off the difference in cost to a Royal bank account."

"You're kidding," Julia said flatly. Her eyes met his again, as if reading him from the inside.

"Nope. Anyway, it ended up being a lot of money. They – Royal – bought a satellite with that money."

Julia sighed, then dropped the pen into a cup on her desk, then leaned back, crossing her thin arms. "Okay. I'm not sure what you want to know from me. Because I didn't know any of this. If this is true, you could bring a major lawsuit against Royal."

"We're considering that. But here's the kicker, Julia," Walter said, rounding to his point.

She smirked again, then said, "I don't think you need much of a kicker when you're working with four of a kind."

He pointed at her, nodding his head. "Indeed. But check this out. Bradley is still alive."

Julia's mouth snapped shut. She might have blanched as she leaned her head forward, looking at him levelly. "Okay, Walter, you have my attention."

⌘   ⌘   ⌘

Callie leaned her head back, closing her eyes against the sun, a jack-o-lantern grin beset upon her pretty face. She was resting on her elbows, trembling with excitement. Chris was sitting behind her, rubbing her shoulders and praising her. She was in heaven. She had survived the dive, and conquered her fear of the great deep. True, she had been the first to run low on air – by a long shot – but she had completed the exercise and made it back to the surface of her own accord, without incident.

The group had drifted almost a half-mile on the healthy current, and Callie was exhilarated by the experience. Her arms felt weak from the energy expenditure, and her heart felt light in her chest, having used up several days'-worth of beats in less than an hour underwater. She looked up through the tops of her shades over her head at an upside-down version of Chris, who looked down at her.

"Aren't you so proud of me, honey?" she said, smiling crazily.

"I really am. That's an amazing feat to conquer something like that." He stroked her hair and leaned down to kiss her forehead. "People who are afraid of water don't just go jump in the ocean to scuba dive. I told you that you could do it though."

"I know. I know you did, Chris. Thank you for believing in me."

The wind blew through her wet hair and the sun shone on her face, and Callie found herself dozing lightly on the high of the trip. She guessed part of her drowsiness was due to the Dramamine she had taken before they got on the boat. The rest was that she lay on the vinyl seat of the boat in perfect harmony with nature and herself, rocking softly in the uncommonly pleasant January breeze. She was in heaven.

Another two hours later, and they were all back on the boat, heading home. The second dive was worlds easier than the first, though she did find a little residual fear on the descent. Once she reached the bottom, she realized Chris had been completely right – there was almost nothing water-like about it. It was like paddling softly through a slowly swaying ecosystem suspended in swishing silence. At one point, she had seen a large sea turtle and took off trying to chase it, but found herself tiring out while the turtle drifted away with almost no effort whatever. The landscape was terrific. They had dropped onto a large coral reef with teems of the brightest, most colorful fish Callie had ever seen. Gorgeous pink and purple plants rocked lazily in the ever-present current. She thought that it would be a brilliant place to setup shop and call home if getting there were made a little easier.

On the drive home, Callie found herself wanting to talk about nothing but the dive. She couldn't wait to get home and update her social network outlets with her experience. She felt the familiar jab of fear when she thought about what she had done, but it was quickly replaced each time with excitement and feelings of personal triumph. She expressed these things to Chris, who told her that the further she took it, the better she would feel about it. They could eventually get training to do night dives and cave dives together, and go deeper. She wasn't sure how she felt about the prospect of spelunking under water yet, but it was definitely not something she was ready to shoot down on general principle.

"You know what's funny?" she said, breaking a long silence.

"What's that, hon?" Chris said.

"I kind of feel excited about the project now. Having seen what's down there and what it feels like to be under the ocean – I think it's going to be cool to be part of that whole thing."

"You mean the trench dive?"

"Uh huh."

"Yeah, that will be super cool. I can't wait 'til you know more about it. And if there's any way I can be on that ship with you, get me a ticket, babe."

"I'll see if I can pull any strings."

⌘   ⌘   ⌘

Codi stood in the kitchen with her hands buried in soft dough while Rebecca verbally guided her into shaping a pizza. She had flour up to her elbows, and her nose kept itching. She cranked her head to scratch it on her shoulder several times before finally giving up and rubbing it from side to side with the back of her wrist. Now she looked like a mime, or at the very least, a cocaine addict with bad aim.

Rebecca laughed out loud at her, and tried to knock most of it off with a paper towel. Codi made a sour face and backed away from the towel, waving her hands comically in front of her face.

"You're making it itch more!" she cried.

"Stand still, darling, you look like a freak!" Rebecca laughed.

"Ugh! Stop! I'll take another bath if I have to!" She shook her head quickly, flopping her hair out of its ponytail and into her face, where it picked up a good portion of the white flour. And Rebecca laughed even harder.

"Ah, God, you're hopeless!" she shouted. She ran water on a rag and began to dab lightly at her face while Codi spat and made bad faces. After she had cleaned up most of Codi's face, Rebecca said, "There, now. You look presentable. Let me put your hair back in place for you."

"Thank you, Bec. I absolutely must look presentable for this pizza."

"You got it, dear," said Rebecca. As she worked Codi's hair back into the ponytail, she looked over her shoulder at the dough. "By the way," she said after a moment, "did you ever hear anything else about your old eye doctor? Like how she died or anything?"

Codi's hands froze in the dough. "No. In fact, I hadn't thought about her until just now. I forgot about that."

"What was her name?"

"Clarissa Steadman. I'd be interested in finding out what happened."

"Well, yeah. That's why I asked. I'll try to look her up online," said Rebecca.

"Well, I don't want you thinking that I attract all this bad luck."

"Don't be silly."

"I was being silly. Like something is happening to all my eye doctors."

"Well, fortunately, I'm not a doctor," said Rebecca.

"What do you call yourself, then?" said Codi.

"I'm a therapist," Rebecca replied.

"Talk about an unfortunate word." Codi finished flattening out the dough and put her hands on her hips, once again transferring the flour unwittingly.

"True that. Ugh, will you stop that! You just got flour all over my black dress!" Rebecca said, swatting at Codi's hips now with the towel.

"I'm wearing your black dress?"

"Yes, dork. It's all I had that would fit you."

"Well it's your fault for not putting an apron on me."

"True again. No big deal. I'll just bleach it out when you're done." They both laughed for a long moment before Codi finally caught her breath and asked Rebecca to guide her hand toward the flute where her wine stood warming.

She leaned against the counter and took a long pull from the sweet red, then swished it around in her mouth before swallowing. "You know, you're really spoiling me here. I don't know how I'll ever repay you, Bec."

"Well, it is not something to be mentioned. I'm happy to have a roommate."

"Roommate?" Codi said, moving her head forward. She was studying Rebecca's face. "Are you serious?"

"Absolutely. For as long as you want to stay, sugar, I will have you."

Codi swallowed hard then licked her lips. "Bec, I don't..."

"Stop. Please. You're so much fun to be around. I completely adore you." She touched Codi's cheek. "In a totally platonic way, of course."

"Oh, Bec. I don't make any money! I can't even help pay utilities or anything!" Codi said. She felt tears welling up in her eyes. She wiped at them with her wrist.

"I wish you'd stop. Really. I make plenty of money to afford this little apartment. And I couldn't be happier with the company. If you like it here, I would love for you to stay. I think we'll get along great together."

"You're serious?" Codi said again.

"Yes, babe. Positively. That's of course, not even mentioning how much I can help you. I work with blind people, you know."

Codi laughed again, and the tears backed off. She sighed and shook her head, then took another drink, finishing off the glass. "Okay. If you're sure, I would love to stay with you."

Rebecca leaned forward and hugged her tightly, then backed away and put her hands on her shoulders. "Yep. But we're going to have to do something about your face. Now you have flour all over it."

⌘   ⌘   ⌘

Walter ran through everything he knew about the failed Oliver mission, checking the notes he'd made on his phone and filling Julia in on every detail he remembered Callie having told him. He had run long over his appointment, but for the better part of an hour, Julia had sat still at her desk, perfect in posture, her chin resting on laced fingers as she listened to him ramble.

"You know, that is so crazy, Walter. We saw a ship out there. One of my interns and I found it while we were prepping for the Atlas mission."

"You saw it?" Walter said, leaning back, frowning. "What? What ship? The Royal ship?"

She shrugged and put her hands in her lap. "I guess so. It had to be. We didn't think much of it at the time."

Walter laughed out loud. "Are you kidding? You see a ship on its way to Mars and you don't think much of it?"

"No, don't be silly. That's not what I meant." She sighed and leaned back, then picked up a glass of water and took a drink. "Of course we thought it was odd. I mean, at the time it frightened me, because I wasn't expecting it. But I didn't think it was relevant to their mission, so I never mentioned it."

Walter shook his head, gripping the handles on his chair. "Wow. That could have changed a lot."

She shrugged again. "Maybe. Maybe not. No one knew who it was or what they were up to. Space traffic is becoming a lot more frequent, you know."

"No, I don't know. I don't know anything about all that stuff. But I think it's crazy you didn't think to tell the Olivers about it."

"Yeah. Sorry. What can I say?"

Walter shook his head again but didn't speak.

She leaned forward and clasped her hands on the desk, and sighed. "Look, Walter. We here are Privatized Spatial Services. We are a space-traffic control service. We're not the only company that provides this service, either. So we see ships sometimes."

"Okay, I see your point. But wow." He blew out his breath and looked around the office.

"What do you need from me? I will help you any way I can, but I just don't think I know what you want to know," she said, levelling her gaze at him.

Walter tilted his head and looked long into her eyes. "Did you know about the forgotten crates?"

She widened her eyes and pushed her head forward. "Crates?"

"Yeah. Apparently Oliver was going to send an extra trip up to the space station or something for some crates that got left behind."

"Oh, yeah. Yeah, I do remember that. It got canceled because they learned last minute that there would be room on the mission or something."

"Okay, so you know about it. But you don't know what was in those crates, do you?"

She frowned at him. "Of course not." She looked blankly at him. Walter thought she was growing bored of the conversation now, and was probably ready for him to leave. Then she spoke again. "I know someone forged Donnie's name on something or other. Something with ETIS out in California, I think."

"Yeah, Callie told me about that. Urn shells?"

"Yeah. Personally I didn't understand why he was so against taking them."

"The guy didn't want to spend time burying people on his first trip to Mars. Who gives a shit?"

"Suit yourself."

Walter nodded slowly, pursing his lips. He looked about the office one more time, then scooted forward, ready to grab his bag and say goodbye. "So that's all you can tell me?"

Julia sat staring at him for a long moment, chewing the inside of her lip before she finally sighed. And then she spoke. "Okay. Look, I'm not supposed to tell you this. But I think you might find it helpful. Just don't credit me, okay?"

Walter sat back, perking up again. "Okay. Sure."

"We used to have a woman who worked here. Named Natalie. Before she came to work for us, she worked for Royal. And since you work for Royal, you might already know this." She waited for him to shrug and shake his head. "Okay, so here's the deal. We ran a couple of missions for them a few years back. Back a few years before the Oliver mission, I mean."

"For who? You ran missions?"

She closed her eyes, then said, "Missions. For Royal. We ran STC missions for them a few times." Walter shook his head quickly, so she added, "Space Traffic Control. They were never officially a client of ours. And they ran the missions under a different name. But it was Royal. There were just a couple of one-offs we did for them. Natalie came to us shortly after we stopped dealing with them."

"Okay, so what?" Walter said. He was scratching his chin absently, wondering where this was going. Her eyes were not giving it away though. He would have to wait for the words.

"So, they've been to Mars, Walter."

"Royal?" he said, sitting forward in his chair. "You're shitting me."

"Nope. I shit you not. They made at least two trips before Oliver Company ever scheduled their first one."

"What is this, attorney-client privilege bullshit? You couldn't let them know?"

She shook her head and knocked on her desk. "No. More like doctor-patient. Some of our clients pay a lot of money for anonymity. For privacy. We sign non-disclosure agreements all the time."

"Well what the fuck were they doing there? Jesus Christ! This is huge!"

"You can't say anything that directly links this information to me, Walter. You have to promise me."

"Why are you telling me then?! You sign NDAs with them but you're telling me?"

"Because information has a tendency to find cracks in the hull, Walter. It leaks. If you ever mention my name I'll say I never met you. I'll deny ev-"

He waved his hands and moved even farther forward in his chair. "No, I'm not going to bust you, Julia. I have no intention of smearing you or your company's name." He pinched his lip and stared at the desk as he thought about what she was telling him. "I appreciate you telling me this. Very much," he added, looking her in the eyes.

She nodded and gave him a weak smile.

"Do you know what they were doing there?" Walter said.

She closed her eyes and sighed again. "You'll have to find that out yourself, friend. I can't go any further with this. But I *do* want you to pursue this. You need to know about this. But I can't be the one to tell you."

⌘   ⌘   ⌘

Callie stared out the window at the trees that slid by on the edge of Route 35. The sky above the trees was a deep crimson that transitioned seamlessly into a dark orange before it went blue. The clouds looked like wisps of white paint from a gigantic artist's brush slapped against the sky. She heard the near-silent whoosh of the telephone poles as they passed outside the window and thought about the pointlessness of roadside memorials as they passed a Styrofoam cross stuck in the grass beside the road. Her phone vibrated in her pocket. She shook her head and sighed, then slid her finger across the screen to answer. She whipped her hair back and crossed her legs, then placed a hand on Chris's knee.

"Hello?" she said.

"Royal went to Mars."

She sat silent for a long moment, staring straight ahead through the windshield, scouring her mind for something to latch on to. Was that supposed to mean something to her other than what the words put together should mean? When she finally answered, it was tentative and slow. "Okay. Walter, we knew this already. What are you trying to tell me?"

"No. Callie. You don't understand. They went to Mars. To Mars. Several times. Like *to Mars*. They've been there. They've walked on the red planet."

Callie sat silent again, but this time she was truly stunned. Could that be true? How had that escaped the news? Or at least the inter-office memos at Royal? Why hadn't Walter known that if it was true? Something so huge should have been common knowledge.

"You still with me?"

"Yeah, I'm here," she said after another pregnant pause. "You're telling me they've actually *been* to Mars? Like landed on that planet and walked around and stuff?"

"Pretty sure that's exactly what I said."

"Coffee. Now. Chris, take me to The Outer Rim please," she said, and hung up the phone while Walter was screaming *Wait, wait, wait!*

Chris breathed in deeply, but did not object. When it came to Walter, he complied with her every demand. He had learned long ago that their unique brand of friendship was not something he could question with hope of any real answers. Walter was extremely important to Callie, as was she to him. And their short-notice meetings were usually to discuss something earth-shaklingly important anyway, so Chris counted himself lucky if he actually got to sit in on one of them.

The Outer Rim was a large coffee shop with a small feel. Instead of the Denny's booth, the owners had constructed a series of small, cozy rooms. Leather couches sat on three sides of actual coffee tables in each of these rooms. Sconces that looked like torches hung on the walls, scattering dim flickering light across the intimate space. Unlike normal coffee houses, this place catered to the coffee connoisseur. They sold gourmet coffees and teas, and each room had a shelf full of games. They also served beer and cocktails, for those in the mood for more than just caffeine. Glancing through the pulled curtains in some of the rooms as she made her way through the establishment, Callie could see people playing chess and dice games, smoking cigars, cigarettes and vapor sticks, while low music emanated from hidden speakers. She glanced at the chalkboards outside each room where people wrote their party name or code word, or nothing at all. She and Walter had their own code word that told one another which room to enter on those nights they scheduled meetings at the coffee shop. But she did not see the words on any of the placards. When she and Chris finally reached the last room, she turned and held her hands up. "Where the heck is he?"

"Are you sure he's made it here yet, babe?"

"Don't be silly, Chris. He always beats me here."

Chris raised his chin as if he understood. "Uh, babe, you did hang up on him. Maybe you had better check your phone again." She looked at him sharply, then started digging in pockets and purse looking for her phone. "What code word do you guys use, anyway?"

"Duh," she said, furling her lips at him. "The Babcock Society." She looked down at her phone while Chris rolled his eyes. She had three missed calls from Walter, and two new texts. She opened the texts and found his messages waiting for her. One said *Answer your phone, goof! I'm not THERE!* And the other, *Callie, I'm in Houston!* brought her up to speed. She slung her shoulders low and dropped her hands to her sides, tilting her head back in defeat. "He's in flippin' Houston, Chris."

"Houston? What the hell is he doing down there?"

"I sent him to investigate something. Darnit, Chris! I'm such a dork."

"Indeed you are, little lady," he agreed.

"Well, let's get a room anyway. I could use some coffee," Callie said. She turned and headed for the first open set of curtains in sight and dropped her purse on the table, then pressed a red button mounted on the end table by the sofa. This would summon a barrista. She immediately dialed Walter back and put the phone up to her ear. Chris faded into the room a couple of seconds later looking defeated, and drew the curtain, obediently succumbing to Callie's lifestyle through force of habit and wisdom alike.

"Walter, why didn't you tell me you were in Houston?"

"You hung up on me, dumb ass! I tried to stop you! And I called you back like thirty times. What the hell?"

"It was only three, dorky onion."

"Oh, and three's not enough? I'll never understand why women have cell phones when they don't answer them ninety percent of the time."

"Whatever. Okay, so I'm here. So talk to me."

Walter filled her in on his two-hour meeting with Julia and what he had learned. He told her everything Julia had said, and how she had reacted when he had told her of Royal's involvement in the Oliver mission. Callie wasn't surprised to hear that PSS had done contract work for Royal on a couple of their missions, but was perplexed like Walter had been that they had actually made Mars. That seemed newsworthy to her. But then, a lot of things Royal had done – temporal delineation experiments being one of them – had never been made public.

Royal was a big enough, rich enough company that if they wanted something kept quiet, they could afford to enforce the code. But with all the freelance astronomers looking for asteroids to name after their wives, and the ridiculous amount of private companies trying their hand at space travel these days, she figured someone would have seen it.

Someone stuck his head through the curtain and said, "Good evening, guys. Oh, hey, Callie. How's it going?"

She smiled at him, then covered the phone and turned to Chris. "Tell him what you want, babe."

"Uh, yeah, thanks. I'll have a tall glass of water with a lemon wedge, please," Chris said, leaning over to slip his wallet out of his back pocket.

"Got it," the barrista said, and disappeared. Chris sat leaning at that angle for a long moment, looking a lot like a tower in Pisa to Callie. Then he shook his head and leaned back on the couch, looking at her.

"So these guys have been to Mars several times, Callie," Walter was saying on the other end of the line.

"Did she just come out and tell you this, or what?" said Callie.

"Well, yeah. After a while. I mean, it's like she finally came to trust me or something, and felt like I needed to know it. For the greater good or some shit."

"You sure it wasn't your good looks, Walt? Did you flash your movie smile at her?" Callie said, winking at Chris as he stared at her.

"Yeah, no, I tried that, honey. It didn't work on this broad."

"HA!" Callie shouted. "You didn't actually call her a broad, did you, Walter?"

Walter made the vocal equivalent of a shrug, then continued. "So hey, do you know anyone who worked at Royal named Natalie?"

"Natalie what?"

"Don't you think I would have told you her last name if I knew it?" Walter said.

Callie sighed. "When did she work there? She's gone now, I assume?"

"Yeah. She quit there and went to PSS for a while. She left PSS a couple years ago."

"Wow. That's like a thread of hay in a needle stack, Walter."

"Not really. How many Natalies could there be at any one company?"

"Well you're the one who still works there, tomato face!" Callie said twirling her hair around her finger. The barrista returned with a tray. He handed Chris his water and set a tall steaming cup of black in front of Callie. She winked at him and patted his shoulder as he set the tray down. He smiled at her, then nodded at Chris and excused himself from the room.

"She doesn't work there anymore, Calcifer," Walter said.

"Yeah. You said that."

"Well then tell me, smart ass. What does my still working there have to do with knowing someone who left years ago?"

"Duh, dorky goof! You can look up former employees!" Callie retorted. She was shaking her head and rolling her eyes for Chris's benefit, but he had grown bored of the one-sided conversation, and was leaned back on the couch doing something on his phone. Callie reckoned he was playing poker now.

"I'm not in HR, genius. I don't have access to employee records."

Callie sighed audibly. "Okay, so what's the point? Who is this Natalie bird anyway? Why do we need to find her?"

"Because she knows why Royal went to Mars."

"You're right, Walter. This *is* like finding a hay strand in a needle stack."

"You're the one who said that, Callie."

"Exactly."

CHAPTER 14

surprise

T he next day a cold front blew in and brought the winter back to its senses. Coats, scarves and gloves were in great abundance on the streets of Neptune City. Callie sat at a table in Dunkin' Donuts looking out into the parking lot and waiting for Walter to show up. They planned to further discuss what he had learned from Julia at PSS, and get their ducks in a row on how to proceed with their investigation. Callie's hands wrapped round a Styrofoam cup of steaming coffee that she had not yet taken a drink from. She sat blowing into it as she stared into the parking lot, her mind wandering like a moth in the darkness of a closet.

When Walter finally came screaming into the parking lot, she shook her head and sat up straight, checking the time on her phone, which lay on a napkin in front of her. It was ten o'clock. She had told Minus she would meet him at the office at noon and go over their plans for beginning phase testing on the prototype. Walter smiled at her through the glass as he approached the door, then whipped it open inviting in another round of frozen New Jersey air.

"Hey!" he said, scooting up across from her at the table.

"Hey, Walt," she said. "How was your trip?"

"I don't miss this cold, I'll tell you that. It was seventy-five and sunny in Houston," he said.

"Yeah it was nice here yesterday too. Just got spitty this morning." She took a sip of her coffee, looking at him through the tops of her eyes.

"So get this," he said. He frowned, then turned and looked at the counter, then back at Callie. "What's it take to get a cup of joe around this bitch?"

"It takes getting off your lazy butt and going up to the counter and ordering one," she said, a smirk forming as she put the cup back to her lips.

"F that. I'll just share yours." He held his hand out and she rolled her eyes before handing him the cup. He took a sip then nodded his approval, pursing his lips. "Hey, that's not bad! I was wondering why we didn't meet at Starbucks."

Callie rolled her eyes again and took her cup back from him. "Way overrated, dude. When have I ever been a corporate whore? So get what?"

"Get this," he said again, jabbing his fingertip into the table. "I called Monica this morning on my way over here."

"Who's Monica?"

"You know, that bird who works at the reception desk," Walter said. He leaned back and slipped his thumbs through his belt loops.

Callie was shaking her head. "No, Walter, I don't know. I don't work there anymore, remember? Anyway, what did Monica have to say?"

"Well, it was a shot in the dark. Just seeing if she knew anything about anyone named Natalie." Walter looked around at the counter again, then said, "F this. I'm getting my own. Hang tight, Calgirl." Then he walked up to the counter and took a decorative pastry from the glass cake platter and ordered a coffee. As he walked back to the table, he looked at the pastry with a frown, then shrugged and took a bite, crumbs immediately moving in on his shirt and jacket.

"So anyway, Monica has only worked there for like two years, so she has never even heard of Natalie. But she does have access to some employee information, since she answers all the phones and has to connect all the calls and whatnot."

"Okay. So she's like a mini HR then," Callie said.

Walter held out his hand to her. "Sure. Anyway, she said she'd do some looking and see what she could find, and hook me up when I got in today."

Callie nodded. "That's good, Walter. I guess this girl likes you, then?"

He frowned and took another bite of the crumbling dessert. "Hmm. What girl?" he said with a mouthful of food.

"Monica. The very girl we've been talking about, Walter. Remember?"

He hiked his chin up, then leaned back and finished his pastry. "Mmm hmm," he said, licking his fingers. "Of course she does."

As Callie and Walter came in the front door of the Royal offices, Walter peeled off, squeezing Callie's arm, saying he'd catch up with her later. He stopped at the reception desk to talk to the pretty girl who was nothing but smiles. Callie felt sure that Monica was smitten because Walter had actually called the corporate line and had spoken only to her. Callie smiled and shook her head as she headed for the elevators.

The doors slid open and Callie made her way down the busy hall to Minus's office. He was sitting behind his desk scrolling through a page on the internet, chin resting on his hand. Callie knocked on the jamb and set her purse down in a chair by his conference table. He looked up and immediately returned his attention to the screen in front of him.

"What's up, Callie? You ready to do this thing?"

"Yep. Ready as I'll ever be," she said.

"How'd the dive go?" he asked, then finally scooted back and put his hands on the armrests, giving her his full attention.

Callie nodded and smiled. "It went well. Well, weller than I thought it would go anyway. I did all right. The first bit was pretty scary."

"What first bit?" he said.

"The descent. That first fifty feet or so was the scariest thing I've ever done. I couldn't see anything! Then the ground finally appeared and I realized I wasn't actually trapped in a water coffin, and I did okay."

He was nodding now. "Good. Good, good. That's great, Callie. This is going to be good stuff."

Callie settled into a chair across the desk from Minus and crossed her legs, then took a deep breath. "Okay, Minus," she said, tilting her head, "How are we going to do this?"

"What? The testing?"

She nodded.

"Well, we take the equipment out on a boat. You dive down as deep as you can go, and I get the readings up on the boat," he said, holding out his hands.

"Yeah, I gathered that. I'm asking where and when. All the finer details."

"I have a trip booked for February fifteenth. Does that work for you?"

"Yeah. That's fine. I have two more dives this weekend, to complete my training and get my certification. Then I'll be good to go," she said.

"Awesome. So what I need from you now is to take the computer and the prototype down to the lab and do as much testing as you can without water. Calibrations, phase readings, interference... everything you can do on dry land."

"You got it," she said. This was one of Callie's favorite parts of the job. Being alone in a lab allowed her to be a scientist. And it allowed her to think. Some of her best ideas came to her while she was immersed in numbers. Being exposed to the science itself behind a project flooded her with inspiration.

When she got to the lab, she set everything up and began wheeling out computers and test equipment that stood mounted on steel-poled dollies like IV carts in the hospital. Then she laid out all the spec sheets on the counter and began reading line by line what had gone into the equipment, and marked off how she would test each aspect of its function. She would be testing the barometer under normal pressure, then in a hyperbaric chamber. The radio receiver and transmitter would be tested in the lab, then in a Faraday cage. They had not yet attached any controls or cameras, or any of the other monitoring equipment to the prototype – and probably wouldn't. These would be added to the first full-size endeavor, and were pretty standard. The initial prototype was the size of a golf ball, and they were mostly concerned with the function of the defensive device. Callie's theory was that it would not hold out for more than a few minutes – maybe as much as an hour. There was just no way to keep that much spare power on the pod.

As she stood at the counter making notes and getting ready to start the testing, her phone rang. She absently pulled it out of her purse with her free hand. "Hello?"

"Hey, baby. What are you doing?" It was Chris.

"I'm working, hon. What's up?"

"Well, I was wondering if you had time for lunch," Chris said.

She frowned, then looked up at the clock on the wall. "Babe, I just got here. I..."

"Okay, okay. Can you just come out to the lobby for just a second then? I have something to show you."

Callie was shaking her head, still frowning. "Yeah, I guess so. Is everything okay?"

"We'll see, babe. Please come out here."

Callie's eyes went wide, but as she was about to speak, the line went dead. A panic began to grow in her chest. *What the heck is he talking about? Is he breaking up with me?* She dropped her phone back in her purse and hurried through the door, and down the hall to the elevator. As she stood waiting for it to arrive, she crossed her arms and began tapping her foot nervously. She was now trembling all over. Callie was not good at surprise confrontations. The elevator dinged and she began the slow ride down eleven floors to the lobby. It seemed to take forever as she stood there wondering what could possibly have gone wrong in their relationship. She knew she wasn't good at relationships because she usually took work a lot more seriously than the relationship itself. And she had lost more than one boyfriend to the wait she required for chastity's sake. Guys were interested in her sexually – no more than other women, but certainly enough to be called her fair share – but it was a rare few who were willing to wait for marriage to take her to bed. And this was how it always started. *"Babe, can we talk?"*

The doors opened and she stepped tentatively out onto the marble floor, heading straight for the welcome desk where Chris waited, leaning against the counter, smiling and talking with Monica. Anger suddenly swept through Callie's heart and now her face was a furious frown. As she got closer, Chris looked up at her and his smile slid slowly off his face. This was looking worse and worse to Callie. She finally stood toe to toe with him. He looked down at her and ran her hair back off her shoulder for her. She stood with arms crossed and shoulders high, head tilted as she stared up at him. This was the best defensive posture she could attain under the circumstances, though she wished she had a baseball bat to complete the picture.

"Hey baby," Chris said. "What's wrong?"

"You tell me, Chris." Her mouth was a small, hard line as she chewed on her jaw and stared up at him fiercely.

He was shaking his head. "I don't know what you mean, honey! Nothing is wrong with me!"

"Oh! Oh, okay. So it's me then!" she said, almost shouting.

Chris stared at her, speechless, and let his hand fall to his side. His mouth hung agape.

"So you're leaving me? Tired of waiting? Is that it?"

He began shaking his head quickly. "Babe, no. I think we've had a misunderstanding somewhere."

"Then what the heck are you doing here?" she said. She readjusted her stance and took a deep breath. Somewhere behind her, the elevator dinged again, and she heard footsteps approaching.

Chris reached in his coat pocket and pulled out a long envelope. "Well, I was just coming to wish you a happy birthday, sweetie," he said. With his other hand, he gripped her shoulder, offering her the blue envelope.

The bottom dropped out of Callie's anger. She looked down at the envelope, still not uncrossing her arms. Now she was defending herself against her own idiocy. Jumping to conclusions was one of her strongest athletic abilities, these days. "What is that?"

"Babe, relax!" he said, stroking her shoulder.

"What's up, man?" Walter said, as he came to stop beside her, looking at Chris. They shook hands. "Sorry I'm late."

Chris nodded, smirking at Walter. "Uh, you're not late."

Callie looked up at Walter, then back at Chris. "You two planned this together?"

Chris shrugged. Walter looked down at her and smiled. "Happy birthday, Cal."

She looked back up at him again and shook her head. She still wasn't smiling.

"What, did you forget it's February first?" he said.

"No. I... I mean," she started, then looked back at Chris.

"You mean you just forgot it was your birthday?" Chris said. He was smiling, but looked a little incredulous.

She stared at him for a moment, still feeling the trembling rush of anger seeping out through her toes. She breathed in deeply, then straightened her head and swallowed. "I thought you were..."

"Babe, no. Never," Chris said, leaning in to kiss her. He then held the envelope up again, which she still had not taken. "Aren't you going to open your gift?"

She stared at him for another long moment before finally reaching out with trembling fingers and taking the blue envelope and opening it. Inside there were two plane tickets to Cozumel International Airport. Callie stared at it silently for a moment, then looked back up at Chris, eyes wide and tears beginning to find their way in.

"Mexico, babe! We're going diving down there! Some of the best diving you'll ever do!" Chris said. He was now holding both of her shoulders and shaking her lightly as he spoke.

"Yeah, we're going with you, Cal," Walter said, lightly punching her shoulder. She looked at him briefly.

"I'm so sorry, Chris," she said, burying her face in his chest. What a fool she had been! He put his hand on her head and held her close. She could hear his heart beating through his jacket. When he spoke it was muffled and amplified at the same time, like a cartoon character on a telephone.

"I thought you'd be happier," he said.

"I am happy!" she said through her tears. She tried wiping them away, embarrassed and ashamed of the way she had assumed the worst with no justifiable reason. "I am happy, Chris. Thank you so much," she said. When she had finally finished her cry, she pulled away and looked at Walter again. "You guys are going too?"

"Yep. Thevi is getting certified as we speak."

"Really? Oh my gosh, that is so awesome!" Callie said, wiping at her eyes again.

"Yeah, she was in classes all last week."

Callie looked again at the tickets, then back up at Chris, and smiled. "I've been such a fool. I'm sorry, Chris."

"Forget about it. We're going to Mexico!"

"Yay!" she said, lifting a weak fist into the air and laughing through her tears.

"Hey, dude. I got you something too," Walter said. He handed her a small card with two blue bells on it. "Happy birthday." She took the card from him and he returned his hands to his coat pockets.

Callie opened the card. It was a ten-dollar gift card for Taco Bell. She laughed out loud and shook her head, then threw her arms around his neck, kissing him on the cheek. "You're the best, Walter."

"Oh, I see. I buy you a plane ticket to the prettiest dive you'll ever make in your life. He buys you a couple of tacos, and he's the best," Chris said.

"Second best," she said, winking mischievously at him.

CHAPTER 15

colOmbia deep

The sky outside the windows was too bright to look at without shades. Looking down, Callie could see nothing but clouds. They had taken off from a cold, dreary New Jersey that morning and had a layover in Atlanta. Now, on the last leg of the trip, they had been in the air nearly seven hours. Callie was drowsy, but ready to get out and get her muscles moving. She hoped the clouds would clear before they hit Mexico. Thevi sat next to her while Walter and Chris sat across the aisle. They had been enjoying the free drinks that first-class travel provided them, and were all beginning to feel the effects.

The clouds did thin out, and then finally disappear altogether as they neared their destination. It was sunny and warm in Mexico, and Callie found herself wondering why she lived in a perpetually cold state. Cozumel was a balmy seventy-five degrees, and was only supposed to get down to sixty-eight later in the week. She thought she was going to enjoy sitting on the beach even more than the dive trip they had planned. She was, of course, a little nervous about the dive, but had been reminding herself constantly how awesome it had been once the world had opened up down there. And how she had even at some points forgotten they were under water. Chris and Walter had been filling her ears with talk about how glorious and majestic the reef was down here in Cozumel, and how it was some of the most spectacular diving in the world. But above the nervousness was an excitement she could hardly explain. She knew it would be beautiful. She knew it would be a once-in-a-lifetime experience. But it was more than that. The thought that she, Callie Simmons, would be subjecting herself to an underwater experience of any kind was so foreign a concept to her that she couldn't quite grasp her feelings on it – even though they felt like excitement.

When the plane touched down on Mexican land, they gathered their luggage and found a resort shuttle outside the airport. As they stepped onto the shuttle, they were welcomed with a chest full of ice-cold beer. Each of them took one and popped them open, and the week-long party officially began. Callie reluctantly sipped from the bottle of Corona, knowing they still had a long day ahead of them, she would be facing jet lag, and they still hadn't even made it to the hotel. But that was what vacation was supposed to be about, she reminded herself. Once they arrived at the resort, Callie had no trouble at all adjusting to the temporary lifestyle. The beers were free and the weather was absolutely perfect.

After they had all unpacked in their adjacent rooms, they all met out at the main pool, where there was a swim-up bar and Mexican music blasted from hidden speakers all around the pool. Callie and Chris waded up to the bar and found stools. The bar stools were raised pillars of concrete spaced evenly in front of the bar. There were two bartenders standing in the well behind the bar, serving free margaritas and beer to the patrons. Bees buzzed around, ever searching for something sweet upon which they could feed. Callie learned quickly that they were no more than a nuisance as they didn't bother the patrons, except by occasionally landing in their beer cups.

They ordered Dos Equis beers, which were served in plastic tumblers, then clacked them together and Callie smiled. "Thank you, Chris. This has been the best birthday week ever." She leaned over and kissed him, her gigantic sunglasses almost getting in the way.

"You're welcome, sweetheart. I've been planning this for ages. It just made it that much better that you got dive certified. Otherwise I would have had to talk you into snorkeling."

"Ha! I think that would be scarier for me than scuba diving now. At least I can always breathe with a tank on my back."

Chris shrugged. "Yeah, I agree. And you get to see so much more."

Walter and Thevi waded up shouting and waving to the music. Callie turned to smile at them and found her eyes moving over Walter's chest, which was massive and muscular, covered with the dark ink of tattoos. She realized in an instant that in all these years she had known him, she had never had occasion to see him without a shirt on, and was almost breathlessly impressed with how modest he had been, not mentioning how well he was built. With the water sliding down his chest in shimmering drops, she noticed he was already starting to brown nicely. She had to turn her eyes back to Chris, lest her face betray her sudden awe of the man she had thought she knew so well.

"What's up, my fine Mexican brotha?" Walter said, holding his cup up to Chris as he slid into the stool next to him. Thevi took her place on Callie's other side. She turned toward Thevi and leaned back, holding her arms open wide.

"Helllllllo, sister!" she said, and they hugged. Thevi wore a very small version of a bikini that did little to cover her at all. Her milk-white skin stood out beautifully against the red fabric of the bikini, her shoulders a smattering of a million tiny freckles that ran down her arms and onto her chest, like someone had dumped a box of matte brown glitter over her head. Her red hair was piled neatly on top of her head, and from her ears dangled long golden threads that sparkled in the sun. She showed Callie two rows of perfect white teeth as she smiled broadly. Callie found herself suddenly jealous of Thevi and Walter. They looked like movie stars out here visiting a pool bar in a nameless Mexican resort – hiding out from the celebrity of the real world in which they lived. By comparison, hers was a very sheltered and unexciting life. She and Chris stayed in most of the time, where Walter and Thevi were almost constantly going out. And they looked the part. She and Chris, though not homely or unattractive at all, could be called plain. And Chris certainly didn't have the large slabs of muscle on his chest and arms like Walter.

"Oh, isn't this just perfect?" Thevi squealed. Callie ditched the revery and tried to get herself back into the spirit.

"Yes. Perfectly wonderful. Thank you for coming with us, Thevi. I'm so excited!" she said, putting her hand on Thevi's knee. Thevi put her hand over Callie's and leaned in close.

"I wouldn't miss it for the world. We're going to have so much fun!"

They sat at the pool bar for several hours, draining cup after cup of almost-cold beer, swatting away the bees and laughing as the sun finally began to creep down past the mountains in the distance. The sky in the west burned dark red and illuminated sparse clouds with golden stroke. They had left for the airport at 4:45 that morning, for the earliest flight there was to Cozumel. Callie's eyes were starting to feel heavy, but she wasn't about to say anything yet.

"You guys getting hungry yet?" Chris said, almost as if coming to her rescue. The beer and liquor was starting to get the best of her. She raised her hand. The others agreed, and they all made their way out of the pool.

"Okay, so we get cleaned up, wash these wrinkles off us and meet back here in say, half an hour?" he said when they were all on the deck drying off.

"Yeah, sounds good. Buffet opens at six, right?" Walter said.

"Yeah. It's open. So let's do this."

They all split up and headed to their rooms to clean up and get dressed.

The night was unmerciful to Callie, but the buffet dinner had been exactly what she needed. She felt a second wind come over her as they were heading to the pavilion next to the restaurant, from which they could all hear loud music emanating. There were tables setup all across the back of the open pavilion, but the front half was dedicated to the dancers, of which there were many. A Latin reggae band stretched across the stage, and a feeling of electricity was present in the air. She knew the night was just beginning, but had told Chris earlier not to wake her in the morning. She planned on sleeping until she could no longer hold her eyes closed. He had smiled and kissed her nose, telling her she was the boss. So if she could just make it through the night, she'd be completely rested tomorrow.

They danced.

They took turns dancing with each other. Walter and Callie, Walter and Thevi, Chris and Thevi, Chris and Callie. Then they all danced together. Several times, Walter coerced the short but beautiful singer into the fray. She would dance around with him for a few moments, but would always shortly return to her microphone with a huge smile on her face. Callie's hands were sore from all the clapping she had done that evening. Not really knowing how to dance very well, she had mainly stood around stomping and clapping to the beat, a smile spread wide across her face. Her jealousy of

Thevi had been dampened slightly when a good-looking forty-something man had appeared out of the crowd and asked Callie to dance. He told her she was the most gorgeous woman in the room with a beaming smile and terrific brown eyes. Her face had lit up with that and she had allowed herself to be twirled about for a song in his embrace. And like a gentleman, he had returned her to Chris's hand as soon as they were finished. Chris was smiling widely at her as she found her seat.

"He told me I was the most gorgeous woman in the world!" she screamed through the music.

Chris's face fell and he began frowning. "So?"

Callie's smile fell too. "Huh?"

Chris leaned forward, shaking his head. "So? What, you didn't already know that? I thought that was well obvious, dear."

The smile returned to Callie's face. She leaned forward and kissed him long on the mouth. "Keep it up, babe, and you'll sleep well tonight!"

Codi sat staring at her reflection in the mirror. The image she saw looked nothing like her, but it was the image she was forcing herself to get used to. She was beginning to recognize it. The blotchy purple and red circles and soft polygons that made up the digital representation of her physiognomy was beginning to look familiar. This provided her only the slightest comfort. But it was at least some amount of comfort. Rebecca sat behind her, hands resting on her knees, guiding Codi through the process of applying makeup.

She had, of course, applied makeup thousands of times before, but Rebecca was showing her the subtle nuances in color and texture that distinguished the difference between too much and too little that her vision could translate. Codi didn't see much point in putting on makeup at all – much less in doing it herself. She was blind. She was already going to attract unnecessary attention with her white cane and slow, fumbling, graceless gait through the world. She didn't want to make it worse by accidentally blotching up her rouge and painting herself up like a clown. Mentioning this to Rebecca, she had been patient, but had prodded her onward.

"Don't be silly, Codi. You'll never look like a clown. And any attention you call to yourself will be rewarded with the vision they have of your beautiful porcelain-doll face. You have the fullest lips and most gorgeous jawline and chin I've ever seen. And that's before you even get to your retardedly awesome eyes." She had run her fingers over Codi's cheek and facial features as she described each of them to her, sending a small row of chill bumps up Codi's spine. And so they had continued.

"What do you want to do when you grow up, Codi?" Rebecca asked after the silence had grown thick.

"I don't know. I think my options are kind of limited now, don't you think?"

Rebecca shrugged. "Maybe a little. But I think you can do anything you put your mind to. Anything you want to do."

Codi leaned her head back and stared at the blankness in the direction of the ceiling. "I haven't thought that far ahead yet, I guess. I mean, I guess I better start getting busy though, huh?"

"How old are you, darling?" Rebecca said.

"Twenty-four," she answered.

"Oh dear, you're just a baby."

Codi turned toward Rebecca. "I know. That's what's so depressing. I mean, I don't mean to complain, but..."

"Oh, honey, come here," Rebecca said, pulling her into a hug. "You have every right to grieve. You have a whole life of this ahead of you. It's perfectly normal for you to feel slighted. Depression is completely rational."

Codi's eyes began to leak. She could feel the tears streaming freely down her cheek, wetting the cloth of Rebecca's sweater where her chin rested. Absentmindedly, she began stroking Rebecca's back the same way Rebecca was doing to her. She noticed there was nothing but smooth cloth. She leaned back as if to look at Rebecca in the eyes.

"Do you ever wear a bra?"

"Ha! No, darling. I don't believe in them. I live a life free of the burden of an underwire," she said, laughing.

Codi shook her head. "Gah. Lucky dog."

Rebecca shrugged. "Why do you ask? Why should I be wearing one in my own house?"

"I don't know. I just know you're dressed for the day, and I noticed it before, too."

"Does it bother you?"

"Of course not!" Codi said. She wiped the final tears from her cheeks and the corners of her eyes. "I was just wondering."

Rebecca sat there with her hands on Codi's knees for a moment, then said, "What say we walk down to the creek and feed the ducks?"

Codi frowned. "What? I thought they all flew south for the winter."

"Nope. Not these ducks. I think you'd enjoy it, besides. It's a really cool sensation to feel their bills as they nibble from your palm."

"Yeah, that sounds great," Codi agreed.

As they walked along the shore, Codi's arm looped through Rebecca's, they looked like a couple. But no one paid them any attention. They found a bench by the water and opened a plastic bag full of old hot dog buns and bread ends and began breaking up the bread into small pieces. Rebecca showed her how to hold her hand, and as the ducks approached, showed her where to put it so the ducks could reach the food. The first time one mumbled across her palm with its hard bill, she laughed out loud, excited and giddy to be experiencing this for the first time. Rebecca laughed with her.

When the bread was gone, they drove down the coast to the boardwalk for an afternoon of popping balloons, eating funnel cake and acting like little girls. Codi had been to the arcades and carnivals many times as an adolescent, but this was a completely new experience. And by the end of the afternoon, she realized she was having fun in spite of herself. The realization that her excitement and pleasure were actually enhanced by her blindness, rather than hindered by it hit her suddenly. The sounds of laughter and shouting, the bells and music from the arcades, the feet on the wood – and the smells of candy and cake and hot dogs and people's breath were all radically intensified by her lack of sight. The stimulation was almost overwhelming. But she found herself fascinated by it. And the best part of it all was that she did not feel like she was missing out on anything. She played the games she could play: she swung the sledgehammer and rang the bell, and the huge padded mallet to knock back the moles that popped up through perfectly round holes sawed in the wood of the game. She threw darts and popped balloons, she rolled ski balls up the ramp and she made it through the house of mirrors in record time. Codi took part in it all like a completely unencumbered patron. She did not wish she had sight so she could experience it more thoroughly – she just simply didn't even think about that part of it. It never crossed her mind.

It was a massive overcoming step for Codi, and by the end of the evening, now turning dark with a bright moon in the sky, she found the only thing she would have changed was Sam. She would have had Sam with her to experience the fun and growth.

⌘   ⌘   ⌘

The next morning, Callie woke with a start and sat bolt upright in bed, drenched in sweat, her clothes stuck to her body like super glue. She looked about the dim room but could see no evidence of other human life. Her head was pounding and her hair was hanging in her eyes. She leaned forward and buried her face in her hands, wiping the matter from the corners of her eyes. Then she stretched long and looked at the clock. It was blinking 12:00 like a digital broken record.

"Chris!" she shouted into the eery darkness brought about by the blackout curtain. The bright Mexico sun was held at bay behind that curtain, and Callie thanked God for small favors. She knew at some point she would have to face the Big Light, but preferably not for a long time. When Chris did not answer, she realized she had been abandoned by those who could handle their alcohol better, and leaned back on her hands, yawning. The thin film of sweat was beginning to run down her spine and into her crack. She grabbed her t-shirt and whipped it over her head, balled it up and tossed it indiscriminately into a corner of the room, then ran her fingers under her breasts, wiping the sweat away, and tried to straighten her hair. It was a wreck. She felt like a wreck. She had not drunk that much in a long time, and didn't remember ever starting that early in the morning and going all day like that. Even before the shuttle had picked them up from home to take them to the airport, the four of them had all had a bloody mary together. Then they had more on the airplane. Then the beers on the shuttle from the airport to the hotel. Then the beers in the pool, and the cocktails after dinner while they were already working on sweating it out on the dance floor. When she finally felt the strength and energy to get out of the bed, she fumbled in her purse looking for her phone. She finally found it plugged in and charging in the bathroom. Callie had no recollection of plugging in her phone. Maybe Chris had done it for her this morning when he got up. She pushed the on button on the side and saw that it was nearly one o'clock in the afternoon. She grumbled and looked up at the ceiling, stretching her neck, then checked herself in the mirror. She was a scary sight.

The steaming shower felt great, albeit a little hot to her lightly burned skin. She stood in the shower for a long time just stretching and enjoying the free heat before finally grabbing her razor and the soap. The stubble under her arms and on her legs was reaching record lengths, and she realized she had not been in the shower for almost two days. She brushed her teeth while she stood in the shower and peed, watching the yellow water turn clear as it sought out the drain. Fully relieved and over being disgusted with herself, she finally spat and rinsed her mouth out, then stepped out of the shower onto a dry towel and began prepping herself for another long day in the sun.

When Callie finally joined the others, they were all seated around an umbrella table by the pool, well into their drinks and full of smiles. "Good morning, princess!" Thevi said as Callie approached the table.

Callie shot her the bird and sat down. "I don't know how you guys do it," she said.

"It takes a lot of practice, babe," Walter said, lifting his margarita and sucking down a good portion of it in one swig. "Hair of the dog. Ahhh!" he said, wiping his mouth.

"You know, I've never understood that phrase. What does a dog have to do with drinking in the morning?"

Walter giggled as he sat back and adjusted his sunglasses.

"It refers to an old belief that if you were bitten by a rabid dog, putting some of that dog's hair in the wound would keep you from getting rabies," Thevi said. "That which made you feel so bad will also bring about your healing."

"Ah. I see," Callie said, though she didn't. The last thing on her mind at the moment was another drink. She still felt swimmy from yesterday's alcohol. "How long have you guys been up?"

"Well Chris here got up at seven to read the paper," Walter said, and looked at Thevi. "Thev and I got up around nine to go for a little stroll on the beach."

"Yeah, you should totally come with us tomorrow. It's so gorgeous in the morning," Thevi added.

"Oh I'd love to. Maybe I won't drink as much tonight," Callie said, making a bitter face and looking toward the pool. "In fact, I think I'll never drink again."

"Ha!" Chris said. "You want a margarita, babe?"

"Ugh. God, no," Callie said, slapping his arm. Chris stopped a nearby waiter and pointed at his drink. The waiter nodded curtly and hurried off. "Chris, I'm serious, I won't drink it."

He grabbed her arm and gave it a squeeze. "So Thevi and Walt want to go out on the town today and bargain with the locals over some fine shell jewelry and ancient Mexican artifacts."

"Now that sounds like my kind of day," Callie said. The waiter returned and set a tall pink drink in front of her on a square white napkin, then nodded and disappeared again. Callie absently put the straw to her lips and started another day in Cozumel.

It was the fourth day when they finally summoned the boat and rented the gear and headed out to the reef for their big dive. Callie and Walter were both fascinated by the fact the boat captain had no depth-finding equipment or any kind of technology at all on board the boat – other than the combustion motor, of course. He just knew exactly where to go. Callie tried focusing on the horizon and the other nuances of the trip to the dive site to keep her mind off the terrifying descent she knew lay ahead.

The water was a crystal blue that gave them a beautiful view of the ocean life on their trek. She could see bright yellow fish trying to get out of the way of the boat as it frothed up the water, and the beginnings of the massive coral reef – Chris had called the second largest in the world. She was both excited and nervous, and reckoned she had better just get used to that cocktail of emotion. Her last two certification dives had been the same way. Standard drop-dives into murky water with not much to look at, and scary all the way down. At least she had been armed with the knowledge that it wasn't a claustrophobic nightmare once they reached the bottom. But the fear was still there, at least in part. It was getting easier though. None of the last three had been as hard as the first. And maybe out here with this clear water and hundred-yard visibility, she would shed the rest of that fear, being able to see all the way down.

When the boat finally stopped, the silence that filled the air was wonderful. Callie's whole body had been vibrating with the rumble of the small boat motor. Now as they strapped themselves into their equipment and donned their snorkels and masks, she was beginning to calm a little. She looked at Chris, who made a funny face before popping the regulator into his mouth, then smiled at her. She leaned forward and popped it out to kiss him.

"This is going to be awesome, isn't it?" she said.

"Oh, God, babe. This is one of the top-five dives in the world. It's going to take your breath away."

"I hope not," she said, and snickered.

Chris rolled his eyes. "Not literally, of course." He smiled again. "You okay?"

"Yup. Doing good." She dropped her mask into place and gave him the okay sign with her finger and thumb. He repeated the sign, then kissed her again, awkwardly, masks bumping into each other. Had he known it was the last time he would ever kiss her, he might have removed his mask.

The descent was uneventful, and – as Callie had suspected – she could see the ground almost the second she ducked under water. It was a completely different descent than she was used to, and her fear and anxiety floated away quickly. As they reached the floor at around thirty feet, she was overwhelmed by the beauty and intricacy of the coral that stretched away in every direction as far as the eye could see. Among and betwixt these fingers of the ocean floor, small animalia and fish darted in and out of existence, playing hide and seek with each other and the humans invading their habitat.

Callie drifted along next to Chris, hands up under the bottom of her tank, attaining neutral buoyancy for the first time without the eyes of an instructor looking on. She felt completely relaxed and comfortable in this water. The water was warmer than the Atlantic, and much clearer. She reckoned a lot of that had to do with the fact that it was a large gulf of trapped water rather than a raging ocean pounding against the shore of a continent. But then, she guessed, she was probably just guessing.

Occasionally she would look over at Chris, who would smile behind his regulator and give her an okay sign. She always parroted the signal and smiled back at him, excited to be on such a magnificent dive so early in her career. She felt like part of the gang. One of the big boys. Included in some elite club of divers who got to experience something no one else in the world was privileged enough to be a part of. She felt giddy and lighter than the bubbles escaping her regulator every time she exhaled.

After a while, the reef turned to a more sophisticated and marvelous form, resembling structure and chaos simultaneously. Tall spires of twisted reef stuck straight up out of the forest of sea flora and live rock. Some of the structures they passed were twenty or thirty feet tall, twisted roots of rock tangling and forming small caverns and tunnels; some of it reached almost back up to the surface. Chris and Walter occasionally ducked down into the shallow chasms, calling the attention of the dive master, who waited patiently, hovering above and keeping track of the time. Each time they would come back to the swim level, Callie would think *Next time. Next time I'll join them.* But each time they would dive to check out another crevasse, she would chicken out and wave off their attempts to get her to join them. It wasn't until Thevi finally went down with them that she finally got the guts to go down and check it out. And the dive master, seeing that the weaker divers were no longer being left alone, joined them down in the makeshift alley between two tall blocks of reef. They came upon a large sea turtle crawling along the bottom of the silty ground, chasing a small group of orange fish. Callie and Thevi looked at each other, and Thevi covered her heart with her hand.

In another natural tunnel, they found a twelve-foot basking shark just hovering above the ocean floor, just looking at them. Callie tried to get behind Chris, as if to use him as a human shield, but he shook his head and rolled his eyes, waving his hand at the shark as if to say, "He's harmless." And indeed, the shark made no move toward them, or even bothered paying them any attention other than the initial glance as they passed in front of it.

They swam on for a while, enjoying the small marvels of the reef before finally returning to thirty feet and drifting along above it again. They had a loose dive plan that involved seeing most of the reef and some tunnels through the small cities, followed by an hour break and lunch on the boat, and then a second dive, where they would get to see the great deep. Callie was completely comfortable and breathing normally by the end of the first dive, even having ventured into some of the alleys formed by the reefs. In fact, when they finished their fifteen-at-fifteen, she had as much air left as Chris and Walter. That made her very proud. She had to keep reminding herself that she was no more experienced than Thevi though. Thevi's last dive had been a cert dive as well, so this was the first real open-water dive for both of them without instructors.

Up on the boat though, Callie started getting a headache. She knew the lifestyle they'd taken to while on this vacation was so far removed from her usual strict routine that she had barely had time to adjust to diving mode. She had wanted to be clear-headed for the dives, but peer pressure spoke louder than any dictum she had given herself about how to act. She was on vacation, darn it, and was going to enjoy it as much as they did. And furthermore, they were all diving with her. It's not like she was the only one who was suffering from a hangover and light exhaustion. She was also a little dehydrated, and drained two bottles of water before it was time to don the mask again. When she leaned over and whispered to Chris, asking where they were supposed to pee, he had stared at her for long moment before looking at the ocean. She then looked at the great water and back at him, catching his drift. Walter then spoke up, having overheard her question.

"Honey, there's two types of people in the world: those who piss in their wetsuit, and those who say they don't."

She laughed out loud and wondered why she hadn't thought of that before. But it gave her a sense of relief. She was just glad she had taken care of her other bathroom business before they'd left the resort. As she was putting her mask back on, she began to feel light-headed and dizzy. She wondered if it was the drinking the night before, or the exhaustion, or just breathing the mixture of nitrogen and oxygen at depth. Either way, she didn't want to speak up and be the one to ruin the party. But when they dropped back into the water and prepared to descend, she was beginning to feel a little claustrophobic in her own head. Tunnel vision began to set in. She took deep breaths, trying to clear her head, and felt a little better, but couldn't shake the feeling of impending doom that seemed to be taking over. She tried to relax, and leaned back, closing her eyes, and then it was time to go.

The descent was slow and laborious. All the way down, her upper sinus cavity kept feeling like it was about to pop. She would slow and make a time-out sign to the others, and wait for the pressure to let up a little, and then drop another three or four feet. At first, it felt like someone was sticking an icepick in her forehead, and Callie worried that she would not be able to make it all the way down. But as she kicked up a foot or two, it would slowly dissipate, and she was able to go down another few feet before the pain returned. It didn't seem life-threatening though, as long as she didn't push it, so she carried on. *Any pain that resolves itself*, she thought, *is a problem that's gone away.* She carried on.

As they floated along with the current in a southerly direction, they could see a reef wall off to their left, while ahead and below them there were gigantic blocks of slate and rock that looked like buildings. Some of these rocks were as big as houses. When the group would reach the edge of one, there was a ten- to fifteen-foot drop off to another just below. The overall appearance was of a long forgotten, underwater city made of brown and gray stone. It was staggering to Callie. She found herself wishing she felt better now so she could enjoy the view. She checked her dive computer and saw she was still doing great on air. They bottomed out at just under seventy feet. It was darker down here, but no less clear. She could still see for what seemed to be miles in every direction. The current was strong, pushing them along at a nice steady flow, but it wasn't offensively strong. She let her bladder go and immediately felt the warmth on her inner thighs, and wondered absently if anyone could tell what she was doing in the dark water. They moved along the edge of the reef wall that ran interminably into the distance on their left until they finally came to an opening in the craggy rock. The opening was roughly circular with a flat bottom that opened on the ocean floor. There were very few fish at this depth, and none were close enough to make out. The few that Callie saw were way off in the distance. She began feeling the dizziness and fatigue settle over her again, and wondered if she should let the others know.

She followed as the group lined up outside the hole in the reef. The dive master stopped and pointed to the hole and gave an okay sign to everyone. Everyone returned the sign, so he entered the hole. Thevi was the first to follow, then Walter. Chris turned to look at Callie and gave her his own OK. She nodded and smiled, trying to hide her sudden fear and uneasiness with the way she felt. He returned her smile and held his hand out, offering her the tunnel. She shook her head and pointed at him, telling him to go ahead. He did.

The tunnel was smaller in diameter than she had thought from the outside. Callie was immediately aware of the closeness of the porous wall around her. It wasn't crushingly claustrophobic, but it was closer than she would have liked. She tried to crane her neck to see up ahead of the group and see how long the tunnel was, but couldn't see past Chris and his tank. He only had a foot on either side of him, and only inches above and below. The tunnel was dark, but not completely lightless, as the porous makeup of the reef let some light in from the top, where there were hundreds of small irregular holes. She felt her chest tightening as the darkness replaced the light, and wondered how long they would be in here. She also noticed the group had slowed down considerably within the confines of the tunnel.

And before she had a chance to object, the light began to return, eating away the darkness like a rock hammer picking away at a brick of coal. One by one they popped out the end of the tunnel, until Callie was the only one left. She had another ten feet left to go when she realized everyone had stopped just outside the opening, and were forming a loose circle, waiting for her to join them. What was going on? She looked up again and made a head count, counting all four of her group awaiting her arrival. But she wasn't about to speed up, either. She had the sudden fear of puncturing her tank on the ceiling above her or something crazy like that. She had to shake her head at that ridiculous thought, and continued on, her breathing now a steady, heavy roar in her ears.

When she finally emerged from the tunnel, she was immediately seized by a magnificent, overwhelming perspective of just how tiny she really was. The world had simply come to an end. She felt herself inhale heavily and tears formed in her eyes as she looked down and realized there was nothing below her but darkness. The depth was too great for the light to pierce. She put her hand up to her chest and stifled her emotion, which threatened to take over her, bringing her to a full cry. It was simply breathtakingly gorgeous. She turned to look back at the hole from which they had just emerged. The tunnel ended in a wall that just seemed to go down forever. There was no bottom out here. Another thought struck her at that point: what if the Bloop was down there? She felt very vulnerable floating here with no world at all below her.

Callie felt a tug on her elbow, and turned to see Thevi floating there beside her, the same emotion in her eyes. It was indescribably beautiful. Even without the benefit of words, she could tell Thevi was saying the same thing Callie wanted to say. They would probably never see anything so awesome again in their lives. Not on this planet. The wall stretched away to the north and south, far beyond their vision, and though the top was only ten or fifteen feet above them, the bottom was nowhere in sight. And there was nothing else out there. In every other direction, there was simply... nothing. Callie nodded and smiled at Thevi, then felt an overwhelming urge to hug her. They pulled close and squeezed each other momentarily, then turned to rejoin the others. Chris was looking down at his dive computer, but Walter was giving two thumbs up – a big no-no in the scuba rulebook, but everyone understood he wasn't saying to surface. He was giving his approval of the scene. He was nodding and smiling too. The dive master hovered nearby, hands behind his back, looking at the group. Callie motioned for him trying to ask where they would go next, and if they would go any deeper. He swam toward her and reached for his slate, then handed it to her so she could write him a message. As she jotted the words down on the slate, he nodded, then looked north, and pointed down the length of the wall, indicating they would travel alongside it for a way before returning to the surface. She nodded and gave the OK sign, then turned to look at the others. Walter and Thevi were trying to communicate in another language. They had both removed their regulators and were kissing. Callie smiled widely and wished she had a camera. She turned to find Chris so she could share such a moment with him.

But Chris was gone.

She glanced around quickly, feeling a sudden panic, then saw him. His arms were out and he looked completely calm. But he was twenty feet below them. And he was sinking. Callie shouted out through her regulator, bubbles and moans the only discernible sound escaping the depth. "CHRIS!" she tried again, knowing deep down the sound wouldn't travel any farther than her immediate surroundings. Something was wrong. She grabbed Walter's arm and squeezed, now completely frantic. She knew better than to drop down after him, but also couldn't sit back and just let him disappear. He was dropping fast. The tiny light on the back of his dive computer blinked every few seconds. What the heck was he doing down there? Walter quickly took note of the situation and ripped his knife from his boot sheath, then wrapped on his tank with it. The dive master looked up, then followed Walter's pointing, looking straight down. He looked back up at Walter and the rest of the group, then suddenly yanked the dive cord on his BC. No bubbles came out. There was no air left to jettison. He turned and dove straight down towards Chris like a torpedo through the dark water, and for a moment, Callie began to feel hopeful that he would catch up with Chris. But it seemed the deeper Chris got, the faster he fell.

Callie was now screaming, grabbing the sides of her mask and shouting at Chris over and over, tears now filling the bottom of her mask. "CHRIS! NO, CHRIS! COME BACK TO ME!" she tried. None of it was intelligible though. Her screams lashed out through the bubbles and dark water, and Thevi came to join her, putting both her arms around Callie, trying not only to give comfort, but also to make sure she didn't get any crazy thoughts about trying a rescue. Callie grabbed Thevi by the shoulders and shouted, "NO! CHRISSIE, WHY?" but Thevi only shook her head and held her tighter.

He was now fifty feet below them, and falling ever faster. The dive master had shot down thirty feet, then began slowing and checked his computer. He shook his head, then, turned head-down and dived another great distance. Callie could see all of this clearly from her position thirty feet above. And she could see that he wasn't catching up with Chris. For all the speed the dive master was attaining, Chris's was more. And it was getting greater. He was just a black figure against the darkness of the water below now. The blinking light was fading with every pulse. And after another thirty feet or so, the dive master had to stop. She knew he couldn't go much below 130 feet, and Chris was way below that now. Callie knew instinctively that the deeper one got, the more compressed he was, and therefore, the faster he would fall. It was a vicious, ugly cycle that no one could stop now. She wished hard for a rope. Her tears were pouring forth so hard now she was beginning to suck in water through the edges of her regulator. Several times she choked on a mouthful of saltwater and had to clear the regulator with a swollen, shivering tongue pressed into the hole. This was no place for a grief- and terror-stricken woman who was losing control. Chris was no longer visible. Only the faintest evidence of his light blinked back at them now, somewhere near a hundred feet below them. And all hope Callie had for his survival was now gone. She knew there was no chance of survival at two hundred feet. Not with the air they were breathing. She reached down toward him completely succumbing to the bawling, wracking quakes that rocked her body, and called out to him, "Chris, I'm so sorry! I'm so sorry, Chris! I love you! Chris, you hear me? I love you so much! Chris, I love you! I'll never forget you!"

She removed her mask and covered her eyes with numb fingertips, shaking and sobbing underwater, trying hard not to let the grip on the regulator slip. Her lips were incredibly tired from holding so tightly against the regulator, and her face hurt from the odd posture of crying with her mouth wrapped around it. What would she do? Would anyone go after him? Would Chris just be left to the cold blackness of the ocean floor? The thought sent another wave of nausea and fear and sorrow shooting through her body.

Then she felt the rest of the group rising around her, pulling her up. They were calling the dive and heading for the surface and Callie felt absolutely helpless. She wanted so badly to turn and dart down into the darkness, heading for one last contact with the man she loved. The man she finally loved. After years and years of saving herself for the right man, she had finally found him, and now he was lost. She would give anything just for a chance at catching him and looking into his eyes one more time – knowing it would be a one-way trip. But she also knew there was no way she could catch up with him. He was by now probably rocketing toward the floor, speed ever increasing as his depth multiplied more quickly than the dials on his computer could keep up with. The glass casing around his gauges had shattered by now, as had his mask.

She allowed herself to be lifted, her mask still dangling around her wrist. That wrist was still pointing downward, reaching out just in case Chris had found a way to make it back to her. He could take her hand and she could pull him back to safety with her. They would climb aboard the wooden boat and never look down again. She knew she would certainly never dive again without him. But she knew he was gone. It was far too late for him to try to come back now. Scenes flitted through her mind – scenes that told her what was happening to Chris at this very moment: his eyes were now ruptured; his lungs were no longer viable; his heart had succumbed to the pressure and stopped beating by now. These thoughts made her sick with grief, but she could not stop them. She finally leaned her head back and let the blackness that had been following her for the entire dive swallow her whole.

When Callie came to, she was lying on her back on the wooden seat of the boat, stripped of her vest and tank, shivering in her wetsuit. Her head was in Thevi's lap and Thevi was leaning over her, cradling her head in her arms. Her eyes were unfocused, staring off somewhere into the distance behind Thevi. After a long moment, she became aware that someone – probably Walter – was sitting at her feet with his hands on her ankles. The boat motor was loud and persistent, and reminded her that they were racing away from the scene where she had last seen Chris. Her body once again convulsed with emotion as another sob broke free and took over. She covered her face with her trembling hands and cried so hard she lost her breath. Thevi stroked her wrists, but didn't say anything. The sleep of the blackout had been merciful and she found herself wanting to go back to it. Back where there was no pain and memory, no fear and solitude. The road ahead in her life looked long and dreary and forlorn, full of fog and pain. She knew these things passed with time, but time was an evil, monumental mountain for the bereaved, and it never seemed to pass with any real urgency. The short future for Callie Simmons was months for minutes, and decades for years. The road ahead was long and lonely, and she hadn't even taken her first step on it yet.

CHAPTER 16

Rebecca and Codi sat at the table in the breakfast nook, drinking coffee and reading. Rebecca held a newspaper up with one hand while Codi had her fingers in a Braille book, reading very slowly and mouthing the words. Rebecca looked up from her paper and stared at Codi for a moment. Codi noticed and looked up in Rebecca's direction.

"You looking at me?"

"Ha! Good work, sugar. Can you tell?"

"Well, no, not really. That's why I asked. I can see you facing me, but I can't make out the eyes." Codi stared at her for a moment, chin still on her fist, then finally said, "Rebecca, can I ask you a question?"

"You mean another one?"

"Gah. I keep falling for that. Yes. Another one. How come your girlfriend never comes around?"

Rebecca laughed out loud, then took a sip of coffee, then set her mug down. "How do you know I have one?"

"Well, I heard you mention her a while back. I just wonder why she's never around. I'd love to meet her."

"To be honest, we've been on the outs lately. We took a hiatus, officially." She took another sip of coffee, then set the paper down and rested her chin on cradled fingers. "She's traveling abroad at the moment. She's been in Europe since the beginning of December."

"What happened? If you don't mind my asking, of course," Codi said.

"Of course not. You can ask me anything, sweetheart." She sat staring at Codi for a long moment, then said, "Nothing really happened, as such. We're just not as compatible as we once thought we were."

"How did you two meet?"

"Well we went to school together. We were best friends all through grade school. Then in high school, she finally decided she was gay. We took the next appropriate step and started seeing each other professionally."

Codi gulped her coffee. "You mean..."

"No, not like as in at work. I mean we went full-on into a relationship. Like two pros would." Rebecca ran her hair back off her forehead and tightened her messy ponytail. "Not like pros like hookers, either. You know what I mean." They both laughed.

"Of course. Well that's pretty cool. So you've known her a long time then."

Rebecca nodded. "Yeah. After high school, we moved in together, and were roommates through most of college. We even worked for the same company for a time." She held her hands up. "I guess the rest is your standard affair. So to speak."

"What's she like?"

"Well, she's very plain, to be honest. She never wears makeup. Her facial structure, I think, is very beautiful. But she's very plain. Nothing really model-like about her. That's I think what turned me onto her, though." She took another sip of coffee, then straightened the paper on the table. "I guess I have a thing about being the prettier one or something. Though," she waved her hand, "that's of course subjective."

Codi laughed out loud. "Sorry," she said, holding her hand over her mouth.

"For what?"

"Well, subjective. I guess you mean 'as long as *she* believes you're prettier?'"

Rebecca shrugged. "Maybe so." She smiled.

"I didn't know gay women thought like that," Codi said. "Sorry. I'm kind of uncomfortable saying you're gay. Is there a better term?"

Rebecca laughed. "No, darling. It's totally fine. I'm not ashamed of being gay, or any of the bullshit that goes along with it."

"Well that's good. I'd never judge you, Bec."

"I know you wouldn't, sweetie. You're too pure. You have the sweetest soul I've ever met. I can't imagine you ever judging anyone."

Codi tilted her head and widened her eyes. "Well, I wouldn't go that far. But thank you." She smiled. "So when is she coming back? Do you think you'll give it another try?"

Rebecca nodded slowly, looking off into the distance. "I don't know." She shrugged. "She was supposed to come back at the end of January, but that got postponed. So who knows how long she'll stay. She said she would call me when she's coming home."

"Home?" Codi said. "Like here?"

"Mmm hmm. She lives here with me. You okay with having a roommate?" Rebecca asked.

"Ha! Is she? I feel like the intruder!"

"Don't be silly. My name is on the lease. Plus, who would object to having a knockout brunette in her apartment full-time?"

"Oh, stop it," Codi said. She felt her cheeks begin to turn red.

"You understand I'm not hitting on you, don't you?" Rebecca said after a moment of silence. "I would never put you in that situation. I flirt, but that's different."

"Stop. You have nothing to worry about, Bec. I've never felt threatened around you."

"Good. I flirt with everyone. Guys and gals alike."

Codi smiled again, then twisted her earrings. "Tell me more about her. What does she do?"

"Right now? Nothing. She's on permanent vacation for the moment. She made a lot of money for a lot of years in a row. She may decide to go back to work at some point, but for now, she's happy just living." Rebecca drained the last of her coffee. "Besides, I make enough to support us both."

"That's great," Codi said, nodding. "What's her name, Rebecca?"

"Natalie," Rebecca answered. "Natalie Reese."

⌘　　　⌘　　　⌘

They finished out the vacation, since they had already paid for the rooms at the resort, and Callie did not want to fly in her condition. The last three days of the trip, she spent the entire time in her room with the TV on, and not much else. Thevi and Walter called on her several times, but she always begged out as politely as possible, saying she just wanted to be alone. On the last night before they left, Callie spent several hours in the bathtub, cycling hot water in every time the temperature started dropping. By the time she got out, her fingers and feet were wrinkled like linens left in a dryer too long. She stared at herself in the mirror, at the dark circles under her bloodshot eyes. Her entire face was puffy.

She had left Chris's clothing and personal effects in the suitcase, just the way he had left it. But now she stood over it, wondering what to do. She would have to deal with his belongings at home as well. And then there was the uncomfortable phone call she would be making to his parents. The only evidence she had of the accident was the report the dive captain had filed with his company. Without his remains, she wondered how difficult it would be to file for a death certificate back in the States. All of these thoughts brought her back to the verge of tears each time they crossed her mind, but she felt all cried out. She knew it wasn't over, but for the moment she was safe. For a little while, at least.

Back on the plane, Callie sat by the window, staring at the squares of land thirty thousand feet below, through her dark shades. She didn't talk much, but neither Thevi nor Walter tried too hard to engage her. They were respecting her space, and for that she was thankful. Thevi sat beside her and held her hand for a big part of the trip, occasionally squeezing to let her know she was still there if Callie needed her. Callie had packed Chris's suitcase and shipped it back home, but she had kept his watch and cell phone and other small personal items that he had carried with him all the time. These were in her carry-on.

When they landed at Newark Liberty, she felt the cold chill of New Jersey's February wind welcoming her home, even on the jetway. She made the long walk up the jetway in silence, pulling her carry-on case behind her like a stray puppy. The three of them opted for a taxi cab instead of the larger shuttle they had taken to the airport on the flight out, and Callie rode up front. The cabby dropped her off first, and Thevi patted Walter's leg, telling him she would be back in a moment.

Thevi helped Callie roll the suitcase up to the door, and load it into the entry hall, then stood by the door, silently waiting for Callie to acknowledge her. Callie leaned her head against the edge of the door, shoulders slumped and hands by her sides, taking deep breaths. After a long, uncomfortable moment, she finally spoke. "It's okay, Thev. I'll be all right. You can go, babe."

Thevi reached up and squeezed Callie's shoulder, but Callie turned into her, and embraced her in a hard hug, immediately letting go again, the tears pouring forth with no reserve. Thevi stroked the back of her head, but remained silent. When Callie had finally finished, she straightened up and wiped her cheeks with the back of her coat.

"You sure you don't want me to stay, Callie? The first night back will be the hardest."

Callie nodded. "It's okay," she said, her voice weak and salty. "I'll be okay, Thevi. Thank you." She smiled weakly and reached for the safety of the door. Thevi stood staring at her for a moment, then nodded.

"Okay, hon. You know where I'll be if you need me."

Callie nodded, then closed the door softly. She leaned her head against it, her fingers resting on the deadbolt, refusing to look back into the dead air of the silent house. What would she find in there? One of Chris's empty beer cans? A book marked on the page he had last read? His slippers under the coffee table? A dish in the sink, his last kiss on the spoon in a cereal bowl? She shuddered, and then jumped as a hard knock rattled the door. She swung it open and fell into Walter's arms as he rushed in and grabbed her, holding her head against his shoulder with a strong hand. She let herself break down again, feeling the comfort of her friend's embrace. He stood there rocking her slowly back and forth, just allowing her to cry.

She looked up into his eyes, tears running across her lips as she said, "Oh, Walter, what am I gonna do?"

He shook his head, a sadness in his eyes with which his words could never compete. And without warning, she stood up on her tiptoes and sank her mouth into his, pulling down on the back of his head. She kissed him long without moving, then finally let go and pushed him away, turning away and crossing her arms. She closed her eyes and waited for his retribution. But it never came. Instead, he turned her back around and looked in her eyes again, and held his hand against her cheek. "Callie, I'm so sorry. I am so very terribly sorry." Then he bit his lip and inhaled deeply, and turned and walked out the door, closing it behind him.

The little things that make up life, the monotony of it, the fine nuances that go unnoticed during the everyday living part of life – the tiny things that no one would remember... all of these were what hit Callie the hardest as she took her first walk into the empty living room. Everything standing where it had been left a week before assaulted her like a battery of cannon fire. It seemed to physically knock the breath from her chest as her eyes took in each little bit of the life that used to be. The remote control sitting on the edge of the sofa arm, a bottle cap resting over the rubber buttons as Chris had fidgeted with it during whatever show he had last been watching; a Rubik's Cube sitting on the open pages of a technology magazine, half-solved with the top layer slightly twisted as if awaiting its master's next command; an open CD case atop the DVD player in the music cabinet, the CD still ready for play; a deck of cards sitting on top of its own box. She refused to touch any of it, but instead only stood staring at each of his artifacts for a long moment before she finally spun on her heel and made her way back to the bedroom where she refused to look at anything. She didn't even turn on the light as she entered the room. She just dropped face-first into the queen bed and buried herself between the pillows for a long sleep.

Three weeks later.

Walter and Thevi sat bundled up in the leather seats of his Bentley, waiting for Callie, who was making no effort to exercise any sense of urgency in coming out of her house. A few nights earlier, Walter had finally heard from Callie, and they had spoken for nearly an hour. And it felt natural. Callie seemed to be in better spirits, at least on the surface. They did not talk about Chris. Walter figured if Callie were to bring him up, he would allow her to vent, or cry or complain, but she didn't bring him up, so Walter didn't either.

He had been watching a basketball game, drinking a beer in the dark living room while Thevi was back in the den working on a scrapbook. His feet propped up on the coffee table, he had an Android tablet in his lap where he played online poker. His house shoes were warm on his feet, the beer was starting to work its magic, and the game was good. The stereo was pulling a light rock playlist from his server in the computer room, murmuring the soft keys of Paul Simon, Peter Gabriel and Phil Collins. All in all, Walter had no complaints, was winning most of the hands he played in the poker game, and was generally content with life. And then the phone rang.

"Hello, Walter," she said when he answered. She had called his land line, so he hadn't had the benefit of caller ID before he answered, and was slightly taken aback by the sound of her voice.

"Uh, well, hey there! What's up, Callie?"

Callie let out a long sigh. "I miss you guys."

Walter nodded, and aimed the remote at the stereo, dropping the volume a few clicks, then dropped the remote on the sofa beside him. "We miss you too, little gangsta. How you holding up?"

Callie made the audible equivalent of a shrug on the other end. "It's hard, Walter. I'm not gonna lie. But I'm getting by."

"Well that's good. You wanna come over? Thevi's scrapbooking, and I'm watching the Nets. You could pick your poison."

"Thanks, but not tonight. I haven't showered in a week. I'm disgusting."

"Yuck. What the hell is wrong with you?" Walter said.

"I've been cleaning house. All... all the stuff that's... not mine... is confined to one room now. So listen. I was thinking, maybe we could all go to Newport Skates this weekend. They'll be closing soon, you know."

Walter was about to say something tacky, to the effect of *What's their closing got to do with my life?* but bit his tongue and decided to hear her out. Callie didn't ask for much. And this might be the least he could do. "Yeah?" was all he said.

"Mmm hmm. We were supposed to go anyway. It was like tradition for us, you know."

Walter nodded and looked up at the ceiling, simultaneously pressing the sleep button on his tablet. He couldn't concentrate on poker while he talked on the phone. "Yeah, I remember how much you guys like the ice." Peter Gabriel's *Mercy Street* showed up on the stereo, and Walter thought of the outdoor skating rink, its beautiful view of the Manhattan skyline, and snow in the air. The picture was wildly romantic. He wondered why he had never taken Thevi. "Sure, that sounds good, Callie. When are you thinking?"

"Well, probably Saturday night. The second."

Walter grabbed his phone off the table and checked his calendar. A completely unnecessary maneuver, since he never actually put anything on his calendar. But it was ritual. And there was at least a greater-than-zero chance that Thevi had added something for him. "We've got no plans," he said after a minute. He looked up and saw that Thevi had crept into the room. He smiled at her, and she sat on the sofa next to him, chin resting on her knees, her arms wrapped round her legs, sitting sideways and facing him. Walter reached over and took her hand then winked at her.

"Good. I think it'd be fun. The Figure Skating Club is performing early in the evening, too."

"Ah. Is that right?" Walter said.

Callie sighed. "Yeah, I know you're not very interested, but it would mean a lot to me."

"You bet, sugar. I wouldn't miss it."

"Thank you. Pick me up at six, okay?"

Walter nodded. "Sounds good," he said, and looked back at Thevi. She was staring at him silently, her face in an expressionless gaze.

"Oh, and Walter?" said Callie.

"Yeah?"

"Bring your flask."

Walter laughed out loud, then shook his head. "All right, sure." They hung up and he tossed the phone onto the coffee table. He leaned back and put his hands behind his head.

"How's she doing, babe?" Thevi said.

Walter shrugged and nodded. "She sounds pretty good! I mean, you can tell she's fighting through it, but she sounds a lot more upbeat than I thought. I mean, it's been what, three weeks?"

Thevi nodded, her chin still on her knees. "Poor darling. What's she wanting to do?"

Walter took a deep breath. "She wants us to take her ice skating."

Thevi frowned. "Where? The Galleria?"

"No. Newport." He rolled his eyes.

Thevi slapped his leg. "Ah, Walter, that'll be nice. That's one of the most beautiful skating rinks in the world."

"Yeah, sure. But it's ice skating, dude. I skate about as well as I paint toenails."

"Oh shush, Walter. If she's asking for this, she needs it. You will be there for her, right out on that ice, supporting her with every inch of your being."

Walter sat silent for a moment, staring at the television, but not focusing. "Yeah, I guess."

"You guess nothing, fart head. You're going, and that's all there is to it."

He shook his head again and leaned it back against the couch cushion. "Yeah, well you're going too, Red."

"Yeah, but you don't have to talk me into it, Walter. I can't wait. And I can't wait to see her."

CHAPTER 17

The snowflakes were gigantic, and soft against her face as they drifted lazily out of the sky, in no rush to meet their end on the hard ice of the rink. The bright white light of the overheads was fogged and muted by the falling snow, and formed stars in their moist eyes as they coasted around the rink. Loud music made its way across the night, easily outweighing the roar of the crowd of excited lovers and children. It was a perfect night for ice skating, and the lighted windows of the buildings across the Hudson looked like small fires in the night, adding to the warmth that enveloped Callie's soul.

Walter held her hand as they slid across the ice, obviously holding himself up as much as steadying Callie.

He looked over at her as they skated, his nose comically red against the white face that peeked out from the toboggan and muffler he wore tucked into his coat. Callie smiled at him and thanked him for coming. He smiled and said, "Dude, I'd never miss it. And hey." He looked up toward the general direction of the music, which was all around them. "Try to stay in a bad mood while you're listening to Frank Sinatra."

Callie's smile widened and her soul felt even warmer. She was glad Walter was actually enjoying himself. She knew he wasn't big on ice skating, but he had kindly conceded, and he and Thevi had taken turns getting out on the ice with her. They hadn't even skated together yet. Callie was the center of attention, but she had a plan to get them on the ice together soon. The colors and sounds around them were all festive, and it seemed to Callie that the only thing missing were the wreaths and tinsel. It looked like a Christmas scene out of season. Two children, a boy and a girl, skated by, tripping and chopping at the ice as they held hands, trying to weave around the rink in a graceless pursuit of speed and adrenaline. Callie smiled again, then spread to the full length of their arms and looked up at Walter and said, "Watch this!" She raised her hand above her head, never letting go of Walter's, and twirled twice, ending up facing backward, skating tentatively with wide eyes. Her arm was now crossed in front of her, still grasping his hand as he looked on with surprise.

"Wow, what the hell?" he said.

"Ha! You like that?" The twirl was a lot more graceful than her backward skating, and she had to spin forward to get going again.

"How'd you do that? You can barely skate, and you're doing pirouettes and shit!"

Callie laughed out loud. "I can skate good, dude! I'm just a little rusty!"

Walter laughed too and shook his head. "Yeah, well you had me fooled." As they rounded the final bend, they looked up and saw Thevi standing there with a camera to her face. Callie pointed with her free hand, then leaned in and hugged

Walter tightly, her face buried in his chest and arm as she smiled for the camera. When Thevi gave them the thumbs-up, Callie looked back up at Walter and dropped her smile.

"I'm ready, Walt," she said quietly.

He shook his head. "Come again?"

"I'm ready. I'm ready to move on. To get out of this funk," she said. She looked around briefly at the other skaters. The attention they paid to the couple standing still in the middle of the lane was minimal – just enough to swerve around them politely. "Mainly, I'm ready to get back into the Bloop project."

Walter raised his eyebrows. "Wow. That's pretty quick recovery, CalStar." He reached up and brushed the damp hair from her forehead, almost like a lover preparing for a kiss.

She took a deep breath and chewed her lip, then answered. "Yeah. I know. But there is no logical benefit to stagnating here. I will only waste away precious minutes of my life when I could be otherwise productive."

Walter nodded soberly. "Yeah. You're absolutely right. But don't deny your heart its time to grieve and heal, Callie." He looked over his shoulder just in time to see a teenage girl bearing down on them with wide eyes and outstretched hands. He deftly scooted forward, sliding Callie back simultaneously so they stayed in perfect relative position. "You don't have to be a warrior. Take your time."

Callie made a resolute face and replied, "Yes, I do. I'm going to bring Brian Bradley down. And I'm ready to get started."

Walter nodded and smiled, then held up his fist. Callie tapped her mittened fist against it and made a mean face before smiling back at him. "Let's do it," he said.

Callie spun around and gave him two thumbs up, almost losing her balance. Then she waved at Thevi, who was still on the sidelines just observing. Thevi waved back. Callie waved again, this time calling her out with her hand. Thevi stood up and made her way easily across the ice, dodging children and couples with a smile on her face. When she got to where they were standing, Callie said, "Oh good. Walter needs you. And I need a break." Then she skated off the ice – not nearly as gracefully as Thevi's skating had been – and dropped on to the bench to watch the two lovers circle the rink together, hand in hand. Callie grabbed the camera and shot some good pictures, then let it hang around her neck as she leaned on the wall watching them. She missed that. Maybe someday she would have her own skate partner again. For now, she was just happy watching the married couple be together. The fog of their breath came out in short puffs as they trekked around the ice, laughing and stumbling and talking, forgetting entirely that the rest of the world even existed.

After an hour an a half, they had all skated their legs off. Winded and sore, they all sat on the wooden bench looking up at the snowflakes that continued to drift out of the shallow sky.

Walter turned his head to her after a long moment of catching his breath and said, "You had enough, Calgirl?"

She nodded, smiling. "Yeah. I think so. My hands are like blocks of ice."

"That's what you need to invent, Callie," Thevi said, pointing a mitten at her. "Gloves that keep your hands warm."

"Ha!" Callie shouted. "I'm on it, sister." They sat there for another long silent moment, then Callie finally said, "Thank you guys so much for coming out with me. I think this did worlds for helping me move forward."

Walter nodded slowly, then said, "Absolutely. I'm glad we came."

"Me too," Thevi said, reaching over Walter to hold Callie's hand. "Now let's go find a fire and a bottle of brandy!"

The three of them retired to the cozy back room of the Lantern House to finish off the night, leaving the cold romance of the snow-ridden skating rink to be forgotten.

⌘   ⌘   ⌘

Codi had not made the trip back to her apartment after all. Rebecca and Maria had managed to gather all her things and get them out with no incident. Tim had scoffed at the idea of releasing Codi's belongings at first, but had suddenly lost his will when Rebecca stood on her tip toes and looked directly into his eyes, leaning in real close. It would have looked from the outside like she was examining his eyes, a hard squint and the lines of determination around her mouth. But it was the reverse of an examination. It was a wordless testimony. And during that brief look, he had swallowed hard and backed up a step. And, never taking her eyes from his, Rebecca had slipped beside him into the warmth of the apartment to collect. Maria slid in quietly behind her without a word of her own, demure and respectful.

Rebecca had not spent too much time trying to determine the rightful owner of everything she saw. Instead, she indiscriminately dropped things she thought might be useful to Codi into a faded red duffel bag. There had only been a couple of "Hey, you can't take that!"s from Tim, but Rebecca had ignored him sternly, and when she went to leave, he made no move to stop her. On her way out, she opened the door and nudged Maria to go ahead, then stopped and looked back at Tim, both hands on the handles of the bag. She said, "I'm taking what I think will suit and benefit Codi in her new state. Consider it the price you pay for her keeping quiet and not pressing charges." She ran her tongue over her teeth without opening her mouth, then shook her head. "I can't imagine the chicken-shit, spineless gall it takes to get a man to intimidate and take advantage of a blind woman. If you're not the sickest asshole I've ever met, then you're pretty close."

Tim sucked in a deep breath and looked at her soberly. "I don't think that's fair. You never even heard my side!"

"Spare me. Please." Rebecca shook her head again and smirked. "Maybe someday you'll realize just how lucky you were to ever even have a shot with such an amazing human being as Codi. But when you do, just remind yourself that it's over. And that I exist. Stay the bleeding *fuck* out of her life evermore."

And with that, she and Maria had strolled off, leaving him to ponder his colossal fuckup, alone and embarrassed.

Over the next few weeks, Codi mastered her internal map of Rebecca's apartment, memorizing the number of steps from each landmark to the next. They had also grown very close, staying up late into the nights sharing stories of each other's childhoods and love lives. Initially Codi was reluctant to say too much about her family for fear of causing concern about how she was going to pay her way, or earn her keep. But she finally warmed to the idea and even felt better getting it off her chest.

Codi's father had left when Codi was an infant, and her mother had grown sick and died in Codi's late teens. Being an only child from a mother who was an only child, left her with no family. Having moved from Detroit only recently meant she had no friends around these parts yet, so staying with Rebecca just seemed to make perfect sense. At least as long as the absentee girlfriend didn't show up and start making changes and demands. Rebecca assured her always that this wouldn't happen.

She told Rebecca of the times and trials she had experienced growing up without a father figure in her life. Her mother was not some wanton single mom who had a series of flings with a series of Mr. Wrongs. Rather, once dad left the picture, mom sort of just locked up and went into a shell. She didn't stop caring for Codi, or treat her any differently at all. She just stopped believing there would be another man in her life. She'd had her one shot, and it was over.

Codi was six or seven by the time she started becoming aware that there was a missing person in her family. Most of her friends had the standard nuclear setup with two-and-a-half kids, a stay-at-home mom and a dad who wore suits to work. She didn't have any of that. She didn't find herself wanting anything, but she was often jealous of her girlfriends, who had daddies who would kiss them goodnight and tousle their hair on the way to the beer fridge. Dads were different from moms. Dads were tough, in her observation. They didn't break down crying or get worried about meaningless stuff. And it was fun seeing moms smile when dads kissed them in the kitchen or pinched their bottoms on the way to the garage. Codi began to wonder why her mom didn't have any of that.

When she asked her why mommy didn't have a man, her mother told her it was a conversation for another time. She'd have to wait until she was old enough to understand before mom would tell her all about that. Well, that day never came. And by the time Codi felt like she was definitely old enough to know what had happened, she had figured it all out on her own anyway. At that point, she was just curious as to why her dad had left at all. And why hadn't mom pursued him? Or even someone else to replace him? And soon, it was too late to ask any of those questions, for her mom had grown sick with Alzheimer's disease. And soon after that, her mother was gone.

After graduating high school she got a job at the local newspaper as an editor, where she did well enough to make a bit of a name for herself within the first year. An old high school friend found her on a social network and offered her a better job, away from the comfort of the relatively small newspaper, to come to work for a literary agency. The grandest of all ironies would set in only two years later, when she started losing her eyesight. That was three years ago. Now, at twenty-four and all alone in the world, she reckoned she had two thirds of her life left to go, assuming all went well, and only eighty percent of her senses.

She would need to find some source of income pretty fast, now that Tim was gone, if she were going to assume anything about the rest of her life, or how long it would be.

Before she had met him, she had made pretty good money at the newspaper. Even better money at the agency. It had been a blessing to have him, at least for the financial benefit; he was happy to let her stay at home while he provided for her. But that was all gone now, wasn't it?

Rebecca, on the other hand, was the oldest of five. Both of her parents were alive and well, and she maintained a pretty close relationship with all of them – even though they were geographically separated by an entire country. Her parents lived in Washington state, as did most of her siblings. Rebecca had been the only one to "escape to somewhere capable of culture" as she had put it.

Rebecca had relayed to Codi during one of these all-nighters how she had come to discover she was gay. "It's not that I didn't know I was supposed to like boys. Or even that I didn't like them. I had a few boyfriends growing up. I've had sex with men. But it just never made me emotional. I never got the butterflies wondering if this boy or that liked me. I never understood what the big deal was about love or going out, at all. So I was a loner most of my way through school. Then on a band trip, I found out what I had been missing all that time.

"I played the cymbals for the marching band, and the concert band. Our band entered a contest that was just over the Washington-Oregon border, in Portland. Well, we played this piece by Giovannini called Overture in C, and it was really good. Most high-schoolers don't get off on concert pieces. You know, classical. But this one was really exciting. And even though I only played the cymbals, which is like the weakest fucking instrument in the band, I still get filled with excitement just thinking about it.

"Anyway, this gal named Brandy played the timpani for that piece. And I remember as soon as we hit the last note on that song, the crowd erupted. And as the sound of the cymbals finally rang off, Brandy turned around and looked at me with this look of victory on her face. But there was also a sexiness there. A look of a little bit of mischief mixed with a little bit of desire. And she winked at me.

"Well, my stomach just flooded with butterflies and I got chills all down my spine. God! I can still feel them today! All during breakdown and cleanup, and all the way back to the bus after the concert, I questioned this feeling. I also questioned the reality of the situation. Like did it really happen? Did she really wink at me? Did she really mean anything by it if she did? Surely she didn't like me. But why did I feel so moved by it? What was this tugging at my emotions? She wasn't even a boy, for God's sake! What's going on with my heart? My guts?

"Well, back on the bus, we were all sweaty and tired, and it was dark. And we had a three-hour trip home. Brandy happened to come sit by me. You can imagine what happened. After talking awhile, and finally succumbing to the heavy eyelids, we fell asleep with our heads on each other's shoulder. Sometime later, my eyes snapped open, and she was staring at me. Looking right into my eyes. And then she kissed me.

"All the confusion in the world came toppling down at once. My understanding of why I am the way I am suddenly made sense. It's like I had this moment of perfect clarity. And I knew that I had been doing it wrong all along. Instead of following my heart, I had been following my head. My head told me what I had heard and seen all my life: that girls go with boys. But I had just this tiny modicum of experience now that challenged that social precept. And I was now a rebel.

"But oh, it felt so right. It's funny: after all the girlfriends – and, well, boyfriends too – that one kiss still hangs with me. Maybe it was because it was my first passionate kiss in a life full of bland reality. But it sure did stay with me. The smell of our uniforms, the smell of the bus, our sweat, her breath... I remember it all so vividly. And it still makes me wet.

"Our first kiss only lasted several seconds, and then it broke while we smiled at each other. And it was so quiet on the bus. I think everyone else was sleeping. You know how a loud bus can be so quiet when no one is talking? It was a very comfortable sound. And I know I didn't want it to end. I wanted us to just keep going. Just drive north, right through Seattle and on into Canada. God, how I wanted it to last. And we just kept kissing. After that first break where I backed up and let the chills fall to the floor, and I smiled at her, I knew it was okay. And we didn't take another break. We kissed for the entire rest of the trip. We didn't touch or otherwise fool around, aside from her putting her hand on my cheek. It was just kissing. But God it was lovely. I was so wet by the time I got home that I spent an hour in the bathtub just reliving the event. I'm sure you can imagine what went on in there. But I discovered myself that night.

"So I guess that's the night I found out who I really was. And let me tell you, sister. There was never a choice in it at all. We are what we are."

Rebecca called these nighttime talks 'Living Room Campfires' and they both looked forward to them fervently. During the days when Rebecca was at work, Codi was left to study, read and practice. But as soon as Rebecca came sweeping through the door, her heart and mind lit up with excitement. A beacon of hope in the dark, dreary cave her life had become. With no job, no real future of getting a job, and no way out of the darkness, she knew it would take a long time for her to feel the thrill of something new again. All but for Sam, that was. Whenever Sam came around, she felt the same excitement and butterflies Rebecca had spoken of in her first love.

They spent more and more time together, but usually only when Rebecca could escort her. Codi was too afraid to go out with Sam alone, since neither of them could see. With Rebecca there, at least someone could make sure Tim wasn't spying on them. Codi wasn't sure he would, but sick fear filled her gut every time she relived her last encounter with him. And she did not want to repeat it.

While it was impossible to surprise anyone at the Royal Research office complex merely by showing up and knocking on his door, there was a brief start for Minus when his intercom spat out Callie's name. After three weeks of absenteeism, Minus was pretty sure she had decided to drop out of the project, and thus had let the project fall onto a back burner until such time as he was able to start headhunting for a replacement. But here she was.

Callie stood leaning against his open door with her purse in both hands, staring soberly at Minus with dark eyes and a dejected look of determination. Minus raised his head and sat still just staring at her before his tact finally got in gear and he stood up, putting his hands in his pockets.

"Hi, Callie," he said. He pulled an unsure hand from his pocket and scratched the back of his head absently as he moved to the side of the desk. He stopped there, as if unsure of the protocol for welcoming back the bereaved.

"Hi."

"I uh..." he started.

"It's okay, Matt. You don't have to say anything," she said.

"I don't?"

Callie shook her head. "No need to be uncomfortable. I'm coping."

Minus nodded, then tried to find something else to look at. He finally cracked his neck and pursed his lips, then cleared his throat. "Okay. Well... I uh, wasn't sure you were coming back."

"Neither was I. But I'm here. And I'm ready to work."

"Well, that's great, Callie," Minus said, trying to find something to which he could transfer his fidgeting. He settled for crossing his arms and leaning against his desk instead. "You were gone almost a month. I'll need to catch you up on everything," he said, and stared uneasily at her.

She nodded slowly, like a mother trying to goad an answer out of a toddler.

"Look. I just need to know what your plan is with Bradley."

Callie frowned and shook her head. "Why? It doesn't really involve you."

"It doesn't?" he said, eyes widening.

She pulled her head back. "Why? Are you hiding something?"

He pointed at himself. "Me? Hell no!"

"Then what are you worried about?"

He sighed loudly and turned away, walking back toward the window. "I'm not! I just want to make sure you don't ruin this thing for all of us! I've wanted this project for the last two decades. I finally have it. I just want to know you're not gonna fuck it up for me."

Callie crossed her arms and tilted her head. "Minus, if you're not part of his scandal, which I don't think you are, then this won't touch you. I just want Bradley," she said, holding her hands out. She pursed her lips and licked her teeth.

Minus stared at her again before answering. "He's funding this, Callie."

"Ha! No he's not! Is his last name Royal? The company is funding it!"

"If you get him fired, we may lose the budget for this!" he said.

"Minus," she said, and tried comforting him by stepping up and putting her hand on his arm. He looked down at it when she continued. "Stop worrying about this. Seriously. We'll be fine."

He stared at her again, reading her. She stared right back at him.

"Have I ever let you down, Minus?"

He smirked at that. "No."

"Okay. So we're good," she said, patting his arm again. Then she smiled. "So, where are we?"

Minus cleared his throat again, clearly having more trouble with this than Callie was. "Right. So preliminary tests are good at negligible depths. They've been able to get the hydroshield to engage, but at anything deeper than a few inches, the pod starts spinning."

"Hydroshield? That's the official term now?" she asked.

"Oh. Yeah. That's their technical term."

"That's ridiculous. It literally has nothing to do with water. That makes it sound like it keeps water off the hull or something," Callie said.

"Talk to the science guys," Minus said.

"Science guys? Minus, I am a science guy!"

He waved his hand, dismissing the argument.

"So what do you mean 'starts spinning'?"

"We lose complete control of its attitude when the barrier is engaged."

Callie frowned. "That can't be."

Minus held his hands out, then leaned against his desk. "Well, it is. You turn it on and the damn thing just forgets which way is up. Just starts rolling any which way," he said, twirling his finger to illustrate.

Callie shook her head, still frowning. "Matt, that would mean we've defeated gravity then, because the pod is heavily weighted on the lower portion. That just can't be." She started chewing the edge of her finger and shaking her head. "There must be another explanation for this. Can I see it?"

The lab was dark and deserted when they entered. Minus flipped on the light and after a few seconds they blinked to life. It looked to Callie as though no one had even entered the room since her last visit before her birthday. She ran her fingers along the brushed steel of the workbench as they approached the prototype. It was still clean as ever, and she reckoned the cleaning crew made their rounds regardless of if anyone was using it or not.

Minus stood against the counter while she fingered the controls absently, trying to come up with an explanation for what he had told her. He unscrewed the cap from his water bottle and took a long drink, then wiped his mouth with the back of his hand. "So tell me, Callie. This is the part I haven't latched onto yet."

She turned and looked at him. "What?"

"How do you plan to steer and control the pod? I mean, if there's a propeller or something, how does it connect to the pod *through* the force fie- uh, hydroshield?"

"I was wondering when you were going to ask me that."

"Ah. Why?" Minus said.

"Because to me it seemed like the most obvious obstacle we'd have to overcome. But come, let me show you," she said, walking toward the white board that covered an entire wall. There was no free space on it though, and a lot of the notations were circled and labeled "DO NOT ERASE!!!" Callie erased through a giant swatch of this while Minus tried to object. She ignored this, but slowed by a long number surrounded by a rectangle, making sure the eraser didn't break that barrier. Written in that box was *OVERRIDE: 308080808445.* There was no other explanation. No obvious reason she should have avoided erasing that, but there it was. She started drawing.

Her doodles illustrated a hovering spherical steel structure that had several rotors on all sides. She then pointed at the center where the pod was, and said, "See, here's the pod. And here's the control system. Of course, the force shield is between them, and, being equidistant all around, it never touches the shield. It's held in check by magnetism."

The design she had proposed for propulsion was an outer scaffold full of rotors with its own energy source. It would completely surround and envelop the submersible, but not be physically connected to it. The two separate entities would repel each other on all sides equally by magnets. That way, if they needed to turn on the force field, the scaffold would still be able to move them, but would be outside the protective field. Made of solid steel, it would not need protection from the shield.

This was an idea Callie had come up with on one of her sleepless nights, which is when she seemed to strike genius more frequently than not. The leather-bound journal by her bedside was full of ideas like this. Her notes from the propulsion system she had designed for the Atlas mission to Mars and program notes for the temporal delineation project – they were all in there. Among so many others. Anything she woke up dreaming of – or things she stayed awake and thought of – would go in that book for review during daylight hours. Chris had once asked her why she had spent two hundred dollars on a Tuscan leather-bound journal when all she did was scribble in it. In his mind, something so rich should be organized and gridded with gold leaf and lettering within. She had walked away, returning several minutes later holding a paystub. She set the paystub down on the nightstand and circled her net pay with a red pen, and then held the paystub and the journal up side by side. No further word was ever necessary on the subject.

Minus took another swig of his bottle and Callie found herself staring at the water bottle, half distracted. She wondered whether it was his loud gulping that bothered her, or the fact that he had a bottle of water in a science lab. He caught her looking at it and frowned, then capped it and set it on the counter behind him. "Okay," he said, beginning to nod slowly. "That's brilliant. So there's no wires or anything actually connecting the control system with the pod, though, right?"

Callie nodded, half smirking, awaiting the next obvious question.

Minus held out his hand and leaned his head forward. "So, uh... Do I have to ask?"

"Wireless. Bluetooth. WiFi. Remote control. Radio. Whatever your flavor of the week."

Minus slapped his head. "Gah. Okay. Duh. I feel like an idiot." He then smiled a wide smile that ended just as quickly as it started. "Wait. But I thought the shield would screw up any signals trying to get through it."

"Nah. You're talking about a distance of less than a couple of feet. You can broadcast that kind of radio with just about anything. Pump a couple of watts at it, it'll break through just fine," she said, and capped the marker.

"You're a genius, Callie. Has anyone ever told you that?"

She smiled proudly, then walked back to him. "Okay. Now show me how we've defeated the law of gravity."

Very quickly, Callie had discovered that anti-gravity had not yet been attained. A flutter of excitement had indeed tickled her belly, only briefly, but then it had disappeared just as quickly with the knowledge that if someone at Royal had breached the law of gravity, she would not have gotten her project back. The lab technician who had built the latest prototype would have mentioned the peculiar discovery to his buddy or his boss, and it would have disappeared like a woman in David Copperfield's jump box. Instead, she had quickly found out that while it was indeed spinning crazily inside the field they had generated, it was most definitely abiding by the known laws of physics. Within this experiment though, she had discovered that her field was working. When she set about it with the tip of her pencil, it had rolled off the edge of the lab table and hit the ground. Completely without sound.

She and Minus had looked at each other, and then simultaneously dropped to the ground to try to peer under the sphere. And though it was much too small of a tolerance to see under, the sphere was definitely spinning crazily a fraction of a millimeter above the ground. A small bluish glow emanated from beneath the object on the cold tile of the floor, but it was the only evidence there was even a field around it. Otherwise, the force field she had designed was completely invisible. She sat back against the counter and dismissed Minus politely, saying she needed to think for a while. He had bowed out quietly and given her space to do what she did best. Then she sat staring for a long while at the crazy object on the floor, frowning, squinting, and considering the ramifications of what she was looking at. And then it died, and dropped to the floor with a nearly inaudible thunk.

Now she sat with her knees folded up to her chest, chin resting on them. She was lightly tapping the edges of the sphere, rolling it back and forth in a space of a few inches, just considering what it meant. Why was it spinning in the shield? Callie took a deep breath and considered it. *Duh! There are no magnets yet!* Once the propulsion cage was built around the submersible, there would be magnetic links to hold it in place. Not only for keeping it steady, but its whole attitude. Of course, she would have to design it so that the magnets could be turned off, lest they be trapped in an odd direction within the cage by accident. Once they righted themselves, which would typically be assumed to happen by simple gravity, they could lock the electromagnets and *voila!* They would be steady.

And what if they saw something out one of the monitors, and just wanted to turn a few degrees to port? The magnets would help with that. Of course, there wouldn't be much to look at through the infrared cameras. Lights or not, no camera in the world would get a very good look at anything when trapped behind thick glass and not allowed to move freely. If they wanted to follow something's movement, they would literally have to turn the sub to keep up with it. Unless... There was a thought there somewhere. Something had slipped through Callie's mind. Something about sight. Something about vision.

She knew it was there somewhere. She just had to think around the corner. She swallowed and looked around the room. What was it that was on the tip of her mind – just waiting to be let out? Callie picked up the sphere and took a deep breath, turning to set it in the cage on the counter.

The cage was not a cage at all, but a square porcelain dish, about sixteen inches to a side and three inches tall. It was porcelain instead of iron so that it would not be a conductor nor an interference for anything magnetic. She leaned her head over and rested it on her fist, elbow on the counter, staring at the steel sphere in its cage, wondering what it was that she needed to get out. Something had sparked but she couldn't trap it now. She was cursed with a thousand thoughts banging around in her head at any given time. Sometimes that meant settling on just one was nearly impossible – especially when it had just escaped. She looked up and saw the square plastic bottle of water behind the cage. Water. Yes. She should be working with water. Callie stood up and twisted the blue cap off the bottle and emptied the rest of Minus's water into the porcelain dish they called a cage. It was, of course, not enough to submerge the sphere. It was hardly enough to cover the bottom of the cage.

As she stared at the thin layer of water screwing the cap back on the bottle, she thought about the content of the water, and wondered if it mattered. Would the salt in the ocean water make a difference? This was purified water. This was... She looked at the square bottle again and flipped it in her hand so the label was facing her. This was Fiji. *Fiji.* Fiji Water Company. *Fiji! Oh my God! I'm so stupid!* she thought, and set the bottle down, racing out of the room in search of her purse.

Walter's phone was buzzing on the table, but he was in the middle of a meeting, where he was the presenter. It wasn't uncommon for people to pick up their phones and decline calls or respond to texts during these executive meetings, but he was across the room from his phone, and was unable to silence it. He was just glad he had at least turned the ringer off. After a few moments it stopped. He was in the middle of a declaration about the plans for the department over the next quarter, and where they would be best investing their efforts. He was close to wrapping up, but not close enough to do so prematurely. So he was visibly annoyed when his phone started vibrating again. He took a deep breath and apologized to the council as he rounded the table to decline the call. He grabbed the phone and slipped it in his jacket pocket, but not before he saw that the face read Caliente. She didn't typically call him to chit chat. If she were calling repeatedly, she really needed something.

Walter returned to the board and picked up where he had left off. His phone went to buzzing again, but he ignored it. He finished his presentation in a few minutes and answered the several questions the board presented him, then thanked everyone and packed up his briefcase, exiting the conference room. As he made his way back to his office, he rounded a corner and slammed head-on into a very hurried and red-faced Callie Simmons.

"Whoa! What the hell, Calgirl? Slow down!"

"Walter, I've been phoning you! Where's your phone?" she said, out of breath. She was already grabbing his elbow and trying to guide him into the nearest conference room.

"Dude, chill the fuck out! It's in my pocket! I was in a board meeting! What is with you?"

She pushed him into a room and closed the door behind her. "Dude," she said, mocking his own tone, "this is important! I really need to talk to you!"

"Okay," he said, putting his hands on her thin shoulders and looking her in the eyes. "But you have to relax. Remember, you don't even work here! You're not supposed to be hauling ass through floors you have no access to, commandeering conference rooms and running people down!"

She was breathing deeply, mouth closed, staring holes through him with laser beam eyes. When she had finally calmed a little, she said as coolly as she could manage, "Okay, Walter. But obviously I have access. I am here." She held up her badge to illustrate the point. Obviously the badge Minus had given her for the tenure she was to be under his temporary employ had full building access. Callie was even able to let herself into the building before anyone else was there for the day – short the security guards. They were always there.

"Look. I need you to get me access to your Fiji project," she said, as patiently as her hauling heartbeat would allow.

Walter let go of her shoulders and stood up straight, picking his briefcase up off the floor where he had dropped it, and setting it on the nearby table. "Callie, what are you talking about?"

"You went to Fiji."

"Manhattan."

"Manhattan." She closed her eyes and shook her head, trying to return to the point. "Manhattan was your Fiji. You said so yourself."

"So?" he said, shrugging.

"You worked on a project there. Something about a camera?"

He tilted his head and sighed resignedly. "Callie, that's a top-secret project. You're not even supposed to know about it."

"Yeah but I do, Walter! I need that for this project!"

"How am I supposed to make that happen? We're dealing with a black box here!"

She straightened up. "What the heck are *you* talking about?"

"You're working on a top-secret project I'm not supposed to know about. And you're asking me about a project I worked on seven years ago that you're not supposed to know about." He stepped back and pulled a chair out, then dropped into it, still looking at her. "How am I supposed to go up the ladder with that? People will ask questions."

Callie crossed her arms and stared him dead in the eyes. "I don't know, Walter. Make it happen." Then she turned and walked out, leaving him sitting in the dark.

CHAPTER 18

Dude. You have to stand still. Seriously. You're rocking like a trailer in a tornado. Look. Stand like this. Feet shoulder-width apart. Relaxed posture. No, no, no, don't lean forward. Stand straight. Keep your back tense. The only part – listen, dammit! The *only* part of your body that is going to move is from the elbow up."

Callie stood frustrated, her mouth pursed in impatience. "Look, Walter, let me just throw the darn darts my own way."

He stood behind her, hands on her hips, so close they could have been dancing. He now put his hands in the air and stepped back. "Okay. Fine. You keep throwing hotdogs. You're just gonna keep losing though."

"You have to let her find her groove, babe," Thevi said, staring at the hot end of a joint as she spoke through held breath.

Callie lowered her head, then looked up at the dartboard and focused all of her will at it. "Yeah, Walt. Let me find my groove. Watch this." She raised and lowered her shoulders then twisted her neck and stretched her fingers, all without taking her eyes off the center of the board. She then raised her arm and closed her left eye, staring down the barrel of the arrow in her slender fingers. She pumped it a few times, then slowed the pump to a nice, even draw, then slung forward and flicked her fingers like she was flinging water off of their tips. The dart sailed through the near-eight feet of air and thunked softly into the compressed fibers of the dartboard.

Walter stared, speechless. Thevi raised her head and let out another lungful of thick, white smoke, then pursed her lips and looked over at Callie. Walter nodded and picked up his pint glass from the bar and took a swig of the dark ale, then said, "Okay, what am I watching for?"

"Shut it!" Callie said. "I still have two more darts." She then went through the same routine, two more times. And as she went to collect her three arrows from the meaningless wedges of the 7, the 3 and between the wires that made the numeral 4, she shook her head and blew her tongue out at Walter. "You know, this just isn't my sport."

Walter shrugged, then took a puff of the magic cigarette and handed it back to Thevi with careful fingers. "Ah, don't give up, Caliente! Darts is everyone's sport! Anyone can be a darts champion. But I'm telling you, you have to find your form. And the only way you can do that is to maintain a structure from which to throw."

Callie turned from collecting her darts and looked at him seriously through emotionless eyes.

"What?" he asked, spreading his hands.

"Nothing," she said, widening her eyes, "just listening. Go on."

"Yeah," Walter said, reaching for his beer again, "If you keep the tower strong and sturdy, you can form repeatable moves. That's what you're going for. If you throw an arbitrarily variable amount of weight at the board every time you throw," he said, making the motions of throwing badly, "you'll never throw the same dart twice."

Callie furled her eyebrows and raised her chin just a little. He definitely had her attention. He soldiered on.

"If you keep the structure still and sound, the only thing moving is your forearm. Everything from your elbow up. Like this." Walter now pivoted his forearm back and forth, the rest of his body and arm staying perfectly still. "See? Once you find your throw like this, you can start honing your aim down. You can start really fine-tuning your throw. Then you'll find your arrows start hitting where you're aiming."

Callie nodded deeply now, and took a deep breath. "Okay. That makes sense. Why didn't you just say that to begin with, dork face?"

Walter dropped his shoulders and turned away. "Bitch, I've been saying that since the first time you ever picked up a dart."

"Well now I'm listening," she said. But her mind was elsewhere. She was perfectly capable of applying the trade he had taught her to the game of darts. To make the connection with her own structure and focus her efforts through moving a single extension of her body. But her mind was making that connection elsewhere – applying the fundamental physics of a rigid structure with a singular moving component to something else. Another science entirely.

She then turned and threw three more darts. One of them hit the outer bull, and the other two were very close to it. And this time Walter's speechlessness was well founded.

He then shook his head quickly, pointing his entire hand at the dartboard as he approached it, stumbling like he was drunk. "Now hang the fuck on. You're telling me that all this time all it took was you thinking about this like a physics problem?”

Callie looked at him silently, her head tilted slightly to one side. “Why? Does that surprise you?”

He rolled his eyes and looked up at the ceiling. “Dear God, woman. Dennis Priestly could take some lessons from you.” He walked up and looked closely at the darts, then back at her, and then back at the board before taking them out.

She widened her eyes. “I’m sorry, who?”

He shook his head again.

Thevi stared, mouth agape, almost not breathing. She finally seemed to catch up with what was going on and turned to look at Callie, straightening her head. “Are you serious here? Did you just do that?” she asked, her wobbly hand moving toward the board.

Callie looked surprised. Not at her feat, but at the disbelief that seemed to be popular opinion in the room. “You guys are acting like this is something I shouldn’t be able to do! I didn’t even make three of the bull’s eyes.”

“Well, you two act like you’ve never played together.”

Walter turned to look at her. “What are you talking about? We used to have absentee games every Sunday when we lived apart.”

Callie rolled her eyes. Thevi rolled her whole head. “Don’t start that shit again.”

Walter smiled and looked back at Callie. “That was pretty remarkable.”

Callie took a deep breath, then finally sighed and grabbed the joint from Thevi’s fingers and dropped it in the ashtray.

The rest of the night was not as impressive. Once they had recovered enough to talk Callie into throwing again, they learned quickly that what she had done had been nothing but a fluke, backed by a well-covered surprise. When they finally caught onto her trick, Callie laughed out loud and widened her eyes, happy to finally be able to celebrate the incredible coincidence that had made her look so precise with the sport.

They had all retired to the booth now, and were sipping hot coffee, snuggling indiscriminately with each other between fits of laughter and truth-tellings. They were back at The Outer Rim, curtain drawn and lights dimmed in their own private room. Walter had tuned in a bluetooth speaker on which he played the entire One Last Orbit discography on shuffle while they talked about everything and nothing. Callie had finally succumbed to the desire of her friends, smoking cannabis and getting high for her first time in a public place. Historically, she had been too paranoid to leave the house with it, thinking someone would notice. But since they all knew her at the Rim and she was with Walter, who was basically best-friends with the owner, she finally felt comfortable enough to give it a shot.

When the conversation finally started feeling stilted, Thevi took a deep breath and looked at Walter. She had told him before that she was worried about Chris being brought up. She wasn't good with awkward conversation, and was worried it would get that way quickly if Callie brought him up. He winked at her covertly and Callie stretched her neck, looking as if she was preparing for just that.

"You know, Walt, Chris was never really comfortable with my coming here."

Walter looked back at Thevi, then took a sip of his beer and made eye contact with Callie. "Yeah? Why not?"

"Because he wasn't in control, I guess. He knew that you and I were really close. And we have this... this strange sort of relationship. I mean," she trailed off, twirling her finger in the air. "How are you so cool with us, Thev?"

Thevi stared seriously at Callie for a moment, then twisted her lips. "You know, I don't know. I just know you're not hiding anything. But I know you're close for mostly intellectual reasons. Like you both share this rich intelligence, and you talk on a level no one else on the planet can understand. But I don't think there's anything sexual about it."

Walter was nodding. "That's the thing. That's the absolute thing right there. I mean, I'm a man. I love boobs. I would never imagine being able to have a gal friend who I didn't want to sleep with on some level. But it's like, with Callie, we've just always had this thing where it was never even a question."

Callie stared at him for a few seconds and then said, "I think that about sums it up. But you know, he was always okay with it. He wasn't cool with it, but he always allowed it, I mean. And I really respected him for it. I don't know many men who would be okay letting their woman have a relationship with a man like you and I have."

Thevi was shaking her head, mouth twisted. "I know exactly what you mean. But you two are just so special. So different than anyone I've ever met. And there's something so genuine about you, Callie, something so..." she trailed off again. She quickly sat up and took a drink of a cooling cup of coffee, then a sip from her glass of brandy. She licked her lips. "There's something so honest about you. I just know that you would never do anything like that with him. Not sure how I know. I just know."

"I kissed him, Thevi," Callie said.

Thevi smiled slightly, then put her hand on Callie's cheek across the couch. "I know. He told me when it happened. But I think that was no more sexual than your conversations about space ships."

Callie tried to smile, and straightened on the couch, pulling her unshod feet up beneath her, Indian-style. "How are you so sure about that? I mean, how are you okay with it?" she asked.

"You were grieving. That kind of shit happens. It's just like some primal response." She took another sip of her cocktail and licked her lips again. "Now if Walter wouldn't have told me about it and I would have just now learned, I would maybe have thought he felt differently about it. Like he felt he had to hide something. But he came right out and told me. And I was like, 'figures'. You know? It's just one of those things. He wasn't even surprised by it."

Walter was shaking his head, staring at the table. Thevi reached up and ran her fingers behind his ear. "I would never want to stand in the way of your friendship. You two need each other. Maybe more than he needs me, Callie... He needs you."

Callie shot him a fierce glance. Walter didn't bother hiding it or looking at anyone. He just pursed his lips and nodded slowly. Then he finally spoke. "So does that mean we're on a level here then, gals?"

Thevi took a deep breath and leaned back on the couch. "No, Double-Dub. You're not getting both of us into the bed."

"Dammit." But they all broke out laughing.

⌘   ⌘   ⌘

The soft strum of the acoustic guitar and Janis Ian's pure, silky voice rang through the dark living room as Codi and Sam stood stepping on each other's toes, moving slowly and softly around in small circles, his hands on her hips, hers on his shoulders. Rebecca had invited an old friend over for the night, and they sat on the couch talking quietly, sharing a short glass of scotch. Occasionally one of the couples would break the code and speak to someone outside their touch, but mostly it was quiet but for the music. The fire danced in the fireplace and the mood was generally warm and completely uninhibited. Codi didn't feel at all like she was being monitored. The couple of times she had pointedly aimed her eyes toward the girls on the couch, she had felt completely at ease – knowing they were caught up in their own game of sorts – knowing she wasn't being watched. Codi hadn't felt so relaxed in years, she thought. The low light was better for her unique sense of sight, and she found that the fire and low light actually helped her discern the shapes on the couch. At one point, she thought she could tell that Rebecca and Mimi were leaning toward each other, hands on each other's necks, foreheads pressed together, occasionally sneaking a kiss. Codi felt warm inside with happiness. Not just for herself, but for Rebecca. Previously she had wondered if Bec had tied herself to the memory of Natalie – wondered if she had reserved herself. But obviously Rebecca found love where – and when – she needed it.

The light 70s pop music seemed to soothe Codi's soul, and she couldn't tell whether the warmth she felt in her loins was from the close dancing with Sam or the perfect atmosphere and the red wine. She leaned her head closer to Sam, feeling his rough cheek against her own. She felt it tickle more than just her cheek. It seemed to reach deep inside her and tug at something internal. She leaned a little closer still, and turned head ever so slightly. It was an incredible sensation when she felt him respond in kind. The front of his jaw met hers, and their chins touched. Tingles ran down her spine. He raised his hand and touched her cheek lightly. She turned her head a little more and felt his whiskers against her lips. He lifted his head ever so slightly. The music changed and the fire popped. Despite her comfort, Codi felt like she had to check on Rebecca. And to the best of her new vision's ability, she felt like she could tell by the firelight that their positions had now changed. Perhaps it was the girls' comfort knowing that Sam and Codi were blind, or maybe a more intimate comfort altogether – but one of them was now completely on top of the other. Codi suddenly felt no reason at all to try to hide anything. And somewhere in the back of her head, she realized that nowhere in life – for the rest of her life – could she guarantee she had any real privacy. Any time she felt she was alone might actually be in question. But in this particular company, she felt no need to care. She felt no shame in the moment, and decided to let herself be swept away. By whatever happened, and whatever Sam might want to do, she would abide. She turned her head back toward him and rubbed her open lips softly along his jawline. Her eyes were closed now. She was now floating on the wine and the music – as well as the emotion. By the time the Hollies made their sonic appearance on the musical playlist, she was tingling all over. Sam had both his hands on her cheeks now, lightly guiding her as they danced circles in the light of the fire.

She raised her chin and thanked God for her fortune in finding Rebecca, and therefore, Sam, and then suddenly she was being kissed. Long and deep, her entire mouth engaged, she was kissing and being kissed by the man she had only recently met – and even more recently yet found she loved. Her feet felt light. She felt like she might be floating. Like maybe he was magic. Sam's fingertips tickled her jawline as his tongue softly danced against her own. And by the time *Sister Golden Hair* began, she had pulled his hands up to her chest.

As they rocked back and forth in each other's embrace, Codi found she had forgotten there was even another couple in the room. The soft smell of cigarette smoke hovered betwixt the night and finally reminded her of Rebecca, but it was different this time than it was before. Before there had been the slightest apprehension – just the tiniest shade of humility and modesty. This time, she found a very subtle jolt of excitement. Knowing that the mother-figure on the couch was not her mother – but an advocate for her love. Knowing that even if Rebecca was watching, it was okay. It was completely comfortable, and Codi found herself more excited than ever. Something so carnal, so *adult* teased her consciousness. Children were not allowed to smoke. *We're all adults here. And everything's okay.* She was not being judged! She was free to be herself. To explore, and be explored.

Codi felt Sam squeezing her softly through her sweater and tried to push more firmly against him – enhancing her kiss. She had, in recent weeks, adopted Rebecca's disdain for the underwire, and so was without any barrier against his hands. She suddenly realized he had been kneading her for quite a long time, possibly as long as an entire song, albeit very softly, and so decided to remove the hindrance entirely. She crossed her arms and grabbed the thick braid of the sweater below her waistline and pulled it up over her head. Tossing it on the ground behind her, she ran her fingers up through the back of his hair and pulled his face down to her bosom. And just as *Third Rate Romance* came on – but before they had a chance to giggle about it, they were both on their knees kissing, hands exploring each other in the dim light of the fire – blind to everything around them – well on their way to the soft carpet with intentions beyond the brass zippers that kept them temporarily apart. Amidst the soft clicks of kissing lips and subtle, almost inaudible moans coming from the couch, they found the floor. And the perfect warmth of the fire negated any need for a blanket. By the time the morning light crept through the window, they would be found snoring softly beneath nothing more than the ceiling, and a warm pillow of air.

⌘ ⌘ ⌘

Callie was the first to wake. The three of them had fallen asleep on the giant Lovesac in the Watsons' theater room. The credits of the last movie had long since left the screen, and she could still hear Walter and Thevi snoring on their side of the beanbag. It was eight feet wide, and large enough for her to get up without waking them. She stood up and stretched, then headed for the kitchen to get a pot of coffee going. Somehow they had managed to make it home from the coffee bar. They hadn't driven themselves – they had called an Uber driver. But still, she had no recollection of it.

As she stood with bare feet on the cold kitchen tiles looking out the bay window at the pool, she knew there was something important she needed to focus on today. As she heard Walter's house shoes scuff on the tile behind her, it snapped into her mind, and she wasted no time attacking it.

"Good morning, sleepy head," she said.

Walter grunted. "Coffee ready yet?"

"Almost. So hey, how are we moving on getting me access to your camera project?"

He stopped by the window and turned to look at her incredulously. "Wow, give me some time to wake up, would ya?"

She shrugged. "Okay. But I want a full report when you have your coffee!"

"Relax dude. Nothing has happened yet anyway." He pulled out a seat with his foot and dropped into a chair at the table in the nook by the window. Callie took a mug off a hook under the upper cabinet and filled it from the steaming carafe, then set the mug in front of Walter and poured her own. "Thank you."

"You're welcome. You know that's not what I want to hear, Walt," she said.

"Okay, well then fuck you instead."

"That's not what I'm talking about. I'm wondering why nothing has happened yet," she said, joining him at the table.

He ran his fingers through his hair and yawned, then took a sip of the coffee. "I think the best way to go about this is to get me in on your project. If we can talk Minus into letting me be in on it, I can bring it up."

"You know what I don't get?" Callie said. "Why is all this so secretive? Both projects are from the same stupid company."

"Don't be naïve, CalStar. You know better than that."

"Better than what?" she said, sipping her own coffee.

"You break your NDA and you'll never set foot in a Royal corridor again. I'm not about to jeopardize my career to take a chance."

"I don't think Minus would pursue anything like that. I mean you were at the table when he brought it up originally anyway."

"You don't *think*. But you don't know. I'm not his favorite person," Walter said.

Callie shrugged and straightened her own hair. It was getting close to her shoulders and she reckoned she had better schedule an appointment to get it cut soon. She took a deep breath and blew across the top of her mug. "Okay. Well, if you think that would help, I'll see what I can do. I mean, it would be neat to have you on the project anyway." She smiled at him.

"You're damn right it would."

The next day, as Callie pushed through the revolving door an into the spacious lobby of the Royal office building, she caught Walter's eye at the reception desk as he leaned over talking to the pretty, petite Monica. Sideways, she thought that if it weren't for rich companies who needed a pretty front thing, girls like Monica wouldn't have jobs.

Walter finished up and patted the counter a couple of times, then jogged to catch Callie before the elevator doors closed. She was the only one in the car, but made no move for the Open Door button, instead opting to let Walter stick his loafer in the closing door. "Woop! One more, please!" he said through the shoe-sized gap. When the door stopped its trek abruptly and started sliding back open, Callie felt the car shake slightly and looked up at the lights.

Walter stepped on and looked out of breath. "Oh. You're the only one on here. Why didn't you wait for me? In a rush?"

"You looked busy, Walt. How is Ms. Monica today? Do her breasts look nice in her striped sweater?" Callie asked, seriously.

"Oh God, yes. Wait. Did you see them?" Walt said.

She rolled her eyes. "It was rhetorical, Walter. I could care less about her boobs."

"You mean you *couldn't* care less," he said, looking levelly at her.

She rolled her eyes again and looked up at the wall where the numbers slowly climbed.

"To say you could care less indicates that there is at least a small amount of..." he trailed off. "Okay. Who pissed on your corn flakes this morning?"

"No one, Walter. It's just disgusting to me. You have an absolutely stunning wife at home who loves you more than words can express and you're up here staring at that bimbo's boobs," Callie said, cracking her neck and trying to avoid looking at him.

"Dude. It's all a game. I flirt. Big deal. It's not like I ever-"

The elevator slammed to a halt. Callie actually felt her stomach rise and lost her balance briefly. She looked wide-eyed up at the digital floor indicator again, a terrified grip on the hand rail now draining her hand of color. "What the flip was that, Walter?"

"I don't know," he said, but he was also gripping the handrail and looking up toward the top of the car. He stepped forward and pushed the Door Open button a few times, to no avail, then started trying to pry the doors apart.

"What are you doing, Walter? Oh my God are we stuck?" she almost screamed.

"It looks like it. I know the elevator isn't supposed to just slam stopped like that." Unable to pry the doors more than an inch or so apart, he began banging on them, and then hit the emergency button. The light beside it began blinking.

Callie was gripping the rail with her left hand and clinching her purse against her breast with a ferocity in the right hand. Her eyes were wide and serious, her mouth a puckered mess that looked like the face of a disapproving mother.

"You can't be serious," Walter was saying, staring at the control panel. Nothing was happening but the steady blink of the LED in the middle of the emergency call button. "All these years and I've never been stuck on an elevator. And it happens now, when Callie is in a shitty mood."

"I'm not in a shitty mood, Walter. I'm scared out of my wits right now. Will you please stop making it worse?"

Walter sighed and turned toward her. "What would you like me to do, princess? How can I make it more pleasant for you?"

She looked at him seriously, shaking her head. "Really? You could start by not being a jerk! I thought these things weren't supposed to get stuck! I thought it was hydraulic or something!"

Walter leaned back against the rail and breathed in deeply, then ran his fingers through his hair. "Negative. You can't do hydraulic over six floors. Sixty feet or so is about as far as you can get effectively."

"Okay, thank you for the elevator education," she said. Her jaw seemed to be trembling now.

Walter looked hard at her. "What would you like me to say, Callie? You mentioned hydraulics and I told you why they can't use them in a thirty-storey building. You sure are in rare form today."

She breathed in deeply and tried to calm herself but it wasn't working. So she kept her mouth shut.

Walter approached her carefully, and put one hand on her cheek. "Look, Callie," he started. She raised her eyes to meet his, expectantly. "I'm not, nor would I ever, cheat on Thevi. You introduced us, for shit's sake. I love that woman like the air that I breathe. Okay?"

Callie almost nodded. But she wanted to wait to see what came next. She was holding her cards close.

"I'm a player, Callie. Always have been. And though that doesn't mean much anymore, it's hard to completely walk away from that lifestyle. But you know how true I am. If I were still actively playing, I would have long ago tried to get into your pants."

She tilted her head and tried to fight back the thought of him standing there at the pool bar in Mexico, tiny magnifying glasses of water droplets on his thick, muscular chest. How she had noticed for the first time that there was not only muscle there, but tattoos. How could she have known him for some twenty-plus years and never known he had tattoos? She swallowed trying to resist the idea that she was actually almost turned on by the idea of him taking her to bed. Now that Chris was gone, the only thing stopping her from it besides her commitment to her chaste cause, was her best friend's marriage to the man about whom she was thinking. It was insane. And it was just a flash of thought. But it had flashed itself. Seeing him shirtless in Mexico in his three-hundred-dollar Ray-Bans had opened a new door of thought for her that she had never before explored. And now it seemed, stuck here on this elevator with him, that it was going to continue to return to mind.

"I love you, Callie," he said, and her heart jumped momentarily. "I would never do anything to damage our friendship." He stood back and spread his hands. "Hey, remember when you kissed me?"

She swallowed and nodded slowly, trying hard to keep her eyes on his. She wondered where he could possibly be going with this.

"I could have slammed you back against that door and kissed you right back. I could have had my hands all up your shirt, gr-"

"STOP IT!" she shouted, cutting him off abruptly both verbally and physically, as she pushed past him to go push the buttons herself. Partly to excise herself from the uncomfortable conversation, but also to hide her face, as she was almost sure that now she was starting to show signs of her inner excitement. She felt a familiar tingle down below and squeezed her thighs together as she started pushing the call button repeatedly. She was sweating now too.

"Sorry," he said, and Callie heard his hands fall to his sides. "I meant nothing by it. I was just trying to illustrate that if it were going to happen with anyone, wouldn't it be you? And furthermore, wouldn't that have been the time?"

She turned around sharply and shot him with her dagger eyes. "No, you pig. That would be the worst time! Or have you forgotten why I kissed you in the first place? Did you forget that my husband-to-be had just died? Or that your *wife* was waiting outside in the taxi?" She began shaking her head and tightening her face up in anger.

"Of course I haven't forg-" he began, but she cut him off again.

"Shut up! Just shut up, Walter!" She swung her purse at him, but he raised an arm and the purse flung madly around it, dumping a pound of eyeliners and change and keys and wallet and gum and other lady things onto the dirty marble floor of the elevator car. She let it drop and buried her face in her hands instead. Immediately the sting of tears started tearing at her eyes. She could feel the anger and rage and sadness and anxiety all building up inside her now. And she began to sob openly.

It was a long moment before she finally felt his light touch on her shoulders, and then, finally, his hands creeping down behind her, pulling her into his embrace. She buried her face against his chest for a second time since Chris had died, and began wetting his shirt with her tears.

"Shhhh," he said softly, his chin resting atop her head. "You're okay, Callie. We're okay. I'm sorry I hurt your feelings."

She didn't respond, but kept crying. And the elevator suddenly dropped a few feet, sending her to the floor screaming. They were on their knees now, amidst tubes of lipstick that were rolling across the floor, scattering in every direction. Aside from the sudden shock of the lurching floor and the pain in her knees from falling suddenly, there was now a pain in her back. A hard jarring fall like that could actually damage something, she reckoned. It was then that she came to her senses enough to realize that Walter was no longer holding her. She looked up and through tear-flooded eyes, realized he was out cold on the floor against the wall, blood dribbling from the side of his mouth. And that was when she completely lost it.

Callie was screaming now. Like a terrified banshee in a hell-bound cart full of fire, she was screaming, slamming her hands against the button, wondering where the help was. "Where the fuck are you?!" she shouted, banging with fists on the metal buttons. The floor buttons were now lighting up, but the call button still blinked steadily. "WHAT THE FUCK IS GOING ON? WHY WON'T ANYONE HELP US?!" she screamed. The terror that filled her now was bone deep. It was threatening complete hysteria, and she could feel her heart rate tripling. Her head was hot and her face was throbbing now. She looked back over at Walter, but he was still motionless on the floor. His chest was rising and falling steadily, but he was otherwise a scarecrow. Fear gripped Callie's stomach like an iron claw and she began wailing, senseless, wordless screams, banging uselessly against the buttons as she slid down to the floor to crumble into a crying wreck. As she sat there sobbing, the lights flickered, and then went out. And as she was increasing the speed of her breathing, on the verge of herself losing consciousness, she heard a knocking on the door. It was light, faint, but it was there. Then she heard a muffled voice, calling out to her.

"Everyone okay in there?" it said. Finally. She was rescued.

Codi was back in the office for her weekly checkup, sitting in a dark room waiting for her eyes to completely adjust. She wondered aloud why there was any waiting involved at all. Didn't she, after all, have robotic eyes now? Would they not adjust instantly? But Rebecca had reminded her that she still had irises that would respond naturally to bright lights. They had not removed her cones and rods, after all. Duh.

As she sat waiting, she thought she heard a conversation going on outside the therapy room door. It sounded like a woman was speaking with Rebecca about something private. Codi's sense of hearing had gotten a lot sharper of late, but not quite sharp enough to hear the conversation through the thick door. She did, however, think she heard her name being mentioned. But there had been no women in the office besides Bec when she had entered. Rebecca was, in fact, the only woman who even worked in the office.

When the doctor came in, it was quick and painless, and all business. None of the usual pleasantries adorned his speech. What was going on here? She wanted to ask if something was wrong, but she was too timid. When he asked her at the end if she had any questions, she simply said, "I guess not," hoping he would inquire what that meant. But he didn't. He just slapped his knees and stood up, wishing her a good day as he exited the therapy room in as much of a haste as he had entered it. And Codi was once again in the dark, literally, and figuratively.

When Rebecca came in a few minutes later, she seemed in good spirits. "Okay sweetie, bright lights!" she said, immediately flipping on the light switch. There was no harsh reflexive penalty for Codi as she had expected – as she had been trained to expect for the first near-quarter-century of her life. It was just a soft rise of red from the edges of her vision, until the whole of her sight was covered with a warm glow, where it settled back and was promptly forgotten.

"Is everything okay?" Codi asked.

"Yup. Everything's great," Rebecca said, "the doctor says you look great." She leaned in real close and whispered to Codi, her hand on Codi's left knee. "I didn't tell him how great you looked last night though."

Codi flooded with warm embarrassment and surprise for Rebecca's impropriety. Never before had Rebecca spoken inappropriately while she was in the office. It didn't so much bother Codi, but she did wonder what had changed. Maybe they had just gotten closer as friends. She felt her cheeks fill with color though and tried to hide it, but Rebecca was already pushing away in her rolling chair, turning toward the small desk and the computer in the corner. Codi took a deep breath and tried to relax.

"So I guess you two were watching last night after all?" she said, trying to sound cheerful and fun.

"Nah. I mean, I won't tell you I didn't peak over a couple of times to make sure you were okay. But no, I had my own hands full. So to speak, of course," Rebecca said.

"Ha! I noticed! It was nice to see you having fun too," Codi responded.

"So who was watching whom then, doll?"

"Uh huh. You know I can't see very well. I think you had the advantage of me there."

Rebecca turned back away from the computer and rolled back to the middle of the small room, then said, "Well, I don't ever want you to feel uncomfortable doing whatever you want to do at home. It's your home too, and if you would rather me leave the room, all you have to do is say so."

"Oh no, not at all!" Codi said. She suddenly felt foolish.

"It just seemed like everything kind of slid into a comfort level without ever really being noticed last night. Like there was no real transition into anything naughty. So, I'm sorry if I didn't extend you the privacy you felt you needed."

"Rebecca, please! I felt completely comfortable. I just meant..."

"It's okay, babe. Don't worry. We weren't watching or anything," Rebecca interrupted, not impolitely. She was now back in front of Codi, her hand back on Codi's knee.

"I don't mean that at all," Codi said. She took a deep breath and ran her hair back behind her ear, then tried again. "What I mean is that..."

"It's okay, hon. You can say whatever you want to say to me. You know that," Rebecca reminded.

"I know. What I mean is that I, uh... I didn't get to see you naked."

Rebecca was silent for a long moment. When she finally broke the silence, she sounded a little stunned. "Don't worry, doll. You're not missing much." She quickly patted Codi's knees with both hands, indicating, at least to Codi, that she was trying to pass the message that the conversation had turned uncomfortable. But Codi fought past it, past her timidity and nervousness.

"No, I mean it, Bec," she said.

Rebecca breathed in sharply through her nose, then said, "You mean what, sugar? You're actually interested in seeing me in the nude?"

Codi shrugged. "I don't know. I'm not sure what I mean. I mean, I do know I don't have any lesbian tendencies. It just... I don't know. It just sort of seemed..."

"Unfair?" Rebecca interjected.

"Yeah," she said, nodding. "Yeah, maybe that's it. Maybe a little. I mean, I guess I am a little bit curious, at least. I've never seen two women making love."

"Well, don't torture yourself," Rebecca said, squeezing Codi's knees gently. "What happened last night was pretty natural. I mean, maybe not natural, as such," she laughed. "But not forced, is what I mean. It was just sort of naturally allowed to happen under the circumstances. But I don't think we'll be making a habit out of it or anything. I really value you as a friend, Codi. I would never want to disturb that at all."

Codi sat nodding for a long moment, then finally swallowed and said, "Yeah. Yeah, you're right. I guess not."

⌘   ⌘   ⌘

The elevator car was stuck halfway between the thirteenth and fourteenth floor, the wall of the hoistway visible in the middle of the vertical space between the bottom and top of the door. It was very disorienting – not to mention discomforting – to Callie, especially in her near-hysterical state. She could see an aluminum conduit running vertically between the floor of fourteen and the top of thirteen's door. There it branched off to each side, trekking somewhere into the darkness outside the horizontal allowance of the doors they had pried open.

The guys in the hallway had lights on their helmets and they were trying to – but not entirely succeeding – keep them out of her eyes. She sat trembling against the back wall with Walter's head in her lap. She was worried for him, but also unsure about what to do next. So she just sat there awaiting orders. The men were speaking Greek in front of her, talking about counterweights and hoist ways and car sills and guide rails. All she knew was that she was seeing part of a wall that no one was ever supposed to see. Except maybe the guys with the miner lights. Peripherally she was aware that it was dark beyond them as well, and she wondered if the power had gone out.

After a period that seemed to Callie to be about a month, one of the men finally slid through the upper opening and dropped down into the car with her. He mercifully aimed the light toward the ground and squatted beside her, placing a calming, albeit blackened, hand on her shoulder.

"Is he okay?" the man asked.

Callie shrugged and breathed in. "I don't know. I don't know what happened. It just fell, and then I looked back and he was lying here like this."

The man checked Walter's pulse, leaving a black smudge on his neck, then reassured her, saying, "Yeah, he'll be all right. Think he just lost consciousness."

After another thirty minutes, they were both out and in the back of an ambulance on the way to the hospital. Walter, it had turned out, had smacked his chin on the top of Callie's head – where he had been resting it – when the car fell, and had bitten a hole in his tongue. Not to mention knocking himself out. He was awake now, and responding to Callie, squeezing her hand. But he had no memory of what had happened. His neck was in a brace, keeping him from moving his head even the slightest bit. Callie had to fill him in on what had happened. At first, Walter was completely skeptical. No way he would forget all that, he had said. She assured him that it had happened. She had the black smears all over her four-hundred-dollar Chanel suit to prove it.

When they had extricated her from the elevator car, they had pulled her up to the fourteenth, whereas with Walter, they had opted for the lower opening, having him on the stretcher and all. He had, therefore, gotten out clean and without a scrape. She had been forced to do some climbing. And was terrified that the car would decide to fall again and cut her in half as she climbed out. They had assured her that this was impossible since they had locked the car against the rails, and had even braced the cable against the wheel above – whatever that meant.

Her hair was frazzled and wrecked, her ponytail a comical bump on the top of her head, spilling her blond hair out in directions it wasn't meant to go, and there was a long streak of black grease on her right cheek. She had to remind him that they were indeed in an ambulance, and why else would they be there if something hadn't happened?

"You should have heard me, Walter," she said, crossing her legs and resting her chin on her free hand, elbow propped on her knee. "I was cussing up a storm. I was really freaking out."

"You were cursing? Okay, I think I found something harder to believe than our being trapped in an elevator that never fails."

"No, really," she said, looking levelly at him. "I think I even used the F word. I should be forgiven and absolved of the blame for it though. It was the most terrifying experience of my life!"

He squeezed her hand again and chuckled. "Oh, don't worry, babe. No one was around – or at least awake – to hear it. It never happened."

CHAPTER 19

Thevi, Walter and Callie sat at a table set with fine flatware and long-stemmed glasses in the dim light of Neptune City's finest Italian restaurant. They were well into their second bottle of wine when the food finally came. Callie hated the waiting, and would rather have gone somewhere faster in lieu of the fine dining experience. But she never won the vote against the two lovers. Majority always won. And she was never in the majority.

"It would," Walter said, "Have to be the thirteenth floor that it failed on, wouldn't it?"

Thevi giggled at him, forking a piece of cheesy broccoli into her mouth. She chewed politely, then covered her mouth with a cloth napkin that smelled strongly of chlorine bleach, and said, "You know, I've never believed all that superstitious horse shit."

Walter shrugged, leaning back in his chair and slinging back another big sip of the wine. "Neither have I. But then shit like this happens, and you start thinking about things like that."

"You know, I've never known what that even meant," Callie said, taking the last bite of meatball on her plate. She still had a sea of noodles left, but had devoured all the meat. "I mean, I've heard the superstitions but what does it mean?"

"What do you mean?" Thevi said, leaning in for another bite.

"I mean, like, what's there? I've seen that most buildings don't even have a thirteen in the elevator. So what's there? Doesn't that just like, I don't know, make the fourteenth floor the thirteenth?" Callie said.

"No dude," Walter said after swallowing the last of his wine. "There's a thirteenth floor. It's just a wide-open empty concrete floor."

Thevi was shaking her head and rolling her eyes, head close to her plate, sucking in a lengthy noodle. Callie obviously didn't see her. She said, "Really?"

Walter nodded soberly, looking thoughtful. "Totally."

"Don't tell me you seriously believe this dipshit," Thevi said.

"Well, why not? I mean, seriously! If there is no thirteenth floor, then the fourteenth *is* the thirteenth. Just mislabled, right?"

"Of course, Cal. He's just screwing with you." Thevi set her fork down and sat up straight, looking around briefly. "You know, they say Rod Piccolo eats here all the time?" she said, changing the subject.

Walter burst out laughing, almost spitting a mouthful of red wine across the table. "Who the fuck is Rod Piccolo?" He immediately started laughing again, and before he could get hold of himself, lost it completely, totally succumbing to the laughter. Callie caught on quickly and started shaking with it herself. It was contagious when Walter laughed. Not contagious enough for his wife to catch it, but who was counting?

Thevi sat staring dumbly between them for a long moment. "You guys are idiots. Or just drunk."

"No, seriously," Walter finally managed, taking hold of Thevi's wrist on the table. "Who the hell is that?"

"You've never heard of Rod Piccolo? The *main guy* in Lucy's Story?"

And Walter lost it again. "Lucy's..." he started, but then roared with more laughter. They were starting to draw attention now. It was a typically classy and, therefore, quiet establishment. They weren't used to having people like Walter in here, who totally ignored the rules of establishment.

The next day, Callie once again found herself sitting across from Minus in his office, taking notes as they discussed next steps with the architect of the prototypes, Dane Silas. He was an extremely tall man, odd angles and a very heavy brow that defied any attempt one might have at trying to figure out his age. He seemed fidgety and awkward when engaged outside of a completely technical conversation, and Callie guessed he was probably incredibly intelligent – perhaps high-functioning Asperger's or something. She knew very little about him, but did know he was a master of his craft, and if it could be built, he was your guy.

"Listen, Matt," Callie said after an hour of discussion, "we need Walter in here."

Minus leaned back and grabbed the arms of his chair, cracking his knuckles and neck at the same time. "Okay, talk to me. This keeps coming up."

Callie bit her lip and tried to roll her eyes to the side, to indicate that she needed Silas to leave. Minus wasn't catching it though. She finally had to just come out and ask. "Are we done with Mr. Silas?" She looked over at him politely. He had closed his notebook and sniffled as he looked up at Minus.

Minus shrugged, then nodded. "Yeah. You're good. Thanks, Dane."

Silas stood up and grabbed his coat, and exited the room quietly. Callie looked toward her lap until she heard the door click closed, then looked up at Minus. "Matt, between me and you, and completely under the radar – he has access to some technology we may find very useful."

Minus's eyes got wide. He was finally interested. "Go on," he said, and began twirling his pen round his thumb.

"He worked on a project a few years ago where they were building and testing a camera that could apparently take full-color photographs in the absolute absence of light," Callie said. She, feeling she had said all she needed to on the subject, reached forward and picked up her cold coffee and took a sip.

"No shit. Wow. Yeah, that does sound pretty useful in our scenario. But uh," he began.

"Because, Minus, it's NDA'd. I can't know about it officially," she said.

"Ah. I see. Well that presents a bit of a problem then doesn't it?" he replied, dropping his pen. He left it and scooted forward in his chair, resting his elbows on the desk and steepling his fingers.

"Why is that?" she said. Callie had thought the case should have been closed.

"Because, if you don't know about it, then how could I know about it?" he said. Then he continued, "And if I don't know about it, why would I bring him on over here? You're putting the cart before the horse."

She leaned back and looked at the ceiling, sighing deeply. "Always something. Look, Minus. I'm not a politician. That's for you to figure out. I'm just telling you on a level that I know he worked on something that could greatly benefit your trench project. Now you need to find a way to learn that officially, and get him over here."

"Okay, there again, Callie, and I'm not trying to be difficult, but..." he started, but she cut him off.

"Just say it and stop being around the bush, Minus."

He chuckled at her misstep, but ignored it otherwise. "Why do we need him on the team? We just need the project, right?"

She sighed again. Then she shook her head and scooted to pick up her mug and grabbed her long coat. "Because, Minus, it's professional courtesy. You know he wants to be here, and I know that may not justify anything, but he's already on Royal payroll, and he did come up with the idea that he could leak the project safely over here, since it wouldn't be breaking company boundaries." She looked at the floor, straightening her shoe and trying to draw attention away from her face so he wouldn't catch her lying. It didn't work.

"He did, huh? Is that how it went?" Minus said through a smile.

"I don't care how it happens, Matt, but he is scratching our backs a little. Or he's at least trying to. It wouldn't hurt to scratch his, back. To scratch his back, back. To back scratch his... To return the favor."

"I'll see what I can do," Minus said as Callie whipped the coat over her shoulder.

"Excellent. Thank you, Minus." She straightened her hair and grabbed her purse. The sun was beginning to set across the bay, visible as a gigantic orange ball through Minus's tinted office window. "I have faith in you. Now if you'll excuse me, I'm going to go home and get in my pajamas."

Without looking up, he waved her out with a flick of his fingertips.

When Callie pulled into her driveway, she felt a sudden sadness, in seeing Chris's car sitting there with a puddle around it. The morning snow had melted off throughout the day and left beads of water standing on every surface. She reckoned she would eventually have to get rid of it if she ever wanted to move on with her life. She turned the key in the door and let herself inside, then flipped the switch on the wall that started the gas fireplace. Twenty minutes later, she was soaking in the bathtub, a glass of white wine in one hand, surrounded by fat candles and relaxing to the sounds of Chopin on the bathroom stereo.

Just as she was letting the day slip down her legs, between her toes and out into the steaming water, her phone rang, buzzing itself across the edge of the tub, and almost dropping into the bubbly water. With the deft hand of a professional, she set her wine glass down and knocked the phone into the water. "SHOOT!" she shouted, sitting up quickly and retrieving it from the hot water. Surprisingly, it still rang. She was, however, unable to swipe her thumb across the screen to answer the call. She quickly brought it up to her nose and ran it sideways, unlocking the phone and connecting the call.

"Hello?"

"Can you and Walter meet me at Brokeback Fountain?" Minus asked with haste.

"What the heck? Who meets there at nine o'clock at night?"

"You do, if you know what's good for you. You can either ask favors or questions, Callie. Not both."

"Okay, okay, I'll call him and ask. Give me a few minutes. Does it have to be tonight?" she leaned over the edge of the tub, resting her breasts against the cold porcelain of its outer rim in search of a towel. "I literally just got in the tub."

"Yes. Any more questions?" Minus sighed impatiently.

"No. Okay, sorry. Give me a few minutes."

She dried her hand off and disconnected the call, then tried to call Walter with it. She couldn't get the screen to move. Maybe the water was beginning to set in. "Ahhhhh!" she shouted, standing up in the tub and wrapping the towel around her. "Shoot, shoot shoot! Why now?"

Fumbling through the house to the kitchen, she opened the pantry and looked for a box of rice. There it was, on the bottom shelf. But someone, probably Chris, had put it back empty. She looked for the next best thing. Finding a box of raisin bran, she popped open the top, ripped open the bag, then dropped her cell phone into the cereal. She shook it around a little and set the box on the counter, then grabbed the house phone and dialed Walter's number from the speed dial button it was assigned.

"What's up, blondie?" he answered on the first ring.

"Walter, Minus wants to meet at the Fountain."

"What fucking fountain?" he said. "And why?"

"The Brokeback, Walter. Can you go or not?"

"What the hell, Callie? What is this about?"

"I don't know, Walter. He didn't say. He said I could either ask questions or ask favors," she said, frustrated.

He sat there for a long time without answering. She could hear him talking to Thevi in the background, and then he finally returned to her. "Okay. I can be there in twenty minutes."

"Good," she said, and hung up. She stood with her hands spread wide on the counter, staring at the puddle she had created on the hardwood floor of the kitchen. She unhitched the towel and let it fall, then scooted it around with her foot, drying the mess. Callie left the towel on the floor and walked naked into the bedroom to put on some clothes. She was not going to get dressed up for this though. She wanted to show Matt how put-off she was about having to miss her bath.

Borbach Fountain was on the shoreline of Neptune City, in the strip mall that was home to all the best attractions in the city. Being owned by Jimmy Borbach, an out-of-the-closet gay, the local joke quickly took over. But he and Ben, his partner, were good sports about it. His business certainly didn't suffer. He sold sodas and ice cream over an old-fashioned solid wood counter top through shiny silver taps that had to be a hundred years old. And he served the sweetest root beer in New Jersey. Callie pulled into the parking lot at a quarter after nine, looking instinctively for

Matt Minus's SUV, but not seeing it. Maybe she was early. But as she sat looking around, someone knocked on her window, startling her. It was Walter, and he was making the twirling gesture with his left hand that said, "Let's get this over with." She killed the engine and got out.

"Your hair is wet," he said to her as she closed the door and thumbed the fob button that made her lights blink and the horn chirp.

"Yeah. I was in the bath tub. What were you doing?" she said.

"You don't want to know."

"Uh huh. You answered on the first ring. I know you weren't having lovey time with the wifey," she said, playfully slapping Walter's shoulder.

"I didn't say that's what I was doing. In fact, I gave no indication at all that that's what you should have assumed," he retorted.

"Uh huh. You were making whoopie!" Callie said again, smiling widely.

Walter stopped in his tracks and turned to face her. Quickly, the smile fell off her face. "Okay, let's just stop right here and get something straight. Number one, I don't *make whoopie*' as you so eloquently put it. Not fucking ever. And two, you and I *both* just said that's not what I was doing."

"Okay. Sorry, Walt," Callie said, sincerely.

"I was expressing the dog's anal glands, for your information," Walter said, still not moving.

"Ooh. What the heck?" Callie said, thinking now that he was toying with her.

"Dogs come from wolves, generally speaking. Wolves have glands in their anuses that excrete a certain smell. It's not pleasant. It's metallic and fishy. You wouldn't like it." He stared at her for a moment, watching her face go sour. Then he continued. "Man has been trying to breed it out of dogs since their domestication. Obviously, unsuccessfully. Therefore," he said, waving his hand around. "You have to occasionally express these glands in your male dogs." He stared at her again for another long moment. "Unless you like the smell of metallic fish."

Callie's face was completely twisted in disgust now. "Are you serious? That's so gross. Oh my God."

"Hey, you asked," he said, and started walking again.

"No, I actually didn't," she said, looking at the ground and shaking her head. Then she jogged to catch up. Then she finally broke free of the disgust and started smiling again, thinking she had him. "Did you at least wash your hands?"

Walter turned and put his hand flat on her face, covering it entirely, then twisting her face around as she shouted and tried to get away, spitting and waving her hands around. Her wet hair flew and flipped about her face as she sank to her knees trying to get away from the awful hand that must surely have dog yuck on it, until he finally stopped. Suddenly. And mercifully.

When she was finally able to regain her composure and stand up, spitting her hair out of her mouth, she looked at him with a mixture of sadness and disgust – a visual question of whether or not she needed to go wash her face with Lava.

"I wear latex gloves, Callie. If you think there's any way I'm sticking my bare finger in a dog's ass, you got me seriously, ridiculously bent." He stared at her for a moment, then added, "Now, let's go. Stop horsing around, and let's get this shit over with."

They found Minus waiting for them at a brightly lit booth in the back corner by the jukebox. "What took you two love birds so long?" he said.

"Well I was on time, Mr. Minus," Callie said. "He, on the other hand, was trying to finger-"

Walter reached out sideways and slapped his hand over her open mouth. "Shut it, princess!" She pulled away, again twisting her face up and fell into the booth. Walter began squatting to sit on her legs, when she finally straightened up and scooted in.

"You done? Can we talk business now?"

"Yes, sir," Callie said, trying on her best schoolgirl attitude.

Walter leaned back and looked around, refusing to play by Minus's rules. He slung his arm over the back of the booth, effecting a complete casual posture, then looked at Minus. "Why Brokeback? Couldn't we meet at the Lantern or something?"

"Listen, dipshit. You're the one who wants in on the project. Let me know now if I'm wasting my time," Minus said. Walter sat staring at him for a long moment, unflinching. When he had finally thought through the threat, he leaned forward and gave Minus his full attention.

"No. You're not. But why the secret spy shit?" He looked around for emphasis. On a Monday night, there was rarely anyone at the Fountain. Tonight was no different. "Do you think people are following us?"

Minus took a deep breath and tilted his head. He was clearly losing patience with Walter Watson. "I run into Royal folk at the Lantern almost every time I'm there, fuckwad. No one would ever expect to run into me here. So I chose here. Now. We could have been done with this bullshit meeting already if you would just stop horsing around."

Walter shrugged, looking at the table. "Okay. Sorry. But did you have to get a root beer float? I mean, for fuck's sake, you really complete the picture."

Callie was staring at him with her lips pursed at an odd angle, not quite sure what to say. So she didn't.

Minus ignored the question. "I think I've come up with a way to get you on the project, Walter. If you're mature enough to handle it. I'm beginning to think it might be a bad idea."

"Oh no," Callie said, grabbing Walter's wrist on the table and squeezing hard. "He can behave. Right Walter?" she said, turning to look at Walter. "I mean, he always behaves when he's working with me."

Walter shrugged. "Sure. Whatever."

"What's your plan, Minus?" Callie said.

Before he answered, he stared at Walter for a long time. Then he took an exaggerated drink from the curly straw of his float and wiped his lips with the napkin. "Well, my thought is that he knows about our project, because in the early phase when I was recruiting, before you were under NDA, Callie, he was there. At the Anchor. I spoke freely about wanting to find the Bloop in front of him. At that point, we had not yet discussed how I was going to go about it."

"Right," Callie said, nodding her head. She looked at Walter to see if he was following. Of course he was, he just wasn't nodding.

"So, it was completely legal for him to know we were going to fund a project to do *something* in that direction. The NDA only covers the force field on the submersible."

"Force field? What the fuck?" Walter said, looking suddenly at Callie.

"Shut it, Walt."

"Oh, you hadn't told him yet?" Minus said.

"Of course not! I signed an NDA, Matt!"

"Well, color me impressed!" he said. "Anyway, since he knows only what he's allowed to know," Minus said, opening his hand toward Walter as if to underline the point, "it's completely legal for him to approach me about the project."

Walter sat back again and put his arm on the bench behind Callie. He was about to speak when Minus held up that same hand to stop him, and continued. "You can ask me if I have ABC Project clearance."

"Oh, shit!" Walter said. "Killer!" It was a perfect idea. That was, after all, the officially sanctioned way to ask someone if he was in the know about a top-secret project. *Are you cleared for Project Whatever?* "So I guess then the only other obvious question is what happens when you say no?"

Minus stirred his float and took another pull from the straw. "You tell me it could benefit the current project I'm on and I ask for clearance. It's all a formality. We all work for the same team. If I request it, they'll give me the clearance. They just need a paper trail to keep track of who knows about it."

"What was the project called, Walter?" Callie asked. "I mean, since we're talking about it."

Walter leaned over and pulled his wallet out of his back pocket, then pulled a thin stack of business cards from a pocket in it, and started fanning through them. After a moment, he tossed one casually onto the table and returned the wallet to his pocket. Callie snatched the card and looked at it. "Project Brightwalk?" she read aloud.

He shrugged.

"You had business cards made up for the project?" she asked, frowning.

"Crazy, huh? That was more like our badge. They weren't really for handing out. I only had the one," he said.

"Yeah, that is crazy." She looked up at Minus. "Are we getting business cards made up for the Bloop project?"

Minus grunted. "Don't count on it," he said.

Callie pursed her lips and nodded, then leaned forward against the table. "Okay, so why did we have to meet tonight again?"

"I don't do these things over the phone." Minus shrugged. "Besides. I wanted a root beer float."

The next morning, Callie woke up and stretched, then reached over to her nightstand in search of her phone. She went over the things she had to achieve throughout the day as her hand fumbled and swept around, knocking the tissue box off the table. Then she sat up and looked around. She bent over and hung off the bed, looking between the nightstand and the wall to try and find her phone. Then she spent another fifteen minutes searching the house. She finally rolled her eyes and sighed and went to finish getting ready for the day. Mentally, she added an item to her checklist: running by the wireless store to buy herself a new phone.

⌘ ⌘ ⌘

Two weeks later, the crate arrived. Minus had the delivery crew drop it in the lab, then rounded the small team up. Walter and Callie arrived together, and they each stood around the palleted crate admiring the mysterious cargo. "It's big," Callie said, very simply.

"I get that a lot," Walter said.

She looked at him with emotionless eyes. And with no inflection, said, "Good one, Walter."

"It's a huge project. There's a lot more to it than just a camera. Obviously," he said, waving his hand over the crate.

On the side of the crate, below the packing slip, a pry bar was wired to the wood. Callie found it interesting that they would include a prybar on the crate itself, and ran her fingers over the cold iron. Minus watched her for a moment, and then said, "Well, let's get to it."

Walter cranked the prybar to the side and began twisting it clockwise, until the wire broke and set it free. Then he made his way around the crate prying up the lid, which was held in place with 20-penny nails. After several minutes, they all pulled and yanked until it creaked free, revealing a perfect puzzle of squares and rectangles cut into high-density foam, each with steel cases in them. They began pulling out the steel cases and setting them carefully on the steel lab table until the crate was empty, except for the thick manual.

The manual was not a standard monochrome print job. It was a full-color publication bound like a paperback book. Minus fished it out and began flipping through the pages. Walter began popping the latches on the steel cases and laying them open. Therein were the components of the Brightwalk Project, each packed in more perfectly cut foam within the cases. The components looked like high-tech mysteries to Callie, which she supposed they were, but they looked nothing like a camera. She wondered briefly if this whole excursion had been an exercise in futility.

"Wow, this looks complex," she said when all the boxes were finally open.

Walter was leaning on his knuckles on the table, and looked up at her. "What did you expect? A fuckin' Polaroid?"

She shrugged deeply and made a face. "Yeah, I guess."

"You don't have business cards made up for a point-and-shoot," Minus said, and picked up a steel faceted contraption that looked like a Chinese puzzle box made from metal. "Yeah, I guess we've got some studying to to."

"Does it work, Walter?" Callie said. Both men looked at her.

"What do you mean?" Walter said.

"You said you were working on the project. Did it run through to completion?" She stared at him for a moment, then added, "I mean, does it work. Like it's supposed to?"

"That's actually a good question," Walter said, standing up straight and scratching the back of his head. "I don't know. My part of the project was the control module. I don't think any of us low men ever got to actually see the final thing. I'm actually surprised they sent the whole thing."

"It helps when you manage an entire research and development floor," Callie said, looking at Minus with a smirk. He nodded humbly but did not say anything.

"Well, we're gonna need to pass that book around then. Minus, just let me know when you're through with it so I can take my turn. Then you can take it after me, Walter."

"Ha! Bullshit!" Walter said quickly.

"Hey, it was my idea to get you over here, tomato butt. I should get to read it before you!" she said, putting her hands on her hips.

"The language!" Minus said.

"No, I mean, I ain't reading that damn thing. It's all yours, Calculator."

"Yeah. I don't think we'd fare nearly as well with it as you would, Cal," Minus said. He tossed the book to her. It hit her flat in the chest, and she had to take a step back. It was heavy, easily three hundred pages of high-tech text and images.

"Oh. Well it's good to see you guys are interested in learning," she said, rolling her eyes and leaving the room.

She spent the next three days at home, curled up on the couch where she and Chris used to sit and watch TV together, face buried in the book, drinking mug after mug of coffee. Learning. Absorbing. Becoming a subject-matter expert on something less than a thousandth of a percent of the human population would ever know even existed – not to mention, being able to understand.

But by the end of the third day, she felt like she had a good enough understanding to start putting her hands on the pieces and making them do what she had read. She spent a day in the lab touching every button, flipping every switch and connecting every cable while cross-referencing it in the book. There was only one piece of the equipment that was left when she was done, and it wasn't covered in the manual. It had a mask like a welder's helmet, and a very dark screen that fit over one's face with a soft elastic headstrap. She stretched it over her head and looked up at the light. It was a very dim green blur in the middle of the screen. What was the point of this? She couldn't see anything through it, and there were no wires or anything that would connect it to any of the rest of the equipment. There were no buttons or circuits or switches or anything apparent on the device, and it didn't have any markings on it. Maybe, she thought, it got thrown into the crate by accident. Maybe... *The crate!*

She hurried out of the lab and down the hall to Minus's office, where he was actively participating in a phone call. He looked at her, but held up his hand and shook his head while he talked. She interrupted anyway, whispering loudly, "Where's the crate, Minus? I need the crate!"

He shook his head impatiently and finally said, "Hang on, I'm sorry, Ben, just a second. I'm being interrupted by the cleaning woman." He then put his hand over the mouth piece and said, "Can't you see I'm in the middle of something important?"

"It couldn't possibly be as important as what I'm in the middle of, Minus. Where's the crate?"

"What fucking crate?" he said, almost shouting.

"The flipping crate that the camera came in! What other crate would I possibly be..."

He cut her off. "It's down in the basement, probably in the incinerator by now. The garbage! Why?" Before she could move to answer, he said, "You know what, I don't care. Get out of my office now, please! And shut the door on the way out!"

She breezed out of the office, leaving the door standing wide open. As she stood waiting for the elevator, her stomach dropped briefly, in memory of her traumatic experience a few weeks before. She had willed herself to get back on the horse though, and had resolved not to be afraid of the technology that rarely did anything but exactly what it was supposed to. Still, it had scarred some part of her, and she doubted she would ever be completely comfortable in one again.

All six of the elevators had been completely out of service for three days following the incident, while they were inspected, repaired and tested. She had, of course, just avoided coming to the building during those days – albeit two of them were weekend days – opting out of the laborious task of walking up some hundred flights of concrete stairs. They had all been assured that everything was back online, and safer than ever. The panel dinged and shortly, the doors slid open like magic. She stepped into the car and ran her badge over the reader, pressing the B button simultaneously. She had never been into the basement of the building, and got a new tingle of apprehension in her belly when she thought of all the horrors that happened in basements in the fiction books she so adored. Basements were dark, poorly lit, scary places full of humming mystery machinery and deadly traps. Horrors lurked round every corner in the basement. Cobwebs in corners, buzzing, popping lights, dripping water and dank smells – the smell of rot and fear. She tightened her fists around the handrail and watched the floor counter dwindle down to 2, then 1, then – after a long pause – B.

The doors slid open. She took a deep breath, and stepped out into a brightly lit hallway where the floors were Linoleum and shiny, clean, waxed. The hallway was wide and clean and neat. Nothing was out of place. There were no cobwebs. No humming machinery. No scary moth-eaten robes hanging on mop sticks. It looked, she decided, like any hallway in any hospital she had ever been in. She let her breath out and relaxed. This wasn't so bad.

She followed the placards on the walls guiding her to the loading dock and trash compactor. It was a long walk, down many hallways. When she rounded the final corner, she reckoned she had walked a half-mile. There, she was faced with two steel doors that had push bars at hand level as well as foot level. Those must be for pallet jacks, she assumed.

Callie pushed open the doors and immediately felt a breeze of cold air being sucked through them. The floor in here was smooth, unpainted concrete, and marred with black marks from the wheels of dollies and forklifts. Across the wide room, she saw the huge steel door of the compactor standing open, and all along the wall, plastic rolling dumpsters full of garbage. No sign of the crate though.

She walked across the room noting the papers stuck to the floor, packing peanuts along the wall where the breeze had lined them up neatly. She reckoned this place must see a lot of traffic. She peaked into the square doorway of the compactor, but saw nothing inside that caught her attention. She sighed and spun around slowly, scratching her mind with her thoughts. Where would it be? She knew, of course, that it was possible it had already been destroyed, incinerated the day they unpacked it. But she had other hopes. Callie pushed through the double doors that led to the back loading dock, and hit pay dirt. There, at the end of the loading dock, where several men were unloading a pallet from a truck, stood a pile of wood crates and pallets. She could see her crate right at the bottom.

The men all stopped and stared at her while she stood in the doorway. They didn't look like they were used to seeing pretty business women down here on this level, and made no moves to hide their approval. One of them, the one with the bushy mustache, finally spoke up.

"Can I help you, ma'am?"

"Yes, actually, you can," Callie said, smiling as she approached them.

After twenty minutes, they had the crate uncovered and sitting apart from the rest of the pile for her. They had all piled onto the job quickly and happily, perhaps hoping for some reward beyond her polite thanks. She crept forward, peered into the crate, and bent over to fetch the leaflet that lay at the bottom, covered with a thin layer of dust. "Thank you, gentlemen," she said, and turned to make her way back upstairs.

The addendum was a three-sheet sheaf stapled together at the top corner, and it was titled, "PROJECT ADD-ON: FOCAL ATTACHMENT". Not very helpful. But, she assured herself, the text within should provide some glimpse into the mystery surrounding the welder's mask. Callie pulled a chair up to the steel lab table and put her reading glasses on, diving into the addendum. After a few minutes, it began to make sense. Apparently, the screen inside the mask would overlay what one would see (if it weren't tinted glass) with a wire-frame of what the camera itself was reading. She didn't find anything about how to connect it, though.

After spending another hour setting everything up and turning it on, she popped the mask on, hoping for something. But saw nothing. She wasn't really sure what she was looking for, either. She had shut the lights off in the lab and looked through what she considered to be the viewfinder of the camera, but still couldn't see anything. She was beginning to lose hope. Then suddenly, by accident, she turned in her chair and knocked the edge of the mask on the table. It spun on its axis and came to rest facing the puzzle-box portion of the camera contraption. And the screen lit up.

Lit up wasn't quite accurate. But it did something. She could tell that it was showing something. She put the mask back on and tightened the straps. When she turned her head, the image disappeared. It reappeared when she faced the steel box again. But it wasn't the steel box she was looking at on the screen. At least, she didn't think so. Then, by instinct, she moved the lens of the camera, which was more like a black window on the side of a steel cube, and the image in her screen changed with it. *Great!* So she had figured out how to use the mask. But it was an addendum. How did they see the images without the mask? How did they use the device before they had added the mask onto the project?

The images that appeared on the mask's screen were not what she had been hoping for, either. It wasn't a full-color rendition of the room she was using the camera in. It was all but impossible to discern anything from it at all. Useless, badly colored imagery. It wasn't even a wire-frame. It was nothing but blobs and pixels of faint red and blue crap. *What a waste.* She slipped the strap off her head and stood up, displeased and losing patience. She sighed loudly and turned the lights on, then slipped out to use the restroom.

In the women's room, she splashed cold water on her face, then leaned on the counter looking at herself in the mirror. And then the door opened, and in breezed a long-haired woman wearing a dark sweater and thick-rimmed glasses. Callie smiled at her reflection in the mirror. The woman smiled back and said hello, then disappeared into the stall. Callie ran her hands under the faucet again, trying to get more water, but it kept shutting off. *Stupid thing.* This was one technology she wondered if they would ever get right. It's supposed to sense motion and turn the water on. So how come it never works like it's supposed to? After a moment, the toilet flushed, the stall door opened, and the woman appeared at the sink next to Callie.

"I hate these stupid things!" Callie said casually.

"I know, right?" the woman agreed. "If you want to get any real water out of it, you have to defeat the system." She grabbed a paper towel and ran it under her own faucet until it was damp, then quickly folded it into a small rectangle, then reached over and smashed it up against the bottom of Callie's faucet, where it covered the motion sensor. The water instantly kicked on. And stayed on.

"Genius!" Callie said. "How'd you figure that out? I thought they sensed motion. That doesn't make sense."

"Nope. Proximity. Things are pissers though." The woman smiled and began washing her hands.

"Thank you," Callie said. "Good to know!" Then she began washing her face again. After a moment, the woman finished and dried her hands, then leaned in close to the mirror to check a spot on her lipstick. And Callie suddenly recognized her. "Hey! Aren't you Rebecca? Walter's friend?"

"I've been accused of a lot worse things, I suppose," the woman said. "Yeah, that's me. I know you?"

"Yeah! We met a couple of months ago. I dropped that girl off to meet you."

"YES! That's right!" Rebecca said, turning toward Callie at the counter. "I'm so sorry I didn't recognize you."

"No problem at all. How is she doing, by the way? What's her name again?"

"Codi. She's great. She's finally getting used to her new vision," Rebecca said, and tossed her paper towels in the trash.

"That's awesome. I always wonder how she fared, but I didn't know how to find out."

"She's here right now. You want to come see her?" Rebecca asked.

"Yeah! Certainly!" Callie said. Rebecca pointed at the paper towel wad she had placed on Callie's faucet sensor, and Callie laughed out loud. She had forgotten to remove it, and had been completely oblivious to the fact that the water had been running steadily the whole time.

She walked beside Rebecca down the hallway to the elevator, then asked her what she had been doing on this floor.

"I had a quick stand-up in the conference room down the hall. I'm up here every Wednesday," Rebecca said. "So were you here when the elevator failed a few weeks ago?" she added, a hint of mystery painting her features.

"Yeah. I was in it."

Callie visited with Codi for a few minutes, holding her hands while they talked, smiling the whole time. She had forgotten how pretty Codi was, and was sad for her that she didn't get to admire her porcelain-doll face in the mirror like so many people took for granted. But Codi was all smiles too. She was in great spirits. She thanked Callie multiple times for introducing her to Rebecca and getting her into the program, reminding Callie that without her help, she, Codi, would still be going completely blind.

Callie reminisced about the chance encounter they'd had at the restaurant and told Codi she was happy to have been able to help. It felt good to make a move that could make such great changes down the road. Then Codi looked in Rebecca's direction and said two words that made Callie frown.

"Butterfly effect."

"There ya go," Rebecca said from across the room.

Callie started nodding. "Yeah, I guess you're right. I walked over to say hi, and now you have new eyes. Wow."

"Wild ride, sister. I'll tell you that," Codi added.

After a few more minutes, Callie squeezed her hands and said her goodbyes, then thanked Rebecca for showing her in, and left.

Callie spent the next hour pacing around in circles in the lab with the tech manual for Brightwalk propped open on her hand, frustrated and perplexed. She did not want this to be a failure. She wanted it to mean something. To be useful in some way to the project. Maybe they could adapt it somehow. If nothing else, maybe they could alter the technology – borrow from it. Use some of it and dump other parts. Find a way to wire it into the existing system. She knew they wouldn't be able to use traditional lens cameras on the submersible, as the pressure would be way too great at that depth. It would be too dark anyway.

They would, therefore, be relying on infrared to get their imagery. It wasn't ideal for seeing the legendary Bloop monster. But it was all they had. Their best hope for getting at least something on some form of media that would put the mystery to rest. She shuddered at the thought of even an infrared image of a creepy monster with tentacles, hiding under the sea – large enough to be heard by microphones three *thousand* miles away. *Dear God.* She was suddenly thankful that she would not be in that submersible, and considered briefly, her safety on board the ship above. Maybe she would be better off back at base camp, in the safety of the building, waiting until they got back. Callie thought she could live with that.

Then the thought surfaced that *what if* they could get a full-color image of that beast? What would it look like? Would it be nothing more than a colossal octopus? A gigantic squid-like monster? Just how big would something have to be to make noises that could be heard that far away? And what were the sounds it was making? Was it a mating call? She shivered again. For surely, where there was one, there had to be more. It couldn't be the only one in existence, could it? If it did exist, that was. That just wasn't how evolution and animalia worked. It surely had to come from something. Something created it. It had, simply put, parents. Whether it was oviparous or live-born, it had to have been *born* somehow.

She then imagined a whole colony of monsters so big they could cause earthquakes. What would it take to live at a depth seven miles deep? Of course she was assuming that. There was no indication or evidence at all that it was at the *bottom* of the trench. Then, trailing on that thought, what if the force field wouldn't work under all that pressure? What if they only needed to go a mile or two deep? Wasn't that the depth of most of the ocean?

Well, it was better to have and not need, she thought. Besides, if the application of her project worked, it could serve so many more purposes than just hunting for mythical giants. Plus, she reminded herself, she was having a lot of fun with it. Not even mentioning the money she was making. She looked up from the page at which she had been staring blankly for the last several minutes and flipped the book closed. She sighed and put it against her hip as she stared at the mysterious equipment in front of her, chewing her lip.

So this thing might or might not be helpful in its current state. We may have to cannibalize it. It was theirs to keep, she thought. If it wasn't, she thought there would be some sort of indication that the owners would need it back. For now, she decided to proceed on the assumption that this was a prototype – one of many – that they had sent her to use at her disposal. She would need to find a way to use it, or part of it, to take pictures at great depth.

She bit her lip and sighed, then dropped the book in a chair and ran her hair back behind her ears. *Think, Callie. This is what you do.* She looked at each piece again, then picked up the Chinese puzzle box that looked completely out of place in the context of a camera setup. It was so heavy and weird looking. What could it possibly do? Well, the book called it very simply, the computer. She squinted at the angles on it, turning it this way and that in her hands, wondering why it was shaped the way it was. If it were just a computer, why not put it in a normal box? A normal rectangular container. Weird, weird, weird.

She set it back down and leaned on the table, then began to talk out loud to herself, to help herself think through the problem. "Okay, so you take the pictures," she said, touching the part that had the square glass on its side. "You're the lens of the thing. And you take the pictures and send them down through this wire," she said, tracing the wire with her unpainted fingernail. "Then the signal comes through here, where it's translated into an image." Translated. That represented language. So the computer was a language box, of sorts. Language. There was something there in that word.

Language. Like English or Greek. Or French or Italian or Spanish or Arabic or Nordic or Chinese or Taiwanese or Hawaiian. Or sign. American Sign Language. ASL. It's for the hearing impaired. Like Braille is to the blind. "The Blind!" Callie screamed, and ran out of the lab, slamming through the glass door and into the hallway where she almost ran the mailman over. She slid around the corner and up to the control panel for the elevator, where she fingered the down button several times. Then she looked up at where the indicators should be that told her which floor the cars were on. There were none. Not on this floor. That was only in the lobby. She couldn't yet hear the cables and the movement of the elevators, and looked at her watch. It was a little after one o'clock. Maybe a bunch of people were just coming back from lunch, so the elevators were busy.

She mashed the button again several more times, before finally cursing it in her own way, and running around the corner to the fire stairs. She slid down several flights of stairs, then burst through the door on the eleventh floor and around the corner into the hallway. She ran down the hallway past the elevator and made a right turn, heading for the end of the hall. She yanked open the heavy wooden door to Rebecca's office and raced over to where Codi was sitting with a mask over her eyes, her fingertips on a plate in front of her on the wall. Callie was silently thankful that Codi was even still here. It had been quite a while since Callie was in here earlier.

"Codi! I need you to come with me!" Callie said, grabbing her by the wrist.

"Callie?" she said, startled. Callie helped her up and started scooting her toward the door.

"Hey, what are you doing? You can't just come and take her away! She's in therapy!" Rebecca said, almost shouting.

"I'll bring her back, I promise!" Callie said, and kicked the door open. She was pushing Codi along while Codi objected with her hands. She wasn't saying anything, but her hands were out in front of her and she was taking stuttered steps, and Callie finally realized it must be terrifying to be in this state. She stopped quickly and took Codi by the shoulders, from the front.

"I'm sorry, Codi, I was being ignorant. Let's slow down," Callie said through her panting. Her own lungs were burning from the rushed trip she had just made down the stairs and through the hallways.

"Okay," Codi said, nodding. She was out of breath too.

The door behind them swung open and Rebecca came jogging out into the hall, shouting, "What is this about?" She came to a stop a few feet from Callie, and looked like she was ready for a fight.

Callie looked up at her calmly. "I'm sorry, Rebecca. I should have talked to you first. But I have an idea."

"Okay, I've called security," Rebecca said, and stepped up to take Codi by the arm.

"Security?" Callie said skeptically. "I'm not going to hurt her!"

Rebecca put her free hand on her hip. "Okay, fine. But when someone comes rushing into my office and basically kidnaps a sight-impaired woman with absolutely no warning or explanation, I get a little fucking ticked."

Callie nodded, her breathing finally beginning to slow. "Okay. I'm sorry."

"I suggest you either explain yourself now, and we do this the right way, or I'll have security escort you from the building," Rebecca said. Her voice was calm but stern. In its light husky flavor there was a lot of authority. Callie found herself nodding again.

"Okay, I'm sorry. I'm working on a project right now. A project that involves..." she trailed off, suddenly remembering the NDAs they had to defeat and work around just to get the camera. "Are you, uh, security qualified for Brightwalk?"

"Yes," Rebecca said, letting go of Codi's elbow and crossing her arms. The elevator dinged from around the corner, and two security guards shuffled around the corner. Rebecca looked up and held a hand out at them, stopping them in their tracks. One opened his mouth to speak but she beat him to it. "Judas, 45491, I was the one who called. Stand by a moment please. Confidential discussion."

"Yes ma'am," the man said, and they backed up a few steps, not taking their eyes off the three women in the hallway.

"Go on," Rebecca said. "I'm clear for Brightwalk. It's the infrared camera, right?" she said, but sounded more like she was just assuring Callie she knew about it, not asking. "But that doesn't mean she is," she added, indicating Codi.

Callie hadn't even thought about that. She sighed and looked at the carpet, then looked back up at Rebecca. "Look. I think she might be exactly the right person to look through the mask."

Rebecca frowned. "What mask? I don't remember any mask."

"It's an add-on. It's apparently a new part. I just had to go down to the loading dock to get..." Realizing it was not important, Callie shook her head and waved her hands. "It's a mask that has a screen in it. When you aim the screen at the computer, images appear on it. But they look infrared. They don't make sense."

"They are infrared. That's what the camera outputs. So how does Codi fit into all this?"

"That's her first language," Callie said.

Codi's posture was perfect. She sat atop a doctor's stool with absolute gorgeous posture, her hands folded in her lap and her feet crossed on the floor like a painting of proper. She was a glamorous vision of femininity and beauty personified by the perfect body below her neck. Above it, a ridiculous looking clapboard of metal and technology covered most of her face. If it didn't ruin the picture, it might well advertise the fluent dichotomy on display. *Hey! Look at the head, not the body!*

Callie had hoped for something miraculous; something akin to a eureka moment for everyone involved when she switched on the camera. She had hoped Codi would shout out something like, "Oh my gosh, it's wonderful! I can understand everything I see here!" So she was a little stunned when she flipped the power switch and watched Codi's head move back on her neck very slightly and then... then, nothing.

The tension in Callie's shoulders finally released and she let her breath out, setting the controller down. "What do you see, Codi? Anything at all?"

"Barely. I mean, it's really hard to explain," Codi said. "It's like... well, like I don't know. But it doesn't look like anything I recognize."

Callie had set the lens portion of the camera under a cardboard box, facing a small lamp. The lamp wasn't plugged in. It was just something to be identified in the dark. Assuming the camera worked correctly. And though it might well be working perfectly, Codi apparently wasn't impressed with the results. Callie had looked through the screen herself and definitely saw something. But it didn't look like a lamp. Of course, she wasn't familiar with how to translate the visual language of infrared. She felt completely let down and discouraged. But hey, it was only a thought to begin with.

"Ugggh!" she said, scrunching her hair up in her hands. "And you're facing the translator, right? Remember, you have to be aiming the screen at that."

"Yes. When I look away everything just goes dark. So I can tell it's doing something. Something, but I don't know what."

"Silly. I don't know why I thought it would be any different for you. I'm sorry, Codi. Sorry to have stormed in there over this... this... failure," Callie said, flapping her hand toward the box in general.

"It's okay, Callie. I really don't mind. I'm always open to experimenting. Especially when it comes to cool stuff like this!" Codi said.

Rebecca leaned against the wall just observing silently. She looked like she had some ideas, but was keeping them to herself. Callie looked at her for a long moment, then put the question to her.

"Any ideas, Ms. Judas?"

She chuckled at the formality, then took a step forward. "Well, not as such. I mean, she sees in digital infrared already. And apparently that's what the camera is supposed to show you. So technically, she's looking at infrared through infrared. A double-whammy of confusion." She stepped up behind Codi and ran her fingers down Codi's neck, just under the hairline. Callie flinched at the intimate gesture, but Codi didn't seem bothered by it in the least. Were they lovers?

"Maybe we need to start from scratch. You said you read the entire manual?" Rebecca said.

Callie nodded and moved closer to the ladies in the middle of the floor. "Yeah. Cover to cover. Actually probably more than once, since I had to reread so many paragraphs. A lot of it is just tech babble."

Rebecca pursed her lips and nodded thoughtfully, agreeing.

"Pretty wild small-world thing though, that you happened to know about this project."

Rebecca looked up at her and smiled, her arms now crossed. "Yeah, I guess so. It was a pretty big team that worked on it though. I would have figured Walter told you."

"You worked on it?" Callie said, eyes wide now.

"Yeah. Of course. How else would I know about it?"

"I... I don't..." Callie stammered, looking for words. "He never..."

"That's actually how we met. My girlfriend was there, too."

Callie looked at Codi, who was still sitting patiently on the stool, full lips slightly apart as she breathed, but made no other indication she was anything other than a mannequin. Rebecca caught the gesture and giggled.

"No, Callie. Codi is not my girlfriend. Much as she would like to be," Rebecca said.

Codi smiled at that. "I'm pretty happy with my boyfriend. Otherwise, sure!" she added.

"Oh. I'm sorry. I meant no..." Callie started.

"Stop. None taken. My girlfriend of many years, Natalie."

Callie's heart skipped a beat as the name fell into place. "Natalie? The Natalie?"

Rebecca pulled her head back, frowning. "Uh, what does that mean?"

"I mean... I mean," Callie said, and trailed off. Her face got suddenly serious. "What's her last name?" she asked.

"Reese. Why do you ask? Do you know her?" Rebecca asked.

"No! Not at all!" Callie said, and realized the last name didn't mean anything to her, because they hadn't known her last name to begin with. But could it be that she was referring to the mysterious Natalie that she and Walter had been silently trying to track down? The very one who had worked at PSS with Julia? The one who knew why Royal went to Mars?

Rebecca was slowly shaking her head now. "Callie, you're a darling. But you're as perplexing as a Rubik's Cube."

"I'm sorry. Okay," Callie said, now pacing and looking at the floor. She was waving her hands like she was trying to shake water off of them as she spoke. "Walter and I were looking for a woman named Natalie who used to work here. We've been wanting to ask her about... something."

Rebecca raised her chin. "Okay. Well, she definitely used to work here."

"Did she go to PSS in Houston when she left here?"

Rebecca stared at Callie for a moment, then said, simply, "Yes."

Too many things were happening in Callie's mind. But she was suddenly full of excitement again. All evidence of the failure she was facing with the camera project forgotten. It looked like she could put this mission on hold and start on her secret mission of investigating the Mars mystery. The one Brian Bradley seemed to be the center of orchestrating.

"That is fantastic! Would you mind getting me her phone number?" Callie asked. She was afraid Rebecca would start asking questions, but she didn't.

She only said, "Sure." After a moment, she added, "She's out of the country right now. She's been in Europe for a while. But I'm sure she'd answer."

Callie made fists and shook them victoriously in front of her. Then she turned and remembered Codi, sitting so patiently on the stool with the uncomfortable apparatus on her face. "Oh, Codi, I'm sorry, you can take the mask off now!" Callie helped her with the strap and took the mask, which had no physical connection to the rest of the equipment, and set it on the steel lab table.

"I'm sorry I couldn't be more helpful, Callie," Codi said, looking in her direction.

"Would you stop? You're absolutely fine. I'm sorry I wasted your time!" Callie said.

Rebecca took Codi by the elbow and began helping her up. And suddenly, Codi shouted. "Holy shit! It's a lamp!"

Walter sat backward on one of the plastic stackable chairs, arms resting on the back while Minus stood against the wall, arms crossed. Callie had excitedly gone and rounded them up, making the announcement that they had made a breakthrough with the camera. Now they were all in the lab to observe the great discovery.

When Callie had brought it up to Walter, asking if he knew anything else about it – any further details that might be helpful, he had shrugged and shaken his head. "No. Sorry, I don't. I knew very little to begin with."

"Well I just remember your saying it was supposed to take full-color pictures in the dark," she said, "so I just wanted to make sure I was using it right. Because it's just infrared."

He had shrugged again and said, "Well I guess they didn't get that far. I know what they got was something pretty serious, but I'm not completely sure what it's capable of. Maybe it's just the kickstarter. A baseline apparatus that someone can come along and build and improve upon."

"Yeah, maybe."

Now they all stood in the lab waiting patiently while Callie went through the unnecessary build up of events that finally led to their success. And Codi sat on the same doctor's stool, shaking her leg impatiently. She was so full of electricity it was almost palpable. Callie thought her excitement might cause her to blow a fuse. The shaking of the leg was causing her rather large breasts to bounce and jiggle freely under the thin fabric of her shirt. Callie had noticed Walter staring at Codi's chest, and realized then that she wasn't wearing a bra. She made a mental note to tell Codi she might want to start wearing one, at least around Walter. He made no move to hide his fascination with the moving picture, and she thought if something wasn't done, he would probably say something to Codi herself. Callie really just wanted to protect her from his nonsense.

When Callie finished explaining how they had gotten to where they were, she finally gave them the show they were waiting for. Though there was nothing for anyone to see, except for the excitement Codi wore all over her body and face. When Callie flipped the engage switch and told Codi it was live, she moved her head slowly until it came to be facing the computer. It was very obvious when it was live. Codi's entire face lit up with joy. And she was able to describe the lamp hidden under the box perfectly. Down to the last scratch on the wood.

Walter's excitement showed too, as he stood up and left the chair behind. "Wow. That's infreakincredible." He looked at Callie and then back at Codi's face, then once again back to Callie. "This is serious?"

Callie was getting the reaction she had hoped for. She was beaming. "Yep. Feel free to put something under the box for her to see."

Walter looked at the box, then back to Callie once again. "Effing wow! WOW, Callie!" he said, shaking his fists. "Do you know what this means?"

She nodded, smiling widely.

Matt Minus was now standing right behind Codi, and really beginning to take an interest. Rebecca was sitting close by Codi, on her own stacking chair, leaned forward with one arm across her knees, propping her elbow up, her chin resting on her palm. She was tapping her teeth with a fingernail, looking very satisfied.

Minus leaned forward, his hands on the back of an empty chair. "So why the hell don't we scale this thing down and just let her carry it around everywhere? I mean, if she can see like normal with it? Why aren't we selling the shit out of these?"

"Two reasons," Rebecca said, then looked at Callie. "If I may," she requested.

"Sure, go ahead," Callie said, crossing her arms.

"It only works in the dark. If you lift that box up right now, everything in her vision will go completely white."

"Ah. Yeah. I forgot that part. Even still, if blind people can see in the dark with this thing..." Minus said. Rebecca interrupted, not impolitely.

"You're forgetting though. The other valuable piece of information here is that she had cornea replacements. She has microchips in her lenses. It's the combination of technologies that allows this to happen."

Callie was nodding. When she saw Rebecca had finished speaking, she added, "Yeah, and we really have no idea why this works. There is nothing in that three-hundred-page tome about this."

"A *hey, install cornea chips first, then look at the weird silver box*?" Walter said.

"Exactly. I guess the designers didn't even know about it," Callie replied.

Minus said, "Wait. I thought you two were the designers."

"No," Walter corrected, "we were the builders. I mean, I designed the small part I took in it. But not the technology."

"And you don't think it's a fluke or something?" Minus asked. "Like it's something that might just stop working if you tilt it a certain way? Or take it outside?"

"Well, that is certainly a possibility. But so far, it seems to stick," Rebecca answered.

Minus was shaking his head, staring at Codi's eyes. "That really is incredible. Well why can't we just shut off the lights and let her see everything?"

"Remember, she only sees what the camera lens is pointed at," Callie said.

"And in turn, she has to be looking at the translator," Rebecca added, looking at Callie, as if for approval.

Callie nodded, just in case.

"Still," Walter said, holding his hands out. "Why the hell not? Can she hold the camera bit and have a little fun?"

"I don't see why not," Callie said. She looked at each of their faces in turn, then moved to grab it from under the box. Before lifting the box though, she told Walter to man the lights. He immediately stepped over to the switch and waited there for further instruction.

"Wait, honey," Rebecca said, standing up. "You can move the box. Just don't look at the translator, Codi, hon."

"Oh yeah. Duh," Callie said. Dealing with several pieces of the puzzle, she was forgetting that it made a picture when put together. She lifted the box and pulled the camera head out, snaking the cable across the floor to Codi's chair, and handed it to her. Then Callie looked at Walter and nodded. He flipped the switch and the world went dark for everyone but Codi.

She sat quietly for a moment, then said, "It's not working. I can't see anything." And then, "Oh wait. Yeah I can. Yes I can!" After a few moments of silence, she said, "I have to keep remembering to look at the one thing while I move the other thing."

She had a few minutes of fun going around the room and looking at the others' faces. In the darkness, not knowing who was being looked at and when, none of them looked at her. She saw Minus rubbing his chin and Walter staring at nothing with his arms crossed, leaning against the wall by the light switch. She stayed on him for a few minutes, admiring his arms and chest before then moving to Rebecca. She spent a fair amount of time admiring her too, for she had taken Codi in and made the most difference in her life so far. She sat with her knees together, raising and lowering them, flicking a thumbnail across her top teeth. Callie, she saw, was squatting on the floor with her chin on her hands, elbows on her knees, rocking slowly back and forth. She suddenly smiled, and Codi guessed she knew she'd be observed at some point. It was a pleasant smile, but Codi didn't say anything. After she had looked at everyone and her surroundings for a few minutes, relishing the ability to see again, she told Walter she was done, and it was okay to turn the lights back on. And she looked away from the computer.

Now they had something to add into the plan for the submersible. The obvious thought was that they should send Codi down in it, so at least someone would get to see the Bloop, were it to make an appearance where it could be seen, that was. Walter had reasoned that if she wasn't afraid to be on the ship itself, at least *someone* would get to see what it really looked like down there. For possibly the first time in history. They all agreed, but none of these discussions took place around Codi, or Rebecca for that matter. They had left shortly after the experiment. The development branch was already beginning work on dissecting the camera, copying circuit boards and schematics, cloning it. They did not want to destroy or otherwise compromise the integrity of the one they had, but wanted to copy it to the point where the images were translated. At that point, it would diverge into a different technology altogether. They were trying to make it where they could pick up that signal Codi was already receiving.

So Callie and Walter got back to the drawing board, literally, mapping out on the whiteboard what they knew and where they could see it going, for a couple of hours. Walter seemed to have gained a ton of interest now that they knew someone could use the camera. Callie refrained from asking him the true source of his excitement, worried he would say something about Codi's tits. Thankfully, thus far at least, he hadn't brought them up.

On the way back to Rebecca's office, Rebecca and Codi discussed the wild electricity that was pulsing through Codi's veins. She was trembling with excitement and the possibilities this new technology offered. When Rebecca asked her what she thought about getting Sam in here so Codi could get to see what he looked like in real-life color, Codi's face got real serious for a moment. And then she had said, "No. I don't want that advantage over him."

She sometimes fell asleep at night wondering what it was like to be born blind – having never had sight at all. The conundrum of it all was fascinating and hard to imagine. Not only did Sam have no sight in his history at all, but he didn't really truly know what sight even was. Did he? He could be told by people every day what sight was, and what it meant. But how do you describe seeing to someone who has never had that capability? It made her sad to imagine that kind of life, and wondered who was the luckier: the person who had memories of sight from sometime in his or her past, or the person who never had it. Each had its own advantages. The torture of knowing you used to have it seemed like Codi to be the less desirable of the two. But she could never know. And now she had found a way to cheat the dark.

The next week, Callie and Walter rode with Minus to the dev lab. In the moderate traffic of the day it took just over an hour. The building was in the warehouse district at the bottom of Brooklyn, right on the bay. It was a large open area warehouse with forty-foot ceilings and sixty thousand square feet of concrete covered with moving scaffolds, air compressors and toolboxes, brightly lit by hundreds of halogens from above.

As Minus coded himself into the steel door, their noses were immediately assaulted by the smell of welding – acrid smoke and hot metal. It wasn't an unpleasant smell, Callie thought, but it had a powerful way of introducing itself. It wasn't so much a handshake to the senses, as a headbutt.

Walter and Minus started emptying their pockets into trays by the door. Wallets, keys and phones were not allowed on the floor. Callie had no pockets, and had left her purse in the car. Following suit though, she removed her watch, a gift from the Oliver Company after her first year there, and dropped it in Walter's pan. They locked the pans in lockers and stamped on the dust trap before heading toward the back wall of the building. It reminded Callie a lot of the hangar at Oliver Company. All the offices were along the back wall, up off the floor, accessible by a steel staircase beside the only windows in the place. The windows were painted over and covered with steel bars. She wondered why they hadn't just been replaced with more concrete and corrugated metal. The offices were all small and rudimentary at best, connected by a steel catwalk that ran all the way across to the far wall, where it came to a dead end.

She stood still for a moment, staring up at that catwalk, calling up a picture from her memory. In it, Donnie Oliver and Mike Thurman stood on that catwalk, arms resting on the steel rail as they watched the action below, laughing, making inappropriate comments and drinking coffee out of paper cups. She smiled with the memory and once again promised herself she would bring down the man who had taken their lives away.

As they approached the project, Callie had a discomforting perspective shift, wherein she realized she was getting closer to the object a lot faster than it was growing. Typically, one expected an object's size to grow in perspective relative to the speed in which it was approached.

But this thing wasn't blending in against its surroundings like it should. She finally stopped and stared for a moment. Minus had wandered off to go talk to someone else on the project, the only man in sight wearing a suit, and Callie found herself surprised by how quiet it was in the large hangar-type building. She could hear the murmur of his voice some twenty meters away. Walter had stopped beside her and was now staring with her at the orb surrounded by scaffolding. She was frowning her typical visage of concentration.

"What's up, babe," he said.

"I don't know. I just thought it'd be bigger," she responded.

Walter chuckled and said, "That's what she... uh, never mind."

She turned toward him and slapped his chest, nearly screaming, "AHA, Walter! You almost insulted yourself, you dumb idiot moron!"

"Wow, Callie, that really hurts. You are so mean," he said, playing hurt. After a quick moment of recovery, he tried to change the subject. "Seriously. Why should it be bigger?"

She made her best Kate Hudson smirk and said, "To better pleasure her, of course."

Walter bent over, eyes wide, grabbing his knees for effect. "Oh shit! Nice one, Callie!"

She stood up straight and looked very proud for a minute, then took a deep breath and reconfigured herself. "I don't know. I just envisioned this massive thing. I don't know. I guess it doesn't really matter."

"You know," he said, "they say it often doesn't."

She rolled her eyes and started for the stairs. The scaffold around the sphere looked as though it had been built and constructed specifically for this project. It butted up against the steel of the submersible right around its equator, about nine feet off the floor. The sub itself stood on a steel stand that had pegs on it Callie assumed were for wheels or casters, in case they needed to move the whole thing easily.

The stairs led up to the back side of the submersible, whereas the entry portal was in the front. She was excited to see the inside of it, though she had no intention of becoming friendly with it. She intended to peek inside, pay her respects and be done thinking about it.

As they made their way to the portal, she ran her fingers along the cold steel admiringly. Walter followed suit. "Does it match your specs, CalStar?"

"Heck, I don't know. I thought this thing was going to be massive. A little disappointed, I gotta admit," she said, peering into the dark hole of the portal.

Walter put his hand on her shoulder and squeezed. "Ah, I think it'll get the job done, Cal. What's it look like in there?" he said, peering in beside her.

Suddenly a light went on inside the pod and someone yelled, "That better?"

They both turned to find the source of the voice. It was one of the technicians, behind and below them on ground level, holding a corded switch. Callie gave him a thumbs up. Walter looked at her for a moment, wondering if she was going to take the honors. He held his hand inside the portal and said, "After you, princess."

She pulled back quickly enough to make her back pop, looking at Walter like he had just insulted her. "Are you crazy?" she said, seriously. "No way I'm going in that fucking thing."

Walter's eyes went wide this time. "Wow, Callie. Chill out!" He put his hands on her chest, just above her breasts and lightly pushed her back a step. "If you're not, then allow me!" he said, and climbed the three steps to the portal. He swung his leg inside, staring her in the eyes, then smiled and winked.

Callie leaned back into the portal and watched him make his way around the small compartment. The grated floor was set about a foot below the equator of the sphere, making it about eight feet across, total. Beneath it were packed a series of batteries and other vague electronic components. In the middle of the floor were three chairs, all back to back in a triangle configuration. They were orange plastic buckets like one would find in an elementary school – clearly stand-ins for the final product. Callie smirked as she thought about the absurdity of the thought, then realized it wasn't absurd at all, and frowned. She backed out and turned to Minus, who was still on the floor engaged in conversation with the man in the suit.

"Hey Minus. Are these chairs the actual chairs that are staying with the unit?" she shouted down.

"Yeah, why?" he said.

"You're kidding, right?" she said.

He dropped his shoulders. "What?" Who gives a shit, you aren't riding in it!"

"You can't be effing serious, Minus. These are plastic chairs!" she said, growing concerned.

Walter said from inside the pod, "Uh, Cal, they're welded to the floor."

She whipped around to see him trying to shake one. It very clearly wasn't budging. "Did you guys forget to put chairs in this thing?" she said, approaching the rail.

"Once again," Matt Minus said, coming closer to the scaffold, spreading his hands, "why do you care?"

"Because!" she shouted. "Minus, tell me this is a stupid joke. I mean..." she started, waving her hand wildly in the air. "Because..."

"Because it's a million-dollar pod with thirty dollars'-worth of chairs in it?" he said, allowing a smile to creep onto his face.

She made a face at him. "Yeah! 'Cause you're clearly not going to fit anything else through that door now!" she said, waving her hand toward the portal behind her."

He held his hands up and shook his head. "Okay, relax, Callie. No, those aren't the final product. The chairs will be assembled inside. Stop worrying about stuff."

She stared hard at him for a long moment, and noticed the man in the suit was trying to hold back a smile. When Minus got bored of her trying to stare holes through him, he turned away. She leaned back into the portal again, seeing

Walter sitting in one of the orange chairs, feet spread wide and hands on his knees, looking up at the electronics above his head. The entire thing was a claustrophobe's nightmare, in Callie's opinion. No windows, and only three small chairs in the middle for living space. The rest of it would be crammed full of equipment and technology. Callie couldn't imagine what the purpose of half of it was. Why would they need all that extra crap? She didn't find she cared enough to ask, either. She had done her part in designing the idea behind the force field, and was almost done with that part. Once they completed the orb, then constructed the navigation cage around it, she would oversee phase testing on the mechanism, and then she would be done. She would wash her hands of Minus's monster-chasing dream and return to work at Bohr, where, she reckoned, they were probably starting to miss her.

"Well, what do you think, Dub Dub?" she said. He looked at her sharply. She had not called him by the silly name in a long time.

He breathed in deeply and returned his attention to the control panels and technological marvels above his head. "I don't know. I think it's pretty bad ass. But I think I'd be a little nervous when they started sealing that door in place."

Callie shivered. "Yeah. Eff that. My palms are sweating just thinking about it." She had to turn away and look at the bigger picture of the hangar for a moment. Her hand rested on the bottom of the portal rim though, and she began to take notice of how thin it was. The entire thickness of the seal, steel and rubber combined, was only around three inches thick. "You think this thing will hold up to pressure, Walt? It's not very thick."

He looked her in the eyes. "Okay, you're just never happy are you?"

"Huh?" she said, wide-eyed.

"You want it big... *and* thick."

Callie had made the visit to Rebecca's house without Walter or Minus. She wanted to talk to Codi alone. In private. She wasn't sure how comfortable Codi would be, being brought into an office to be surrounded by several people she really couldn't see. It may or may not be intimidating. Callie wanted her to be comfortable and in her own environment when she made the proposition.

When Rebecca let Callie in with a warm smile, Callie realized for the first time that it was Rebecca's house she was visiting. When she had asked Rebecca for the address so they could meet, Callie had naturally assumed it was Codi's own apartment she would be visiting. And she wasn't sure she knew how she knew. But she did. Maybe it was the décor. Blind people wouldn't put a bunch of fancy artwork on the walls, would they? Or was she being prejudice? The place itself was warm. Callie stood on a rich rug in the entry nook and took her wet coat off and allowed Rebecca to hang it on a hook by a large mirror on the wall. Rebecca then held her hand out low, waiting for Callie to take it. Callie felt a little awkward about it, but didn't want to offend her, so she took it and allowed Rebecca to guide her into the living room, where a fire burned in the fireplace and two standing lamps glowed very softly behind an overstuffed sofa that faced... Nothing.

Her eyes swept across the room in search of something. But the couch was only opposite a great opening that led into the kitchen. There stood an ornate coffee table in the middle of the room, upon another very expensive looking rug, and on the wall facing the fireplace, a very large Lovesac like the one Walter and Thevi had. But that was it. As Rebecca let go of her hand and approached Codi, who sat on the couch with one knee pulled up, Callie noticed what it was that was missing. A television. There was no entertainment cabinet with a large television in it. *Nice!*

Rebecca bent over to whisper something in Codi's ear, putting her hands between her knees as she leaned in close. This stretched her blouse very tight across her back, so Callie was able to see her backbone. She noticed there was something missing there as well. Though Rebecca was still dressed in what was obviously her work clothes, complete with stylish black knee-high boots, she was without a bra. Callie squinted into the dimness of that side of the living room, watching as Codi lifted her chin and turned it slightly toward Rebecca as Rebecca spoke softly in her ear, glancing back at Callie. It was very subtle, but it looked to Callie like Codi was either in love with Rebecca, or just very enamored of her. That might explain her following Rebecca's braless protocol. Rebecca always wore classy sweaters or scarves or shawls, which covered her relatively small chest. But Codi had no business going without the support.

When Rebecca finished speaking to Codi, Codi turned her head directly toward Callie and said hello. Callie smiled and moved in closer, then sat next to her on the couch, extending her hand. "Hey sweetie. How are you?"

Codi nodded. "I'm well. You look very nice, Callie," she said.

Callie looked quickly up at Rebecca, but Rebecca only stared back, almost smiling, head slightly tilted, and squeezing Codi's shoulder. What was going on here?

"Thank you, Codi. You can see me that well?"

"Oh, I've gotten a lot better at my new eyes. We keep it pretty dark in here. I can see a lot better in dim light," Codi said, and Callie realized almost with shock that Codi and Rebecca lived together. *We?* Now the intimate touch on the neck made a little more sense. They were close friends at the very least, and the possibility of lovers was still not off the table, as far as Callie was concerned. Something was definitely going on here.

"That is amazing. I'm so happy for you. I would love to see through your eyes once. I'd love to know what you're seeing," Callie said, trying to be polite.

"No you wouldn't," Rebecca said, turning away from Codi. She picked up a package of long cigarettes off the mantel and lit one with a cheap lighter. "It's fucking terrible."

Callie was taken aback by the language, as well as the insinuation that she was somehow belittling or mollifying Codi with the comment. She looked up at Rebecca again and stared at her for a time, rethinking what Rebecca had said, wondering how to take it. Callie didn't know her well enough yet to know if she was being insulted. "I'm sorry, have I said something out of line?"

Rebecca pursed her lips and shook her head slowly. "Not at all. But I promise, you don't ever want to have to see through her eyes." She took a long drag of the pencil-thin cigarette, then said, "It's fabulous technology, and she gets a second chance at sight. But count your blessings."

Callie wondered why she was defending Codi at all, when there had been no overt threat made. No insult, and no harsh comments in any form or fashion. Beyond that question though, was why was Codi *letting* Rebecca speak for her? She decided to drop it and try starting over. She straightened her back and decided to concentrate solely on Codi, which was exactly what she had thought she was doing before.

"Codi, I'm sorry you lost your sight. I meant absolutely no offense by saying I would love to see through your eyes once. I don't propose to know a single lick about the pain and suffering you've been through. I only meant it as an intellectual curiosity – that's all." Callie sat silently just looking at Codi for a moment. "I apologize if it came across that way."

Codi smiled. Her eyes were a powerful, beautiful blue, her lips thick and luscious. Callie had no trouble understanding how someone would be attracted to her – even another woman. The thought of Thevi putting her thumb in Callie's mouth – an almost-experiment in their sexuality suddenly came to mind. Callie had to shake the thought away. It did not repulse her at all, but maybe that was the problem. Codi was breathtaking. But Callie had never before found herself gazing upon another woman with any kind of sexual curiosity. Was her allure just that powerful? Or was Callie just that vulnerable? Codi's pale lips moved with voice and shook Callie back to the present.

"It's really okay, Callie. Bec here is very protective of me because I've recently been hurt. But she means no harm." She smiled toward the mantel, and gave very faintly a hint of being blind. Otherwise, Callie thought, she was hiding it pretty well. "Tame, tame, Bec! Callie's good people."

Callie glanced at Rebecca, wanting to see her reaction. "Whatever you say, sister," she said, her cigarette against her mouth. She did not look at Callie when she said it.

"So why are you here?" Codi said, smiling widely, and Callie found herself now staring at Codi's teeth. Was this girl a super model in a former life? She was perfect! A tinge of jealousy shot through Callie's stomach and she squeezed Codi's hand, which she wasn't sure how long she had been holding. *What the hell is wrong with me?* Briefly, the thought of being under a spell crossed her mind. She shook it away.

"I've come to ask you if you would like to join our project."

Codi looked back toward Rebecca; Rebecca shrugged and Codi looked back to Callie. *No wonder she defends you, you goof! You keep looking to her for all your answers!*

"What project is that, Callie?"

Callie realized they had not told Codi – or Rebecca for that matter – anything about the underwater part of the project at all. As far as these two women knew, it was something involving the use of the fabulous sight-giving camera.

Callie cleared her throat. "Well," she said lightly, "that's what I'm here to tell you!"

The mood finally settled in the room, and Callie finally started to feel more comfortable, like she wasn't having to ask Rebecca's permission to engage Codi. She understood protective nature, and someone's desire to look after a disabled friend, but it had gotten pretty tense for a moment or two, and it had only been words. Soft, rounded, sweet words at that. It wasn't like Callie had come in here trying to pick a fight with a blind girl. Maybe they were lovers after all. Maybe Rebecca was jealous of anyone trying to talk to her love. It was clear that Codi was much better looking than Rebecca, though Rebecca herself surely turned no shortage of heads, either. There was just something a little more rough about her. Something about the eyes... She always seemed to be squinting very slightly. Like Julianna Margulies. She was definitely attractive, but there was some room for a little jealousy there, Callie thought.

They talked for over an hour about the project and what it meant and the dangers involved. Rebecca had eventually even made coffee for the threesome. Callie had explained that there would be no privacy in the submersible. There would be a tiny curtain in the corner where they could do their necessaries, and the other two crew members would likely be men. She had told Codi that they could be trapped in that windowless shell for as long as twelve hours at a time. And there would likely be more than one 'time'. She had explained that, unless there was some really deep-seated interest in mythological beasts and phantom sea monsters, there would likely be no real reward in it for her. And throughout the whole process, with Callie doing almost all of the talking, Codi never said one word about her interest level in the project. She asked several questions and asked Callie to repeat a couple of points, for clarification. But she gave Callie no indication whatever whether she had any interest in it. Therefore, Callie had begun to lose hope for what she had thought was a fabulous idea – to bring on the only gal who could see in the submersible's native language.

Of *course* she wasn't qualified. Of *course* they didn't need her. It was more of an honorary thing upon which Callie had insisted to Minus, since she was in charge of design, and she had been the one to make the introductions that had eventually led to Codi getting her new eyes. It was all just such a special coincidence to Callie – that she had learned about the project and met Codi, literally within the same hour – that she felt she had to connect them. There had to be a reason it had played out like that. She had made this argument to Minus, and he had asked her why the hell Codi would deserve to be on the sub. Callie had reminded him that if she hadn't been there that day, Codi would probably be completely blind today. Minus had almost spread his hands – Callie could see the movement readying itself in his muscles – but he had abstained. He had been ready to say, "Who gives a shit?" or something similar. But he had known Callie would fly off on him for his tacky disrespect. And in the end, he had approved it. The original plan was to have two people on the submersible. But Callie had shown him effectively that the extra oxygen involved in putting a third chair in the sub was negligible. They would have to surface and recharge the batteries every ten hours or so anyway – far earlier than it would ever run low on oxygen.

So here she was, about to ask Codi if she wanted to be a part of one of the richest, but possibly most pointless endeavors in human history. Up to this point, Callie had introduced the idea in sort of a storyboard way, telling her all aspects of the project in such a way that it would gain her interest, without actually letting on that they wanted her to be a part of it – though it was probably obvious by now to Codi. And now she was out of words. All she had left was to ask if Codi was interested. So she did.

She spread her hands, hoping Codi could see well enough to take the gesture, and asked, "So, do you think you'd be interested in joining us?"

"Of course," was all Codi said.

Callie swallowed and tilted her head. "You don't need to think about it or anything? I mean, this is a pretty serious commitment. It's okay if you-"

"No. It sounds like an amazing adventure. I would be honored to be a part of it."

"Wow. Okay then," Callie said, dropping her hands into her lap. "I guess that's that, then."

They went over the rituals of bringing someone into the project. Callie told Codi she would have to come in to sign the NDAs and the releases and all the other paperwork required for such an excursion. She offered that Rebecca could come as well and assist her with the signing. Codi would now be invited to all the project meetings, and Callie would take her to see the prototype soon, so she could tell in person whether or not being sealed in a steel ball would work for her. Codi assured Callie she had no claustrophobia, to which Callie had replied by saying, "Better you than I. I won't set foot in that thing, even with the door nowhere near it."

At the end of the meeting, as Callie was slinging her purse and putting her coat on, Rebecca approached her in the hallway. Callie had already said her goodbyes to Codi, and was standing near the front door. Rebecca leaned against the wall and crossed her arms. "I was unsure about you at first, Callie. But you seem like good people."

"Well, I'm glad I passed the vetting process," Callie said.

Rebecca smirked. "I am pretty hard on people. You just have to get used to it, at least until you know me."

Callie shrugged. She didn't see why she had to get used to anything. If she didn't like Rebecca, she would just avoid her altogether. She didn't feel like she had to pass anyone's test. This wasn't a two-for-one deal. She could easily bring Codi into the project and just shut the door on Rebecca. But at this point it didn't seem necessary, and the hostilities looked like they had been confined to the first few minutes of their meeting. All seemed peaceful now. And as she was getting ready to turn the door knob, Rebecca actually leaned in and hugged her. Callie was so stunned she didn't even hug her back.

Walter took Callie's call on his Bluetooth hands-free in the car, on his way home from work. She told him the news about how quickly and surely Codi had came on board once the question had finally been posed. He shook his fist and said, "Awesome, Cal. Good work, soldier." The rain was pounding on the windshield of his Bentley Continental. He was driving unusually slow, and leaning forward in his seat, trying to get the most out of his perception for the short but timely drive home. Traffic was terrible on the highways, so he was sticking to the back roads, cutting through neighborhoods and down long alleys where trucks were likely to back out and end his trek in the most concise manner possible. And the back roads always took longer. But at least he was moving.

"Yeah, I thought she'd be a shoe-in all along. But then I got there and started telling her all about it, and she just – well, she seemed interested, but just not like chomping at the bat or anything," Callie was saying.

"Bit," Walter corrected.

Callie either didn't hear, or wasn't paying attention. Or perhaps, more likely was the thought that she was so used to hearing his quick corrections mid-sentence that she didn't feel the need to stop down and acknowledge it anymore. She misspoke a lot, and that was just going to be that. "Either love me or leave me," she had said many times. He loved her. He was her *knight and shining armor.*

"But when I finally laid the question to her, she said, 'of course!'. Just like that. No thinking, no, 'hey I'll have to think about it' or 'let me call you in a few days' or anything. Just 'of course'. Pretty cool."

"Yeah," Walter agreed. "Remind me again why we need her?"

"Walter, we've been through this a hundred times. She's-" Callie started, but Walter cut her off.

"Listen, I have to go. This shit's getting dangerous out here."

Callie sat in silence for a moment, then said, "Aren't you on hands-free?"

"Yeah, babe. But dude, I need to concentrate. Meet me at The Rim if you wanna talk."

And there they met.

⌘   ⌘   ⌘

Callie looked for the familiar Babcock Society label on the chalkboard, but didn't find it. She came to a closed curtain that had a single letter on it, though, and knew instinctively that it was him. She stared at the W for a period, then shook her head and threw back the curtain. "What the heck, poppy cock!" she said. Walter was standing in the middle of the floor with his shirt off, leaning over with his head to one side, wringing the rain out of his hair.

"What?"

"What's with the W?" she said, staring at his chest. It was covered in small drops of rain.

"What W?" he said, frowning. He caught her looking at his chest, and so returned the favor, looking down at her rain-soaked white t-shirt. She followed his gaze and suddenly whipped her hands up to cover her chest. At least she had a bra on. If she hung out with Codi and Rebecca too much though, she thought that might change. Rebecca had a powerful effect on people, Callie included.

"What? You get to look but I don't?" Walter said.

"No! That's totally different!" she said.

"Tell me how," he said. He turned his back to her to grab his wet shirt off the couch, where it hung over the arm close to the space heater.

"We are not having this conversation. You know it's different," Callie asserted.

"No," he said surely. "It's not. If a woman can look at a man's chest and have some sort of favorable reaction to it, then it's no different."

"A favorable reaction? Ha! Don't flatter yourself, Walter!" she said, but her cheeks were beginning to brighten. She dropped onto the opposite sofa and dropped her shoes off, crossing her feet underneath her.

"I'm not. You were the one who was looking."

"Whatever. You want to see my boobs, Walter?"

"Nah. It's cool," he said, slinging the shirt back over his well-muscled chest. He then dropped into the couch and picked up a tall glass of pale ale.

Callie sat staring at him, a little stunned, and perhaps a little hurt. And she wasn't doing a very good job at hiding it. She wasn't sure she would have gone through with showing him, but did see his reasoning. It did make at least some sense. And she had really enjoyed looking at his torso. If all it took to keep his shirt off while they talked was whipping her shirt up for a moment, then really, what could it harm?

Since Chris's death, she had been thinking about things a lot, and had come to think that maybe it was time to do some changing. Here she was, pushing forty, and she had still never been laid yet.

Maybe she was just doing it wrong. It being life. Maybe she should just change her ways. Maybe she had been dumb to wait. Her faith told her it was the appropriate thing to do. But then, she almost never even went to church anymore. What good was the practice of a faith if you didn't practice all parts of it? Maybe, she thought, she should just go out and find some cute younger guy to take her home and bring her into the twenty-first century. Just throw her on the bed and fulfill every fantasy he's ever had with a virgin woman. Just so she would be current. So she would know what the hell she had been missing.

And maybe sex wasn't the right, or at least the *full* right answer. Maybe waiting for sex was still the right thing to do. And there was the thought that she had waited this long, so she might as well hang on now. But maybe she didn't have to go out and get herself laid just to be part of the culture club. But maybe she should lighten up a little bit. Callie Simmons still felt guilty when the occasional S-word slipped from her pretty lips. Maybe she should hip up a little and have a little more fun. Not be such a prude. Maybe that would get her a little more attention. And heck, maybe even a little more respect! Maybe people would take her a little more seriously!

She considered that and then considered what Walter had just said. Clearly he was playing right back at her little game, because through all the years she had known him, she had never been loose enough to show him her breasts. And the fact that this was apparently a landmark in a female-male relationship was ridiculous. But it seemed to be a thing. A real thing. And Walter, of all people, was someone she could trust. If there was anyone she could – and did – trust in the world, it would be him. So why not reward him a little, occasionally? Maybe not everyone, but why not him? He had gotten so used to her purity that he had even given up asking for it, or – in this case – saying things like, 'of course I want to see them!' Because he knew she would never really show him.

Well, screw it, she thought. She was going to change. She was going to become more interesting. And she would start with Walter. He deserved it. He had never taken advantage of her. Never touched her when he thought he could get away with it – and she knew there were probably many times that he could have. He had never chastised her for keeping her chastity and class. The least she could do was flash the poor guy. He definitely deserved it, if anyone did.

Callie reached back and unfastened her bra, then pulled it off through the arm holes of her t-shirt.

"Callie, what are you doing?" Walter said, looking closely at her.

"I'm gonna show you my tits. I think you've waited long enough," Callie responded, and grabbed the bottom of her t-shirt. She started pulling it up, and he was off the couch like a firecracker. Before she could uncover the pale flesh of her belly, he was there, in her face, hands on her chest, holding her back. His hands, she realized dejectedly, were on her chest by accident. Not in a sexual or grabby way at all. Not to touch her breasts, but rather, to keep her from going through with what she had been about to do.

"Callie, no. Stop," he said. He did not try to reposition his hands, but it was so non-sexual that it wasn't an issue. His palms were flat against the shirt across the tops of her breasts, not moving, not exploring, not closing over them. And she stared up into his eyes, brown eyes meeting blue, a look of curiosity and wonder in her visage. She wondered if he was going to kiss her. And maybe she would let him do that as well.

"Stop, hon. Seriously. You don't have to do this," he said.

She resisted a little, and started trying to raise her shirt again. "I know I don't, sweetie," she said, looking straight into his eyes. She was feeling the sexuality now. "I just want to. It's okay," she assured.

"No, Callie, it's not." While keeping his hands on her, he rounded to the side and sat backward on the couch, right beside her, and facing her. "Callie, you are special. And what we have is special. You are a very cool, very, very cool girl. And you are classy!" he said, squinting while he spoke. "That's my favorite thing about you. Don't ruin that just because you think I need to see you topless."

She just stared at him. Was he serious? All these years and he really *didn't* want to see them? Did he truly have no interest in her at all? She had to admit that she had scarcely ever considered him in that light either, at least until she had seen him in the pool in Mexico. That seemed to have changed everything. Had she been wrong all along? There really was no sexual tension from his side? Or had she ground it into the dirt with the heel of her prudishness? Had she killed his spirit? Turned him completely off of her? The one man in the world who should definitely think she was attractive, now come to find out – didn't? So no one did? A tear pooled up in the corner of her eye. And Walter finally took his hands off her chest.

"Callie, we're not that shallow, baby," he said. He wiped the tear from her eye, then leaned in and kissed her on the tip of her nose. She had moved her chin up slightly, hoping to be kissed like a woman. But he had been the ever-gentleman. Rejected by the last hope of sexuality in her life, she now sat here looking like a fool, shedding tears in front of a man who had no interest in even seeing her naked. There was no commitment in that, she thought. It would change nothing for him. He didn't have to touch or judge or comment or think about it. It would be a completely free show for him. And he wasn't even interested in that.

He smiled very slightly at her. "What's going through that pretty head of yours, Cal?" he said.

Her breath stumbled and caught, and suddenly she was holding back – choking back tears. He put his hand on her shoulder and stroked her collarbone with his thumb. "What is it?"

Callie breathed in deeply and rolled her eyes, trying to look cool. Trying one last-ditch effort to maintain some sense of her dignity. She looked up at the ceiling and ran her hair back behind her ears with one hand, the other still resting on her stomach. Her bare stomach. The shirt was bunched up above her wrist, still waiting to be put back where it apparently belonged.

He put his powerful hand on her jaw and gently turned her head to face him again. He then slid his thumb across her face and across her puffy lips. She closed them, trying not to embarrass herself any further. "What's wrong, sweet face. Tell me," he said. Walter didn't sound like he was asking. He was saying it. "What's wrong."

"No one wants me!" she cried. He pulled her face down to his chest and wrapped his arms around her while she cried. She buried her face against his t-shirt and bawled, hands trying to quell the terrible sound of her choking and tears, but he just sat silently, rocking back and forth and holding her tightly. He reached back behind him to the trunk that stood at the end of the couch, and grabbed a thick blanket. This he whipped over her and pulled it up to her chin, then rewrapped her with his arms.

It was a long, long time before he finally spoke. And all he said was, "Oh yes they do, Callie. They all do." She had no idea what that was supposed to mean, but somewhere deep down inside, in a place she wasn't even sure she had access to, she felt some tiny stirring of hope.

⌘   ⌘   ⌘

When Walter got home, he tossed his keys on the counter and whipped his shirt off as he rounded the corner into the bedroom, where Thevi waited under the comforter, face buried in a book. She looked up at him and smiled as he came into the room, and removed her glasses so she could see him better. It was instantly evident that something was going on, because she frowned and put the book down, then sat up, letting the thick cover fall away from her chest.

"It's Callie."

"Yeah? Did you have a beer with her?" Thevi asked.

"No. Well, yeah, I mean, no, I had a beer. She didn't," he said. He sat on the corner of the bed and absently grabbed her foot.

"What's wrong now? Chris again?" she asked, tilting her head to him.

Walter was shaking his head. "I don't know. Yeah, I mean, I think so." Then he looked at her. "Thev, she tried to show me her tits."

"Huh?" she said, more perplexed than surprised. "What do you mean, 'tried'? Haven't you already seen them?"

"Ha, no. I've told you, babe. All we've ever been is absolutely straight platonic."

She sat up straight and took his hand on the covers, and said, "I'm not mad, honey. I just figured that by now you would have seen her naked just due to natural circumstances."

He shook his head. "She feels like no one wants her. I know she's super-depressed about Chris but she's been hiding it so well, you'd never even know. And I think it's weighing on her. She's finally cracking under the pressure."

"So why was she trying to show you her boobs?"

He shrugged. "I don't know. I think like just like you said, since I've never seen them, she was trying to change that. She wanted to feel like someone wanted her."

"And you didn't look?" she said, shaking her head, looking skeptical. Walter looked at her seriously. "I mean, that seems like the least you could have done!"

"What the fuck?" he said, standing up. "I can't believe I'm hearing this. My wife is chiding me for not looking at another woman's tits."

"No, not at all. But under the circumstances, it seems like it might have made her feel better about herself."

Walter coughed. "Dude. Babe, if she's reached a point where she needs to show her naked chest to someone to feel okay about herself," he said, spreading his hands palm-down, "then she needs more help than someone just looking."

"Yeah, you're right," Thevi said, pulling her hair up on top of her head, and turning toward the nightstand to retrieve her tall insulated cup of ice water. "You're right. So what should we do?" she said after she had taken a drink.

"I don't know," Walter said, pacing and scratching the back of his head. "But this is fucked up. I feel really bad for her."

"Well, yeah, me too," Thevi agreed. She sat staring at her pacing husband, red hair disheveled and falling in her face, but making no move to set it straight. "And she hooked us up together. Maybe we should return the favor."

Walter turned on her sharply. "What does that mean?"

"Nothing, hotshot. It means we introduce her to someone. I have some single guy friends who are cute."

Walter sighed and stopped moving. "Are you sure that's what she needs? Don't you think we should wait until she gets over Chris? I mean, isn't it a little quick to be playing cupid?"

"No, Walt. We're not talking about an arranged marriage. Just a date here and there. She needs to get out a little! See what's out there! She needs to see that people do want to be around her. Most of all, she needs to feel wanted."

Walter found himself nodding. "Yeah. Okay. I can see that. Maybe some double-dates?"

"Yeah! That kind of thing." Thevi sat there for a moment, frowning. "Who's the guy you have beers with sometimes? The one who sold you the Dodge?"

Walter hiked his chin and grinned. Then he shrugged. "Yeah, I mean, I see your point. But it just feels weird hooking her up. She's always seemed so robotic to me. Like she doesn't need sex."

Thevi lowered her gaze at him. "Or companionship?"

He nodded and sighed. "I know, I know. She's human. I just don't look at her that way."

"Did you hear what you just said?" Thevi asked, smiling.

"Sexually. I don't look at her sexually." Walter stood staring at the ground for a minute, hands on his hips. He went into the bathroom to brush his teeth, then returned and she was back under the covers. He looked at her over the top of the book for a moment, then got undressed.

"What?" she said, dropping the book momentarily.

"I would like to see *someone's* tits tonight," he said.

She took her glasses off again and tossed the book on the nightstand. "You can do more than see them, baby."

CHAPTER 22

"O kay, we've come a long way," Minus said. He stood in front of the white board in the conference room, a marker held between his hands. They were all gathered at the tables, watching expectantly, with excitement and fervor. Everyone from the design team to the physicists to the actual manufacturers of the orb were all present at the meeting. All told there were nearly twenty-five people in the room. "We've been approved by the guys in the white suits."

Everyone applauded. There were a few shouts in the room. Callie looked around at the other faces in the room, smiling broadly. Everyone already knew they had been approved for phase testing. That meant that the prototype in the hangar had now become the beta product. And that meant she could begin testing with the real thing. And once that was complete, they were a go for the dive.

"So Callie and her team will start their testing next week. We're looking at three weeks for testing, then another three weeks for any changes and upgrades. Beyond that, we start packing for the big trip," Minus said. He was smiling wildly, too. Callie knew how excited he got when they were this near the end of one of his projects. He was beginning to show it.

"Not sure if everyone's met Codi, Codi raise your hand," Minus said, completely unnecessarily. Everyone in the room looked directly at her before her small hand shot up in the air. "We've brought her on for a very important but oft overlooked part of the project. She's going to sit in the submersible and record her feelings."

Everyone had a good laugh at that even though there was quite a bit of truth to it. "No, seriously, she'll be manning the collection magnets and traps, observing, and recording. The journaling of such an historic event as this is very important to me. She used to write for a newspaper, so she's probably a better writer than all of us. And she will be the only one of us who actually gets to see this thing, if we see it at all, with her own eyes. I have asked her to sketch, draw and write everything that comes to mind about the experience. If she wants an interview, give it to her. This will be a publishable document when we finish this thing up. She's in charge of all that. Come to her with any press you find about us, any ideas and any thoughts you think might add to a coffee table book. This shit's gonna get big." He stared at their faces for a few seconds and then added, "Anyone who has any qualms with her being on the submersible needs to come see me. Is that clear?" Everyone nodded.

Callie looked at Codi and squeezed her hand. Codi glanced at her and smiled with excitement, shrinking down into her shoulders. She could hardly contain herself, and that made Callie happy. At the same time, Callie tried to avoid thinking about what Codi would actually be going through down there. Every time Callie thought about being trapped in that death coffin several miles beneath the cold water, she got shivers down her spine, and sweaty palms. She did not envy Codi her position on the sub, and had a pretty good idea that not many other people in here did, either. But there were always likely to be those who disagreed with the decision made on who gets to go along. Codi went back to staring at the white board. She was squinting at something. Callie glanced over and saw the rectangle with the override number in it, written like a conviction in terrible purple ink. She looked back at Codi, who took a deep breath, readjusted in her seat and turned her attention to the floor in front of her. She was fun to watch, Callie decided. Just trying to figure out what was going through her pretty head was an interesting puzzle. Callie reckoned it could keep someone busy for quite a while.

"We've also brought in Jack Carpenter, a contractor, to man the vessel. With six years piloting subs in the Navy, he has spent more time under the ocean than ninety-nine percent of the population. Jack?" Minus said, extending his hand.

Jack stood up and waved. Everyone clapped again. Callie glanced at him, then did a double-take. She looked him up and down real good, then returned her attention to Codi. "He's cute!" she whispered. Codi smiled again.

"Okay, so does anyone have any questions?" Minus said. After he answered a few, mainly to the scientists, who took avid notes of everything he said in response, he clapped his hands together. "All right then. I guess it's time for everyone's favorite part of the meeting! Drinks!"

"Wait! Mr. Minus?" a small voice said from the middle of the room. It was Suzanne, the project bookkeeper. "The jackets?"

"Oh, shit! Yeah, thank you Suze," Minus said, and waved a hand at a couple of men who sat at the edge of the group by a large cardboard box. "Everyone get your mission jackets!"

They all applauded again and made their way to a line that generally led toward the box, where the two men handed out leather jackets that had the participants' names on them. Codi looked at Callie. "Jackets?"

Callie squeezed her shoulder. "You weren't here when they fitted us for them, but yeah, we all get leather coats with the mission badge on them. They're very nice. Come on, we'll get you hooked up."

"You think they have one for me?" Codi said, very skeptical.

"Of course! You have one of the most important parts on the mission, goof ball."

The jackets were brown Egyptian leather, soft and luxurious, the kind of leather that you could mark with your fingernail, and they smelled like heaven to Callie. Each of them had a circular patch on the breast that read OPERATION: MONSTER HUNT and the year. In the center was a squid-looking beast in gold relief. Everyone had a good laugh at the light-hearted, yet take-serious approach of a five-hundred-dollar jacket with a cartoon patch. But there was no talk from anyone about removing it. No one in the world had these patches. They were real. Funny, sure, but real they were.

Throughout the testing, which was done twenty miles off the coast of Galveston in the Gulf of Mexico, the team would be living in a hotel. The company had rented out most of the rooms on the ninth floor of the Hilton Galveston for all the members of the team. Callie and Walter got adjoining rooms on the east side with a fabulous view of the ocean. Callie had come to Walter's house on the morning of the departure, to have breakfast and coffee with Walter and Thevi before taking an Uber out to the airport with three gigantic suitcases in the trunk. Two of them were hers. Walter was a habitually light packer, opting instead for buying whatever he needed when he got there, and shipping it home.

Most of the morning and well into the afternoon was spent unloading and unpacking the submersible, down at the bay. When Callie and Walter arrived, they had the shell around the sub removed, and it sat on its steel pallet. A crane stood silently, hook hanging directly over the pallet's lift ring. The entire apparatus would be loaded onto a ship where it would stand right against the port side of the prow. The ship they had commissioned for the task itself had a crane built into the prow, so it could lower the submersible into the ocean, as well as retrieve it.

The hustle and bustle of the workers was interesting to Callie, who stood on the pier with a steaming paper cup of coffee with an orange and pink double-D on it. The weather was far different down here on the Texas bay than the bay in Neptune City, and she realized as soon as they stepped off the plane that she had over-packed. Most of her second suitcase was full of sweatshirts, hoodies and even an extra coat. Now she had on a light wool jacket and gloves with the fingertips cut out. A black cossack covered her crown and most of her ears, and her short blond hair poked out the bottom. Walter stood beside her, hands in the pockets of his mission jacket, watching the ships come into the Galveston Channel from the west.

Men in hard hats were in thick abundance around the scene, preparing the submersible for its trek to the ship. Callie looked at Walter. "You know, I thought it was small before. Look how freakin' big it looks now."

"Yeah, sorry, Cal, but I never followed that logic."

She shrugged. "You excited?"

"Hell yes I am. I'm just ready to get to the real mission," he replied, taking a sip of his coffee.

"Patience, young gunslinger," Callie said, patting him on the chest. She was smiling pleasantly at him, looking like she was about to tell him something nice.

He turned to look at her and shook his head. "Patience? Fuck patience. The entirety of my career has been nothing but a prelude," he said, holding his hands out in front of him, much like he were holding an invisible volleyball, "to this. This right here." He shook his hands. "Everything has led up to this. I've waited my whole life for this shit."

She was still smiling, head tilted, mouth closed, eyes halfway there. "Walter, do you remember how you came to work for Royal?"

He held his hands in the air for a moment, staring at them, before finally dropping them to his sides and looking at her again, perhaps a little disappointed with the subject change. "Of course. What, you don't?"

She made a duck face and frowned. "Of course I do. I'm just wondering if you do."

He shrugged then straightened up. He reached out and grabbed a passerby's jacket sleeve. "Hey, buddy. Sorry to bother you, man. You got an extra one of them?" Walter said, pointing at the stranger's cigarette.

"Sure," the man said, a little perturbed. He pulled a cigarette out of his pack and handed it to Walter. "I suppose you need a light too?"

"Of course. I don't smoke. Why would I have a lighter?" Walter replied. The man lit his smoke then Walter thanked him and let him go on his way.

Callie was shaking her head. "You take cigarettes from strangers?"

"Yeah. Sure beats the shit outta buying 'em," he said, looking at the glowing end intently. He finally looked up at her and took a deep breath. "I was twenty-six. Right out of college. I was standing on the pier with a fifty-five Plymouth between my legs. I had my hands on Cindy Holloway's thighs and my mouth was about an inch from hers. She was sitting on the hood," Walter said, reflecting. His eyes were gone now, lost in the unfocused recollection of the world of long ago. Callie crossed her arms and looked at him like a starstruck little sister.

"We were there watching the sun set. But I think we had forgotten about the sun entirely at that point." He took another pull from his new cigarette. "And I hear this car pull into the parking lot behind us. I turn to look back at it, but see nothing exciting. So I turn back to Cindy. And her nose is right on mine, but her eyes are looking over my shoulder. And next thing I know I hear the footsteps stop behind me. Her eyes get real wide and this guy behind me says, 'Excuse me, partner.' Can you believe that shit? I'm making out with the hottest chick in Santa Monica and this dipshit sneaks up behind me and calls me partner."

Callie laughed out loud. "Yeah, who talks like that?" she said through giggles.

He took another drag of the smoke and blew it out the side of his mouth. "That was it, really. He said he was sent to talk to me about a job. That was that."

"What?" she said, incredulously. "Why the heck did he come find you on Santa Monica Pier?"

He shrugged again. "You know how important they think their shit is. Obviously I was so good they couldn't wait to catch me on a Monday morning." He finished his cigarette and dropped it on the asphalt, scuffed it out with his boot toe. "Why? How'd they get to you?"

She looked off into the distance at the freighters coming into the harbor and stuffed her hands in her pockets, blew a lock of hair out of her eyes. "Minus," she said. "He walked up to me while I was on a payphone in the dorm hallway at ASU."

"What the fuck? Isn't that a girl's dorm?" Walter said.

"Seriously? Guys come in there all the time," she said, frowning. "He came in while I was talking to a girlfriend from back home on the phone. Holds up this piece of chalk."

"Chalk?" he said, pushing his head forward as if to hear better.

"Yeah. Chalk. A fat chunk of chalk. See," she said, scuffing her toe on the ground, staring at her shoe. "I had a sponsor all through college. Sort of a mentor, really. Harlan Mayor."

"Is that name supposed to mean something to me?" Walter said. He leaned his bottom against the waist-high pole of the car lot fence.

"No. He, I guess had been meeting with Minus for weeks. Feeding him information about my GPA, work ethic, all that other horse shoot." That got a big sigh out of Walter, but he kept quiet vocally. "So I guess he told him about this story from my childhood. So he brought a big piece of chalk in, thinking it would get my attention."

"Well, did it?" Walter said, grabbing her by her shoulders. She looked up at him."

"Heck yes it did. I told my girlfriend I had to go. I hung up almost instantly," she said. She sat staring hard at him for a minute, like she was trying to find the answer to a complex equation on his face. "Why do they do that?"

"What? Bring chalk into dorm buildings?" Walter said. She hit him on the shoulder with an open hand. He stared at the spot on his arm, frowning, before returning his gaze to her.

"No, dork. Why do they come at us like that?" she asked.

"To make it more personal," said Minus. Callie and Walter both turned in the direction of the new voice.

"See? That's exactly what I'm talking about. Do you guys just sit there listening to people's conversations, waiting for an in?" Callie said.

"Sure. Look, we're getting ready to launch. Are you guys coming, or what?" Minus said.

"What?" Callie said, looking out into the bay at the ship. "Right here? It's only a few feet deep here, isn't it?"

"I'm sure he means launch the boat, Callie. Not the sub," Walter said.

"Oh." She looked back at Walter, then Minus. "Oh yeah. Yeah, okay. We're ready."

As they boarded the boat and eventually headed for deeper waters, Callie and Walter leaned over the aft rail watching the sun set over the continent behind them. The Galveston skyline burned orange beneath thick gray clouds that hung like smoke high in the sky. The last of the city's heat caused the lights in the buildings to blink like distant stars. From this distance, there were no bad guys. No car wrecks. Nothing but faraway beauty. Distant music blared from somewhere in the direction of land. It was all very romantic to Callie, who had not spent much time in large bodies of water.

"I want to hear about this chalk," Walter said above the gurgling churning of the motor.

Callie turned and leaned back against the rail, wrists dangling, foot propped up on the foot rail. "It's not that interesting, Dub Dub," she said.

"Bullshit. Harlan thought it was interesting enough to slip it to Minus. Minus thought it was interesting enough to approach you about a job with a piece of chalk in his hand."

She rolled her eyes and swallowed. "Okay, well it's not that interesting to me, I guess. When I was younger, maybe twelve or thirteen, a bunch of my friends went wandering under the city in the sewer drains. Well, my friend Rachael, or at least at the time I thought she was my friend, talked me into going in there with them. Said they had found a cigarette and were going to smoke it or something."

"And you give me shit for smoking?" Walter interrupted.

"Walter, really? I was thirteen."

"Oh, shit. Yeah. Sorry. It's so much better for you at thirteen. Carry on," he said.

She slapped him on the shoulder and rolled her eyes before continuing. "So we all went under there to check it out. But I had a piece of chalk in my pocket. So I'm following Rachael through these never-ending tunnels. There's light occasionally from the storm drains, but pretty soon I was lost. Well, I would have been if I would have had to navigate out by myself. But every time we made a turn, I marked on the wall with that piece of chalk. Nothing big or anything, just a subtle little mark."

"Did you try to hide it from Rachael?" Walter asked, seriously.

Callie shrugged. "Yeah, I think so. But it might even have been subconscious distrust or something. I had a hard time trusting anyone at that age," Callie said, making wide eyes. "So I think maybe I was preparing for being left or something, and yeah, that deeper part of me probably wanted to be the only one who could find her way out if something happened. So I could get out and leave them trapped."

She stood silent for a moment, watching the sun disappear behind the buildings in the west, pensive. Walter leaned back with her against the rail, clasping his hands together and leaning on an elbow. "Is that what ended up happening?" he asked. She looked at him directly, but ignored the question.

"So I followed Rachael deeper and deeper into these tunnels until I finally started getting a little worried. I mean, we had probably gone like a mile or something. Well, we finally came to this room where there were like seven other tunnels going off of it. And everyone was in there. They were all smiling." Callie took a deep breath, then held it. She stopped talking for a long while. Walter stood patiently, allowing her the space. A tear formed in her eye. She wiped it away finally, then said very softly, "Needless to say, it didn't turn out the way I had hoped. They started throwing rocks and mud at me. And when they started chasing me, I led them down the wrong set of tunnels until I finally came back down the right one and found my marks. I lost them pretty quickly, and made it out."

Walter nodded soberly, still clasping his hands together. He still didn't speak.

"I saved that piece of chalk a long time. It seemed like my savior for many years afterwards. I put it on a shelf. I just about idolized it." She sighed and took another deep breath, wiped another tear away. "Harlan came into my dorm room when I was in college and picked it up. Asked the significance of it." Callie shrugged. "So that's how Minus came to know about it."

Walter nodded again. "So what happened to the other girls? Did they fuck with you after that?"

"I'd rather not talk about it, Walt," she said.

"Okay. You okay, Callie?" he asked, and gingerly pushed a bit of hair up behind her ear.

She looked at him with glassy eyes, and nodded quickly. "Yeah. Maybe someday I'll be able to talk about all my demons. But for now, I'm stuck."

"I hope you don't believe that, Callie. I know you better than any human being on the planet. I hope you know that's not true. That you can talk to me about anything," Walter said. He had his hand on her cheek, slowly running his thumb across her jawline.

She stared at him for a long time. "I know, Walt. Thank you."

After a long moment of silence from his side, he finally shook his head and said, "I can't believe you've never told me about the chalk. I thought I knew everything about you."

She blew air out and rolled her eyes. "There's a bunch you don't know, babe." She put her hand on his chest and pushed away from the bars. "A whole ton of stuff I've got locked up in here," she said, tapping her head with a short fingernail. "Stuff I just can't air out. Maybe someday you'll be the guy I break down and tell."

The first time they dropped the submersible in at any kind of depth, it was only a hundred feet, well within reach of the cable. And two divers were down there with it, watching. Recording. They had cameras attached to their masks. They made shorthand notes on slates and circled the submersible, observing the way the force field reacted with the water around it, the magnetic interference it produced, temperature, and a whole host of other things. The propulsion cage seemed to have no issue controlling the direction as well as the attitude of the orb. The pilot was able to make it do exactly what he wanted it to do, within centimeters of tolerance.

They had built small pockets into the orb all around its equator. They were round cutouts a couple of inches deep that were covered in thick glass. Beneath the glass were cameras. In all, there were eight of them around the unit.

These recorded anything they could see in the visual spectrum, when the lights were illuminating anything interesting. And evenly spaced around the orb within these cameras there were three of the special full-dark cameras. These were covered with the same black glass that made the lens on the prototype camera. All of the cameras fed into a computer in the core of the submersible that had enough space to store about twenty-five hours of video total from all the cameras, as well as the other monitoring equipment like depth, temperature, barometric pressure, and so on. This computer was much like a flight data recorder on an airplane. Every single movement and control change was recorded. In this way, if anything went wrong, they would be able to tell what had been going on when it happened, and therefore, probably why.

It went smoothly. The divers learned that there was a slight difference in what their dive computers read as opposed to what the computer on the sub was reading. But other than that, it was almost a perfect dive. There seemed to be no problems with it at all.

Codi was in the Charlie seat, mostly silent for the test dive. She had no real mission here but to make sure she could look at each of the three translators, all in front of her seat on the wall, and see what the cameras were picking up. Since the infrared cameras were spaced equidistantly, two of them were behind her. But that didn't matter, as she only had to twist her head slightly to change views. And with a 120-degree vision field on each, she could see every direction around the equator of the submersible. The only directions not covered were the up and down.

She was comfortable in her seat, though she felt a little nervous when the portal had first closed. When that seal had been made, she felt an eerie butterfly tribe set to flight in her stomach. It left after about a half-hour though, and she refused to say anything about it. Richard Baltey was in the Alpha seat, and Jack Carpenter was in Bravo. They were good company. Jack was the quiet type, but polite. Richard almost wouldn't shut up. That comforted Codi. To have someone talking almost non-stop, excited about everything he saw, took her mind off a lot of the potential worries, like what if they lose control and sink to the bottom of the ocean, for instance. In a ridiculous scenario like that, there would be no way out. There simply wasn't enough strength between the three of them to push the door off against the pressure of all that water. All those atmospheres put literal tons of pounds per square inch against any hope of escape.

Jack, having done a stint in the Navy, was full of reassurance that they would be okay. So long as they didn't sink to the bottom of the ocean. Codi at first had a hard time reading him, then finally determined that he probably wasn't exercising a weak sense of humor. He was probably as serious as the situation. He was endlessly nurturing to Codi though, very attentive to her disability. Part of her wondered if he had ulterior motives, but she overlooked it if for no other reason than to shut down that cynical side of herself. And she needed the assistance. But she did find comfort within the relatively small cabin of the spherical sub. There was not much to see in the spot of ocean they had chosen for the phase testing, but she was able to see that the cameras were definitely operating correctly. She saw fish and the occasional turtle and octopus, but nothing spectacular. Everything, it seemed, was giving the freakish orb a wide berth.

The magical force field she had heard so much about was completely invisible. But according to the two men in the cabin, it worked when it was on. It acted like a buffer that literally kept the orb safe from anything that might get too close. They turned in on only briefly, and only a couple of times due to its power drain. But on one of those times a large fish had been too close and they heard the loud pop as it set off the defenses. On the outside, the shield crackled and arced and shimmered. But they could not see any of that from the inside.

Day after day, the crew awoke before the sun showed itself and made their way down to the pier to load up for another long day of testing. The ground crew would make minor adjustments, sometimes calling the sub back to the surface several times just to tweak and adjust settings. It was tedious, and after the third day, really started to be a drag. Codi was bored to tears and was beat down by the whole thing, mostly because she didn't really feel much need to be on the sub now that she had fulfilled her obligations in testing the cameras.

After the fifth day, she was finally relieved. They admitted there was no further need for her to be on the sub if she didn't want to be, and actually even allowed some others to go down in her chair just to experience it. One of the scientists took a turn in the seat, but had to return to the surface after only fifteen minutes due to severe panic and claustrophobia. She would never say so, but secretly, this made Codi feel superior. The fact that she, a disabled girl could do something a fully able science-minded man could not do made her feel on top of the world.

The testing continued for another week, then ended on the thirteenth day, when the project lead determined they were good to go. All the tests that could be done outside of the water had been done in the previous months, and so the water tests were wrapped up quickly. On the evening they finished the testing, the entire group had dinner at Pablo's Italian, taking up the entire party room. Most of the group also attended the after-party, which was down the road at the Chandelier – an industrial dance club with a big floor and two hundred feet-worth of bar. And that is where Callie finally put her new self into action.

realignment

The Chandelier was an industrial-style warehouse with concrete floor and visible ducts and pipes in the ceiling. There were no televisions or karaoke bands, just a small raised stage at one end of the dance floor, upon which stood a DJ's booth with turntables and a mixing board. The bar literally wrapped around the opposing side of the dance floor, two hundred feet long, and was crowded with bartenders on one side, patrons on the other. Callie guessed there were twenty bartenders back there, none of them idle.

Then, of course, there was a chandelier in the middle. It clashed badly with the industrialized ambiance of the place, but somehow was attractive at the same time. It was giant –

maybe eight feet across, and hung low enough that one could touch it if one were to jump up with a hand raised. It was beautiful, covered with hanging crystals and lit from within by glowing candle-like flickers of light. These lights would change color on command from the DJ, and would sometimes pulse and flicker with the beat of the music.

Callie had allowed herself to be talked into drinking beer with Walter instead of her typical vodka-based cocktail, and was beginning to feel the effects of the alcohol. The ease in which the beer went down had a lot to do, she thought, with the fact that she was drinking it in thirst as well as pleasure. And before she stopped to think about it, she had already had quite a good bit of it in a relatively short amount of time. This was also perhaps why she pulled Codi out of her seat and dragged her to the dance floor. She did not, however, have to pull very hard.

Friday nights at the tavern were ladies' nights, and it began to fill up quickly. Callie called Walter to the floor, and he came obediently, but only stood rocking back and forth and holding his beer. It was good enough for Callie though, to see him participating. He kept tilting his head toward Jack, who was watching from the table with hard-to-hide interest. And perhaps a little jealousy.

After they had danced for a few songs, Callie thought she might be ready to sit down for a while and take a breather, but she saw that Codi showed no signs at all of slowing down. Callie herself stared at Codi for a moment – Codi, who was off in her own world, dancing with reckless abandon. She was leaning her head back, squatting and snapping, flowing like wine, merging and meshing with the single and singular guys and gals on the dance floor like she belonged. Callie found a twinge of jealousy in her throat as she watched that perfect body sway and wave and twist like a physical representation of music. It was absolutely beautiful. She looked like a professional dancer. How could a man *not* be looking at her?

The music was loud. It was this year's version of what electronic dance should be. A lot of female operatic endeavors laid down upon transient beats and heavy bass lines. Sonically, it was very attractive to Callie, and she had no trouble understanding the allure of the floor in a place like this on a Friday night. Loud passion filled every cubic inch of the night, blasting from the heavy speakers hanging above them and all around. The beer was the right temperature. The air was hot. The lights that danced around ignited motes of dust and beads of sweat flung from whipped hair and writhing bodies. Callie felt like a million dollars.

She kept looking back at Jack though, and wondering why he wasn't dancing. Obviously, he had the hots for Codi, because he was fascinated by her fluid movements on the dance floor. Maybe that jealousy she had pinpointed was a little closer to home though. Callie wanted a man to look at her again. And Jack was a fine specimen to start with. They had spent a few minutes talking over the last few weeks, but Callie had scarcely thought anything more of it than just casual conversation. They were there together in a professional capacity, so there was no reason he should be interested in her, after all. But now that she was here twirling and sweating on the dance floor, why wasn't he looking at her? She discovered that maybe she had a little bit of a crush on him, and was hoping for some attention. Maybe Walter could be her wing man. She finally leaned in and touched his ear and said, "Dude, Jack has been staring at Codi for half an hour. Why doesn't he ask her to dance?"

Walter put his hands on her shoulders, stopping the bounce, and looked at her levelly. Soberly. "Callie, he's not looking at Codi."

Callie stood there sweating, breathing heavily, and looking around without moving her head. She could now see that there were plenty of lookers. Plenty of the singulars were looking at Codi. Watching her flow and ripple like the smooth waves of a dark sea. And then her eyes returned to Jack, sitting sideways in his chair, one arm over its back, and the other on the table, holding a bottle of beer. He was bobbing his head at the end of his neck, acting like he was really into the music. And then she saw it. Jack was looking at Callie. Instantly, her spirits rose a notch. He was unmistakably staring at her. Not Codi.

She started moving again. Keeping her feet glued to the floor, she moved her body in slow circles and pulsed up and down, grinding an invisible dance partner. Snapping her fingers and whipping her sweaty hair back from her face, she began to feel like a dancer. The spotlight was for her. The music was for her. She pulled her arms back and pushed her chest out, advertising the fact that – like Codi – she, too had gone without her carriage. Just tonight. After so much exposure to Codi and Rebecca and their freedom, she had decided to try it out for herself tonight. She had come to the bar to enjoy herself. And now, even though the evidence of her excitement stood out on her chest in vivid dark shadows of contrast in the purple light, she felt uninhibited. This was her new chapter. Those changes she had decided to make were now in effect. Walter said no more. He stood watching her, head slowly moving with the thick beat that vibrated her chest and rattled her guts. He was almost smiling. Like a father, proud of his daughter after her first stage performance, he stood watching, approving. And without Callie seeing, he pointed at Jack. Jack looked up and pointed at himself. *Me?* Walter nodded and called him out. Without hesitation, Jack took a swig of his beer and set it down, rising to meet Walter on the dance floor.

That air of legend and leadership that Walter exuded during the entire tenure of their phase testing, that mythical awesome that the other men tried to emulate and women tried to appropriate, was working its magic. Jack came to him on the floor. Walter put his hand on Jack's shoulder and held his other hand out as if he were offering Callie. And though Callie saw this part of his show, she paid them no attention. She was too into the dance. In a drunken and dreamy state, she absorbed without looking. Her eyes were open, but they weren't entirely seeing. She was grooving and moving with a freedom she had not previously felt. She felt like she was the queen of the evening. And when Jack finally turned to face her and started moving with her, she reached up and grabbed the back of his head, pulling him close. Before he could object, she had his right thigh between her legs and her hand on his rear. Her other arm was then around his neck and she was looking him in the eyes. He was a full foot taller than her, and solid with muscle and stout. Callie thought he might give Walter a run for his money in that department. She was grinding her thighs against his and whipping her head with the music. It was as if she were possessed by dance itself. Completely unashamed, the antithesis of timidity pulsed through her veins.

Callie looked closely at him as they made moves that were normally saved for the bedroom. Jack was grinding her just the right way. She was governing his movements with the careful placement of her hand and her own legs. And in staring at him, she began to appreciate, up close, how pretty he really was. He had movie-star hair. Not short, but standing about his head like he'd found an electrical outlet. It was stylish and perfect. He had two days'-worth of growth on his jaw, the dark brown that matched his hair and the alluring lake-at-night eyes that gazed back at her in amazement and questioning. He was unsure how to act around her. She was teaching him though. It was so sudden, and she reckoned quickly that it was the beer doing most of the forward movements for her. But she also decided it was okay. She trusted, for once, her instincts. She was going to allow herself that loose that was typically reserved for bad words and bad women. She might well regret it tomorrow, but not tonight. Tonight, Callie would regret nothing.

And with that, she pulled his head down and kissed him.

The night played out in perfect rhythm with the beat of the dance music, and Callie, standing covered in sweat and breathing heavily, looked at the venue with new eyes. She had not danced this hard since college. And she still felt like she was just getting started. Jack was stuck to her like a strip of hook-and-loop on a wool couch. He obviously wasn't going anywhere. And every chance Callie got to look back at the lovely Codi Cohl, she was reassured that Jack's eyes were only for herself. Callie and Codi had come in close together several times throughout the night, dancing like party stars as the crowd circled around them hooting and hollering while they grinded like lovers. Somewhere at the bottom of the thought pit that was Callie's alcohol-soaked brain, she knew she would be sleeping in when the sun rose. She knew she would pay for tonight with pain and regret. But she let it go.

As the hour grew late, the dancing finally began to slow for Callie. She finally found herself in a booth leaned back against Jack with her feet stretched out on the vinyl seat, watching Codi out on the dance floor. Codi was still going at it. And furthermore, Callie noticed, she was commanding it. The men were gathered about her in a loose circle as she moved from one to the next, making each feel important – worthy like he was the one who would end the night with her. Callie wondered if she would go home with one of them. Callie didn't really know much about Codi, all said and done. She didn't know if this was the type of thing she did regularly. The only thing she did know about Codi was that she was single. Callie wasn't even entirely sure Codi was straight.

When Callie had finally had enough to drink, she finally stood on shaking legs as the club blew imitation fog onto the dance floor, the lights switching about like lasers in a sci-fi movie. She made her way unsteadily back out onto the floor, breaking through the circle of sweating males – she actually put her hands on two of their shoulders and lifted her feet off the ground momentarily for a high kick – to join Codi. Her dress was sticking to her in ways she wouldn't typically allow, and without shame, she noticed Codi's was doing the same. Callie put her hands on Codi's waist and started grinding with her. Codi immediately clasped her hands behind Callie's neck, and they made a spectacle on the smoky dance floor.

The crowd around them was thick with men and women alike. But the women were standing with the men. Not trying to get into the circle with the two stars, but happy to observe and judge from the sidelines. Callie was not naive enough to think she had any control of the power. It was completely under Codi's hand. Callie just happened to be the mentor – the cool older sister who let Codi into the cool clubs. And that bought her the spot on the floor. But there was no doubt that the eyes were really all on Codi. She was bouncing and jiggling in all the right places – in her normal braless form, but wearing a tight little black nylon dress that accentuated every curve and contour of her body. It looked almost as if she were naked, but spray-painted with black nylon. The men were eating it up. Perhaps even the women were. And, Callie noticed, so was Codi herself.

Hands on each others' hips, they danced and grinded through another song, whipping their heads back and forth, making the men think things they had no business thinking. And then they walked off the dance floor. They walked toward the table holding hands and shaking their hips. Callie downed a tall glass of room-temperature water and ran her hair back off her forehead, looking back at the crowd that had now filled in to replace them empty spot the two girls had left. She met eyes with Walter, who stared at her unblinking. She wondered if – had she been sober – a message would have been passed there. But sober she wasn't. She stood swaying on her feet and surveying the crowd. She put her hand on the corner of the table and tried to act like she was still in control. And finally, Walter stood up. He came around to her and put his mouth against her ear.

"Callie, you're going to make a mistake tonight."

Callie pushed back from him, offended, and shoved him on the shoulder. She tried to make a face to match, but couldn't tell if she reached her desired effect. It might have fallen short. Peripherally she noticed Codi was looking up at them, trying to focus in the unsure light – and then remembered that this was Codi's prime light. Her best vision came in the dark. Callie and Walter had an audience. And then she had to ask herself why she was offended. She was so drunk she had already forgotten.

"Fuck you, Walter!" she said, safely.

He breathed in, but didn't respond. Just looked at her. And then she remembered what he had said. Was he right? What mistake was she going to make? Jack? At this point, she didn't even have any plans with him. What mistake could she be about to make? She didn't plan on sleeping with him, though if that were to start looking like the path she was traversing, would she object? Wasn't this 'the new her' in play here tonight? It had certainly made her feel on top of the world for most of the night. Or was that the alcohol? She suddenly had a sick feeling in her stomach. Dammit, Walter! She turned and tried to make her way casually and gracefully to the bathroom. She knew she had plenty of time to make it, but knew also what was in her short future.

As Callie rounded the corner into the restroom, she shouldered past a couple of ladies who were on their way out, laughing and smiling, having a lot more fun than she was, and pushed into a stall where the toilet was running. Trying to maintain some sense of sanity and dignity, she stood with her hand against the stall wall and leaned over the toilet, closing her eyes. It didn't take her long to finish. She rinsed her mouth and face at the sink, then fetched a piece of gum from her purse. Callie checked her eyes in the mirror and sighed. She could pretend she was sober, but she would only be fooling herself.

Taking a deep breath, Callie steeled herself. Reminded herself that she was not a sixteen-year-old girl at the dance bar with her father. She was her own person. A full-grown woman. She was free to make her own decisions. Her own mistakes, if it came to that. She splashed cold water on her face and then made a mean look in the mirror. "F you, Walter. It's not a mistake."

Callie Simmons walked out of the bathroom with her arms swinging, gum popping, and head on a mission. She walked directly up to Jack, sitting there at the end of the booth nursing his bottle of beer. "You ready?" she said, looking him directly in the eyes.

Jack swallowed and then looked around the table, as if for permission. No one was paying him any mind though. The only person not engaged in conversation or kissing was Walter. And he was looking at Callie. Resignedly, he was staring, arms up on the back of the booth seat, lips pursed, disconnected. Jack looked back up at her and smiled. "Yeah, sure."

She held her hand out for him. He took it and followed her out of the bar. As they donned their coats and pushed out the front door onto the sidewalk, the music and the temperature dropped like bricks from the sky. It was windy and cold out here. They had been surrounded by sweat and music for the last several hours, completely oblivious to the weather outside. Callie grabbed Jack's hand and pulled it over her shoulder, wrapping herself in his warmth.

Callie used an app on her phone to call an Uber driver. Estimated time of arrival: five minutes. Plenty of time to contemplate what she was doing. And then she decided to set herself a net. Suddenly she turned to Jack, pointing at him, seriousness set upon her pale face. "I may or may not go through with this tonight. More than likely, I will chicken out."

He stared at her wide-eyed, not quite knowing what to say, she suspected. She tilted her head to the side and breathed in, reading him. Judging him. Listening to what he wasn't saying.

"Listen, Jack," Callie said, placing a small hand on his chest, and staring at it instead of his face, "I am taking you back to my hotel room tonight. I plan to get naked. I plan to get naked between the sheets with you. I want you to snuggle with me and keep me warm."

She straightened up, rising to her bravery. "That may be all that happens. I can't guarantee anything else. You don't plan to take advantage of a drunk girl, do you?"

He shook his head slowly. "No, Callie. I'm not..."

She put a finger against his lips. "Just know this, Jack. I may or may not be ready for anything to happen." She turned to look down the street and sighed. "I just want you to respect whatever I decide to do," she finished.

"Of course, Callie," he said, taking her hands in his. "I'm just thrilled to be spending time with you. How about this?" he said, and paused for a moment. "How about I don't put my hands on you until you move them there? You just pulled my arm around you a minute ago. So, just like that. You are in complete control of what I do and what I touch." He smiled at her reassuringly, and then added, "And if anything 'untoward' happens," he said, making quotes with his fingers, "you say stop at any time you need to. And I stop." He snapped his fingers. Was he trained in talking to women? He sure was saying exactly the right things. Her want for him rose another notch. Callie found herself getting excited in more than just her chest.

She stared at him through half-closed eyes for a few seconds, then squeezed his fingers and stood on her tiptoes, kissing him on the chin. "Thank you for being cool, Jack. I'm not normally like this, but -"

He tried to speak, but she opened her eyes wide and lifted her chin. "Listen! I've never done this. But that doesn't mean I don't want to." She stood still a moment, staring at the ground between her feet. She felt his hands on her shoulders. They were not idle. She was thankful for that. His thumbs were making small loops on her shoulder bones.

"I've been stagnant in my life – really, for my whole life. And listen, I know I'm drunk. But I know where I am. And I know who I am. And I didn't just single you out to be the lucky guy." She stood still a minute and played back what she had just said, in her head. "I don't mean it like that. I just mean that I didn't come out tonight looking to pick some random guy to go home with."

Jack chuckled. "I didn't think that at all, Callie. So that means you've been looking at me for longer than just tonight?" he asked, wide-eyed.

She bit her bottom lip and squeezed his hands again, and nodded. "Uh huh." She stood up and kissed him again. "Just be patient with me, okay?"

Jack nodded. "Okay, Callie. You're the boss."

She looked long into his eyes. And then she smiled. And then she pulled herself into his arms, burying her face against his chest.

Codi did not go home with anyone. She shared an Uber with Trisha, one of the other girls on the team, and allowed Trisha to help her get to her room, but then went inside alone. Codi went into the bathroom and sat on the toilet, elbow on her knee, resting her chin on her hand, staring at the giant tub across the marble floor from her. It was then that she decided to take a bath. When she finished, she stripped down and turned on the hot water, then brushed her teeth and stepped into the quickly filling tub. She tore the top off a foil package of hotel-supplied bubble bath and dumped it into the steaming water, then leaned back and slid in.

After a few minutes, Codi shut off the water and wet a rag, putting it across her sweaty forehead. She splashed the water around for a few minutes, and then closed her eyes to relax. And promptly fell asleep.

CHAPTER 24

Callie awoke with a snap, and twisted her head to the side to verify what she had dreamt of. Had she really just slept in bed with a man she didn't really know? And yes, there he was, back toward her, brown hair a disheveled mess on the white pillowcase. Callie took a deep breath that turned into a yawn and lifted the sheets up, looking down the length of her torso to see how undressed she was. There was nothing to see. She clapped the sheets back down and looked up at the ceiling. She remembered the whole night. She remembered everything.

She sat up and wrapped the sheet around her chest, then reached over and put her hand on Jack's shoulder. He rolled softly over and smiled at her. "Good morning," she said. He responded in kind, and sat up. Then he ran her hair back behind her ear with his strong hand and pulled her in for a kiss. It was indeed a good morning. Jack was only the second man with which she had ever slept in a bed. And they were both naked. She felt comfortable and excited. She wasn't afraid of his seeing her, either. What had changed? Was it really that simple? All she had needed to do was just – well, to just do it? Maybe so.

She hopped up out of the bed and scribbled across the floor to the bathroom, her bare bottom completely visible to Jack, who, she noted in the mirror, did not look away. She stopped at the doorway and stared in the mirror. He caught her eyes there and smiled again. He was quite obviously lusting over her naked body. And she was adoring the attention. "Feel free to stare as long as you like," she said, then blew him a kiss and disappeared around the corner to pee and brush her teeth.

When she finished, Callie stood again in the bathroom doorway, this time facing him. And once again, not covering any part of her. And Jack sat there again, taking it all in. He leaned back on his hands and took a deep breath then smiled at her. "Callie, you let me, and I'll sit here and stare all day."

"Don't tempt me," she said, and ran and jumped into the bed, straddling him. There were covers between them but it didn't much matter. One could feel everything through a sheet. She kissed him hard on the mouth, then sat up straight pulling her hair back into a messy pony tail. "What are we gonna do today?"

He rested his hands on her hips and looked her in the eyes, then shrugged. "I think we should go hit one of those little restaurants on the beach for breakfast."

Callie looked toward the window where the sun was streaming in, but a little higher in the sky than she would have thought it should be. "What time is it?" She leaned across the bed, across Jack who was in her path, reaching for her phone on the bedside table. He did not object to the smothering, and put his hands up on her ribcage, holding her in place.

She rested her chin on one hand, elbow on the bed beside him while she scrolled through her morning routine on her phone, checking emails, texts and the weather. Callie was also just taking her time, allowing Jack to enjoy himself. His whiskers tickled her chest but it made for a stunning sensation in her loins. Parts of her were waking up – parts that she hadn't known existed.

It was after nine o'clock, and Callie said so. Jack sighed and stretched and said, "Seriously? Good God. I haven't slept that late in years."

"I know, me neither," Callie said, hopping up off the bed. She grabbed a t-shirt and panties and made her way back to the bathroom. "I'm going to shower real quick. I still smell like last night. Do *not* join me in that shower, Jack. I'm warning you."

"Okay, Callie," he said. "I promise."

Callie stood leaning against the door jamb outside Walter's door, waiting for him to answer. He had called out something affirmative after she had knocked loudly for half a minute. But now it was taking a suspiciously long time for him to answer. Callie's stomach began to sink a little when she thought of what that might mean. When he finally opened the door, clad only in pajama pants, Callie pushed past him into the room.

"Whoa, what the hell, Calgirl?" Walter said. He frowned and shook his head, then turned back to Jack and hiked his chin. "What's up, man?"

"Walter, how are you?" Jack said, accepting Walter's invitation to come inside.

Callie came into the room expecting to find one of the pretty girls from the club in his bed. But there was no one there. The bathroom was dark and dead too. She immediately felt better, and then felt ashamed of herself for suspecting the worst of her friend.

"We're going to eat breakfast on the pier. You interested?"

Walter ran his fingers through his messy hair and looked at his watch. "Shit. It's almost lunch time."

Callie shrugged. "Yeah, we had a heck of a good time last night. I think we deserved to sleep in a little."

"Sure, sure. You getting anyone else?" Walter asked.

"Yeah, I thought we'd go get Codi and maybe Minus," she said.

"Yeah that's cool, you can grab Codi." He stared at her for a moment then looked back at Jack. "Why don't you two love birds go grab her and get her going, then come back and get me. I need to run through the shower real fast. I smell like hookers and cocaine."

Callie rolled her eyes. "So you don't want me to get Minus? Don't you want him to pay for it?" she said, smiling broadly.

"I'll pay for the damn breakfast, Callie. If I could eat my Alabama omelet without having to look at his face, it would taste a lot better."

"Suit yourself," Callie said, and grabbed Jack's arm on her way past him. "Let's go, bubba."

"See ya in a few, Walter," Jack said, nodding at him. Callie saw that there was a high level of respect there, perhaps bordering on idolatry, and felt a quick giddiness for Walter. She was proud of him. He was a great guy, and a great guy to have as a big brother. She pulled Jack along behind her and closed the door on the way out.

When they got to Codi's door, she answered quickly, but was standing there in a towel shivering. "Good morning, princess beautiful!" Callie said.

"Hi Callie," Codi said, teeth chattering. None of her usual bouncy enthusiasm was present.

"What's wrong, sugar?" Callie said.

"I fell asleep in the tub last night. This morning. Whatever. The water was freakin' freezing when I woke up. God, I think I caught a cold."

"Oh my God! Come here!" Callie said, letting herself into the room. She guided Codi to the bed and sat her down on the edge of the mattress, then wrapped all the blankets around her. "Jack, babe, grab that other blanket in the top of the closet," she said. He complied and tossed it to her. Callie wrapped that around Codi as well, all the way up to her chin, then reached into the mess and undid the wet towel, pulling it free and tossing it to him.

"Ooooohhh," Codi purred, still shivering. "So much better. Thank you!"

Callie looked around the room, then back at Jack. "Jack, sweetie, would you be a doll and excuse us girls for a while? Maybe go wait with Walter?"

"You got it. Hope you warm up, Codi," he said, and showed himself out.

Codi looked at Callie, a mischievous grin on her face. "So?" She leaned toward Callie, nudging her with a shoulder thick with blankets.

"So what?"

"Did you sleep with him?" Codi said.

"Ha! Wow, you're a nosy one aren't you?" Callie said, but she was smiling. She went to the mirror and played with her hair, borrowing Codi's brush and a pony tail stretch. "He stayed in my room with me last night. It was so nice, Codi, waking up with a man in my bed."

Codi's mouth was open wide, her face full of smile. "That is awesome! How long has it been?"

Callie's smiled dropped off. "How long has *what* been?"

"How long has it been since you slept with someone?" Codi said. She then slapped a hand over her mouth and widened her eyes. "I'm sorry, I'm being awful, aren't I?"

Callie breathed in and looked at her, smiling again. "It's okay, sweetie. You're not awful." She made her way back to the bed, where she started grooming Codi's hair for her. "But I didn't say I slept with him."

"You said you woke up in bed with him!" Codi said, and this time a hand came out to do the shoulder-nudging.

"Yeah but I didn't say anything about sex!"

Codi frowned for a second, and then said, "Well, yeah, technically neither did I. But whatever! So how was it?"

Callie shook her head. "I said it felt great to wake up with a man in my bed. But since you asked, I have to tell you, I've never been with a man before."

Codi's eyes got wide again. "Are you a lesbian, Callie? I had no idea!"

Callie rolled her eyes and stood up again. "No, dork. Wow, this is so off-track! I didn't mean that. I meant, very simply, that I'm a virgin."

"You are?" Codi said, scrunching her face up into an incredulous stare. "Well, I guess you mean until last night, anyway," she added.

Callie laughed out loud. "Ha! No, Codi! Again, I didn't say any of that! I've never been with a man. I've never been with a woman. And I'm not telling you if I slept with Jack!"

"I bet you did. You're all smiles!" Codi said.

Callie put her hand on Codi's shoulder. "I'm always all smiles, darling. I love mornings. Now let's get you dressed. We're going out to eat."

"Yay!" Codi said, clapping her hands and letting the blankets fall away. Callie was instantly jealous.

"Good God, woman! And you go without a bra?"

Codi looked down, spreading her hands. "What? What do you mean?"

"You are stacked, sugar! How in heck do you go around with no bra?"

"Oh. Yeah. That. I've just gotten to where I hate them. I hate their restrictive nature. Rebecca kind of turned me onto the whole free-chested thing."

"I'll bet she did!" Callie said.

"What does that mean?" Codi asked.

"Well, you're a treat to look at, Codi Cohl. You have the most amazing body I've ever seen. And Rebecca is gay."

"Yeah but she never hits on me or tries anything with me!" Codi said, almost sounding offended.

"Look, I'm not saying anything bad about her," Callie said. "But don't you think gay women enjoy looking at beautiful women naked?"

"Well of course! But it's not like I walk around nude over there!" Codi said.

"You don't have to, sugar." Callie tossed her some clothes from the suitcase by the dresser, noticing that they were all shades of gray and black – probably for ease of color-coding. "You don't have to."

They ate at Jimmy's on the pier, each filling their plates from a long steamy buffet full of all the favorites. Callie drank three tall glasses of ice water, and began to feel human again by the end of the breakfast. When they all finished, they leaned back and looked out at the water while the wait staff bussed the table. Walter looked at Callie and said, "You wanna go drinkin' and dancing tonight Cal?"

Jack laughed out loud. He was holding Callie's hand on his thigh, discreetly under the table, though everyone there knew about it. They weren't hiding anything. "My thighs are pretty tight today," he said. "I can't imagine what's going to hurt tomorrow."

Walter looked at him over the top of his glass. When Jack's eyes met his, Walter lifted his chin and leaned back. Callie had been watching Walter for most of the morning, trying to gauge his thoughts. She was wondering if he approved of Jack. She still looked up to him like a big brother and found herself seeking his approval on a lot of things, maybe without even consciously knowing it. She saw this little look over the glass thing and wondered what it meant. It looked ever so slightly to Callie like Walter might be a little jealous. Typical. Be jealous of a girl you couldn't have anyway.

"So is everybody packed?" Jack said.

"None of us are packed yet, dork," Callie said. She was chewing on a piece of ice, looking out over the water again. "But we have like an hour to checkout before they charge us another day."

"Well I'm ready when everyone else is," he said. Walter was looking at him again.

Codi smiled, sitting with her hands in her lap. She had not said much this morning. Maybe she was just shy, Callie thought. "I might need a little hand with mine, if someone doesn't mind," Codi said.

Walter slapped his hand down on her knee and squeezed. "I got ya covered, sister," he said. But he was looking at Callie when he said it. Callie frowned at him in turn. What the heck did that mean?

"Thank you, Walt," Codi said, looking in his direction. She had giant shades on that covered a lot more than just her eyes, and they were very dark. The sun was probably very uncomfortable for her, Callie guessed.

"Yeah I guess we should probably start heading that way," Callie said. She was having a staring battle with Walter, and she didn't even know what it was about. "Jack, would you be a dear and walk Codi back so Walter and I can talk for a minute?"

Walter rolled his eyes and tossed his glass back, sucking on more ice.

"You got it," Jack said, and kissed her on the cheek.

After the two were gone, Callie leaned her chin on her clasped hands and looked Walter dead in the eyes. He was still leaning back, nonchalant as ever. "What the F is your problem, Walter?" she said.

"That was expedient, don't you think?" Walter returned, looking at her like a displeased father.

Callie shook her head, holding her hands out. "What are you talking about?"

He finally leaned forward and closed his eyes, took a deep breath. "Look, Callie. I love you. You know I do. But dude. You met him last night, and he's already shared your bed?"

Callie raised her chin high and closed her eyes. "Okay. I get it. You're jealous. But I didn't meet him last night."

Walter laughed. "Last night… You think I'm jealous? Callie, you know I could have had you many years ago! Long before all the Chrises and Thevis and Jacks, you could have been mine."

"That's a little arrogant, isn't it?" she said, actually offended.

"No," he said, shrugging. "I don't see it that way. You could say the same thing. You could have had me if you wanted me. It just didn't move that way. Big deal!"

"Yeah! Big deal!" she said. She was shaking her hands now. "So why are you jealous?"

"I'm not jealous, Callie," he said, looking back out at the water.

"Then what's the problem?"

He shrugged again. "Like I said. I just think it happened a little fast. And I don't want to see you get hurt."

"Well, big brother, I don't see how it's any of your business who I share a bed with. And furthermore, who says I had sex with him?"

"Callie, come on. Two adults – two *drunk* adults – don't share a bed together and not have sex. That's just not how it happens," Walter stated.

"Okay, hot shot. Well I'm glad you think you know everything. But you don't. Thanks for worrying about me, but I'm a big girl." She began gathering her things and buttoning up her purse.

"So are you saying you *didn't* sleep with him, Callie?" Walter said, leaning in again. He was looking at her intensely.

"Wow, what is this? Some grand inquisition?" She stood up and brushed the crumbs off her linen pants. "No. I'm not saying that, Walter. For your information, I believe in this thing called discretion. And privacy. I'm not saying I did or didn't sleep with him. And you'll never know."

He shook his head. What was his problem?

"And I'm not even sure why you care! I'm happy, Walter! For the first time in months, I am happy! Can't you be excited for me? Serendipitously this guy just happens to be on the sub crew and I get lucky enough to meet him!"

"I assigned him, Callie," Walter said. He was twirling his knife on the table, staring intently at it as it made its shiny circles.

"Huh?" she said, slinging her purse over her shoulder. "What does that mean?"

He looked up at her. "I put him on the crew. He's here because of me."

"Okay? So?"

"So, I got him on the crew because I wanted you two to meet. I hooked you up, Callie. I orchestrated the whole thing."

Callie was speechless. She had her hands in her coat pockets. She didn't know what to say. She instead opted for staring at him, wide-eyed and curious.

"Why do you think he was sitting there staring at you last night while you were dancing?"

She looked closely at him, now hurt, shaking her head slowly. "Walter, you are so mean. You are mean like a snake!" And she turned to walk off before she started crying. She got fifteen or twenty feet away before he caught up with her, stopping her from behind with a strong hand on her shoulder.

"Stop, Callie. Stop. Listen. I didn't mean it like that," Walter said. She finally stopped, but she did not turn to look at him. He came round the front of her and lifted her shades up onto her head. She slapped his hand away and returned them to her swollen and leaking eyes.

"You're beautiful, Callie. He wasn't the only one looking at you. Not at all," Walter said. He ran her hair back with a fingertip, then returned his hand to her shoulder. "What I meant though, was – didn't you find it odd that he was just there staring at you all night? Like there was nothing else for him to do?"

She tilted her head. "Are you serious? You're not making this any better, Walt! Are you trying to crush my heart right now?"

"God! Dammit, no, Callie!" he said, looking at the ceiling and holding his hands out. "I'm not trying to hurt you. I'm just trying to say that he was sitting there staring all night. At you. He was there for you. He was wondering when you were finally going to notice him. And ask him to dance or something."

"Well I'm sorry. I don't notice men looking at me, because it doesn't happen very often. So I stopped paying attention."

"Well that's just stupid, Callie. I'm sorry, and I hate to be a pig, but dude, you looked so hot last night that I wanted to take you to my bed."

Callie swallowed and chewed on her lips. Reserving the right to speak. Checking her play.

"I'm not sure what got into you last night, but you were dancing like crazy. Your tits looked incredible in that dress."

She felt a giggle rising up in her throat. "You noticed?"

"What?! Of course I noticed!" he said, holding his hands up again, then dropping them at his sides. "How could I not! You were jiggling like five-dollar Jello out there!" He made the motion to illustrate, as if she had trouble envisioning what he was saying. "And you looked like you were smuggling raisins! You were hotter than a Texas sidewalk last night, dude."

Callie said, "Thank you, Walter. That means a lot to me." She felt warm inside again.

"Yeah. It's not really my job," he said, looking around the restaurant, "to make you feel good. My job is to make Thevi feel good. And now, it's apparently Jack's job," he said, waving and looking in the general direction of Jack, "to take care of you. But sometimes you're just so damn dumb that I have to come out and remind you how awesome you are."

"When you want to make a person feel good, you really do a good job, Walter. You should talk like that more often," Callie said.

"Ha! No. If I talk about your tits all the time, you're gonna have to start showing them to me."

"I tried to. You shut me down, remember?"

He laughed easily and smiled at her, then put his hands in his own coat pockets. "Yeah. One of the biggest fuckin' regrets of my life," he answered.

She hit him with her purse. "So what is it about Jack that you don't like then, Dub Dub?" She looked pleadingly at him. Just then, he remembered that he hadn't paid for the meal, and dug out his wallet. The waiter was standing politely behind Callie.

"Here, bro. Sorry, I wasn't trying to stiff anyone. Totally forgot," Walter said, and handed the man a crisp one-hundred-dollar bill. The man bowed politely and was about to speak when Walter added, "Keep it."

Walter watched the man disappear through the double doors of the kitchen, then looked back at Callie. "It's not that I don't like him, Callie. Like I said, I brought him on board because I wanted to introduce you two. I just didn't think you'd..." he started, waving toward her, but wised up and stopped talking.

"And so what if I did, Walt?" she said, leaning in toward him and widening her eyes.

He stared at her levelly for a silent minute, and then finally swallowed and said, "Did he treat you with respect?"

She nodded slowly, still not willing to betray anything that might or might not have happened.

"Good. Yeah, that's good," Walter said, turning to look about the restaurant again, briefly. "I just know he really likes you. Every time you're not around, you're all he talks about."

"Huh? What? When?"

"For the last two weeks, Callie!" Walter said. He put his hand on Callie's arm and guided her over a step to her right to let a bus boy through. He moved with her, then continued. "Almost like obsessively. So I started wondering if I had made the wrong call."

"Nope!" she said, still staring up at him.

"Okay. Well, fine then. That's all that matters. I just..." he said, looking very uncomfortable. He sighed then cracked his neck. "I just think," he started, then scratched the back of his neck. All ticks betraying discomfort about the subject matter.

"Spit it out, Watson," she said forcefully.

He laughed out loud, breaking the tension a little. He finally met her eyes again. "I just wanted your first time to be right, is all." He held out his hands for approval.

Now Callie laughed. "Walter, your concern is noted! I'm still not telling you whether or not we did anything! But to put your mind at ease, and since I love you like a brother, I will tell you that he was a perfect gentleman in everything he did. Sex or no sex, everything from the dance club to the hotel room, opening my door, walking me in with his arm around me, carrying me to bed, covering me up, the way he kissed me, everything. Everything he did was completely cool. You need not worry about it!" she said, putting her hands against his chest and acting like she was going to push.

"Good. That's great, Callie. That makes me happy."

"You sure seem jealous, Walt."

He shrugged. "I've never known someone like you, Callie. And whether or not anything happened, it *could* have happened. And yeah, that's a real special thing. And it's like... Well, with my knowing you as long as I have, that's sort of like history being made. And I just..." he spread his hands again. "I don't know."

"Want to be a part of it?" she said, grinning.

They both laughed out loud this time.

The flight home was long and quiet. Minus slept the entire flight away. Callie envied him his ability to sleep on the plane. Codi and Walter sat talking. She could not hear his words over the purr of the engines, but he was using his hands a lot, so Callie guess he was talking tech to her. Explaining something very high-tech and important. Callie smiled to herself. She at least had someone with whom she could hold hands on the way home. She kept leaning her head on Jack's shoulder, looking up at him and smiling. She felt so good when she was with him. Walter was right – it was very expedient. Callie felt like she could be falling in love with him already. She knew better, of course, but that infatuation was an important part of the relationship. And she could tell Jack was smitten by her as well. How had she not noticed him before? He was perfect!

They spent the flight getting to know each other – catching up to their apparent relationship with the behind-the-scenes necessaries like family talk, discussion of where they came from, and all the little things that typical couples would have discussed before they ever had their first kiss. Callie and Jack were simply doing it in reverse.

Near the end of the several-hour trek, Callie squeezed Jack's hand on the seat handle. "Jack, I need to talk to you."

"Okay. What have we been doing all afternoon?" he said, smiling and frowning simultaneously.

"No, dork butt. I need to ask you something."

"Go ahead, Callie." He squeezed her hand back.

"I was engaged before. I had-" she started.

"I know. And I understand if you need space. Or if we're moving too fast."

She looked at him seriously. "Did Walter tell you my whole life freakin' story?" She looked over at Walter across the aisle. He and Codi were laughing. She was trying to get something out of his hands. They sure looked comfortable together.

Jack shrugged. "You really like him don't you? I mean, you look up to him, right?"

She squinted at him. "So do you."

Jack nodded. "Yeah, he's an amazing guy."

Callie put her hand on Jack's chest and looked him in the eyes. "I don't think we need to slow down. I haven't cried in a long time now. But I do still have some of Chris's stuff in my house. And in my driveway. I was wondering if you could help me get rid of it."

"Sure thing, Callie. If you think it's appropriate. I mean, if you think you want me to be associated with the act of getting rid of your ex-fiancé's stuff, then I'd be glad to help."

Callie half-rolled her eyes. "Yeah. It's just stuff. It has no sentimental value to me, except that it reminds me of him constantly. The stuff itself can come or go." She looked out the window, then back at Jack. "I just know nothing about selling a car."

"I do."

Callie looked closely at him. "Okay..." she said, waiting for more.

"I'm the director of new auto sales at Neptune City Dodge," he said.

"What the fluff?" Callie almost screamed, hitting him on the shoulder. She instantly looked over at Walter, who had heard her yell and was looking back at her, almost bemused. *What?* his expression seemed to say.

"How the heck did he get you on the project? I thought you worked for Royal!"

Jack smiled easily. "Nope. You know that orange Challenger he has in his garage?"

Callie shook her head, frowning hard. "Yeah! What the heck?"

"We've been friends for a few years now. And to tell you the truth, I've been jealous of Chris since the day I first came to Walter's and saw a picture of you on his end table."

Callie now looked back at Walter, who had forgotten about her, and was back to talking with Codi. "What effing picture?" she said, now leaning way forward so she could look back at Jack from the front.

"There's a picture of you two sitting at a table in the airport. I don't know anything else about it. I think it was LAX though," he said.

"Oh my God! Yes! I hadn't seen him in several years and he flew in while I was out there for a meeting. I only got to see him for a little while, but I took a selfie of us. And *that* made you jealous of Chris?"

He nodded slowly. "Yeah. You're absolutely gorgeous."

"Yeah, I was also about five years younger there. You know I'm pushing forty, right?" Callie said.

"Got ya beat, babe. I pushed through that last year."

"You're forty?!" Callie said, again, almost shouting. "Here I thought I had found a younger man!"

"Nope. Turned forty in March," Jack said.

"Wow! Okay, well that means you have a birthday coming up." Callie pulled out her phone and opened the calendar. She asked his birth date and added it, then realized she didn't even yet have his phone number. "Holy shoot, we're doing this backward," she said.

CHAPTER 25

They had a few weeks off before the launch date. They were scheduled to fly into Osaka on April 14th. With the free time, Callie opted to go to work on nailing down her case against Brian Bradley, rather than returning to work at Bohr, only to have to take leave again.

On Monday, Callie had her suitcase open next to the washer, as standard protocol dictated. Jack was going to come over this evening and she had a little catching up to do. But with a newfound fervor for life and love, she was steadfast in getting all of Chris's stuff packed up and moved out to the garage, where it could be pushed out of her life forever. If she couldn't have Chris, she didn't want any part of him. Even his valuable watches and other belongings, she decidedly put out of reach. Rather than suffer the regret or remorse or remembrance of dealing with each item just to have its worth in money, she put it all in the boxes. Rather than collect the several thousand dollars for her effort, she just wanted it gone. That was the price she would pay for the comfort of not having to deal with it. What if she looked at his watch and remembered a special time with him, and her depression resurfaced? What if she had to go through all that pain and sadness again? Why not, she insisted, just move on with her life and let the past stay in the past? She had what was looking like a boyfriend now, and was doing just that. She was moving on. No need to dwell on little things like watches and wallets, knives and belt buckles, photographs and files. All of it went into the box, indiscriminately.

As she loaded clothes from her trip to Galveston into the washer, Callie realized she was handling it well, and wondered if there was part of the grieving process that she had not gone through yet. What if it all came crashing down on her? What if the worst was still to come, and it happened while she was with Jack? She grabbed the edges of the washer and looked straight ahead at the wall, willing herself to come to terms with all of it. It was time, she reassured herself, to lay Chris to rest. Completely. That was a chapter in her life that she had finished. And she had no intention of rereading it.

Callie slammed the washer lid and snapped off the light, making her way into the kitchen to get some breakfast. She pulled a box of raisin bran from the pantry and set it on the counter, staring out the window at the small bird feeder that no bird had ever visited. She picked up a glass with her other hand, one hand still on the cereal box, and ran some tap water into it. Then she took a drink and wondered if that meant anything. Where had she even gotten that bird feeder? She used to buy food for it. She didn't anymore. Maybe that was why the birds never came.

She finished the glass of water then grabbed a bowl from the cabinet and opened the cereal. As she poured from the box, a gigantic white rat fell into the bowl and Callie shrieked, jumping back several feet, heart slamming in her chest. "Dear God!" she screamed, covering her heart. But it was not a white rat that now sat in her bowl. It was her long lost phone.

Shaking her head, Callie stepped back up to the counter and picked the scary phone up out of the flakes and raisins. "Seriously? I looked hours for you. How the heck did you get into my box of raisin bran?" She smirked, then tossed the phone into the trash can beneath the sink. "This is how my life is defined," Callie said out loud. "Phones falling out of cereal boxes."

⌘   ⌘   ⌘

Codi was in the living room listening to music on the big stereo. While Rebecca was at work, she enjoyed blasting the high-dollar stereo. Codi connected her phone to the Bluetooth receiver attached to the stereo and pumped out Coldplay and Muse and One Last Orbit, and all her other favorite music at high-volume. And today, she was dancing. She was revisiting in her mind that special spot she had found Friday night on the dance floor at The Chandelier. It was not the first time she had ever let loose at a club. But it was the first time she had ever been surrounded and put on a figurative pedestal. It had been marvelous. She had not once felt uncomfortable or shy, but found herself asking why she had never experienced it before, if she had it in her all along. Whatever the reason was probably unimportant. But Codi had found her special place. Some people had the stage, some people were in movies. She had the dance floor at a club. Just letting go and becoming part of the music had made her feel royal. But seeing a crowd gather around her, appreciating her dance – that was magnificent.

So Codi stood here in Rebecca's living room, twirling, snapping, convulsing with the music, singing out loud. She was reliving the fifteen minutes of fame. She was relishing the spotlight. Losing herself in the music.

The doorbell rang.

Laughing out loud at what someone would think if they were to walk in on her, Codi breezed to the front door, smiling widely. She didn't bother with the peephole. Those things didn't work for seeing-impaired people. Instead, she swung the door open, forgetting that she was in nothing but a tank top and panties.

Codi did not recognize the face that stood looking at her across the threshold. "Hello?" she said timidly. But she did recognize the pain in her throat as Tim stepped through the doorway and put her in a choke hold, bringing her almost instantly to her knees.

⌘   ⌘   ⌘

Walter stood in a conference room, showing numbers and stats for the new month. His tie was eating into his neck and he was feeling very tired. The previous Friday night was still working in his system, despite the fact that he had been drinking water like it was a rare commodity since last night. Clearly, he was getting too old for the all-nighters. He wondered sideways how Callie had bounced back so quickly. They were the same age! And Codi? You couldn't even tell she'd had a sip the night before. Of course, Codi was almost two decades their junior. But still, it didn't seem fair. How had he gotten so old so fast?

His mind wasn't in the game. Walter wondered if he still even had it in him. He was enjoying the shit out of the underwater project, but this numbers game he played during the rest of the week was starting to get to him. Was it too late for a career change? Was that reserved for people still in their twenties and thirties? Shit! He wasn't even in his thirties anymore.

"What does it mean for the stock? Oil futures?"

"Huh?" Walter said, turning toward the voice, a sheaf of papers held rigid in his hands. Where the fuck was his mind? Was he still in Galveston? What had he been thinking about?

"Walter, are you okay? Are you with us?" his boss asked from the other end of the table. Walter met his eyes and tried a wan smile, but it fell flat.

"Man, I'm so sorry, Roland. I just can't make it happen today. I had a really rough weekend."

A lot of shuffling in chairs and sighs could be heard. One man got up and coughed. Roland was staring at Walter, leaning back in his chair, pen bouncing on the table between loose fingers.

Walter stared back. *Hey, shit! At least I'm honest with you!* Finally he added, "Sorry."

"Okay guys. Let's look at this again next Monday. Walter spent the weekend taking care of some very difficult personal things," Roland said. He then stood up himself, smiling politely at the other executives now making mass exodus from the room.

Walter didn't waste any time. He pulled out the chair at the opposite end of the table and plopped down into it. When everyone had left, the last man had courteously pulled the door closed. Walter looked at Roland and said, "I'm sorry, Roland. Thanks for covering."

"Listen, dick head. I'm tired of your attitude. Either you want to work here or you don't. I don't mind you spending evenings and weekends getting wet. But during normal business hours, you're mine. You belong primarily to this department. I'm going to give you the rest of the week off to get your shit in order. Get your head straight, Watson. Don't come back here Monday in the same state you're in today."

"Yes, sir," Walter said. He was now staring at the table. He didn't think he could have cared much less about the conversation. He was acting humiliated and sorrowful, as a good employee should. But that's not where he really was. He was still trying to find where his mind was, actually.

"Go home. Take a nap. Take a smoke. Call a hooker. Whatever you gotta do to get your head straight. Are we clear?" Roland said.

Walter finally smirked and stood up. "Really, Roland? A hooker? I'm sorry I let you down today. My mind is in other places. That, I give you. But a hooker? Who the fuck do you think you are?" He grabbed his briefcase from the floor by the white board, noticing peripherally the shock on Roland's face. As he grabbed the door handle, he turned back to look at his boss.

"You're a cool guy, Roland. But don't think for a second that I'm a pushover. Just because you sign my paychecks doesn't make you better than me. Don't ever fucking talk down to me again. Okay, asshole?" And before Roland could answer, the door was closed again, and Walter was seven feet on the other side of it.

On the drive home, Walter revisited where his mind had been. And it was getting more and more uncomfortable every time he brought it to the front of his mind. Had he really been thinking about Callie? It wasn't just her beautiful tits bouncing on the dance floor. The way her nipples stuck out of that thin black dress. No, he could see that anywhere. And over the years, he had seen her nipples poke through the fabric of a hundred different blouses and dresses. It was most definitely not that. But what was it then?

Was it simply because she had taken a man back to her room with her so quickly after meeting him? The primal part of him recognized the primal call of that situation. If she had taken someone back to her room, she had almost certainly slept with him. And what of that? Well, if she had gone back to her room with a good-looking guy she had only just met, then that meant that Walter truly did have a chance. Maybe not anymore, but definitely before. Proximity breeds want. One begins to covet what one is close to on a regular basis. Surely, after fifteen years of knowing each other, he could have slipped into an easy relationship with her – if nothing more than a sexual one. Hell, it had been she who had offered to show him her breasts the last time they were at the Rim! Women don't just do that! Well, at least not classy women. Not friends, either. There had to have been something more there. Callie, of course, was very aware of Thevi and her importance in Walter's life. Callie had spoken of her many times when worried about whether Walter was cheating on Thevi or not. Why was this Jack character bugging Walter so much? Why did it feel like he was encroaching on Walter's space? Why did Walter feel like it was his space at all? Why was he having this conversation with himself? Why was he asking himself these questions? Why did he give a shit? He knew Chris had gotten closer to Callie than Walt himself ever had. But he had never been jealous of Chris. Why Jack, all of a sudden? Walter knew for a fact that Callie and Chris had gone farther than just a little dry-humping in the backseat of a Chevy. He believed strongly that she had still been saving herself when Chris died. Those are the kind of things that guys are okay talking about. And Chris and Walter were close. But she and Chris had gone right up to that oh-so-naughty all-the-way state. They had never actually closed the deal, but they had gotten close. Close enough to know what the end result would feel like. And here she was telling him that she may or may not have even done anything with Jack. So why was Walter deliberating about whether or not he even cared? In short, why was he jealous? Did he feel like he was missing out on something he should have taken himself, long ago? And *should he* have taken her long ago? Well, if anyone were more deserving of her virginity than Walter, there could really only be one contender. And that wasn't Jack. But why? If they truly were just friends, then why did he even give a fuck?

Quickly, he changed the subject in his mind. He thought about Thevi. And was sad to see that, at the moment, at least, he didn't get that jolt of excitement like he used to. Walter thought about the dark freckles all over her chest and shoulders that he found so attractive. The way her breasts stuck out at him when they were making love. The way she looked at him like he was the only man in the world. The way she would tell him he was the most magnificent thing ever created when he was bringing her to climax. And how he believed it. None of it felt like anything right now. But Callie…

Maybe he needed a litmus test. Maybe he should think about something neutral…

Walter let his mind slide over what he had seen Friday night. Not Callie. The other one. The raven-haired gal with the d-cups and the aversion to covering them up. The one with the mystery in her robotically enhanced eyes. The one who moved like oil through gears on the dance floor. The one with the perfect full lips and gorgeous, pointed chin and wide blue eyes. That girl with the semi-wide hips and the almost non-existent waistline, who looked like a porn star. That girl they called Codi Cohl, who looked like something out of a fantasy rather than real life. She was hot. The definition of hot, in fact. He imagined his hands grabbing handfuls of her chest as she sat on him with those piercing blue eyes setting fire to his skin. She was leaning back with her hands on his knees, sliding back and forth on him like a well oiled machine. He tried, anyway. But it wasn't working.

Sex was good. Sex was great. Walter had had a lot of sex in his day. That, he discovered, was clearly not what this was about. He could find himself alone in a locked room and take care of any fantasy he could ever imagine, and never look back. There wasn't much point on dwelling on emotion and want when it came to sex. Sex was just the coupling of two bodies. Thevi did plenty for him in that department. Would Codi be fun in the sheets? Dear God, seriously? He shook his head. She would be probably the most magnificent thing on the planet. Stellar. He, in fact, found that he could not imagine anything more alluring – more perfect. She was like liquid sex in a bottle. All he had to do was think of her to unscrew that cap and get her flowing into his thoughts. But that's not where he was this afternoon. This afternoon, on his way home from a job he might, in all actuality, not even have anymore, he was not with Codi. He was not with

Thevi. He was with Callie. And that was the most intriguing thought yet. Because he had no idea why. Maybe, if he searched his mind and heart and soul, he could produce an answer pretty quickly about why he thought of Callie occasionally. But what he couldn't pinpoint was the temporal side of that equation. Not *why*, but rather, why *now?*

It wasn't her body that his mind was stuck on. She was small up top. Compared to the well-packaged Codi Cohl, Callie was flat-chested. She had skinny thighs and skinny arms and no ass. She was unremarkable at best in body. Not unattractive, but certainly not something men pondered about when the lights went out, like it was with someone like Codi.

It was something more than that. And that was what frightened Walter the most. Because the 'why now' part of that question was the most important thing in his life right now. If he was in love with Callie Simmons, then his and Thevi's marriage was in serious danger.

He pulled into his driveway and shut the car off, then leaned back and stared at his garage door. Home. Thevi. Lovely red-haired Thevi with the flat belly and the gorgeous waltz. Thevi – the one who had stolen his heart from the first moment he had laid eyes on her in that Mexican restaurant so many years ago. She with the toxically beautiful green eyes. She was right there! Right on the other side of that wall in front of him. She was inside waiting for him. And she was still madly in love with him. No one could doubt that. People told him all the time that they loved how she looked at him. She was smitten. So why wasn't he?

He pulled the keys and got out of the car.

⌘   ⌘   ⌘

Rebecca dropped her cigarette in the pot outside her apartment door. Before pulling her keys out of her purse she decided to try the door. She liked those times when Codi had it unlocked for her. It reminded her of home. Made her think of love and happiness and family. It also made her think of Natalie. Rebecca was silently missing her like crazy.

The door was unlocked. As she swung it open, she tripped on Codi's legs, sticking straight across the hallway. Rebecca took a hard fall and yelped as she landed on top of Codi, knees cracking against the ceramic tile of the entry hall. She quickly recovered though, and rolled over so she was sitting with her legs bent over the prone body of Codi. Codi was sprawled out on her stomach in nothing but a tank top. What the hell was going on?

She was instantly frantic, up on her knees and talking in Codi's right ear. Codi's eyes were closed. "Codi, wake up baby. Codi! Codi are you okay? Codi, talk to me!" Now she was slapping her cheek lightly and moving her head by the jaw. Had she fallen down and hit her head? Rebecca looked around the hallway but saw nothing out of place. The table still stood with the potted plant and the candles, all still standing. Everything looked normal.

Rebecca felt for a pulse and found one quickly. And Codi was warm. That was good. Immediate relief flooded into Rebecca's veins, but tears also quickly rushed to her eyes. If she had not hit her head, then something worse was going on. Had she had a stroke? Suddenly, she frowned and sat up. Why was Codi not wearing any pants? Or for that matter, no underwear? Rebecca propped herself up to a squat and, on a sudden instinct, put her hand in Codi's crotch.

"Oh my God. Mother fucker!" she shouted, standing up. She slipped her phone out of her trouser pocket and was immediately scrolling through the list of contacts. She found the number she was looking for and hit the call button. Within five seconds, Walter answered.

"Walter, I need you. Something has happened to Codi," she said.

"Bec, now is really not that much of a good-" Walter started, but she wasn't having any of that.

"Walter, get the fuck over here now. I need you. Codi needs you. Something is bad wrong."

He sighed, but she could hear movement. "Okay. Give me ten minutes." He disconnected.

Now Rebecca was pacing, running a hand through her hair and trying to think of what to do. She had come from a place where you did not call the police to handle your problems for you. They were not to be trusted. This looked like maybe it might be time to break that tradition, but she would let Walter help her decide that. She was now seriously worried. She squatted back by Codi again and went to put her fingers on her neck. That was when she noticed the purple bruising. "What the fuck?!" she said loudly.

Rebecca rolled Codi up onto her side so she could get a better look. Frantically, she moved Codi's head back and forth, and began slapping her cheek lightly again. "Oh Codi, baby, wake up! I need you to wake up, sweetie!" she was saying, leaning down and combing Codi's hair back from her ear, her own tears dripping on Codi's head.

It did not seem like ten minutes later, but suddenly there was a knock at the door. She stood and opened it, quickly pulling Walter in. His coat was wet and a light steam was drifting off of it. "What's going on?" he said, urgency evident in his voice. As he came in the door, Rebecca saw that she wouldn't have to spend a lot of time explaining. He closed his eyes and then looked up as he evidently noticed that Codi was naked below the waist. "Good God, what the hell?" he said.

Rebecca put a hand on his chest and talked frantically, "Walter, I don't know what to do. She's been raped. That mother fucker came over here and choked her and raped her."

Immediately, she saw the fury flood his eyes. "Where does he live, Rebecca?"

She held her hands up defensively and shook her head, closing her eyes. "Walter, no. You have to help me with Codi. Forget about him for now."

Walter took her hand in the air and stopped the movement. He wasn't exerting any force on her, but she could feel the strength and seriousness in his hand. His chest had bowed up and it was now obvious he was holding back a rage thick with physical strength. He was mad in his blood. "You call an ambulance, Rebecca. This girl needs medical attention right now," he commanded, pointing down with a stern finger. There was no arguing with his intensity.

"Okay. Walter, I don't want you going over there. You really-"

He grabbed her shoulder – again that strength telegraphed itself through gentle fingers – and spoke lowly, looking her in the eyes. "Rebecca, now is not the time for what you want. You tell me where he lives."

She took a deep breath and stared him in the eyes. She saw no fear there. The fear she saw was a reflection in the lenses of her own eyes. She was now afraid for what was going to happen to Tim. She shook her head as if to clear the nonsense and realized who she should be feeling sorry for. She was right there on the ground at her feet.

"Grandview Apartments. Unit 208."

Walter squeezed her shoulder and gave her a half smile. "Call an ambulance. Then call the police."

"Walter!" she started, sounding a lot like a whine. But he was out the door and it clicked closed softly.

The rain beat heavily on his windshield as he drove the twelve-mile route down 35 to the apartments she had told him. Walter had been there before, but couldn't place why or when at the moment. He maintained his calm enough to make it there safely, and even looked cool as he stepped out of the car, his boots splashing in the cold water. He swept the door of the Bentley closed smoothly and walked calmly up the walk to the stairway. Anyone watching him would have no idea who he was or what he was doing. But a man about to engage in conflict was probably at the bottom of the list.

As he walked down the outside walkway of the second floor, he passed a small table and two chairs outside someone's front door. Without so much as an instant of hesitation, he lifted the thick marble ashtray from its place on the table and whipped the ash and butts out of it over the rail. He continued to 208 with it held low beside his thigh. The rain was sliding down his hair now. He was completely soaked.

Walter knocked calmly on the door of 208 and put on his best sweet-guy smile for the peephole. After a minute he saw movement on the other side, then heard a muffled voice ask who it was. Walter had the ashtray behind his back now. He had his shoulders pulled up and tried to look as if he were small and shivering. He just needed to come in out of the rain. "Hey buddy, my name is Ryan Parker. I found your wallet!" Walter held his own wallet up between his thumb and first finger, smiling."

"That's not my wallet," the voice said.

Walter frowned and flipped the wallet open, looking closely at the ID inside. He smeared water on the picture from his thumb and held it up to the peephole. "Are you Tim? Isn't this unit 208?" he said. But he was holding it too close to the peephole for the man on the other side to actually be able to read anything.

The lock suddenly turned and Walter pocketed his wallet. Then the door opened and the man was talking. "Listen man, I said," he started, but that's all he got out. And it would be weeks before he got anything else out at all. Walter pushed his way into the entry hall and closed the door behind him. He wanted Tim to know why he was here. He wanted to make sure he made an impression and said his piece. But he also wanted to make sure Tim understood there would be no fighting back. Not this time. So before he began his crude exercise, he brought the ashtray up and slammed it hard into Tim's mouth. An explosion of teeth and blood sounded out and splattered the walls. Some of it might have gotten on Walter as well, but he was too busy to notice.

Within the instant, Tim was on the ground, moaning in pain. Walter squatted down and dropped the ashtray on the floor. It broke in two with a loud clunk and Walter clapped the dust off his hands, then wiped them on Tim's pants. "Listen, Tim. Can you hear me?"

Tim wasn't responding. He was still writhing and moaning. There might have been some incoherent cursing in there, but Walter couldn't make any of it out.

"Listen, buddy. I need you to acknowledge that you understand what I'm saying. If I don't get your attention I'm going to get violent. And I'm going to injure you."

"Fuck you!" Tim said, spraying blood as he made the f sound. He leaned up on one arm long enough to look at Walter though.

Walter smiled. It was a genuine smile, too. He was getting his way. "That's fine. Just wanted to make sure you were hearing me." He adjusted his squat and looked deeper into the apartment. "Is there anyone else here?"

Tim was breathing heavily and blood was running freely from the open mess on his mouth. He was staring at Walter, but he wasn't talking.

Walter looked him in the eyes. He reached up and took hold of Tim's cheek with his full hand and squeezed like a vise. Terror filled Tim's eyes and he screamed out in pain. Walter's point was making its way across.

"NO!" he shouted. "Dammit stop!" He fell back grabbing his face with trembling hands.

"Okay, sorry, bro. I thought I'd made myself clear that if you didn't respond to me then I was going to get violent. Apparently you didn't understand that part." Walter looked around again, but saw no other signs of life. No purse on the dining room table, no open beer bottles on the counter down the hall. "Is there anyone else here?"

"NO, asshole, I live alone!" Tim said.

"Okay, buddy. That's good," Walter said, patting Tim's leg. "Listen. I just came to let you know that your involvement in Codi Cohl's life has come to its end. Do we understand each other?"

"You think you can intimidate me, you piece of shit?" Tim said, returning to his elbow to look at Walter again.

Walter shrugged and made an oops face. "Shit, I don't know! I guess I don't really care if you're intimidated." Walter, without cocking, slapped Tim across the face. And it wasn't a soft slap. It was the kind that would leave bruising and potentially detach corneas. Tim cried out again and fresh blood hit the wall. "I didn't come to intimidate you, Timothy. I came to give you a message."

"I have nothing to say to that bitch whore," Tim said, now looking like he was tired of the game. Like he just wanted to be done with this charade.

"Good. Because I'm not good at remembering messages. I'm not much of a messenger, actually. No. Like I said, I came to deliver a message. But it's not from her. It's from me. I've known her for only a few months now, but I like her a lot. And I like to take care of my friends." Walter smiled again.

"I just want to be clear here, bud. If you ever come within a mile of her again, you had better do an about-face and high-tail it out of there. Consider this a friendly restraining request. Because if I ever hear about your getting close to her again, or – much less – hurting her, I will come back and kill you. I will take your fucking throat right out of your neck." Walter reached out and clasped Tim around the neck, in much the same way Tim had done to Codi not a couple of hours before. And he squeezed until Tim's eyes started bulging. "Do you have any doubt that I could make that happen?" The fear in Tim's eyes was answer enough, but he managed to shake his head very slightly. Walter let go, and patted his shoulder now. "Good. Good. Okay. Just making sure."

Walter stood up and brushed his hands against his trousers and looked around once more. Then he saw the phone on the ground just behind Tim. The screen was still on, and it showed a connected call to 911. Walter shook his head and looked up at the ceiling. Then he chuckled in his throat. He lifted his foot and smashed the screen, breaking the phone almost completely in two. "Good move, Tim. Listen, I'm not a bad ass. I don't do this for a living or anything, I mean. But if you fuck with her ever again, I'll find you. Do we have an understanding now?"

Tim stared at Walter for a long moment, perhaps considering a riposte. He apparently thought better of it though, because he nodded. "Yeah. I get it."

"All right. That's good. Glad we got that cleared up. Sorry about your mouth, man. You know, that shit just happens sometimes when you rape and strangle defenseless blind women." Then he stepped on Tim's outstretched hand and twisted his boot as he turned for the door, not liking at all the crunches and pops he felt through his heel.

As he closed the door behind him, he raised his hands above his head and got down on his knees for the police, who were coming up the walkway, calmly covering their sidearms with gloved hands. "No trouble here, officers."

"Oh, there's trouble, partner," one of the men said as he clicked the cuffs on Walter's sweating, blood-covered wrist.

⌘   ⌘   ⌘

"Walter's in jail."

"What? What the hell are you talking about?" Callie cried. She covered the mouthpiece and mouthed to Jack, *Walter's in jail!*

"Look, there's a lot of bad shit going on right now," Rebecca said. "I could really use some moral support if you're not too busy."

"Sure, sweetie! What can I do? Do you want me to come over?" Callie said.

"Oh that would be wonderful. I don't have a ton of friends around here, and-" Rebecca started.

"Stop it. No excuses. You can call me any time. I'll be over in a few minutes," Callie said. "Do you need anything?"

"Do you have any vodka?" Rebecca said.

"Got you covered, sister," Callie said. "See you in a few."

"Great. Thank you. Oh, and Callie?"

"Uh huh?"

"You can bring Jack too if you want."

They sat at the kitchen table. Callie sat directly across from Rebecca. Jack stood wandering around the living room for a bit until Rebecca pulled out the seat next to her and patted it. "Come sit, sugar. We're not talking about anything you can't hear," she said. Before she had done that though, she had looked at Callie with eyes wide as saucers and mouthed the word *Wow!* Callie had smiled brightly and nodded, widening her own eyes. *I know!*

But then as Jack took his seat next to Rebecca, she sat with her elbows on the table, twisting the rings on her fingers. Callie sat staring at this for a few minutes. Jack pulled the paper bag up from the floor and set it on the table. "We brought you some Stoli, Rebecca."

She leaned in and put her arm across the front of his neck, pulling him in for a face-to-face hug. "You're a dear. Thank you."

Callie stood and started for the bar but he held his hand out. "I'll get it, babe." She smiled at him and he fetched a glass, then returned to the table.

Callie looked at him blankly. "I'm sorry, but does she only have one glass?" she said.

"Yeah, seriously? When women cry together, they drink together," Rebecca said, spreading her hands and looking at him.

Jack stood again quickly and said, "Sorry, I didn't realize..."

"Grab yourself one too, gorgeous," Rebecca said. She reached forward and took Callie's hand on the table. "Callie. Callie, Callie, Callie. Thank you so much for coming. I am so screwed up right now."

"I can tell. What can I do?" Callie said, squeezing the hand she held. Jack returned with two more glasses and set them up.

Rebecca pulled her hand out and took a deep breath, twisting the top off the Russian special. She poured it tall into the short glasses, then screwed the cap back on and took a long drink from it. Callie had been waiting, thinking there would be ice, or olives, or… something. She made an internal shrug and picked the glass up. Neat it is, she thought. "Cheers, Bec."

"Oh. Shit. Sorry, yeah. Cheers, guys," she said, holding her now half-full glass up. They clinked them together and took sips.

"So yeah. Walter is in jail." She held up her fingers in the air, elbows still on the table, and said, "But that's the least of it. Codi is in the hospital."

Callie covered her mouth with her hand. "Oh my God!"

Jack sat sipping, politely quiet.

"Yeah." She breathed in deeply and twisted her head around, stretching her neck. "I came home earlier and found her unconscious on the floor in the hallway. She was just about naked."

Callie now had both hands on her mouth and she was staring with fiery intensity at Rebecca. Her heart was pounding in her chest.

"Tim, her ex-fiancé, apparently forced his way in while I was away, and choked her."

"Good God," Jack said under his breath. He was staring at his glass on the table.

Rebecca looked at him for a minute, and went back to twisting her many rings. "Yeah. He also raped her."

"Jesus, Rebecca!" Callie said. She felt her face drain of color. This was too close to home.

"So I'm guessing that's why Walter is in jail?" Jack said, his first real addition to the meeting.

"Yeah. I tried to stop him from going. To talk some reason into him, but he wouldn't hear it. He instructed me to call an ambulance while he went to Tim's house. Apparently fixed him up real good."

"Well, that's Walter for you. He's a good man, Rebecca. If he believes in something, you can't stop him from standing up for it."

"Fuckin' A," Jack said, still looking at his glass.

Both women turned to look at him. After a brief silence, he realized it was quiet, and looked up. "Sorry. I uh..."

The girls looked back at each other. "So Tim is also in the hospital."

"I know I'll regret asking, but..." Callie started, but trailed off as Rebecca raised one eyebrow.

"They won't let me see her." Then she opened her palms, as a *there you have it* gesture, and added, "Hence my calling you. I'm a wreck. Needed someone to calm my nerves."

Callie squeezed her hand and smiled wanly. "God, I'm so sorry, Rebecca. Anything we can do, just let me know. Let us know," she added, looking at Jack with the same weak smile. No one was expecting reality behind the smiles. Not here, at this particular table. It was just a reminder that there was always sunlight after the storm.

"You're doing plenty just be being here, sweetie. Believe me. And this," she said, lifting her glass and draining it. "I really needed this."

"Oy," Jack said, and drank the rest of his. Callie thought she detected a sense of duty there. He would not have drained it had Rebecca not done so. He probably didn't even drink vodka. Another thing Callie still did not know about her new boyfriend. Callie smiled a little more easily at him and took a swig from her own glass.

"I'm sorry, Rebecca. I'm not tough enough to drink it like this. Can I get some ice?" Callie said.

"Ha! Oh my God, of course, sugar. I can't believe you think you have to ask!" she said, scooting out from the table. She went to the freezer and filled a bowl with ice and came back, slinging it on the table. "You guys don't have to drink it like me. Hell, you don't even have to drink!"

Callie was about to speak up when Rebecca added, "Well, you do. I need you to drink with me." She was looking at Callie. She turned to Jack. "You don't have to drink. But I need a sister right now."

"I'm at your service, Rebecca. If you want me to drink, I'll finish the bottle with you. If you want me to leave, I can do that. Anything you need. A friend of Callie's is a friend of mine."

Rebecca smiled at him and let her gaze linger on him for a long moment. "You're a doll, Jack. Easy on the eyes, too, I might add," she said and patted his hand on the table. He held back a smile and just did a courteous nod instead. "You got yourself a good one, Callie."

"So what's our game plan?" Callie said, now feeling like a team. She dropped a few ice moons into her glass and stirred it with the tip of her finger while Rebecca watched, seemingly very interested.

"Well, I think maybe we finish this bottle first. Maybe we'll come up with something by the bottom." She was back to twisting her rings. "They're supposed to call me when she's stable. If anything changes at all."

Callie nodded slowly.

"They won't let us see her any time soon, it doesn't look like. They're doing a rape kit on her, and there's an investigation and all that. So we won't do much good there." She was looking at Callie. "Are you okay?"

"Me?" Callie said, hand against her chest. "Yeah, I'm okay. A little in shock, I guess, but I'm okay." Callie tilted her head and squinted at Rebecca. "Are *you* okay?"

She shrugged. "That's the big question. Unfortunately, one I can't answer right now. Maybe after another drink," she said, and screwed the cap off the bottle again.

Callie then frowned with a realization. "So how did you know Walter was in jail?"

"One free call," she responded, absently. She was looking out the back window at the gray, rainy sky. Callie felt her heart miss a beat, definitely from jealousy. Walter, her friend of almost half her life, gets one call, but he uses it to call Rebecca instead of her? That hurt. And Rebecca must have seen it. Because she looked back right at that moment, and took Callie's hand again.

"Don't be hurt, honey. He didn't want to scare you. He told me to let you know in as serene a way as I could manage. He only called me because he had just left my place to go after that jerk."

It helped a little, but Callie still felt a little dejected. But Rebecca was right, she would have been scared. She probably would not have handled it nearly as well as Rebecca had.

"Okay, well what *can* we do then?" Callie said, trying to change the subject.

"We sit and wait. And drink. Strength in numbers, right?"

"Is there any way to get Walter out?" Jack asked. Good thinking, Jack, Callie thought. Why hadn't she thought to ask that? She was too busy being hurt by who he had called instead, that's why.

"Not yet. He has to see the judge first, which probably won't happen until tomorrow morning, at the very earliest. Then they'll set his bond and schedule a hearing," Rebecca said. She was about halfway into her second glass now, still drinking it neat. "I did call his lawyer for him though. So things are at work behind the scenes."

"That's just flipping great," Callie said, exasperated.

Rebecca frowned at her. "Never learned to cuss, darling?"

Callie tightened her mouth and raised her eyebrows. "I slip up sometimes, but I try to keep a clean mouth."

"You got a good woman there, Jack," Rebecca said, pointing at Callie but looking at him. Callie felt flutters in her stomach. It was a banal compliment at best, but Rebecca seemed powerful. Intimidating. To be considered good by a good woman seemed a pretty great accomplishment.

Jack smiled at Callie and took her hand. He didn't say anything. His eyes said it all.

Callie finally finished her first glass, and was reaching for more ice when the front door opened. She glanced sharply at Rebecca, automatically thinking it was Tim, returning for more of Codi, but instantly remembered how impossible that was. Rebecca met her eyes over the table and frowned, herself. Then her frown fell as she looked up over Callie's shoulder. She leaned back and let go of Callie's hand, and swallowed. It took every bit of willpower Callie had not to turn around. Somehow it felt inappropriate to look. Voyeuristic.

"Hi," said a female's voice behind her.

Rebecca cleared her throat. Callie could see the faintest hint of glass in her eyes. "Hi, Dommie."

Jack, Callie saw, looked at Dommie and watched in silence. She could tell that Dommie wasn't looking at Jack, because he would have smiled or nodded or something. That meant she was staring at Rebecca. But who the hell was she?

"Introductions?" said the woman behind Callie.

Rebecca cleared her throat again, then stood up. "Oh yeah. I'm so sorry. This is my friend, Callie, and her boyfriend, Jack." Callie twitched at the appropriateness of that statement and its technically accurate depiction of their entire situation. And then she turned to greet the newcomer.

"Hi," Callie said, standing and sticking her hand out through the arch window that separated the kitchen from the living room where Dommie stood.

"Jack, Callie, this is Natalie," said Rebecca from behind her. Callie's heart skipped a beat.

W alter made bail the next morning. He stood in the courtroom lobby in yesterday's clothes, tired and disheveled. He had not slept a wink the night before. He hadn't even been processed before he was released. Having spent the last fifteen hours sitting in a plastic chair in the processing room of the correctional facility, he was humiliated and in a bit of a cranky mood. In this room a large group of future inmates sat in perfect rows, males across the room from the females, overlooked by a long table with three officers doing the paperwork. They would laugh and joke and lean back in their rolling chairs, stretching and walking around, enjoying their freedom while all the pre-processed sat quietly fearing their futures.

Now here he stood, waiting for Thevi to come pick him up. His clothes had been soaked with rain the day before, and then had dried. They still smelled like the rain. Sitting in that room where the officers had about as much of a sense of urgency as a set of snails on an uphill run, he had begun to wonder if he would freeze to death. Cold, miserable and angry.

When Thevi arrived, she came into the lobby and stopped when she saw him standing there. He had been pacing, silently cursing himself. There were several other parolees in the room with him, and it was more than just a little obvious when she breezed in the door. Every head turned. She stood there with the door behind her, red hair pulled back into two small piggy tails on the sides of her head. Her hair wasn't long enough to make a real tail. The freckles on her face stood out bright and beautiful in the offensive light of the lobby. They stared silently at each other for a brief instant, and then Walter saw her breathe in deeply and lower her chin, ready to take on the brunt of his bad mood.

When she came toe to toe with him, she looked up slowly. He could see anticipation and unsure in her eyes. He put his hand on her jaw, slowly stroking her cheekbone. "God are you a sight for sore eyes," he said. "I haven't seen anyone this beautiful since… Well, since last time I saw you."

She smiled weakly. "Are you okay, baby?"

He nodded. "Yeah, I'm okay. Have you heard anything about Codi?"

Her eyes got wide. "Who's Codi?"

"What the fuck? Seriously? No one had the courtesy to get you in the loop?"

"What loop? Walter, I don't even know why you're in here."

He shook his head and breathed in deeply. Unbelievable. "Let's go." He took her hand and led her out the front door, into the shitty morning weather.

"Walter, I am so sorry," Callie said. She was holding Thevi's hand. "Thevi, baby, Rebecca called me and told me he was in jail. I made probably a thousand assumptions in that one second. I don't consciously recall wondering whether someone had told you. But I think somewhere deep inside my mind I must have assumed that if she knew, you knew. There's no way it would have trickled down to me without you first knowing."

Thevi was nodding. "Look, it's not a really big deal, Callie. You guys are making a big deal out of it, but I was just kind of like, what the fuck, right? I mean," she said, and spread her hands. They were standing on the front porch of Rebecca's apartment. Callie was in borrowed pajamas, having spent the night on the couch keeping Rebecca company. That was her story, anyway. The truth was that she had been too drunk to get home safely. Jack, ever the gentleman, had slept on the floor next to her, holding her ankle. Much the same way Walter himself had done, once upon a time. The further truth was that Rebecca no longer needed keeping company. Natalie, or 'Dommie' was back. Whatever that meant.

"I'll tell you why it's a big deal, Callie," Walter said, rounding on her. "When a man spends the night away from his wife, she tends to get worried. She had no fucking clue where I was." He was raising his voice a little, and his hands were doing a lot of talking in Callie's face.

"Walter, chill the freak out, dude," Callie said. "You're making me uncomfortable."

"Uncomfortable? Really?" he said, turning away.

"Uh, yeah, butt hole! Think about what happened here yesterday! In this very hallway!" she said, waving her hand at the door.

"You think I would hit you Callie? Choke you? Rape you?" Walter said, getting right in her face.

She breathed in slowly and swallowed. "No. Of course not. I'm sorry it sounded like that. I'm just saying that I'm a little freaked out about violence right now," she said, crossing her arms to put a little distance between them without having to take a step back.

"Here's the thing, Walter. Thevi didn't call me either. She could have called her best friend if she was worried about you."

"I'm standing right here, Callie," Thevi said, waving at her.

Callie grabbed Thevi's arm and said, "Thev, honey, that's not what I mean. I'm just-"

"What do you mean, Callie?" Thevi responded, yanking her arm away.

Callie stood shaking her head, speechless now. *What the heck is going on here?* She grunted and raised her hands. "Look. I'm not the only one to blame for your not knowing. Why does it fall on me? Why am I the primary communicator of events here?" Callie said. She was beginning to get loud.

"Because you knew where I was. Thevi is your 'best friend' as you just said yourself. Why wouldn't you call her? Ask if she needed a shoulder to cry on? Ask if she needed help? Hell, ask if she knew about it!" Walter said.

Callie shook her head, disbelief in her eyes. "Seriously? Why didn't you call her instead of Rebecca? Jesus, Walter!"

He turned away again, pacing. This didn't look like something she was going to win. She saw his argument, and it was valid. But so was hers, and they were both refusing to see it. "Whatever, guys. I explained myself. If that's not good enough, then leave me out of it from now on," Callie said, holding her hands up in defeat and turning for the door. She was sick now with disappointment and fear that she was about to lose two good friends over something as stupid as a forgotten phone call.

"Wait." It was Thevi. Callie stopped at the door, but did not turn around. "Walt, Callie has a point. I didn't call her either. Which lends even more to the point that she thought I already knew. Let's not get so sideways here that we start doing stupid shit."

"Why *didn't* you call her, TJ?" Walter said. Callie turned to look at them again. He stood crossing his arms.

Thevi took a deep breath. "To be honest, hon, I fell asleep. I was watching court TV and just sort of dozed off on the couch."

"For fifteen hours?" Walter said.

"Of course not. But when I woke up, it was middle of the night. I figured you were out drinking or something. I didn't worry. Like I said earlier, this was not that big of a deal."

"Thanks," he said.

"Okay, shut it. Now you're being obtuse on purpose."

Callie stood with her own arms crossed for a minute, looking back and forth between them. When she felt like the air had cleared a little, or at least enough to move on, she finally spoke. "Walt. Guess who's here."

Her initial impression was that Natalie was pretty. She certainly wasn't stunning like Codi. Or heck, even like Rebecca. Rebecca had her way. Her loose spirit, her hippy attitude and casual style – she was a very attractive person. And pretty. Natalie was just your average girl-next-door, Callie thought. She had choppy shoulder-length mousy hair and brown eyes beneath thick, dark eyebrows. Her lips were thin and unremarkable, and her face was mostly round. She watched Walter's reaction carefully, but only saw curiosity and interest on his face, as they had suddenly happened upon the mystery woman they had been chasing. Of course, chasing wasn't the right word, as they hadn't started the chase yet. But they had planned to. And she would have been their pursuit. Convenient it was, then, that she came to them instead.

They all sat on the living room floor, simply because that's where Natalie had been when they walked in. She was sitting Indian-style with the fire at her right, a funny-shaped orange ashtray just at her feet, and what was left of the bottle of Stoli within easy reach. Callie saw no glass and reckoned she must be partaking direct from the fountain. She looked up at them when they walked in, but didn't question what they were doing there. She had, of course, been aware of Callie's presence already. They had spent most of the morning talking already. But apparently it was cool for Callie to invite in her friend and his wife. So they all followed suit, kicked off their shoes and formed a circle. This was, of course, after the introduction.

Callie had come in and propped back down on the pillow directly across from Natalie, where she had been before Walter had banged on the door with Thevi in tow. She then looked up and said, "Walter, Thevi," swinging her hand from them dramatically over to Natalie, "this is Natalie."

Walter had looked at her for a moment, studying her, perhaps wondering why that name should have meant anything to him. And then he looked at Callie, and saw her smiling. He looked at her mouth, and then his eyes widened. He looked back at Natalie and they got really wide. Then back at Callie. "Natalie? Holy shit, *the* Natalie?" he said, and bounded around the couch to shake her hand.

Natalie had watched all of this with detached interest. She was almost smiling, but that might have been the music as well. She was bobbing her head to One Last Orbit and their spooky, spacey melodies. Walter bent to shake her hand, which she accepted with a smile, and then he sat down between Callie and her. "Babe, have a seat!" he said, offering her the last quarter of the circle, which was directly across from him, back to the fire. Thevi breathed in deeply, then dropped her purse on the couch and took the seat happily. She had been shivering, Callie noticed.

"Oh man, it's so good to meet you," Walter said.

Natalie looked at him through smoke-squinted eyes, pulling from a short joint between her thumb and two fingers. "Yeah, I'm a real legend around these parts," she said.

Walter suddenly looked around. "Is Bec at work?"

Natalie and Callie nodded at the same time. She finished her puff and passed it to Thevi. "Wrong way," Walter said, and held out his hand. Thevi laughed and slapped his hand away.

Callie rolled her eyes. "We're used to poker," she said. Then Callie looked at Walter and said, "You'll be interested to know that she knows a little bit about our quandary."

"Oh yeah?" he asked. "Like what?" He looked at Natalie, hoping she would do the talking. But Callie spoke for her.

"Royal has been going out to Mars for the last two decades. Is that right?" Callie asked Natalie. Natalie nodded.

"Yeah," Callie continued, "so tell him how you know."

Natalie frowned. "Well I used to work there."

"Wait. You worked at Royal and then at PSS, right?" Walter asked, pointing at her. He then took the proffered joint from Callie and took a lengthy hit.

"Yeah. But that's uh…" Natalie began. "Wait. You know they're the same company, right?"

Walter and Callie looked at each other. He shook his head slowly and his mouthed dropped open. "You've got to be fucking kidding me." He passed the joint to Natalie, completing the circle.

She took it and just shook her head. Walter pointed at the bottle, which she handed to him without speaking. "So are you saying Royal owns PSS?" Walter said. Thevi sat looking pleasant across from him, just happy to be there. She didn't need to be involved. Callie loved watching them be together, and was glad they had been able to get past the earlier BS.

Natalie shrugged, then offered the joint to Thevi. Thevi shook her head and leaned back on her hands, looking expectantly at her, as if she were as interested in her answers as they were. Natalie dropped the roach in the orange ashtray and blew smoke out sideways.

"Okay, so here's the thing. They don't directly own them. At least not technically. But Royal is the only reason PSS exists. Let's just say that."

"Okay, we're saying that," Walter said. He was leaning forward, waiting patiently. Well, as patiently as Walter could wait.

"Kim Coyin – you know him?" she said, pausing. The others shook their heads. "He's the CEO of Royal. Well, he was at the time," she said, looking like she was losing patience with herself. "Anyway, he saw the need for a private corporation who would provide those services with absolute and perfect discretion." She took the bottle back from Walter and took a big swig, Callie noticed, without even bothering to wipe off the mouth from where Walter had chugged. Callie reached out, asking for it when she finished. She wanted to be part of this.

"So skip ahead, you know the rest of the story. You already know why he needed that," Natalie said.

"So Royal could go to Mars? Jesus. That's insane." He sat shaking his head for a few seconds, just soaking it all in. "Twenty fuckin' years?"

Natalie raised her eyebrows and gave him a passive smile. "That I know of. Shit, I guess it could have been fifty. But yeah, when PSS was founded, that's when they started officially going. However, it's always been top-secret. So I guess that's not very 'official', is it?"

Walter put his hands on the sides of his head, trying to squeeze some sense into it. This was all making too much sense. "Fuck! I think that's what Julia was trying to tell me. Man," he said, leaning back on his hands like Thevi, and looking at the slow-spinning ceiling fan. "I wish I could talk to her again now, knowing what I know now."

"I doubt she'll talk, Walter. She's a company gal. She's pretty true to her NDAs," Natalie said.

He shrugged. "Okay, so what else do you know?"

"Honey, I know more than I want to know." She leaned forward and opened a small zipper pouch and began rolling another joint. "Pass me that bottle, Mr. Jones," she said, holding her hand out. Callie handed it to Natalie, who drank deep from it, then set it back in the middle.

"You know Brian Bradley?" Walter said.

She waved one finger at him while her other hand continued effortlessly on the joint. Natalie was quite skilled at this, Callie saw. "No, I don't. Callie already asked me that. I don't know him, but I don't think he matters, based on what she told me."

Walter looked at Callie, but Callie, having already spoken at length about all this with Natalie, just shrugged and smiled wanly at him. She wanted all the answers as badly – or worse, even – than Walter. But they just weren't there yet.

"Okay, you're gonna have to explain that one to me. I thought he was the bad guy in all of this."

"No!" Natalie shouted, holding that pointer finger up in the air now. She started slinging it to the beat of the music. "God damn I love OLO." She finished rolling the new joint and licked it, then lit it. "He was the bad guy, perhaps, in your little event. The..." she looked at Callie and twirled that same finger in the air, asking for help.

Callie prompted her. "Atlas to Mars."

"Yes. That!" Natalie said, pointing at Callie before putting the hand back down on the floor where it supported her swaying body. "The Atlas mission. But he's not my bad guy."

"What the fuck does that mean?" Walter said, frowning. He looked at his wife, who now had her eyes half-closed, still vaguely smiling at Natalie. He held out his hand to her, and she looked at him, then took it. Walter pulled her closer, and then guided her head down to his lap. She complied and curled her legs up, going fetal in the middle of the now-broken circle to rest a while. Walter put his hand over her head, playing with her hair, rubbing her neck, touching her ears. Callie adored watching all of this love.

"What it means," Natalie said, leaning real close to him, "is that you're chasing a different bad guy than I am."

"You're chasing someone too?" Walter asked.

"Would be. A different bad guy than I would be, if I were trying to bring them down," Natalie corrected.

Walter looked back at Callie. "What's with all the fuckin enigma here? We're not trying to bring down the company. Just the guy who brought down our favorite mission."

Natalie shrugged. She was obviously very high, Callie saw. Callie took the joint from her and pulled from it, hoping to reach the same level soon.

"Suit yourself," Natalie said. "I'm just saying, there's a lot more sinister shit going on in that company than just some guys trying to keep your mission from making Mars."

"Mind blowing," Walter said.

"I told ya," Callie said, smiling at him.

"Huh? What the fuck. You didn't tell me shit!"

"Well," she shrugged. "I was going to tell you. That's what I meant. I wanted you to hear it from the horse's mouth."

Natalie took another swig from the near-empty bottle. "I've been called worse."

"Okay. So where should we go? I mean, what should we do? Who should we be after?" Walter asked. His hands were now clasped over Thevi's shoulder. She was out.

"Which one of those do you want me to answer?" Natalie said.

"The most important one," Walter said. He took the bottle from her and put his mouth on it. "Your choice," he added after a big swallow.

"Okay then. Simple. Fiji."

Callie sat up a little straighter. This part, she had not yet heard. Fiji? Fiji what? There was that damned word again. She looked at Walter. He was staring back at her. He looked drunk. Walter was already swimming in the vodka, and she tried to remember how many pulls he'd had from that bottle. Four? Five? She couldn't remember. But then, she was now having trouble remembering much of anything. She was higher than the exponent at the end of a big number. But this stuff was important! She hoped she would be able to recall it later. Callie leaned over onto her elbow and put her hand on Thevi's shoulder. "Walter, are you going to remember all this?"

"What, are you stoned?" he said, frowning at her. Then he returned his gaze to Natalie. "Which one was that?"

"The where. You go to Fiji, you'll find everything you're looking for," Natalie said, nodding slowly, the joint glowing red against the backdrop of her thin lips.

⌘　　　⌘　　　⌘

The next day, they were allowed to see Codi. So they all did. Walter drove and Jack sat up front with him while Callie and Rebecca rode in the back. They had to take turns as couples going in to see her, so Jack went in with Rebecca, and Walter with Callie. Rebecca was excited to see her. She had felt like a piece was missing from her heart. She did not dare question whether this was displaced emotion caused by the absence and now reappearance of Natalie, her Dommie. Not yet, at least. She would have to search those feelings later.

She leaned in and cupped Codi's face in her hands, leaning in real close, just about touching noses. "Codi, baby, I'm here. It's Bec. How you doing, beautiful?"

Codi reached up and grabbed her hands and squeezed. "Rebecca? Oh, glory, it's so wonderful to see you!"

Rebecca laughed, closing her eyes. "Oh, I know baby doll. I missed you so much!" Her eyes were filling with tears. "I was so worried about you!"

Codi smiled, looking, searching with her eyes. But at this close proximity they were almost worthless. Rebecca didn't want to back away though. She loved being this close to Codi. Codi was the sister she had never had. There was nothing untoward about her desire for closeness. It was a mother-figure desire to protect, to love, to nurture. And Codi was well worth every ounce of love she could pour into the relationship.

"I'm so glad you came to see me! I missed you too!" Codi said, still searching Rebecca's face with her eyes, now touching her cheeks with soft, tentative hands.

Rebecca leaned in again and put her forehead against Codi's. "Are they treating you right in here?'

"I think so!" she said. Her voice was cracking and weak.

"Good. Good, good, good. Do you know why you're here?" Rebecca asked.

Codi closed her mouth and her face went sad. She nodded slowly, twisting her mouth in anguish. "Yes. They told me."

"Don't you worry about him, Codi Cohl. He's not gonna bother you no more," Rebecca assured. She was still head-to-head with Codi, but now was running her fingernails through the hair above Codi's ears. "Big bro Walter took care of him real good," she said.

Codi had a single burst of laughter. Her breath right against Rebecca's face smelled thickly of hospital. Rebecca kissed her on the lips, then stood up. She held onto Codi's hands though. "Honey, Jack is here with me. You want to say hi to him?"

"Who?" she said. Her eyes looked sad, longing. Perhaps she didn't remember Jack, but it looked as though she wanted to. She was trying to.

Jack stepped forward and took her other hand. "Jack Carpenter. Hi Codi. You don't know me very well, but we're in the sub together."

Her face lit up with memory, and it warmed Rebecca's heart. She had been worried that there might be memory loss. This was definitely refreshing.

"Hi, Jack. You're Callie's boyfriend now, right?"

He nodded, looking at Rebecca. For what? For approval? "Yes, I am."

"Well why didn't you just say that, silly goose?" Codi said. They all giggled at that. Then the door opened and Walter and Callie came waltzing in.

"Hey, hey, hey!" Walter said. "Is that Codi Cohl over there?"

Her face got serious as she no doubt tried to place the voice.

"Hey CoCo!" Callie said, smiling and clapping. "So glad you're back with us!"

"Is that Callie?" Codi said.

Rebecca looked up at Callie and smiled widely. She took Jack's hand and led him out.

⌘   ⌘   ⌘

Callie drew a stool over and sat on it so she could be close to Codi. She leaned in close and rested her chin on the rail, one hand holding Codi's weak right hand, where an IV tube disappeared under a thick patch of tape. Walter sat on the other side, twirling back and forth on his stool. He was busy looking around the room though, where Callie was watching every expression Codi made as she spoke in her scratchy voice.

"Tell me about you," Callie said.

"Well," Codi said, raising her eyebrows, "I'm not sure what there is to say. I remember dancing in the living room. I was listening to good music. Dancing. Being free. I was wearing..." she stopped and thought for a minute. "I know, I swear I was wearing underwear. But apparently they found me without any on. So maybe I wasn't."

Oh my God! They haven't told her! Callie looked sharply at Walter. He had stopped the motion and was staring at Codi. Then he looked up and met Callie's eyes. It looked like he was thinking the same thing. He shook his head subtly and looked away, returning to what he had been doing.

"Anyway, I was dancing. Dancing..." she said, putting her hand on her chest, looking at the space directly in front of her face, searching for answers.

"Walter, turn down the lights," Callie said. He wheeled across the room and flipped a series of switches. Most of the lights went out.

"Oh my God, that's much better," Codi said, turning her head toward Callie. "Oh, hi Callie. You're beautiful."

Callie smiled broadly. A tear touched the corner of her eye. "Thank you, sweet gorgeous. You are too!" She felt warm inside. "I wonder what I look like to you."

"I remember you, Callie. I looked at you through the machine. I will never forget what you look like. And now my memory is associated with that look. Not this shitty pixelated fuckery of vision. Don't worry. I've got you stored as one of those beautiful flowers."

Callie's eyes let go. "Codi, that's the sweetest thing anyone has ever said to me."

Codi smiled. A wide, big, genuine smile. "Thank you for coming to see me, Callie. Jack is a lucky guy to have you. I'm so glad you guys found each other."

On the way out, Callie was drying her eyes, trying to maintain composure. But she felt herself cracking. She felt like she needed to finish crying. Like it might happen when she got home, whether she wanted it to or not. Codi had stirred up a lot of emotion in her with that soft broken voice of hers. What a powerful girl she was to go through this hell and still be in good enough spirits to be complimentary to her friends. Callie was humbled. As Walter drove them home, she found herself doing a lot of soul searching. Here she was with perfect eyes, but had no doubt that Codi saw the world with a lot more clarity than Callie did.

After staring through the window at the gray rainy world outside for a long time, Callie leaned forward and put her arms on Walter's seat in front of her. "Can you believe they didn't tell her, Walt?"

"They will. If the rape kit comes back positive, they have to tell her," Walter said.

"Oh. Okay, good. Just wondering why they hadn't already," she said, leaning back in her seat again.

Rebecca said, "Those things take time. But the main reason is probably because they don't want to traumatize her any more than she already is."

"When is a good time to tell someone that?" Callie said, frowning and furling her mouth. This didn't make sense to her. She knew that if she woke from a coma and they waited several days to tell her that she had been raped, she would be angry they had withheld it.

Rebecca put her hand on Callie's, calming her. Callie looked at it. "Callie, sweetie, they're not keeping it from her. They have to be sure it's positive, for one thing, and they also have to be sure she's ready to hear it. Right now she doesn't even remember Tim coming over there. So if they want to prove there was a rape, they may have to go to trial."

"Oh my God!" Callie said. "They know she was choked! They know she was unconscious! If they found any evidence then it *had* to be rape!"

Rebecca looked levelly at her. "You tell that to the judge. In a court of law."

"I wish it were all that easy," Walter added.

"Speaking of courts of law, Walter, how's your thing going?"

"I bonded out. I'll be back in front of the judge within the next month or so. Jennifer says it's unlikely to go to trial, but I will probably face probation and maybe community service."

"Well that's good," she said.

"What did you do to him, Walter?" Callie asked.

"I just showed him what it felt like to be Codi," he said. Before anyone else could speak, he raised a finger and said, "Short the sexual assault."

"Ugh, Walter," Rebecca said. Then, "Hey, drop me at my car instead of my door."

Walter nodded.

"Where you going, Rebecca?" Callie asked.

"I'm gonna go grab Sam. He just got back in town, so he's anxious to go see her."

CHAPTER 27

Walter's ship came in on exactly the wrong day. The certified letter came the week after he had bonded out – not a month later, like he had hoped – and instructed him to appear on February 28th at the Monmouth County Courthouse for arraignment. When he signed for the letter, he turned and leaned back against the wall, dropping his chin to his chest. "This is bad," he said to himself. And then Thevi had come into the room and seen him standing there. She instinctively knew what it was, and went to hold him. She put her head on his chest and wrapped her arms around his waist.

"When is it?" she said softly, without looking up.

"Last day of the month," he answered.

For a moment she was silent, and then said, "Good wow, that was fast.

"I guess it's not their busy season."

She looked up at him, chin on his chest, staring into his eyes. "Walter, no matter what happens, I want you to know that what you did was extremely brave. Codi is lucky to have you as a friend. Anyone would be. That was an amazing act of defense."

"It was fucking stupid is what it was. The court's not going to see it as defensive at all. If I would have been there when he attacked Codi, that argument might have held up."

"Brave, Walter. That's the old-school way. Back when men handled shit for themselves without chicken-shit calling the cops," Thevi said.

He took a deep breath. "I know what you and all my friends think. Unfortunately my case is different than his."

"What do you mean?" she asked, frowning.

"He will be arraigned for assaulting her. But not at the same time. If it all happened in the same appearance, his might cancel mine out."

For the rest of the month, Walter's stomach was in knots. He had trouble keeping his appetite, didn't want to socialize, and found himself moody and quick to anger. The not knowing part was the hardest thing for him. If he knew he was going to jail, or not, then it would be easier to prepare for it. At this point, he was preparing just to prepare. He had no idea what to prepare for. So, he decided, he would start planning for the worst.

Walter called Callie the morning after he received the letter, and let her know that he was being arraigned, and it might interfere with the trip. He also asked her to notify Minus in some discreet way, that Walter might not be available after all, and to start planning to fill his spot on the ship. When Callie called Minus though, he told her he already knew what was going on. "The papers," he had said, "Are still a pretty reliable source for news." He had not sounded worried though, Callie told Walter afterward. It wasn't something Walter should worry about from the company's perspective.

The ship crew, different from the mission crew, was already on their way to the site with the submersible on board. They had spent three months customizing a used 440-foot cargo vessel into the *Scylla Scout*. Every crew member would have his or her own cabin instead of the small shared bunks originally installed. Minus was also adding a few 'surprises' as he called them, even though he had already spilled most of the secrets. One of them was a full-scale theater. It had fifty chairs in stadium seating with a 200-inch screen and surround sound. He had the tech team install a computer with twenty terabytes of drive space in it, and had them load it full of high-definition movies for the crew's entertainment. But the real reason for the theater, everyone knew, was that during the dives, the screen would display what the cameras were seeing in real-time. Any non-essential personnel were free to sit in there and watch the dives on the big screen.

Another of the so-called surprises was a fully stocked arcade room. Minus loved arcade games, and had personally donated ten from his own house as well as ordering fifteen others. His friend Brad built custom computer-based pinball tables. Minus commissioned him to build two special for this trip. The themes? Well, Call of Cthulhu, obviously.

There was also to be a fully stocked bar with, as Callie had specially requested, a dance floor for the girls to let loose in the evenings. Minus had agreed with a smirk. "Sure thing, Cal. I'll make it happen." He was completely into this thing, she and Walter had noticed. Obsessed might be a tame word to use for it.

The eighteen-man crew whose job it was to captain the ship, provide maintenance and janitorial services, and also cover the cooking and wait-staff had left port about the time Walter was paying Tim a little visit. They would arrive about a week before the mission crew. The mission crew were all making the long trip into Osaka on a chartered 787 jumbo jet.

Things were quiet for the few weeks up until the end of the month. Callie had gone back to work at Bohr just to get caught up on the projects she had put on hold for the Monster Hunt. Her boss, a wiry old man with bushy white eyebrows named Charles Lancey, was happy to see her. He came into her office after she had been there for half an hour or so, and sat on the end of her desk, smiling at her. Charles carried himself like royalty, and dressed in nothing but perfectly tailored suits and bow ties, but was otherwise known for his kindness.

"How is the Royal engagement faring, Ms. Simmons?" he asked.

She leaned back in her chair and propped her feet up on the edge of the desk, twisting a pen in her fingers. "It's swell, Mr. Lancey. I haven't had this much fun in a long time!"

He raised his chin and pursed his lips. "Ah. I don't suppose it is within your allowance to discuss anything specific, is it? I would be very interested in hearing anything you have been granted permission to discuss."

She grinned at his formality. He had once, long ago, told her it was fine for her to call him Charles, but he would also never object to the more formal Mr. Lancey. He also insisted on the latter when they were attending functions or meetings together. So to alleviate confusion and embarrassment, she just always used the full formal.

"All I can tell you is that I helped design a submarine."

He nodded. "Well I look forward with great anticipation and child-like excitement to hear the reports upon your return." Mr. Lancey stood up and straightened his coat and shook his wooden cane. He tapped its tip against a five-hundred-dollar Italian leather loafer and said, "You take as much time as you need." Then he leaned in close as if privacy were in danger within her office, and said quietly, "And let me know if they aren't covering your expenses while you are away from your home company. I can have Trixie write you a check by this afternoon to get you by for a couple of months if you need it, Ms. Simmons."

Callie knew the accounts payable clerk's name was not Trixie. It was Diane, or Diana. She couldn't quite remember it herself, actually, but always got a kick out of Charles's unsparing use of Trixie for anyone he had no interest in remembering. Thus, about three hundred Trixies worked in this building alone.

"No, thank you, Mr. Lancey. They are paying me," Callie said.

He nodded, looking satisfied. "Are they paying you well, though?" he asked, raising a thick, unruly eyebrow.

Callie nodded, closing her eyes and tightening her mouth. She was trying not to giggle. A man with such immaculate attention to his personal appearance would seemingly take his eyebrows to the barber occasionally. Maybe he did it on purpose.

"Good," he said, patting the desk and standing on stern but twisted legs. When he left, Callie logged into her computer and checked her email. There were only eleven new ones that had come in over the last couple of months, and she found herself surprised that there were that many. Her job did not involve much interaction with other people. Those with whom she did interact typically traded information verbally. So email was almost a rare occurrence in her inbox.

However, one of them caught her eye. It was from an account at a domain she recognized as a temporary email service. A 10-Minute Mail account, typically used for site registrations and other services where someone needed a disposable or anonymous account. And there were no words.

Only a video.

Callie came running up to meet Walter, never once wondering why he was standing in the rain. She ran with her coat clasped closed with one frigid hand, the other holding her hair out of her eyes. It was sticking to her cheeks like tape. The rain had come from nowhere. One minute it had been cloudy and looked like a good snow was on the way. The next, it was a torrent.

"Oh, Walter, why?" she said through shivering but smiling teeth.

"I know. It's fuckin' terrible," he said, grabbing Callie by the elbow and helping her up the courthouse steps. They hurried up the stairs and under the high overhang, then finally into the dryness of the lobby. "What the hell are you doing here?" he asked in a hushed voice once they got inside.

She looked around for a towel rack. She didn't find one. "Walter I have really, really important news to share with you."

He raised his eyebrows at her and she raised hers, monkeying his look. "Well, what is it?"

"Thank you for asking!" she exclaimed quietly.

Walter rolled his eyes and shook his head.

"Watson, Walter," someone shouted behind them.

He looked over his shoulder, saying, "Dammit. Already?"

Callie looked at the bailiff who was calling Walter into the courtroom. She held up a finger and mouthed, *just a minute!*

The bailiff looked squarely at her and shouted, "Watson! Walter! Now!"

"Okay, dude! Hold your freakin' horses!" Callie said, tilting her head and speaking sideways at a place somewhere between them on the floor. She looked up at Walter and grabbed his shoulders as he was moving toward the courtroom. "Walter, I got a video!"

"Callie, that's-" he started.

"Someone sent me an email from an anonymous email account."

He was walking his normal long stride, and Callie was bouncing along beside him like a stumbling bunny, trying to keep up, waltzing sideways in her heels. Walter held out his hands. *So what?*

"Stop, Walt, Walter, WALTER! Just STOP!" she shouted. Even the bailiff stayed his persistence momentarily. Walter made eye contact with the man, and then stopped.

Obviously, the man could see that Callie was in charge here, and that she wasn't some random gal off the street. She wasn't the week-old girlfriend or the drag-along little sister. Callie probably looked more like a lawyer than Walter's own attorney.

Walter looked down at her, and she stared right back up, her brown eyes meeting his blue ones. She showed him the seriousness of the situation without saying anything. She might lose a few seconds to the grand, but the scheme of things would profit. He would understand better with that look than any words her fumbling mouth could ever string together that fast.

"Walter, someone from Atlas sent me a video."

"Atlas?"

She shook her head quickly. "From the Atlas. It's..." she waved her hands and closed her eyes against the stress as the bailiff shouted again.

"His honor is in a hurry Mr. Watson. If you please," said the man.

"What are you saying, Callie?" Walter said, now moving again. And to the man, "Coming, sir, I'm very sorry."

"It's been five-" she started.

"Today, Mr. Watson!" the bailiff shouted again.

She was running again. "God dammit!" Callie shouted, stopping and throwing her anger full force into her eyes, directly at the bailiff.

"Callie, you're gonna get us both thrown in jail!" Walter said, grabbing her shoulders. "I'm sorry sir, she's just lost a loved one and she's hysterical."

"She's about to lose another one, Watson!" the man shouted. Walter was now within easy reach of the man. And reach he did. He stuck his hand out and grabbed Walter's coat shoulder, narrowly missing Callie's nose with his watch.

And before she realized what had happened, she had stopped, and was watching Walter being walked to the front of the courtroom by the bailiff, and the doors were swinging shut in her face. "No!" she yelped, and grabbed the stainless steel door handle, yanking it open, and ran down the aisle to Walter. The bailiff turned right as she got to him, seizing her by the shoulders.

"Walter, the video shows the crash! You can see the ship crash into Mars!" she shouted, and suddenly there were hard steel cuffs round her wrists.

The man walked her out of the courtroom as Walter stared at her, dumbfounded. When they got into the hall, the man kicked the door closed behind him and twisted Callie up against the wall, where her wrists slammed into the tile, feeling as though they would break against the steel of the cuffs.

"I don't know what the hell your problem is, young lady, or what you think is so urgent, but you're lucky you didn't get shot!" the man said.

Callie tried to talk, but he held up a finger. She had never been in handcuffs before.

"Listen! I don't have the time, nor the desire to lock you up. But if you turn toward that door one more time, you'll be sleeping on a metal rack tonight."

She looked at him soberly, breathing heavily through her nose. She swallowed hard and blinked. "Okay. I'm sorry. I just thought this was really important."

"I see that. But running into Judge Turner's courtroom like that will get you either shot or arrested. Nothing is that important." The man pulled up his trousers and looked about the lobby, recomposing himself. "Besides, he'll be out in five minutes." The bailiff put his hand on Callie's shoulder and spun her like a ballerina, then pushed her up against the wall. Her teeth hit the tile and she whimpered.

Then the cuffs were being removed. So it came to be that Callie Simmons had handcuffs on her wrists exactly one time in her life. And they had been on for less than sixty seconds.

Three and a half minutes later, the doors swung open again, and a tall woman with dark, serious eyes, came out, hurriedly seeking Callie. "Ms. Simmons?" she said, already knowing Callie's identity. She was the only one waiting in the lobby. And she had obviously already seen the craziest side of Callie, inside the courtroom. This woman looked like she never experienced crazy. She was always in control. She would sit calmly and take care of business while the tornado tore through the neighborhood around her.

Callie breathed in deeply, seeing up close that the woman was beautiful, and made a mental note to ask Walter why his attorney was so stunning. Then she had a lighting-fast thought beyond that. *Of course he does. That's just how Walter rolls.*

"Ms. Simmons?" the woman said, and Callie extended her hand. The woman got too close too fast though, and paid no attention. She had no interest in formalities with Callie. Callie, who had come into this courthouse looking like a rocket scientist come to warn a man of the end of the world, now appeared to be the batshit mental clinic escapee from Folk Lane Hills, up the road.

"Jennifer Cambria," the woman said quickly. "Walter is being detained."

Callie's mouth dropped. "What? That man said he'd be right out!"

Cambria shook her head. She stared at Callie with disbelief. *What the hell does Walter need with this bimbo?* Then she said, "He's being charged with felony aggravated assault, and the prosecution has recommended detainment until the hearing. Well, the Page Turner agreed."

Callie gulped, looking at Cambria like a dumb fish.

"He's called the Page Turner. The judge. Because he slings people through his courtroom like hockey pucks.

Turns the pages in his docket like he's reading a comic book."

Callie still stared wide-eyed.

"Fast. He turns docket pages fast. It's hyperbole. Connect," she said, looking off around the lobby, swinging her hands out. "I tried, Walter."

Callie shook her head. "What? Walter told you to try to *connect* with me? Like it would be hard or something?" Callie looked like she had sucked on a lemon. "Look, I'm not stupid, you vapid C word!" Callie said.

That got her attention. Cambria stood up straight and swallowed, then pursed her lips. Callie apparently didn't even have to say the real C word to make it feel like she had.

"You don't have to connect with me, Jennifer. I think we got off on a bad foot," Callie said. She held her hand out again, looking down at it. Insisting. "Which is why I always start an introduction with a handshake."

The woman looked down at Callie's hand.

"I like to remember we're both humans," Callie said, looking Jennifer Cambria straight in the eyes.

"You're right." She grasped Callie's hand firmly. And did not let go. "I'm sorry. After that display in there, I was unsure how to approach you."

Callie breathed in and looked at Cambria, trying not to revel in her ascendancy. "I understand. I'm just... I'm just so shocked that they arrested Walter, that I lost my ability to speak for a moment. But it's okay. I'm okay. I'm good," Callie said, holding her hands out, removing her right one easily from the firm grip.

"I've a predilection for intellectualism. I'm just not quick and witty."

Cambria nodded, smiling. "Okay. Well, I was just trying to say that if you don't impress this judge in the first ten seconds, you're probably heading west."

Callie frowned at her. She thought she recognized that colloquialism.

"Instead of coming out the double doors, you'll be going through the side door, where the undecorated hallways are. That's where the steel doors and wired windows are."

Callie nodded.

"But Walter told me to come out here and find out what you were talking about. He said it was of earth-shattering importance."

"Really?" Callie asked, furling her mouth and wrinkling her nose.

"Yes. He said if you came busting in anywhere like that, then the world was either about to end, or someone just came back from the dead." Cambria tried a very faint smirk. "I'm inclined to agree, of course."

Callie straightened up. It made her feel good that Walter understood how important she thought this was. But she also thought that what she had said to him was more than obvious in its meaning. What more could 'you can see the ship crash into Mars' imply?

"So which is it?"

Callie looked at her sharply again, then said, "We have video of the Atlas crashing into the surface of Mars. So it's safe to say someone came back from the dead."

⌘ ⌘ ⌘

Over the next two weeks, Callie tried to carry on in her life like a big part of it hadn't gone missing. Without Walter to ping her ideas off of and to tell about the critical information she had learned, she was going crazy. The thought had occurred to her that maybe it was Natalie who had emailed her the video, because she had only recently been talking to her about it. It would be an awful strong coincidence for the two to line up being from different people. Maybe it was obvious.

But if it were from Natalie, why the secrecy of an anonymous account? Was she just protecting herself from the powers that be? Callie knew the government monitored every email transmission, but was that a reality for worry? Was that a real, close-to-home threat against their privacy? Well, a video showing an actual crash of a spacecraft into the surface of an extra-terrestrial plant was pretty damned important. If anything 'threatened national security' this could certainly be it.

But Callie didn't really believe it was Natalie. She did not seem the type to exercise that kind of distance when talking about conspiracies. Of course, Callie had only just met her, so she couldn't be a reliable character witness. But she was a pretty good judge of character. And not only that, but Callie didn't think Natalie had that kind of insight into the Atlas mission anyway. She had long been gone from PSS, and – therefore – Royal by the time Atlas left for Mars. So unless she was on the ship itself, she just didn't have that kind of access.

One part of Callie just wanted to ask her, to alleviate any question. But then if the hunch was wrong, she would be sharing the video with just one more person who didn't need to see it. But was Natalie really one of those people? She was, after all, the one who had shared so much with Callie and Walter that they hadn't known before. So she definitely seemed like one of the good guys.

Walter's hearing was set for April 14th, which was the exact date the Monster Hunt was to take flight. Callie would be among the clouds, somewhere over the North Pacific, by the time Walter reported to the courtroom that day. It made her stomach sink as she thought about not only facing the entire project without him, but his facing the court without her in attendance. That just didn't seem right. He was her best friend on the planet. She should be there for him. But this was also the biggest project she had ever taken part in, and she was obligated to the tune of several hundred thousand dollars for it.

She spent an entire afternoon over at Rebecca's and Codi's, helping Codi pack for the big trip. Callie had to keep reminding her that just because it wasn't a vacation didn't mean she shouldn't pack like it was one. There would be many a night, Callie assured her, that she wouldn't be locked in a bubble under the ocean, but where she would be in the theater, or the bar, dancing her booty off.

Codi had been released from the hospital with a light warning to take it easy, but no bed-rest recommended. She was free to travel and explore and do whatever she wanted, as long as she took frequent breaks and took it easy when she was feeling tired.

On the thirteenth, the night before they were to leave for Osaka, Codi spent the night with Callie. When Callie picked her up, she was wearing pajamas and slippers, a big bag waiting by the front door, ready to be picked up. She reminded Callie of a little girl ready to go to her friend's house for a sleepover. Callie had to admit though, she felt a little of the excitement too. Not only was it rare for her to have a single friend over for a late night, it was even rarer for her to spend an evening with someone so intoxicating as Codi. Something about her was attractive, even across party lines. Callie had to keep reminding herself that it was not a sexual thing, and so it was okay to feel attracted to her. Though there was something about her being able to look at Codi uninhibited without being noticed. Codi had gotten to where she could recognize people with her weird perception of reality. But she couldn't see fine details like whether someone was looking at her or not. The eyes were just another blotch of color lost in the everything-painting that was normal sight. Callie could literally stare at her eyes or mouth or teeth or breasts – or whatever – with no fear of being caught. Why, she asked herself, did she need to stare at Codi? It was a little like being star-struck. Codi was one of those rare human beings who just so far exceeded the standard allocations for beauty that it was hard for people to keep their eyes off her. Callie reckoned it was a good thing Codi was legally blind – for Sam's sake. She had heard Walter say it was hard to keep a woman like that down.

As they rode to Callie's house in the warm air of Callie's Unlimited, Codi sat forward in her seat, rubbing her hands together and staring at the floorboard. "I thought you did better in the dark," Callie said, after a while.

"Well, I do," Codi agreed, "But not at distance. Not this kind of dark. The highways and roads are just a confusing mess for me. If you think about it, it's not really dark. It's kind of a bright dark. A darkness made of lights."

"That's an interesting thought," Callie said. "A darkness made of light."

"Yeah. Haven't you ever noticed, "Codi said, looking over at Callie, "How right when the sun is setting, it's not at all dark, but you can't see shit?" She returned her gaze to the front. "It's the worst time to drive. Your headlights are useless."

"Yes. I have definitely noticed that. I just never had such an eloquent name for the phenomenon."

Callie's alarm clock was set for three-thirty in the morning. They would have to be at the airport by six a.m. So when they got home and Callie started a fire – by throwing a switch on the wall by the fireplace – and made hot chocolate for both of them, they both agreed they should just stay up. There would be a ridiculous seventeen hours on the plane. They would have time to sleep on the plane – twice, if they wanted to.

So they stayed up, sitting Indian-style in the living room floor, playing games and drinking wine, Callie subconsciously trying to recreate Rebecca's apartment in her own living room. It just wasn't as cozy. Here there was maturity and structure. The furniture you were supposed to buy when you were getting ready to get married. The L-shaped couch and the glass-topped coffee table, the entertainment cabinet with a big TV for the to-be-husband to watch, and a couple of standing lamps.

Rebecca still had that eclectic taste and sense of freedom that only a single woman could get away with. Someone who was still in vogue, but not so much as to be considered hipster. Her living room was one of those places that couldn't be duplicated by an imitator. You either had it, Callie realized, or you didn't it. There were no fakers in this sport. She could pay to have someone come out and decorate it for her, but then she'd likely lose the warmth that came with do-it-yourself. The personal touches Rebecca had put into her décor were undeniably present.

Still, Callie had a blast, and Codi never complained. It was cozy and intimate, and they enjoyed themselves. She was pleased with herself for talking Codi into joining her for the night, even though it was easily the most pragmatic decision anyone could be expected to make. People just didn't get up that early only to drive somewhere and meet someone to go somewhere. At least not in Callie's life. Callie had watched Rebecca stand there in the hallway of her own apartment, hands on Codi's shoulders while Codi stood there with her bags and blankets, talking softly to her like a mother might a new teen going out for her first date.

Callie stood there feeling happy that Codi was leaving the comfort and safety of Rebecca's place to come to the unknown territory of Callie's. That spoke, at least to Callie, volumes about her trust in Callie. When they finally made it to Callie's she realized she was battling herself inside. Half of her was ecstatic to be spending the evening with Codi, and knowing she was going on one the biggest trips of her life, starting tomorrow. The other half was sick with worry and fear for Walter. Every time her mind would flip over to Walter's Channel, she would take a deep breath and try to force the thoughts away. Reminding herself that there was absolutely nothing she could do to either assist Walter or better his situation at all, she was able to get away from it each time. But the big picture kept presenting itself. She was going basically alone on her life's journey. The first project Walter and she had gotten to work on together in over a decade, and he was locked up.

As the shuttle picked them up for the airport, long before the sun was even a thought in the eastern sky, Callie found herself checking her phone to make sure she had not missed any calls from him. One last-ditch effort to say goodbye to her and wish her luck on the dive. Callie knew he would if he could. But her phone stayed dark.

"I'm turning a page," Callie told herself. "I can do it without him." She reminded herself that she was the one who had gotten Walter on the project, but it didn't serve her much relief. At least she would be traveling with Codi and Jack. She could have been on the sub with them though! That thin piece of her mind that didn't deal with reality wondered why she had not volunteered for a seat on the submersible. The realistic side didn't even get that far before the claustrophobia set in and her palms started sweating. Callie was positive she had made the right decision.

CHAPTER 28

departure

T he flight to Osaka was markedly different than the short flight to Texas had been. Obviously, there was the difference of about twelve hours in flight time. But the mood was different as well. Callie kept looking across the aisle where Walter would have been and seeing an empty seat instead. It broke her heart. She was seated in the middle between Jack and Codi this time, giving Jack the window. She wanted to sit beside both of them.

Callie had visions of a flight full of fun sitting between the two of them. She had brought a deck of cards and Sushi Go, a card game, in her purse. But they never made it out. The mood was somber and quiet rather than playful and bright. Codi spent a lot of the time listening to music on her phone and sleeping. Callie also noticed that Codi almost never got up to use the restroom. She either had a huge bladder, or just didn't drink enough to make her need to go. That was, Callie reckoned, probably a pretty useful trait for being on a submersible.

They were flying into Kansai International Airport, about thirty miles outside of Osaka, where they would have a layover before boarding another flight to Guam. The thousand-mile flight to Guam would take another three hours, whereupon they would shuttle over to the port and get on the Scylla Scout – home for the next few weeks. The trip out to the trench area, the Challenger Deep, as it was called, would take a few more hours still. There would be no plush hotel this time. Callie wondered how she would fare on board a cargo ship. She had never been on the open ocean before. No cruise liners, no deep sea fishing trips, no pirate ships. She had always been a terrestrial girl. What if she got seasick? What if, God forbid, she got claustrophobic? There would be no escape.

No one else had brought up anything about being on the ship. The only things they mentioned were positive things. Never anything bad about being trapped or anything like that. Callie must have been the only one, therefore, who had any of those thoughts. So she kept quiet about them. She did not want to be the only one who had those kinds of feelings. To be a whiner. A complainer. She would suck it up and make the best of it. How bad could it be, anyway?

The weather was supposed to be really nice for the next ten days. That was as far out as they could see, but according to the almanac, it was usually nice this time of year around Guam. Guam was about two hundred miles from the trench. She just hoped they saw something when they were out there. She hoped this wasn't a wasted trip. There were other things Callie could think of that she would rather be doing. Lying on a beach with Jack was one of them. A chance to lie in the sun sneaking occasional glances at his broad chest and being a little high on martinis did not sound bad at all. Maybe she would get some time for that in a lounge chair on the top deck of the Scout.

When they landed, Callie had to wake both her neighbors. Jack and Codi, damn them, had both been able to sleep for the last seven or eight hours of the flight with not even a twitch toward waking. It was one o'clock in the morning when they landed, and the runway was full of a warm fog. They spent the next four hours sitting in uncomfortable chairs in the airport before their flight left for Guam.

When they landed at Guam, there was no jetway for them to walk down. There was a staircase wheeled up to the small commuter plane. As they made their way down the steel steps, Callie looked up at the sky and had to stop to catch her breath. It was about an hour before sunrise, and the sky was magnificent. She could see stars she didn't know existed. There were billions and billions.

"You okay, hon?" Jack asked softly, from behind her.

"Yep. I'm good," she said, and continued down.

Codi was behind him, holding onto his shoulder for guidance. As they reached the concrete they moved to the side and looked up again. Codi stood still, patiently waiting for them, staring straight ahead at nothing while Callie and Jack had their necks cranked back.

"Codi, honey," Callie said, reaching out for her hand. "I am so sad in my heart that you can't see this. We are looking at the stars. And there are so many. So, so many."

Callie felt like a ghost. A zombie. She was working on about an hour of sleep and felt like all of this might just as easily be a dream, or a figment of someone else's imagination. They dragged their way to the bus that would take them to the other side of the island, where, hopefully, rest awaited.

Unfortunately, that was not meant to be. The bus had a flat tire. They had to wait for another to take its place. There was, therefore, an hour of sitting on the tarmac with the mist of a coming storm blowing in at them from the side. While the sun had not yet come up, the eastern sky was beginning to lighten. The wind was capricious and uncertain, but not entirely uncomfortable. During the times it decided to blow at them it was refreshing, tinted with the slight moisture of the coming rain. The air was a comfortable seventy degrees and was laden with the scent of far-away flowers. Callie was excited to be so far from her home, but wished she was in a better state of preparedness to take on the day. The way things were shaping up, it was going to be an extremely long one.

When the bus finally arrived, they trudged up the steps and found seats that stank of old sweat and a floor rusted through so badly in places they could see the street below. Callie couldn't find the strength to care though. She slunk into the seat next to Jack and laid her head against his shoulder. As she began to close her eyes, the sun crested the sea and made its grand entrance into the day. Callie knew she would not be forced to do any real work today, but the thought of being called upon set a fear writhing in her stomach. Anticipation, she gathered, was her worst enemy. That was her biggest reason for not being a good napper. If she knew she only had twenty minutes to nap, she would lie there anticipating the alarm for nineteen of them. And the last minute she would spend getting up and turning off the alarm before it went off.

The forty-minute trek to the dock on the east side of the island was bumpy and loud, warm in the bus. She and Jack flowed down the steps, not so much like humans descending, but rather like cold oil being poured from an icy glass. But then there was a spark of excitement in her belly as she saw the ship. It wasn't some ugly old rust-bucket, decrepit and scary and discolored by the sea. The Scylla Scout had recently had a paint job and now stood bright white in the harbor, glistening like a new car.

Jack said, "Nice!" and squeezed her shoulder as they approached the gangplank. Callie noticed peripherally that there was no one there checking credentials of any kind. It seemed anyone who had a slight desire had everything he or she needed to board the boat. She paid it little mind though, and asked Jack to help her with Codi's suitcase, while she carried her own.

Callie and Jack were given rooms next door to each other, but Jack quickly removed the paper nameplate from his own door and slid it in the plastic holder next to Callie's. He didn't want to ghost it and waste valuable space. But with this, he looked at Callie for a moment. She stared back at him, shoulders drooping with the weight of sleeplessness, wondering what could be the hold-up.

"You cool with this?" he asked.

She frowned. "Of course!" she said, brightening up a little. That spark of excitement returned as the thought occurred to her that she would be spending her nights wrapped in Jack's embrace. "Don't be a goat!" she added, slapping his shoulder, then twisted the door handle.

The bed was a double. She would later learn that all the rooms had double beds. A double was plenty big enough for Jack and her, who could almost have gotten by on a twin with their method of cuddling. They were still in that phase of their relationship where they craved each other's warmth and closeness rather than rejecting it. Callie slung her suitcase against the wall by the bed and spun round, falling backward onto it. Her legs bounced up comically and she slid off the side. Jack helped her back up and joined her on the tall mattress, their legs hanging off the side, then turned his head to kiss her. And that was all she remembered of that day.

When she awoke, it was late in the evening. Her watch said 2:21, which sent a jolt of fear through her veins. But then she sat up, noticing the slant of sunlight coming through the small window above the bed and looked again. Of course, she had forgotten to set it when they landed in Guam. She reached for her purse, dug her phone out of the side pocket and looked at the screen. No service. She had not upgraded to an international plan. What the hell time was it? She turned and shook Jack, who still lay in the long light of the evening sun, legs hung over the edge of the bed, his hands clasped on his stomach, lightly snoring. "Wake up, babe!" she said softly. His eyes finally popped open and he sat up, running his hand back through his hair.

"Hey, baby. What's up?" he said.

"I don't know what time it is, Jack. I'm freaking out here," Callie responded.

"What? Why? It's okay!" he said, running her hair back for her. She brushed his hand away and stood up.

"No, it's really not. I don't do well not knowing what time it is. I don't even know what day it is!"

Jack slipped his phone out of his pocket, dropping back onto his back to do so. "No service. I'm sorry, babe, but I think we'll be all right. Let's venture out and find out what's going on."

Callie found a remote control on the night stand and aimed it at the television. Shortly it blinked to life and she found a news station. The time read 8:32. She quickly set her watch, then turned her phone off and tossed it on the bed. "Okay. That sounds good. Let me brush my teeth though."

"Good idea," he said. They dug through the bags and found their toiletries, freshened up, then slipped out into the hallway where there was absolutely nothing going on.

Callie had this weird idea that everyone would be down partying in the bar or something, but that simply wasn't the case. Everyone was apparently as whipped as they were. There was one man sitting at the bar enjoying a tall glass of iced tea, no doubt tricked up with something strong. That man was Minus. He looked at them as they walked in.

"Hey, kids!" he said, raising his glass. "Ollie, pour them a drink!" he said, turning to the bartender. Ollie was a friendly looking guy who stood leaning on the bar, completely casual. Callie had assumed the wait and service crew would be dressed in uniform or something fancy. This spurred her memory of whom she was dealing with. Minus would have insisted they dress as comfortably as the mission crew. This was his project, after all.

"Hey, guys," Ollie said with an infectious grin. "Everything's on the house. What are ya having?"

Jack looked at Callie. It didn't feel right to have a drink this early. But then, it wasn't early, was it? He looked back at Ollie and returned the smile. "I'll have a glass of single malt, if you got it," he said.

"Friend, we have it all. Do you have a preferred poison?" Ollie returned.

"Glenlivet?" Jack tried, extending an open hand.

"Twelve or eighteen?"

"Oh, God. I get that much choice?" Jack asked.

"Eighteen," Callie said for him, then slung her purse up on the bar and pulled out the stool next to Minus. "I'll have a vodka and water on the rocks with a pepper-cheeny."

"She means pepperoncini," Jack said, looking at her as he pulled his own seat out.

"Got it," Ollie said.

Jack nodded his approval when Ollie slid the glass of scotch in front of him on a square napkin. He was secretly happy, Callie could tell, that Ollie had not asked him how he took it. She had already heard his lecture about bartenders who offered options when it came to single-malt. It was okay, he had said, to fuck-up a blend with ice or water, but a single-malt was sacred. Any man worth his salt would drink it neat. No question. Callie smiled at him.

"Did you get any sleep?" Minus asked Callie, though he did not look at her. His focus was on the television above the bar where a soccer or football game or something was on. Callie couldn't be bothered to check again to pin down the proper sport. She just knew there was a lot of green and a lot of uniforms running around. That meant she could safely ignore it for the rest of the evening.

"Yes. What time did we get here this morning, Minus?" Callie asked, looking at her watch.

"Six-fifty," he replied.

"Okay, well then we slept for about thirteen hours," she said, looking at Jack.

Minus only nodded. He then turned on his stool, one arm on the bar. "Can you believe it's finally here?"

Callie shrunk down into her shoulders and smiled, yawned. Her hands were between her thighs on the barstool. "Yeah, crazy."

Minus stared at her for a moment. "Wow. You really couldn't care less, could you?"

"Oh, she could care less," Jack corrected. "Just not enough to register on anyone's meter." He held his finger and thumb apart about a centimeter.

Minus chuckled. "It's really sad, Callie. This is history in the making."

"That's what I keep telling her!" Jack said, holding his glass up toward Minus. Minus raised his own and they clinked them together. Some of Minus's tea sloshed over the edge and dropped onto Callie's lap.

She looked down at it silently, then returned her attention to Matt. "You guys are stupid. Even if we do find the legendary sea Bloop, I don't think it's going to make history books."

"Well, suit yourself. Party pooper. But since you're already here, and you're pretty well trapped on board for the next however-long-I-see-fit, you might as well get into the spirit," Minus said, holding his glass up to her.

Instead of lifting her glass to his, she leaned forward and rocked her head to the side, acting like she was toasting with her nose. "That's fine, Minus. I'll get into the mood. I'll be fine. But don't expect me to do anything stupid, like walking around talking like a pirate or some shit."

Jack choked on his whiskey. Minus laughed out loud. "Callie, did you just say the S word?"

She looked him in the eyes and squinted – displaying her best Clint Eastwood. "I did. Get used to it, boys."

Jack widened his eyes and nodded slowly. "Whoa, there, cowgirl. She's getting serious, Minus!"

"Turning over a new leaf, are you?" Minus said, taking a drink of his Long Island.

"Yup. Better get your rake. The new Calligator is in town. I came to chew bubble gum and kick ass."

Jack laughed out loud this time, leaning so far back in his barstool that he almost tipped over backward. Ollie was laughing too, head rocked back, obviously enjoying the vulgar display from the dainty blond ditz.

They were, of course, up all night. Once the mood set in and the drink started to work, the general malaise began to wear off and they came alive. They quickly found the dance floor and the disco ball and the loud music. And as the night wore on, more and more folk awakened from dead naps and joined them in the bar. Even some of the off-duty ship crew joined them on the floor under the awkward lighting. Minus had let on to Callie that the real workdays wouldn't even start until they started hearing some signs of movement from below. They would take the sub out just to test it and have a look around at some serious depth, because, he said, why the hell not? But for the most part, most of the monster crew was free to roam the halls, the bars, the dance floors and do whatever they wanted.

The music that got them shaking on the first night was southern rock. Upbeat music wore them out long into the early hours of the morning. Codi seemed to have found her calling. Callie noticed she seemed to be moving more comfortably on the floor, even more so than at the Chandelier. That night seemed like a distant forever ago to Callie, who had to stop and remind herself that they hadn't even been on the ship for a full twenty-four hours yet and she was already drunk and partying like it was the end game.

Codi was moving fast and hard, elbows bent and hands up in the air, snapping and clapping, gliding around her little space on the floor like grease on a hot pan. She wasn't paying much attention to anyone else on the floor. Nor, though, was anyone. It was mostly a free-for-all of a bunch of science dorks and singles. There wasn't a lot of grinding going on. Even Callie and Jack were staying respectfully distant, not wanting to set forth any impressions that might taint their image – at least not on the first night. With an open bar, the drinks were a lot more attainable, and Callie found shortly that she had a problem. She wondered sideways if it was something she needed to start taking a personal inventory of, and if she had a real problem. While she was bouncing and hopping and shaking it on the floor, she was not feeling the effects of the alcohol at all, and was downing them like this might be her last chance.

It was when they finally turned in – Callie grabbing Jack's hand and leading him through the thick crowd amidst pats on the back and kisses on the cheek from some of the gals – that she realized just how drunk she really was. She bounced off the walls down the hallway until they found their room and she popped the door open. She whipped her shirt off over her head and turned to Jack, covering her chest with small hands. "I'm probably not sober enough to shower off tonight. Is that going to be a problem?" she asked, swaying. She reached up and steadied herself against the low ceiling.

Jack reached back and closed the door gently behind him, throwing the lock without looking. "Not a problem for me. You gonna be okay?"

"That depends," she said. Then she tilted her head seductively at him.

The next morning they slept in, but not as late as she had expected. Even the short five hours they were asleep was so much more than she had gotten in the two days of travel that it refreshed her almost entirely. Callie knew they would be returning to the room after lunch – if they could make it that long – for a nap. But until then, she felt pretty good, considering. She even had a bloody mary with breakfast. Jack joined her.

After breakfast they wandered the upper deck, having a look at the view. The sun was well up, but obscured by large puffy white clouds that looked more comforting than threatening. The breeze was light and cool, and it felt like the perfect weather to be unsure about. It was that exact temperature that was wrong for planning. Too warm for a light jacket, too cool for a tank top. Callie carried a sweater, but never put it on. Instead, when she found herself under a slight chill, she would pull Jack's arm around her shoulders and bury herself in his warmth.

The mood around the ship was festive and friendly. Callie knew most of the people they encountered, and was even surprised by a couple of them. Candy Hanning, for instance, was someone Callie had not expected to see on board. But it was a telling experience, Callie realized. She was here with Simon, one of the guys on the dive team. While there was nothing strictly wrong with it, they had never advertised their relationship during the tenure of the project. Of course, Callie didn't work at Royal, so maybe they showed up at a lot of functions together. Either way, she was pleasantly surprised to see Candy, and made a promise to hook up with her later.

She didn't. In fact, Callie only saw her one other time during the entirety of the trip.

CHAPTER 29

Callie looked at Jack in the mirror where she had been splashing water on her face and raised her eyebrows. He was sitting on the bed shirtless with his legs crossed, reading the latest Rolling Stone. It was the thirteenth day of the mission. "What'cha thinkin' about?" she said, turning off the faucet. He had grunted with laughter and caught her attention. The last several days had become monotonous. There was dancing and drinking every night, good music in the early evenings, fabulous breakfasts, remarkable tea-times followed by power-naps and breezy lunches on the deck where they sipped bloody marys and got ready for another night. There was nothing at all unlike a vacation about it. It was wonderful, Callie thought, and she could see herself retiring to a ship quite like the one they were on. But there was no excitement in it. It was just relaxing. It was now routine. Awesome, yes, but routine. Nothing stuck out from the monotony of it all.

He looked up at her and smiled, then returned his eyes to the magazine. "Nothing in particular. This is incredible though. Have you ever seen these guys live?" Jack asked, turning the folded magazine so she could see it in the mirror. She squinted, then dropped her glasses down from her head into place. She still couldn't make out the details of the inset though.

"Who?" she asked.

"One Last Orbit. This Randall Cameron guy went and saw them. He's writing about it here. They sound pretty bad ass," Jack said.

Callie nodded, then squeezed toothpaste onto her brush. "No. But I love their music. I would love to see them live. Why?" She stuck the toothbrush in her mouth and turned to face him.

"They don't come out and say 'welcome' or anything. They don't take breaks between songs and shit. They just play music. It's supposed to be like an incredible, fully immersive experience."

"What's that mean?" she said around her toothbrush, dripping onto her open hand.

"Immersive? Well, they put more into it than just the sound. You're supposed to like, become part of the music. There's like a whole experience to it. A light show. I don't know exactly. It's just more than them standing up there playing instruments."

"Well, we should go see them then," Callie said, turning to spit.

"Definitely. This guy calls the singer one of the last true sirens in the dying art of operatic trance. I think I'm in love," Jack said, scratching his chin as he read.

"So do I need to learn to sing, Jack?" Callie said, hands on her hips.

"Ha! No, babe. You're good. I just have a thing for chirps."

"I see that. What's her name? Candice something?" Callie said. She moved to the bed and sat down beside him, resting her chin on his shoulder.

"Tanis," Jack started. He was interrupted by the speaker in the ceiling though. An announcement was coming over the common channel telling all mission-essential personnel to report to the command center. Callie looked at Jack, not three inches between their noses. Her eyes were wide as they listened to the whole message. They had fifteen minutes to get ready and get down to the command center. They were already ready though.

"Holy cow!" Callie said. "This could be it! You think they heard something?"

"Well obviously they did!" Jack said, standing and digging through his suitcase for a shirt. Callie had unpacked her suitcase on the first full day of being awake on the ship. She had neatly and carefully placed all her things in the small assortment of drawers around the room. Jack opted instead for the convenience of the suitcase. All his stuff was wrinkled. "I just wonder if it's what we came to hear."

In the hallways there was suddenly a snap in the air – an excitement that was palpable. People were rushing around, dipping into doors to change and get their business faces ready. Everyone was smiling. Callie wondered quickly how many people would be showing up drunk. No one was really on the clock out here. She supposed the real science guys would have to be sober. And, of course, Jack. But how sober did one really have to be to pilot a submersible that only really went in two directions?

They were not the first ones to arrive in the command center. In fact, it was already packed. Minus was standing up on what passed for a stage facing a crowd of almost a hundred people. There was some laughing going on as Callie edged her way into the door. Minus almost immediately spotted her, and called her out.

"There she is. Callie come up here."

The people directly in front of her turned to look, then cleared a path for her, smiling and clapping, patting her on the back, shaking her hand.

"This here is Callie Simmons. No, seriously, everyone, go ahead! Give her a round of applause!" The applause was deafening. "SHE'S THE REASON WE'RE HERE!" Minus shouted over the roar. He had a microphone in his hand, but it wasn't doing much good.

When Callie was finally up front standing beside Matt Minus, she was smiling and blushing, embarrassed and shy. She had not expected any of this fanfare. He put his hand on her shoulder and said, "It wasn't even a year ago, friends! Seven months, sixteen days, to be exact. This woman," he said, squeezing her shoulder. She suddenly had her answer for how much alcohol was allowed. She could smell whiskey on Minus's breath. "This woman came into my office and told me how to build this submersible." The crowd applauded again. The excitement was thick in the air. They seemed willing to clap about anything. She made eyes with Jack, who stood in the back, nodding and clapping. He had a special look for her.

"So now here we are, floating about four miles above what we think is something huge, and – well, possibly dangerous!" Minus said to a roar of laughter. When they finally quieted down, he continued. "It was over twenty years ago that we first began hearing the sounds of something large beneath the surface of the ocean. They say we know less about the surface of the ocean than we do about the surface of the moon. So it's not, at least to me, that far-fetched to think there could be something big under there that we've no idea about."

Minus paused and leaned over to a stool that sat on the stage. He picked up a glass with something orange in it and took a heavy sip. There was scattered laughter at this, and someone shouted, "Atta boy, Minus!" He smiled broadly. "Well, ever since then, I had it in the back of my mind that I would someday go search for the source of this sound." He squeezed her shoulder again, rocking her back and forth slightly. Callie could tell he was warming to his thunder.

"This woman here," he said, looking directly at her. "She made my dream a reality." He nodded slightly. A few awws scattered through the crowd. "I knew two things going into that meeting in my office seven and a half months ago." He lifted the microphone above his head, raising a finger away from it, and spoke without the amplification. "I knew," he said, returning the mic to his mouth, "that Callie could solve the mystery of how to go deep for me." He looked at her again. She could see the whiskey in his eyes. Maybe it was better this way. Part of her envied his drunkenness.

"And secondly, I knew that if I didn't have her on my team, it would almost certainly never become a reality."

Again the applause.

When it died down he said, "I threatened her once. I told her she was replaceable. Walter Watson was there to tell me how fucking stupid that comment really was."

He got his thunder. The applause was deafening. It shook the floor and the walls. Callie could feel it in her guts. She was definitely a darker shade now. She could feel the hot blood in her cheeks. She wasn't used to this kind of public doting. And Minus still had her by the shoulder.

"Ladies and gentlemen," he said, once the applause had finally died down, "I know you're all here because you believe at least in the idea of closing off a mystery if there isn't one. I know some of you don't believe in the Bloop. I know some of you have your glacial calving theories. Some of you think we're wasting our time out here. You're just here for the paycheck." Minus looked around the room. Hand still on Callie's shoulder. "And that's fine. That's fine," he said, nodding. "But I thank you for being here anyway. And shit! How much fuckin' fun have we had?" he said, almost shouting.

The applause was back, full force, accompanied by a lot of hooting and hollering, whistling and chanting.

"I knew some of you I'd have to twist your fuckin' arms to get you to come out to the middle of the damn Pacific!

That's why I wanted to make it worth your time! That's why I had this old boat turned into a luxury liner!" More applause. "I hope you all have had some fun out here. Have you had fun?"

It just never ended. He was rounding to his finale now, too. Callie expected this little room was going to come down with all the excitement and celebration.

"Well, I thank you all for joining me on this great expedition. Childish? Maybe a little. But when you have the money of a small country backing you, why the hell not?" Minus waited for the applause to die again. Then he finished. "Thank you all for joining me. But also, I want to make sure we all recognize Callie Simmons for her contribution to the project. Because literally, we would not be here if it weren't for her noggin." He finally took his hand off her shoulder to tap a finger on her head. It kind of hurt. She tried not to wince, not wanting to spoil his speech.

"So, Callie Simmons, I would like to present you with a token of our appreciation." He reached back and took a blue envelope off the stool. He held it close to his chest for a moment, then looked out at the crowd. "Suzanne? Where are you, Suze?" he said, standing tall to see over everyone. Finally, Suzanne emerged from the crowd, carrying a small box. She handed it to Minus, then stepped up to hug Callie.

"Sorry I was late, dear," she said. Callie smiled. She couldn't think of anything to say. She was, in fact, on the verge of tears already, and she didn't even know what was in the box. Or the envelope for that matter. Suzanne then stood aside as Minus opened the box and dropped it at his feet. In his hands he now held a glass plaque.

"This is just a small token of our appreciation, Callie Simmons. It says," he said, holding it away from his eyes a bit to focus, "To Callie Simmons for once again saving the world… One monster at a time!"

There was a deafening roar of applause and shouts, this time for longer than all of the previous ones combined. It was almost as if each person in the room appreciated Callie as much as Minus himself did. Like every single one of them truly believed in her. And the tears began to well up. She was on the verge of losing it completely. When she had heard the announcement less than an hour ago, she had no idea she was about to be honored. And now here she was about to cry in front of a hundred people she only knew in passing.

"Oh, honey, don't cry yet. You still haven't seen the envelope!" Minus said. There was a fair amount of laughter, and then he opened the envelope. He glanced over at Suzanne again, then back at Callie. "Like I said, the money of a small country," he mumbled. Callie frowned. And then he was saying something else. "I want everyone to quiet down for a second. This is real. This is serious."

Minus waited patiently up on the stage, his left hand now back on her shoulder, his right holding the microphone and the now-open envelope. When they had finally attained a quiet he could deal with, he continued. "Okay. Are we ready?"

Everyone shouted similar versions of affirmatives in the confines of the room. Callie was beginning to feel dizzy.

"Now don't anyone get any funny ideas. And let me remind you, this is not a joke." Minus looked at Callie. "Callie Simmons, this is real. You have earned this." He stared at her for a long time in complete silence. The crowd was even silent. She could have heard a sock drop in the back row. "Callie Simmons, I present to you a check." And now he was reaching into the envelope with trembling fingers. "This check, Callie." And it was free. He held it up, whipping it back and forth over his head. "Callie, this is a check."

The crowd waited silently, patiently. It was a ridiculous show for a check, Callie thought. A thousand bucks? Ten thousand? That would be a great little gift. But did it really need this kind of fanfare? So this was why he had insisted on her coming on the big trip with the entire crew, she thought. It had just now occurred to her.

"Callie, this is a check," he said again. And then he handed it to her. Callie's eyes blurred up immediately.

Without even seeing the figure on it yet, her eyes were full of clouds, and the rainstorm was on the way. She held the check with both hands, trying to look at it, but she still couldn't see it. Somewhere in the background, she was aware of Minus speaking again. She tried to look up and face the crowd, but she was overwhelmed with emotion.

"Callie," Minus said. She turned to look at him, but wasn't seeing him very well. She gasped, her torso now spasming with the cry she was trying to hold back. Her lips were furled and trembling. "Callie, darling. This is a check for a million dollars."

There was music playing. There was shouting and hollering and clapping and whistles, and Callie was being crowded by a hundred bodies. There was no longer any safe distance between her and the crowd. They were all swarming her. Lifting her up. Clapping her on the back. Kissing her on the head, the cheek, the lips. Men and women alike. She had been told that she was well-known throughout the company, even though she didn't even work for them anymore. Callie was like a legend in the halls of Royal. But she had never believed it. Not until now. Now she believed it.

As her eyes flooded with tears and her body wracked with pent-up emotion, she felt hugs and squeezing and kisses and shakes. And within a short moment, she felt a familiar sensation. The arms of Jack Carpenter wrapping round her waist. She turned toward him searching for spots in the crowded lenses of her eyes, feeling a little bit like Codi must feel when trying to process her new vision. And she was in his arms, crying freely.

Jack lifted her up, spinning slowly in circles as the crowd continued to applaud and shout her name. They seemed to be more excited than she was. She didn't truly understand what was going on though. "What's happening, Jack?" she said with a broken voice.

"Callie, you're being honored here," he said quietly in her ear, following it with kisses all down her neck and cheek.

"Did you know this was gonna happen, Jack?" she asked. She was gasping now, fighting back the flood of tears that threatened to break her dam.

He just kissed her again and held her tight, spinning her slowly around. Somewhere in the distance behind her, Callie heard Matt Minus's familiar voice saying congratulations, and that the party was in the ballroom. The classy music was turned up, and suddenly, she was almost dancing to Norah Jones while Jack held her close. Somewhere in the human part of her that was still not trapped by emotion, she was wondering what this was all about. Wondering if she would remember in the morning what this had all been about. Wondering if she would misplace the check. "What if I lose it?" she said, but not really caring if she did. Callie didn't even think she wanted to cash it. She wanted to frame it. A check for a million dollars? Who had ever received something so cool? She made plenty of money. But a check for a million dollars? That seemed cooler than the money it was actually worth.

"The real one is back in my office," Minus said in her ear. "Don't sweat it, Callie. Just have fun. Congratulations." He squeezed her arm just above her elbow, then he disappeared into the crowd.

Callie laughed out loud and let herself be swept away on the emotion that had suddenly become too much to hold back. And then she cried. She cried while she danced.

⌘　　　⌘　　　⌘

Codi sat with her legs curled up, sideways in the uncomfortable chair by the day room phone table. Her flip phone, like almost everyone else on board, wasn't in service out here in the far away ocean. There was no line of people waiting to use the phone. There was no one else even in the day room. In fact, Codi had noted, no one ever used the day room. Being a former serviceman himself, Minus still believed in the day room. He'd had one of the private dining rooms converted, so it wasn't big, but it was nice. Codi found it to be her favorite room on the ship. It was cozy and familiar somehow. The light wasn't too harsh, as the window could be covered by dark curtains. There was a television in here, which Codi liked to turn on for background noise, though she never watched it. There were also a couple of plush sofas and a stack of blankets in the corner.

She was talking to Sam, who did have the benefit of his cell phone. She had commented to him about the irony of technological advancements in the communications field. Technology had brought them smart phones. Small computers one could carry in her purse and use to do anything from read a book, listen to music, to mapping a location and having it direct you there. One could look up something on the internet, check her social media networks, make flight reservations, rate a good restaurant experience, and, if one still had enough battery at the end of all that, even make a phone call. But this technology everyone craved came at a price: somehow in all the hubbub to get their hands on one, people had completely neglected and given up comfort and ergonomics. Now everyone cared about the thinness of the device. Could it be carried in a purse or a pocket? That's what mattered. So now, in lieu of comfort, one held a flat piece of glass up to his face. Codi much preferred the throwback phone Minus had dropped in the day room. It was the typical old clunky push-button handset from the 1980s, complete with a spiral cord. And it was comfortable. It was, she had said, almost like someone had designed it to be held up to your ear instead of worrying about whether it would fit in a pocket.

"I should write magazine articles, Sam," she said, matter-of-fact. "I have all these contrary-to-popular opinions."

"You should, Codi. That's been your biggest question since you lost your sight. What will you do?" Sam replied.

She was nodding. "I have been doing a lot of writing here. It's been exciting. Since I kind of had this thing just pushed on me, it's really pushed me to do something I haven't done in so many years. But I think I'm really good at it."

"I can't wait to read some of it," Sam said. He was, of course, referring to the unique brand of reading that blind people did. If it wasn't printed in Braille, they listened.

"Some of it?" she asked.

"All of it," he corrected. "Well, at least all the good stuff."

"Ha! I hope it's good! I think I'll need an editor. But I'm really putting down everything about the trip. Everything I experience. I've been talking about the ship and the feeling of being out in the ocean looking for this stupid thing, and the experience of being away from the mainland and your loved ones. The taste of the food, the feel of the sheets on these beds, the smell of the air, the feel of the floors beneath your feet as you make your way down the main hall, the sounds of the creaking hull in the middle of the night..."

"Man, that sounds fantastic. It sounds like you're really gathering all of it. What makes you think to capture all that?" Sam said, the awe evident in his voice.

"I'm so much more perceptive than most of these people, Sam. I think since I have to move so slowly through here, I'm aware of so much more. I take my time with everything."

"I know that's right," he said.

"Most of these people just seem like they're here to party."

"Haven't you been dancing with them every night?"

"Absolutely! I'm not gonna miss out on the dancing! And I don't dislike them. They just have different goals than I do," Codi said. She was twisting a lock of hair between her fingers. The bumper music of a soap opera sung quietly to her from the TV across the room.

"What is your goal, Code?" Sam asked seriously.

She breathed in deeply and thought about it. "You know, I really only signed on to be part of something. Didn't matter what. Just being invited to participate in anything, I knew that I would get some good experiences, and really get to test some of my functionality in a completely different environment. I knew it couldn't be bad for me."

"So you're saying you don't really believe you're going to find the Lovecraftian beast beneath the dark waters," Sam said casually.

"Pssh. Of course not. This is such a silly bullshit joke. I can't believe they're spending all this fucking money on it. Callie got a check for a million dollars last night."

"Wow. Good God," Sam said.

"Yeah. Pretty awesome for her, but man. That just shows how arrogant and flippant this stupid company is with money. They could be donating millions of dollars a day to feeding the hungry or finding a cure for breast cancer or something."

"Gotta save the breasts," Sam said. "Are you writing all this too?"

"No. No way. I just feel like such a damned hypocrite. I hate what this company stands for. Buying a whole ship and having it completely refurbished for this one mission? God it's maddening. But I also don't feel like I could have gotten my new eyes without them. A bunch of tiny things fell into place like dominoes and Royal was one of them. That damned butterfly effect." Codi sighed, then added, "Anyway, I feel like I owed it to them to help with this thing, even though it's a ridiculous waste of money."

"I agree. But like you said, when would you ever get an offer like this again? To be on a ship out in the Pacific, getting to go down in the sub to look for a monster? Such a neat experience, even if you never see what you're looking for."

"Yeah," she said. She was nodding and chewing on her hair, staring off into the warm space in front of the couch. "Yeah. That's what I feel like. I owe them this much. But I feel like I'm sleeping with the enemy."

"That's what you could name your book," Sam said lightly.

"Yes. Totally," she said. She sighed and looked at her watch. It was almost noon and she was still in her sweats. Her pajamas. "As soon as this shit is over with, I'll be done with Royal."

"I don't blame you. Well hurry up and come home to me, Codi Cohl. I miss you terribly."

"Aww, sweetie, you can't miss me! You're gonna make it too hard for me!" Codi said.

"That's what you do for me all the time," Sam said.

"You're bad, Sam. I hope we get done with this stupid trip soon. I can't wait 'til you're holding me again."

"Likewise," he said.

CHAPTER 30

The seat felt tighter this morning than she was used to. The five point harness made her feel more like she was in a baby's car seat than a high-tech monster-hunting submarine. And it was cold. Her stomach was full of nervous tension, and she worried that would translate to a necessary privacy she simply couldn't imagine fulfilling within the confines of the tiny vessel.

Technically, this was no different than the test dives they had made many times before. But something just felt different this time. Perhaps it was the most simplistic, basic reality of all of it: that this time they were actually fulfilling the prophecy of the mission. Maybe it was that they had been called to "man their battle stations", a ridiculous misuse of a military protocol, because they finally had a hit on the mikes. Maybe it was just that she was sick of all the charades, chasing after a monster that obviously didn't exist. She had listened to the accessible terminal at the library as it read to her the article she had discovered in Scientific American, breaking the myth of the Bloop. It was glaciers breaking up. Gigantic sections of ice were cracking off the face of the glaciers and scraping the bottom of the ocean. There really was no mystery to it. Maybe it was this ludicrous play she had a major part in – to act like it was real. To act like it mattered. To act like they didn't really know what was down there, all to justify spending a quarter of a billion dollars to go take a look at the deepest part of the ocean on the planet. Whatever the reason for her anxiety, she wasn't happy about it.

Codi had enjoyed her time on the ship, but not to the extent most of the other workers had. She had become reclusive in the last couple of weeks, spending almost all her time in the day room or her own quarters, only coming out at night to dance and drink with Callie. Callie, God bless her, was the only real reason she ventured out at all. Codi believed she had found a real friend in her. She wasn't sure she would have survived the long, monotonous days without the release she got from dancing and spending time with Callie. And Callie wasn't even supposed to have been on the ship. She had said she was done as soon as she finished the design of the sub. Minus had all but forced her into being there. Codi was silently thankful for that. She didn't have any other friends on the ship. How nice that Callie had her boyfriend on board with her. But Jack didn't do much for Codi. He was quiet. A true gentleman, and always there to help, but too quiet for Codi's taste. She just wanted to be done with this and back home where things made sense. Back where people did things because those things mattered. Those things had true meaning. True goals she could shoot for. Not like this traveling circus of scientists chasing a rumor through the most expensive terrain in the world.

The call had come in at four o'clock in the morning. An animated and very excited Matt Minus had broken through over the common channel, announcing that contact had been made, and they had fifteen minutes to prep and man their battle stations. Codi had not been awake enough to really know what was going on. But she had definitely had the presence of mind to roll her eyes. She had rolled out of bed, brushed her teeth and slipped into her jumpsuit. At least she was warm. And now that it was real, that they were really diving, she wondered what it was. What was this elusive sound they had picked up? What contact had been made? Had she been wrong all along? Of course not, the realistic part of her mind asserted. But there was something that had made them decide now was the time. So here she sat in the dark submersible, where all the lights were red and calming, easy on the eyes. Jack was behind her to the left in the B seat. Rick Baltey was on her right, fidgeting and blabbing like a high-school girl, as usual, in the A seat.

Jack said her name, and she heard snapping off behind her to the left. Low. She reached back and found his hand. He squeezed her fingers reassuringly. Had she made it that obvious she was uncomfortable?

"You're doing great, Codi. Try to relax. You got this," he said.

"Whoa! Is someone scared? Man, is this ever the time not to be scared! Codi, this is gonna be the most awesome thing you-"

"Will you please shut the actual fuck up, Baltey?" Codi said calmly. "The most awesome thing ever would be if you would just keep your childish excitement to yourself."

"Wow. Sorry," he said, not without a little self-pity. "Who pissed in your-" he started, but was interrupted again.

"Dude. Can it." That was Jack. Codi leaned her head back against the headrest and closed her eyes, took a deep breath. She really did need to relax. Her heart was racing. She knew the medical team would be piping up shortly, asking her if she was okay, if she didn't get her heart rate under control. The sensors taped to her skin under the jumpsuit monitored everything from her temperature to her blood pressure. She had to unzip the soft cotton suit and sit half-naked on the prep table in the launch room while they quickly pasted the itchy patches all over her torso. She was wearing a light tank top, but the doctor – or nurse, or PA, or whatever the hell she was – had to lift it out of the way. Humiliating. Cold. Unnecessary. Another in the long list of complaints Codi had with this whole "mission".

She was thankful Jack was here with her. At least he knew what was going on. He had probably, she reckoned, dealt with many fearful seamen during his time on Navy subs. He had a good calming effect. She continued breathing deeply as she felt the machinery around her vibrate. They were being hoisted into the air, over the edge of the prow, hanging by a thick chain that would lower them gently down into the cold water of the foreign ocean.

Codi could feel every little bump and movement from the outside. Someone's hand touching the propulsion cage, steadying the swing of the sub. Every link in the chain as it rounded over the wheel of the pulley in their slow trek down to the surface. She could even feel the vibration of the launch crew's voices through the thick steel as they shouted to each other. And when the sub finally reached the water, she felt that too. A calming, yet spooky emblem of finality that told her it was real. *We really are going under. In less than an hour, we will be several miles beneath the surface of the ocean.* Millions of tons of water would separate them from the rest of the world. And she had already made enemies with one of the others in the cabin.

As the submersible, aptly named Scylla, dropped past its equator into the water, it began to steady. The movement tapered off and became a smooth, silent descent. She could now hear the silent roar of the ocean around them, and terror suddenly set in. She squeezed Jack's hand, hard. "Jack!" she said, stern and full of apprehension.

"It's okay. It'll pass, Codi," he said.

"Why am I so scared? This isn't any different than any of the other dives we've done!" she cried.

"It's okay, Codi. You're perfectly safe. Just keep taking deep breaths, and remember, you've done this. This isn't your first rodeo, girl."

She tried to smile a little. Her eyes were still closed, her head pressed hard against the headrest. And suddenly they were falling. It was a sudden and sickening jolt that sent her stomach up into her diaphragm, and before she could even cry out, they were spinning. A crazy, horrifying dance through the ocean as they sank ever deeper, rolling like a bowling ball down the gutter of a lane. There was no longer any up or down. It was all the same. Everything was mixed up. And she was getting dizzy. The spin was so fast and out of control that her head was swinging back and forth, round and round on her neck. She tried to keep it pressed against the seat.

"JACK!" she was shouting now. "What the fuck is happening?!"

"Standby," he said, calm but strong. "Trying to get control of her."

"Scylla, base, what's with the attitude?" she heard through the speakers in the ceiling.

"Don't know, base. This hasn't happened before. Can you see us?"

A new voice came in over the speaker. It was Minus. He was speaking to someone else in the room, then he turned to the mike. "Hold cool, Scylla. Callie is on her way in. The cable snapped. We dropped you."

"Great fucking Scott," Jack said.

"Holy shit, are you kidding?" Rick Baltey shouted.

"What's happening, Jack?" Codi screamed. "What does that mean? I thought it was a chain!"

"There was six feet of cable between the cage and the chain. That cable must have broken."

"How does that happen? That's not supposed to happen!" she shouted.

Rick voiced his agreement.

"Standby, hon. It's going to be okay. Just stay calm."

Suddenly, Callie's voice was on the speakers. "Hey guys. The propulsion cage is fine. You're spinning in the cage."

"Okay. What do we do, base?" Jack asked calmly. Codi admired his ability to stay professional. He was talking to the woman he loved.

"This happened during proto-testing. You have to lock the magnets. There's an emergency switch between the Alpha and Bravo seats. It's got a black guard over it. Flip that guard and flip the switch underneath it."

"Got it," Baltey said. Codi heard the click of the metallic guard, and then the crazy sickening spin was gone.

"Good. Now adjust your attitude. You're still falling, but you're almost inverted," Callie said.

Servos spun and motors whirred. And then they were turning back upright. Though now, it didn't feel like true up. Like maybe the sensors had gotten screwed up. She could see the artificial horizon on the instrument panel in front of her. The orange half was down, so they were definitely upright. But it sure as hell didn't feel like it. She had heard of private pilots, those without instrument ratings, plunging into clouds and getting disoriented. Not trusting their instruments because of the crazy visions outside the windows, they would come rocketing out of a cloud straight for the ground. This must be what it was like. Some of that sickness she attributed to the fact that they were still falling like a stone. Why was that? She knew they were supposed to have control of their descent. But she opted to keep her mouth shut and not get in the way of the professionals. She had put her trust completely in Callie and Jack, and wasn't about to start freaking out now. She hoped.

"Attitude normalized," Jack said. "Still falling. My rotors aren't working."

"They worked in pre-flight," Minus said. Was he just covering his ass?

"I know that, sir. But that doesn't help me much here. Because they're most assuredly not working now."

"You guys need to slow down somehow," Callie said. "I don't want to state the obvious, but we're way out of tolerance here."

Codi knew the maximum descent rate was supposed to be nine hundred feet per minute. That seemed, on the surface, unbelievably fast. But here, they were well above that.

"I can engage the shield," Jack said.

There was silence from the control room for a long moment.

"Base, Scylla, do you copy? Can I engage?"

"Why would you do that, Scout?" Callie responded.

"I don't know. Just throwing stuff at the wall. Maybe it might help," Jack responded. He sounded exasperated. Meanwhile, they were still falling. Fast. Codi opened her eyes and located the vertical speed indicator. They were approaching two thousand feet per minute descent rate. And the needle was still climbing. Her ears popped. They were already at three thousand feet. Over half a mile between the sub and the ship. She swallowed as fear gripped her stomach.

After a minute of silence, Jack spoke into the microphone, "Still waiting, base."

Another thirty seconds passed before the speaker crackled and Callie replied, "Affirmative, Scout. If you think it will help, engage. Just turn it right back off. Hold onto your seats."

Codi gripped the edges of her seat with terrifying strength, already exhausted from the expensive energy expenditure of sudden fear. Her eyes were closed again as she waited. But there was no sudden jolt. No sudden stop in their motion. She heard clicking and realized the lights were flickering. *Please God, no. Don't let the lights go out.* Still, they were falling.

"It's not engaging, base," Jack said, still calm as a pond at midnight.

"Are you serious? What the hell is going on, Minus?" Callie said. "It's like Atlas all over again."

"What's it doing, Carpenter?" Minus asked.

"Nothing. It's clicking. The lights are flickering like it's trying to power itself on, but nothing is happening."

"Okay, that's the safety lock," Callie said, and sudden excitement flooded into Codi's stomach. Someone who knew what the hell was going on had finally come online. The surety in Callie's voice had been wonderful. "I forgot about that. We put in a safety to keep it from coming on during a fast descent."

"If it's not supposed to have any effect, then why would there be a safety to keep it from coming on?" Baltey asked.

"Because," Callie said patiently, "if you're dropping like a brick you might hit something. You could really cause some damage with that shield. It was designed as a Hail Mary. In case you are being attacked by a whale or something."

Codi heard Jack sigh, then there was silence for a moment.

"Okay. Is there an override?" Jack asked.

"What's your vertical speed, Scout?" Callie asked.

"Why does that matter?" he asked.

"Because there's something else at play here, Scout," Callie said. Her patience was admirable.

"And what would that be, base?" Jack asked, sounding like he was losing his own patience.

There was a long pause from the base before Minus finally came in over the speaker. "Jack, that thing vaporizes about a thousand cubic feet of water around it. Instantly."

"What does that mean?" Baltey asked.

"Think about it," Minus said. "It could create a gigantic pocket of air beneath it."

"So?" Baltey asked.

"Is there an override or not, guys? We're still falling fast." Jack said.

"Scout, read me your vertical speed. I cannot authorize override over a certain descent rate. The vessel could implode."

"Callie, I think you're forgetting the urgency of the situation here," he said, now sounding more stern.

"Just tell us how to override, Goddammit!" Baltey said.

Everyone ignored that.

"I am not forgetting anything, Scout. You are forgetting we have safety protocols. We've lost connection with your instrumentation, so I cannot see your attitude. I'm going to need you to read me your vertical speed and depth before I can tell you how to override the safety lock," Callie said, still maintaining her professional posture. "If you create a pocket of air beneath you, then you'll slam into the bottom of it when you hit the water again. It would be like slamming into concrete."

"We're at twenty-five hundred feet per minute. Seven thousand feet."

"Was that seven thousand?" Minus asked.

"Affirm," Jack responded.

Minus had forgotten to let go of the mike key though. They heard him say, "Dear Christ. They're dropping like a stone. Authorize it, Callie."

"I can't Minus! It could kill them all!" she said.

"That's a chance we're gonna have to take, base! My rotors are ineffective at this speed. I'm way underpowered here," Jack said.

There was a long pause from the other end.

"Callie, we're sinking here," Jack said.

"Why is this happening?" Rick Baltey asked, plaintively.

At that moment Codi felt sorry for him. She was scared out of her wits, and had no time to worry about anyone else. But she felt sorry for him. He sounded like a little boy. It did nothing to help calm her own fear though. If anything it enhanced her fear. Justified it. Intensified it.

"Jack, I think it's too dangerous. But you're the captain. If you pull that trigger, I don't think we'll see each other again."

Codi heard Jack's solemn sigh. Felt the light bump as his head hit the headrest behind him. Clearly he was thinking this over.

"What are my options, base? If I hit the floor like this, I mean."

"You're a long way from the floor yet."

"Dear God. This is unbelievable," Jack said.

"Are we going to die, Jack?" Codi asked.

"Yeah, no shit. Is this it? Why the hell did I sign up for this?" Baltey cried.

Jack did not answer.

"Scout, can you create drag?" Callie asked suddenly.

"Fantastic. Here we go again, guys. Hold on," Jack said, not on the radio though. Then the world tilted to the right. They were falling sideways again. But Codi could immediately tell they were slowing. The VSI now read 2400. And the needle was dropping. Slowly, but it was dropping. Gradually working its way anti-clockwise, back toward the safety of the lower numbers.

"Dragging," Jack said over the radio.

The altitude was now at negative thirteen thousand feet. That was two and a half miles deep. Codi's instruments were digital. Large red numbers and needles on black backgrounds, custom tailored to her robotic vision. They were also slightly larger than the others' instruments. But right now, she didn't want to be seeing what they were telling her. She cursed her vision and closed her eyes.

She took a deep breath and let a thought roll around on her tongue. Testing herself, asking whether she wanted to let it be spoken.

"Roger that, Scout. What's your depth now?" Callie asked.

"Thirteen-five. Falling at 2200. Seems to be riding there."

"That's still too fast, Scout," Callie said. "Can you make more drag?"

"I don't know how I would. I would welcome any ideas," Jack said. After a moment, he said, "Is there a parachute on this fucking thing?" Codi realized he had kept that off the radio.

Codi finally tightened up and turned her head toward him. "Jack, I know the override code."

"Huh?" His voice was slightly closer. He was turning to his right, cranking around to try to communicate better with Codi.

"I know the override code. It was written on the white board in the lab."

"Really? How do you know?"

"What do you mean?"

"How do you know that's what it was?"

"It said override! And then a long number!" Codi snapped. She was scared. Jack didn't snap back.

"You're sure?"

"Yeah, what if you got it wrong?" Baltey said. The fear was still thick in his voice. Jack was the only one who still sounded calm. She guessed if they hit the bottom of the ocean, thick with the silt of a million years, and survived… Well, he could make do until they ran out of oxygen. He seemed completely comfortable down here.

"I don't get numbers wrong," she said simply.

"Pssh."

"If you guys want to try it, I'm game," Jack said. "If we hit the bottom at this speed, they'll be sopping us up with sponges."

"This fucking thing is made of steel, dude," Baltey said. "It's not gonna break against sand or rock or anything. And that's, what… like twenty-five miles per hour?"

"You know why they put airbags in cars, dude?" Jack asked. "Hitting a solid wall with no deceleration at twenty-five… If it didn't instantly kill you, you'd be writhing around in your seatbelt with a broken back. Furthermore, under this kind of pressure, I can't guarantee that we wouldn't break up. If nothing else, it might pop some welds on the prop cage. Break some rotors. If we lose control of our cage, we'll never see the sunlight again."

Codi's stomach sunk again. She was beginning to feel very nauseated.

"I think you're forgetting, we've already lost control!" Baltey screamed.

Jack sighed audibly. "We haven't lost control. Our rotors are working. They're just ineffective at this speed. We have to slow to use them. We weren't supposed to fall this fast."

"So, you fucked up then?" Baltey said.

"Will you shut up?" Codi shouted. "The cable snapped! None of this was supposed to happen."

"Let's try it, guys," Jack said. "We're accelerating again. We have to do something soon."

The altimeter now told her they were at twenty-one thousand feet deep. That was four miles. Codi shivered.

"Give me the code, Codi."

"Wait." That was Baltey. "Are we sure we want to do this?"

"I don't see any other choice," Jack said. "Codi. The code."

"30808 0808 445," she said.

She heard Jack's fingers clicking on the keypad beside his chair. Then she looked at the translator box in front of her. The one that sent perfect-clarity pictures to her computerized eyes. And she nearly jumped out of her seat.

"Jesus, oh my God!" she shouted.

"What is it?" Jack asked. The ship slammed to a stop with an audible creak and a severe bang that echoed like a hammer on a bulkhead. The picture skipped and everything went dark momentarily. Codi's chin slammed down against her chest when they stopped, and her back cracked as she flew forward against the harness. Had she not been buckled in, she might have just flown forward. But as it was, her back felt like a spring that just got stepped on. She cried out in pain.

At the same time, peripherally, she heard a loud pop from behind her on the right, and then a sort of over-exaggerated snoring. A deep growling aspiration that sounded like someone with severe asthma.

"Baltey, you okay?" Jack shouted. He was unbuckling his harness. The outside world swam sickeningly in circles.

Orbits. Revolutions in an unspecified direction. They were holding perfectly still vertically, she saw, but the ship was again spinning, although much more slowly. Something whipped past the camera, which she now thought of like a window. There were three of the translator computers just in front of her, mounted above the instruments. She was the only one in the ship who could see them. So she was the only one with windows. There were other monitors in front of the two men, but they were translated infrared imagery, not the full-color picture she was getting.

"Codi, are you okay?" Jack asked.

She was trembling so hard she could hardly speak. "Yes. Yes, I think I'm okay. My neck hurts really bad. I think I've got whiplash."

"Okay. Try to stay still. I'll be over there in a minute. Don't unbuckle. You'll fall to the ceiling."

"Got it," she said, nodding quickly. She was breathing fast now, holding tightly to the straps above her chest, trying not to pay attention to the sickening roller coaster that was putting her upside down and backwards every two minutes.

Baltey was still snoring, and Codi was beginning to get frightened. "What's going on?" she asked. "What's wrong with him? Is he okay?"

"Oh my God," Jack said. "I don't think so." And then, "Base, Scylla, come in?"

"Base copies."

"We need help. Richard needs medical attention right away," he said.

Codi's heart dropped. "What is it?" she shouted, trying to crank her head around enough to see. But the angle in which the seats were placed was too obtuse.

"What's his status, Scout?" someone said over the speakers. It wasn't Minus or Callie.

"Snapped windpipe," Jack said. Then he cursed silently to himself as the sub made another revolution, switching the ceiling for the floor. He was holding on back there like a gymnast on the monkey bars. "Never mind, base. He's not gonna make it."

The snoring sound Codi was hearing had grown deeper and slower. It was now loud and low, haunting in its unquestionable meaning. Codi's eyes were wide, searching for safety somewhere around her. It was getting really dark in here. Dark in her soul. Claustrophobia, which had never been a familiar feeling to her, began to introduce itself. It started in her stomach, and tightened against her bladder.

"It's all right, man. Just relax. Here," Jack was saying quietly. "Here, dude. Hey. Goddammit!" he said. There was a struggle going on back there, and Codi could only guess what was happening.

"Say again, Scout," base said through the radio.

"Richard Baltey is dying," Codi said, depressing the talk button on her seat handle. "Can I help, Jack? I'm so scared. Is there anything I can do?"

"Yeah, sure. You can stop this fucking ship spinning like a top," Jack said.

She took several deep breaths quickly, trying to steady her nerves. Codi didn't want Jack to be the only calm one on the ship. She knew he was going to need her to be in control. "Okay, how do I do that?"

"You're gonna… shit!" he said. Something metal banged against something else. "Can you move to my seat?"

The thought both frightened and excited her. "Yes. I think I can!" she said.

"Okay, wait 'til the ship's upright if you have to. But come to my seat and buckle in as fast as you can. Got it?" Jack said.

"Got it!" she said.

"What's happening down there, guys?" Callie said over the speakers.

Neither of them could answer now, though, as Codi was already unbuckled and moving toward the other seat.

"Go to your left, Codi," Jack instructed.

"I am. You turned the shield off, right?"

"Yup. Good. Careful. There's a console there somewhere."

"Got it," she said. And then she was in his seat, strapping in – just as the world was beginning to tilt sickeningly forward again. She got the last tab in the buckle just as the pressure fell full force against her chest. She was now hanging by the harness, which was adjusted for Jack's masculine body size. He outweighed her by almost a hundred pounds, and the webbing was loose like a sweet remark on a birthday card. It didn't fit, and barely held her in.

"Okay, how do I do this?" she said. Callie broke in on the radio again, and suddenly, Codi remembered what she had seen on her monitor. And with that remembrance came the realization that she was now blind. She could no longer see her monitors – the only ones in the ship that she was able to read at all.

"Grab the yoke in front of you. It's right between your legs," Jack answered.

"Got it. Uh, Jack? I saw something out there a minute ago," she said.

"Pull back on the yoke very slightly. Feel it. Make it do what you want it to do. Can you tell which way is up?"

"Yes. Your harness doesn't fit. Makes orientation a cinch."

"What did you see, Codi?"

"I don't know, Jack. But it's not something I ever want to see again."

There was silence from her left. The struggling had stopped. So had the weird death-rattle snore. Had Baltey just died right beside her?

"What did you see?" he asked again.

"I think I saw our monster."

CHAPTER 31

Walter stood in the hallway, leaning against the wall. The concrete felt good. Cold, to the top of his head. His neck cranked up so he could stare at the ceiling and feel this cool against his head. It was the closest thing he had felt to comfort in the last era in his memory. He heard the echoes of footsteps as people casually strolled from place to place with no real sense of urgency. Why? Why did they have no rush about them? He felt like he was rushing headlong to the end of his life in a four-alarm hurry, his feet leaving trails of flame behind him on the floor.

The cuffs were tight on his wrists. Jennifer Cambria stood silently beside him, face lit by her smart phone. She was respectfully quiet, honoring his unspoken wish for solitude – inasmuch as he could attain such a thing in his arrested state. They had been standing here for almost an hour. He needed to piss. He wanted a smoke. He needed a shave. He dropped his head, looking directly forward at the side door of the courtroom and ran his hand through the month of stubble on his face.

"How much longer is this bullshit gonna take?" he asked quietly, looking down the hall toward the steel doors at the end where a police officer stood on guard. These were the undecorated hallways, as Cambria called them, in the back of the court. The parts that didn't have to look appealing to the tourists and casual comers and goers. Back here was all business. The parts he didn't imagine himself ever having to see.

"Not much longer. I think I hear movement in there," she responded. She looped her left hand through his right elbow, grabbing his arm and squeezing slightly. "Try to relax if you can. I know that's hard," she said, face still buried in her phone, "But you're gonna worry yourself sick."

"I'm not worried. Just want this shit to be over with," he said.

When they were called in, Walter felt the sting of anger he had become familiar with over the last two months. It had become close enough to call a friend, though he hated it worse than the shackles on his wrists. The case had been open and shut with an expedience he would have laughed at, had he read about it in the paper. Sideways, he wondered what Thevi would think if this one aired on one of her court TV shows. She was there, in the courtroom. He had been facing the judge, the jury during the reading of the verdict, so he had not seen her reaction. But he had heard her gasps and silent sobbing, all the same. That wrecked him. He had instantly felt tears welling up in his eyes. Not those of sadness, but those of that hateful friend called anger.

He had been convicted of felony aggravated assault and battery in the first degree and obstruction of justice. That had been bullshit. His stomping on the guy's phone had kept the 911 operator from doing her job, they had said. He had silently rolled his eyes at that one, but couldn't say anything. Could not escape that anger. He feared for the next person who crossed him. With all this pent-up aggression, he was ready to take it to the next level on the next person who pissed him off. And the jury – who the fuck had selected those dick bags? There were nine men and three women, and all the men were the sweater-wearing type. Those liberal idiots who thought guns should be reserved for the military. Those who thought the government had everything under complete control, knew what they were doing. Those who thought laws provided physical safety. These thoughts ran full-speed through his crowded, confused head as he tried to process what type of person it took to look at his case and think it was anything other than defensive. Of course, he had been the aggressor. He had driven across town in the pouring rain to exact a carefully planned – ha ha – revenge on this poor defenseless man. It was sick violence. The kind of thing that made this country a dangerous place. Like guns.

Not one of the men in the jury would make eye contact with him. How had it come down like this? The women, he saw, were looking at him with that vacant sadness in their eyes. That sympathy for a man who would go after someone who brought harm to a woman. Where were the men? Where was the chivalry? Where was that burning core that made a man a man? He saw it in not a single one of them. These were guys who would call the cops at the first sign of trouble. Neighbor making a little too much noise? Call the cops. A woman getting beat, raped, choked in the street? Dear God! Someone call the cops! That attitude was like rocket fuel splashed on the fire of his anger.

"Watson," a man said, leaning out the door in front of them. He stepped out and held the door as Jennifer Cambria walked Walter into the courtroom, still holding his arm like a love, whispering positive words to him as they walked. Walter was, of course, ignoring her. He was done with the system. The system had betrayed him. He wished for that time machine so he could go back to somewhere that made sense. Ancient Rome, perhaps. Medieval England.

As they approached the defense desk, he felt the full weight of his anger. That slimy fuck Tim was sitting at the prosecution desk, hands in his lap looking forlorn. The poor guy. He just raped and strangled a woman. Not a big deal! Why should he have to suffer?

"Mr. Watson, the court has agreed with the prosecution on your punishment. The despicable act of rape and battery against a woman is not something this court takes lightly. Mr. Blisk will be tried for his own crime, and dealt with accordingly. But it is when we as citizens decide to take the law into our own hands, to forgo the process and the laws, the very cogs that turn the gears of the justice system, that we become a society of imbeciles. A society with no law and order quickly crumbles under the chaos. When any man can exact his own judgment with no due process, with no fair trial by jury, then we are rendered helpless in the face of evil. It is, therefore, the opinion of this court that you should serve time for your assault of Mr. Blisk."

Walter looked up at the ceiling, rolling his neck, cracking it. Trying to maintain his calm. Every part of him wanted to climb over that prosecutor's bench and sock Tim's teeth through the back of his head. He made a silent pact with himself right there. If ever he crossed paths with this leech again, he would end him. Walter would arrange for him to see the silky side of a coffin. Forget Codi. Forget the rape. All that was behind him now. Tragic and unnecessary, and completely unforgivable. But that was no longer Walter's problem – if ever it was in the first place. No, his anger burned from the setup he had walked into. While he had been knocking on the door, hiding the picture on his driver license with a wet thumb, Tim had been dialing 911 on his phone already. He was so weak in the face of conflict that he had arranged for a team of police officers to handle his confrontation for him. And that itself should be punishable, Walter thought.

"This court, in finding you guilty of first degree felony assault, hereby sentences the defendant to eighteen months in a medium security correctional facility to be determined by availability. Bailiff, detain the defendant." The bailiff did as he was told, taking Walter's arm from the preferable grip of the altogether softer Jennifer Cambria. She tried to say something to him as they were separated, but he could not hear her. He now heard Thevi sobbing loudly in the row behind him. Walter refused to turn and look at her though. Shame filled his heart and soul. Not shame for his crime. But shame for the way the state had gone about handling it. This was so unfair. So weak. So unabashedly and unapologetically pansy. Lock the real men up while the rapists are coddled by the state. He shook his head.

Un-fucking-believable. He did not want Thevi to see him like this. He knew she was looking at his back right now. But he did not want her to see his face. Or was it that he did not want to see hers? He had a moment to think about it as they forcefully removed him from the courtroom. As he went west, out the wooden doors and into the ugly part of the courthouse, he thought about his marriage. His sweet red-haired wife sitting there bawling in the courtroom as he was taken to the back to be locked away like so much street trash. Like the scum that actually belonged back here, he was being thrown into a cage.

Walter silently, quickly, wondered which it was. Did he not want to see her face? He was disgusted with himself for getting caught, for being treated like a criminal. But was he maybe disgusted with her? That primal human instinctive reaction to mourn when one's loved ones are mistreated — that cry she tried to hold down but that broke free and escaped into the eerie static silence of the courtroom. His lovely wife had broken down. Maybe his anger was to blame for his embarrassment of her. He found himself wanting to say, "Pull yourself together. Look at you!" But as he got to the door, she threw her inhibitions to the floor.

"I love you, Walter! I'll love you forever! Stay strong!" she cried.

That stopped his heart cold. He turned and looked over his shoulder. A brief, lighting-fast moment, stunning in its clarity but deadly fast and inevitably over, he saw the weight of the world in her green eyes. The sadness of a thousand deaths, her trembling hands covering her small mouth, tendrils of her red hair hanging in her face, tears streaming down her reddened cheeks. She looked at him pleadingly, and he realized in that tiny instant that it would be a long, long time before he kissed those lips again. Held her hand, smelled her perfume, stroked her back. And then he was through the door and into the hall, in that part of the courthouse he should never have to be.

CHAPTER 32

Jack sat up straight. Codi pulled hard against the loose harness, turning to look at the man with whom her new friend Callie had fallen in love. He sat staring seriously at her, eyes wide, but skeptical. He was chewing on his lip. His hands were on Richard Baltey's knees as he sat on the ground in front of the dying, or possibly dead man. Codi had the yoke in her right hand, steadily pushing against the weight she felt in whatever direction it came. The shifting current of the sea was a constant push against her. Not a hard one to control against, but it was there. It was that pressure she felt from one direction or the other that comforted her. It told her which direction, and how firmly, to press back. She was almost doing it peripherally now. Second-nature. Forgotten. Had she mastered it that quickly?

"What did you see, Codi?" he asked for the third time. "Describe it."

"I don't know," she said, suddenly unsure of herself. She felt a fear and yearning down in her chest. Something she could not pinpoint was coming at her from the inside. That unsurety – was it of what she had seen? Had she really seen it? Would she be taken seriously? She was, after all, the only seeing-impaired person down here. Could her sight – *would* her sight – be trusted by the others, if she were the only one to have seen it?

"I don't know. It's like an apparition," she said, voice trembling now, much like the fingers with which she so carefully and expertly grasped the yoke. "It was like... like..." she trailed off as Callie cut in on the radio again.

"Turn that damn thing off," Jack said.

Codi looked up at the display in front of her. Then she keyed the mike again. "Callie, this is Codi. We have something going on down here. Can you give us a minute please?"

"Negative, Scout. You said you have a man down, we need to assess and assist. This is not the time for radio silence."

"Where the hell did she get this professionalism?" Codi asked Jack, off-radio. "Where did she learn this?" Her thoughts were quickly scattering, and she began to seriously doubt what she had seen. Could it have been real? Regardless of whether or not what she saw was a real thing, had her vision of it – even if it had been digital interference on the camera – been real? Had she only *thought* she saw something?

Jack looked up at the screen in front of her, twisting his head to make the angle. There was nothing but blackness on the screen as far as Codi could tell. Perhaps that was true for him as well. He looked back at her. "Describe this apparition please."

She gulped. "Jack, I'm afraid. I am very, very afraid right now."

He raised up on his haunches, looking again at the screen. "Codi, you're okay. Talk to me. I need you right now to talk to me."

"Respond, Scout, are we making contact?" Callie asked from the radio.

"You are," Codi said. "We hear you. Callie, we need a minute. Richard is dead." She didn't know if that was true or not. She just didn't know what else to say.

There was a long pause from the other end. "Are you guys okay?" said Minus, after a bit. What had happened to Callie? "Do you have control of the vessel?"

Jack breathed in and looked back up at Baltey, then stood and put his hands on his hips. He was nodding slowly. He walked over to Codi and squatted down in front of her. She followed him closely with her eyes, trying to follow his gaze in the dim red light. She straightened in her seat, once again facing forward, holding tightly to the harness straps in front of her shoulders. "I'm so scared right now. Is he really dead?" she asked. Her voice was even shaky now.

"Scout, do you copy?" asked Minus.

"Yes, we copy, dammit," Jack shouted, keying the mike on the end of the handle upon which Codi's hand rested. "Can you give us a few minutes? I'm tending to my live passenger right now." That seemed to finally buy them some time.

Jack grabbed her knees and looked up at her calmly. "Have you ever been around someone who has died?"

"Ha! God, not while they were dying!" she said loudly. She was breathing too fast now. "Are you saying he's dead? For real?" she looked over, trying once again to see Baltey, but again to no avail.

"Codi, calm down," Jack said. "It's going to be okay."

"How can you say that? He's dead!" she said, throwing a finger toward Baltey.

"Your losing control is not going to bring him back, Codi. I really need you to maintain your cool. It's going to take both of us to regain control of this situation." He was speaking very calmly himself, running his thumb back and forth over her knee.

She took a deep breath. "I've never been there when someone died," she said. She squeezed the straps and swallowed. "How did he die?"

Jack looked over at Baltey. He could see him from where he was sitting, though Codi could not. Maybe that was a blessing. Jack looked back at her, then tilted his head. "His neck broke when we stopped. Looks like his head somehow snapped backwards. His trachea," he said, touching his own neck, "must have popped."

"Good God," Codi said, covering her mouth with a trembling hand. Tears began filling her eyes. "That is so terrible. I feel horrible for how I talked to him," she said, shaking her head. She was beginning to sob openly now. She bent her head and let herself cry. Jack, she noticed, was making no moves to stop her either. He did, however, reach up and stroke her cheek once. Then his hand fell to her shoulder.

"Okay, I really need you to be strong right now, Codi. We're going to take care of Richard. But for right now, I need you to help me. Can you do that?" He was sitting right behind the yoke. He took it from her and stood up.

"Okay," she said, nodding. She tried to tighten herself up, to get control of her emotions. Jack was right. There would be time for tears later. For now, they still had a ship to command.

"Okay?" he asked again.

"Okay. Yeah, I'm okay."

Jack helped her back to her seat. He put the ship on auto-pilot and helped her buckle in, then asked her again to speak of what she had seen. "Can you tell me what you saw now?"

She was shaking her head. "It was like a tentacle or something. But it was so... *big*." She replayed what she had seen in her head, questioning her memory. Her sanity. "I just don't think it can be, Jack!"

"Remember what we're out here to find, Codi. We knew it would probably be really big," Jack said.

"I know! But I didn't believe! I still don't know if I do!" she said, wiping her eyes with the butts of her hands. "I've thought all along this was just a joke."

Minus chose this time to interrupt. "You guys okay down there?"

Jack sat looking at her for a minute, then put his hand over hers, fingering the button on her seat handle for her. "We're making it work, Minus. We'll be heading back up in a little bit," he said.

"Copy that," Minus said. It sounded like there might have been a trace of disappointment in his voice. Codi could not have cared less. Someone had already died in the first hour of the drop. He could find someone else to man his stupid sub for him. Codi was no longer interested.

"Look, Codi," Jack said. "You know they just only recently confirmed the existence of the colossal squid, right?"

She nodded. She was pretty sure she had heard something about them.

"Well those things are like fifty foot long. Is it really hard to believe there's something bigger than that in the ocean?" Jack asked.

"I don't know," she said. This was not a subject she had done much thinking on before. She never imagined she would need to know the sizes of sea creatures. Perhaps she should have planned better, being on one of the first dives down the Challenger Deep.

"Well trust me, dear. There is. We've spotted blue whales before around the hundred-foot mark."

Was that true? She did not know. But she didn't think Jack was lying to her. Certainly not here, not about this. "Really?" she asked, tentatively.

"Yes. Absolutely. And there has always been the thought that there might be something even bigger than that. We really don't know that much about what's going on in the deepest parts of the oceans. There could be things that make the colossal squid look small. We just don't know. But I would start trusting your eyes a little more! It's okay to believe in what you saw."

"But God, I don't want to, Jack," she said, quaking with chills as she said it. "It was so big! If that thing was real, then the colossal squid… the blue whale," she said, waving a hand toward the general outside, "those are little guys."

Jack straightened up. "Well, if you saw it on that screen, our computers recorded it."

She nodded, breathing in deeply, steadying herself. Trying to recompose.

"So, start believing in yourself!" Jack said, squeezing her knee.

"Thanks, Jack. I appreciate you trying to make me feel better."

"Sure! You're my teammate. My first officer! I need you healthy, girl."

"Okay," she said, trying a laugh. It felt better. "What are we gonna do with him?" she asked.

Jack smiled. "Well, we can take him up right now. Or we can go find this son of a bitch!"

"Ha!" she said, laughing out loud. "Okay, you made me feel a hundred times better. But I don't think you're gonna talk me into wanting to go after that fucking thing. That was the scariest thing I've ever seen."

"Okay," he said easily. "I respect that. And we do have a fallen comrade on board. We need to get him upstairs." Jack sat there for a moment just looking at her. Making sure she was going to be okay. Then he stood up and made his way back to his seat. She could hear him sit and buckle back in.

"You ready, Code?" he asked.

She nodded. "Yeah. I'm ready. Let's go," she said.

"Base, Scout, we're heading up," he said in the mic.

And they started rising.

⌘   ⌘   ⌘

Callie was sitting on the stool in front of the command console, head bent over, massaging her own neck. "How the heck did things go so wrong?" she asked to no one in particular. "So fast."

Minus was leaning against the desk beside her, watching as a technician scanned through the recording of what had happened so far. So far, it was a whole lot of blackness. The sub had not yet even gotten down to the depth they were supposed to start searching before everything had gone out of control. And thus they had not yet even turned on the outside spotlights. An occasional flash of white would slip by on the screen – a fish or a bit of detritus passing close to one of the infrared cameras – but nothing noteworthy. They had been scanning through on fast-forward for fifteen minutes now. Nothing.

Callie was feeling the effects of staying up too late too many nights in a row, and reckoned it was simultaneously a blessing and a curse that she and Jack were together now. Being on a cruise together would be one thing. Being on one where they would be called to work with little or no notice, might be an entirely different other. She was running low on sleep, and trembled slightly with the caffeine she had been pouring down her throat like water all morning. It was almost seven a.m. now. The sun was well on its way up the sky, another race across the heavens under way. It seemed like so much later, since they had gotten started so early this morning.

"So go over it again. I have my coffee. I've taken my pee break. What happened?" Callie said to Bill Murphy, the technician beside her. Bill was looking at the vitals of the submersible, studying the complex graphs and readouts from the central computer like he was reading a novel. Callie could make no sense of the gibberish herself. He had run through what had happened, a sort of play-by-play, with Minus, but Callie had only caught the tail end of it.

"Okay, so when the cable snapped, they started falling. This in itself isn't a real big deal. But no one was ready for it. So he didn't have the rotors on. By the time they got their feet under them, the thing was falling too fast. And spinning like an eight ball dropped from a tall building."

Callie nodded, sipping from her coffee, staring into the blank space on the desk in front of her lowered head. She was trying not to look at anything that might distract her. "Okay."

"Well, the motors are really ineffective when you're falling that fast. Think of it like a boat propeller. Those tiny little things can get a ski boat going pretty damn fast, pretty quickly. You can get up to thirty, forty miles per hour, in just a few seconds, right?"

"Right," Callie said, having no idea if it was right or not.

"Well, if you take that same motor and put it on something heavy like this – something that doesn't float – and drop it in the water, it's gonna start sinking. Spinning. Twisting, twirling, whatever. Well, that motor isn't going to do anything for a while. It has to defeat the momentum of the fall. And the real problem is that the rotors themselves are underpowered already. They weren't meant to make it haul ass. It's not a fast boat. They push it along at maybe three or four miles per hour."

"Uh huh," Callie said. She turned and leaned her head on a hand, looking at Bill as he spoke. He was sitting sideways in his chair, hands out in front of him, using them to help with his lecture.

"So when the thing is already dropping at, say, twenty miles per hour, and spinning too, well... Those little rotors just don't do much. We never planned on having this thing be out of control like that. It was a scenario we never encountered, so we didn't build accordingly."

"Okay. I follow all that. What I don't get is why it was spinning," Callie said, running her hand back through her hair.

"Well, just like any stone you drop in the water, it's probably going to develop an unbalanced attitude as it falls."

Callie shook her head. "How did I miss this?"

"Ms. Simmons, you really shouldn't beat yourself up about this. This wasn't your design."

"I designed the propulsion cage, Bill."

"You sketched it out, sure! But you didn't attach numbers to it! The horse-power? The torque of the engines? That wasn't your department. You drew out what you wanted the thing to look like and the engineering guys took it from there. They made assumptions based on the weight and the size of the vessel. Totally not your fault."

She sat staring at him for a moment, trying to allow herself to feel better. It wasn't working. She knew it wasn't entirely her responsibility. But she also kicked herself for allowing it to happen.

"Listen, Bill, I know I didn't write the numbers in. But I should have known this was possible. I should have accounted for an emergency."

"So should they, Ms. Simmons." Bill said, looking her straight in the eyes. "Again, not your fault."

She sighed. "Okay. I'm not interested in pinning blame here. I just... I just," she started.

"Guys, we have a problem," someone said from the other side of the room. It was Nathan. He was running the mission control, watching several screens at once.

Callie shot up out of her seat and dashed to his console, along with several others.

Minus was right behind her, hand on her shoulder, trying to gain a vantage point. "What the fuck is that?" he shouted. "Is this a live feed?"

"Yes, it's live," Nathan said.

Callie's heart skipped a beat as she realized what she was looking at. She had a hand over her mouth, looking wide-eyed at a twenty-three-inch monitor where a very clear picture of something... alien hung like the chills from a bad dream upon waking.

"It's an arm. A tentacle. Something big," said Nathan.

"What the hell is it doing?" Callie asked. Her heart was now beating very fast. This was turning quickly into that nightmare. That movie where you know the ending but you can't do anything to stop it. You can't walk away. You can't stop it. It's still going to happen whether you witness it or not. She had asked what it was doing, but it was well obvious. Whatever had the submersible in its pale pink grasp was taking it down. Everything was happening so fast it was hard to focus on any one thing. But in small wisps of time, she was able to discern that they were going down. The direction of the bubbles was wrong. And during some of those brief flashes of clarity, she could see down the long arm of this beast that had a hold of the ship. And it was a long way down to the body. The body, at the far end of the spotlights' reach was just a silhouette. The spotlight was good for about a hundred and fifty meters. The water looked like blue background to the horror that took up most of the screen. The deep royal blue hue of the water was interrupted by the silhouette of a terrifying shape.

"He's got them!" Minus was shouting. Suddenly, his hand was off her shoulder and Minus was turning around, grasping for a microphone on the desk at an empty station. He keyed the mike and spoke into it quickly. "Scout, do you copy?" Without waiting even long enough for someone to respond, he keyed again. "Scout, come in! Tell me what's going on!"

"Tell them to engage the force fi-" Callie started, and her mind went blank. Minus was hunched over the desk. He turned his head slightly to listen to her, but did not look at her. "The..." she started again, snapping her fingers. "What the hell is it called?" she shouted.

"The shield!" Nathan shouted from behind her.

Callie's hands were in her hair as she stared at the screen in front of Nathan. "The shield, Minus! Tell them to engage!" she was shaking hard now. "Turn on the force field, guys!" she shouted at no one.

"Scout, do you copy? Scout, come in! Scout, if you can read me, turn on the hydroshield! Engage it now!" Minus said into the microphone.

"Look, look, look!" Nathan was saying, tapping a finger on the screen. Purple ribbons danced away from his fingertip as it left the LCD of the monitor. Callie was looking. The image on the screen was twisting like crazy – a sickening roller coaster spin – as the being rolled the sub up in its grasp, and then suddenly, the entire screen was covered with the disgusting pale flesh of the being. It had no suction cups, but rather, it appeared to have what Callie could only later describe as sphincters. The muscle at the bottom of the stomach, she recalled, the muscle that closed off the stomach from the duodenum – that's what these looked like. Tiny muscles like mouths that could open and close at will, ugly, obscene openings that humans should never have to look at. They lined this tentacle-like arm with such ridiculous frequency that she wondered how it was possible to digest anything they took in. If, indeed, that's what they were. Maybe they were just suckers. The very sight of them made her feel sick at her stomach. The ones close to the camera were writhing and moving like sentient objects searching for evil to ingest in the deep darkness – a place where humanity was never meant to venture. This was the devil himself. Callie had to turn away.

"Oh my God," she said, covering her mouth again. "Do something!" She was beginning to feel the stirrings in her stomach of an overload. A true, unabashed panic was setting in. "Somebody do something! Get that terrible fucking thing off my ship!" She was crying now.

"We're trying, Callie," Minus said, still not turning to look at her. "Scout come in!" he shouted into the microphone, over and over, all with no response. All to dead air. "Jack! Codi! Can anyone in there hear me?"

Callie remembered at that moment that a third of the dive party had passed away, and her cries became terrible, wracking quakes of her body as she fell into a rolling chair, completely consumed by emotion. She was bawling the kind of cry a human experiences when she has seen too much – when her mind is on the verge of shutting down because it has been overloaded with emotion and trauma.

Candy Hanning was there now, wrapping her arms around Callie. "Come on, baby. Let's get out of here for a minute. Let these guys do their work," she said calmly. She was pulling Callie out of the seat.

"NO!" Callie screamed between sobs, "NO! I can't leave my team! I can't desert them! They're trapped at the bottom of the ocean!"

"Let's go. Come with me, sweetie. Let's take a little walk. You're not gonna do them any good up here in this condition."

Two hours later, everything was quiet in the command center. Everyone exhausted, all options expended. Everything that could be tried had been tried. They had lost complete control of the situation. They no longer had eyes on the ship, ears inside it, or any way to communicate. There was absolutely nothing left to be done. Nothing was visible on the screens any longer. This had gone past the state of just being a nightmare, to something far more sinister. Something reserved for horror movies. The worst possible thing anyone could imagine.

Matt Minus had left the command center an hour ago, and was now sitting in the theater, staring at nothing on the big screen in front of him. Everyone who had tried to enter the theater in the last hour had been told to leave. Unless they had an urgent message for him – which no one had yet – they had been excused immediately. He sat scratching his chin, his knees bent, feet up on the seat back in front of him, just thinking. He had lost control. He had lost his submersible. His entire project had gone to hell. He had lost the crew. Little did he know, they would spend the next fourteen hours doing absolutely nothing.

There was simply nothing they could do. So that's exactly what they did do. The coffee makers were working overtime, and there was a lot of pacing going on. Some of the most brilliant minds in the world were on this ship, but no one had much of a plan to bring to the table, because any real plan would have to start with another sub. And they only had the one. The one they could not possibly lose because it was so highly advanced. So high-tech. Every computer in the world would have to get in line behind the one they had built and installed on the Scylla Scout submarine. It was outfitted with some technology that wasn't even known to anyone but a select few on the ship itself. Minus and a couple of others, including Callie, knew about it. It was so classified it wasn't even in the schematics of the ship.

But, like the computers and the force field and the rotors and the propulsion cage itself – all of it was completely useless. What good was technology of any kind when it was in the grip of a monster? A beast so gigantic it made the word colossal sound cheap and dainty. When something of that scale and magnitude had your technology in its hand, and was playing with it like a Matchbox car, who was number one? None of it mattered. Thus the pacing. The coffee. The ideas that sputtered out like bad fireworks thrown in a dirty puddle. Everything was a dead end. They were hanging above the deepest trench in the world, feeling extremely vulnerable and useless, staying in place with a soft anchor. That was a quick label for a fantastic series of motors on the bottom of the ship that took commands only from the boss computer when they were turned on. And that computer was controlled by its connection to a GPS satellite.

Hanging steady in that one spot, rocking with the light waves of the ocean, they stayed for fourteen hours, deliberating. Hoping. Praying. Pacing.

Callie had been reclusive herself, hanging mostly in her room, only coming out to get coffee and use the bathroom, to stretch occasionally. A grief so deep had settled in on her soul that she feared she may never recover. She had now lost two loves in less than a year. And love was not a strong word when she thought of Jack. She had fallen hard for him, in just a short amount of time. Letting a man into her bed, she had realized, was a fast track to the heart. And this had nothing to do with sex. Just that closeness – that bond that comes from sleeping naked next to someone you adore – that intimacy one can only achieve by standing naked and bare in front of someone, no secrets, nothing to hide, all emotions bared... That closeness she had never given anyone else a chance to attain – she had attained with Jack. And now she had lost him, too. Right on the heels of Chris, her first true love, she had now lost another. Depression seemed to be seeping in from every direction.

Deep into the night, Minus sat in the theater. Callie knocked lightly on the door and let herself in, hoping mostly to learn what his plan was. How long would they be sticking around? Was there a plan for coming back? How long would they wait, in short, until they all admitted the inevitable had happened? Or had they all admitted that to themselves already, in private? Were they just waiting for the word to execute the evacuation? To count their losses and move on with their lives?

As Callie walked up the short ramp to the theater, still hidden from the seating area by a wall built to keep the light out, Minus shouted out, "Go away."

She rounded the corner and came into the room. "I said go-" he said, turning to look. His words trailed off as he saw who it was though. "Callie."

"Minus," she said. She chose the row behind his and walked to the seat behind and to the left of his.

"I didn't know it was you. Sorry," he said.

"I know, Minus. I'm familiar with the limitations of light."

"Doesn't do corners well," he said with a wan smile. He turned back to face the front as if they were watching a movie. The screen was on, still broadcasting what could be picked up by the cameras on the sub, lost some seven miles below them. Which was, at the moment, absolutely nothing. Just the same as it had been for the last whole day.

"What is our plan, Minus?" she asked.

He sat silently for a moment, his fingers steepled under his chin. "That's all I've been thinking about for the last forever. It's killing me. I have no idea what to do."

Callie nodded. She crossed her legs and looked for some dust to pick off of her trousers. She could find none, and instead decided to twist her ring like she had seen Rebecca doing. She only had the one, and it wasn't a real important one – just a cheap hundred-dollar bit of bling that made her feel pretty sometimes. But it twisted nicely on her finger when she set to it. It made a good fidget stone.

"I'm open to suggestions," Minus said. He was still facing forward. They both were.

"God, Minus, I don't know either. I'm going to leave my personal feelings out of this. But I just keep thinking that there's something I'm not thinking of. Like an option I've overlooked."

"Why would you leave your personal feelings out of this? That seems every bit as important to the situation as anything else at this point."

"Because it gets us nowhere. Nets us nothing but hurt."

"Good God, Callie."

"What."

"You lost both of your loves to the ocean."

"Thanks for putting it in words, Minus. You really have a way, don't you?"

"I'm sorry, Callie. I'm just…" He spread his hands then dropped them to his raised knees. "I'm not trying to be crass. I'm just crushed for you. I can't imagine. Not even having a bod-"

"Minus!" she shouted. During that instant it took for the one word to come out of her mouth, she felt her anger rise, hot and fast, into her head. It almost made her dizzy.

"I'm sorry, Callie."

"I sat here and told you I was leaving my personal feelings out of this. I would do a lot flipping better for you to not pick up the slack for me. I have my own way of grieving. Talking about it with a man who doesn't even know what love is just isn't – and never will be – part of it."

He nodded, breathing in slowly. "I'm so sorry. You're right, Callie," he said, spreading his hands again.

"Fine. Just drop it." She was staring at the ring as she twisted it on her finger. Looking at the tiny reflections of light it threw off. Reflections of the can lighting recessed in the ceiling of the theater. That lighting was dimmed to a level that was comfortable for the eyes, but was actually terrible for seeing. When she tried to focus on Minus, she found her eyes shifting in and out of uselessness – dark splotches of shadow appearing in all the wrong places. It was, in fact, when she thought about it, almost nauseating. So instead, she stared at the ring. "I can't think of anything else we can do out here, Matt," she said. The tiny reflections of light spun in her eyes, crazy patterns and movements as she spun the ring.

The ring was gold. It wasn't real gold, of course. Not for a hundred dollars. But it was fourteen-carat-gold-plated. It was pretty enough. She never got compliments on it. But it made her feel special. She had secretly been hoping that someday someone would put something more substantial on her finger. That hope seemed silly now. Two in one year, to the same terrible fate – there was something to that. Was she supposed to be seeing the signs? Was this an omen? Was the ocean telling her to keep to herself? To her studies, her work? "Stay out of this game of love," it could be saying. "Leave the love to the people who know how to handle it."

She lifted her chin and rolled her head around, stretching her neck. Peripherally, she noticed movement on the screen. Her eyes darted back to it and she frowned. Then she was leaning forward, squinting at the picture. "What the hell is that? Minus, Oh my God! What is that?" she screamed.

He was up and alert again, standing in front of his seat. She stood up and jumped over the seat, to join him on his row. "What the fiery fuck?" Minus said, almost too low to hear.

"Minus what is going on?" she said. The screen showed a toppling, turning, splotch of light spinning out of control crossing from the upper right of the screen to the bottom left, then coming from the top left to the bottom right. Then across from the side. Shooting across the screen in crazy directions. The light itself was dim – almost as dim as the lights in the theater ceiling. It was almost hard to tell it was a light. Something was there on the screen. Right in the middle of the light. Something long and dark. It was impossible to tell what it was though, because of the ridiculous spin. But it was getting bigger.

Suddenly she heard footsteps outside the door. The door slammed open, sending chills down her spine. She turned to look at the doorway atop the head of the ramp.

"You seeing this?" asked Nathan. Then he stepped around the corner. There was no need to answer him. He joined her on her row, but stayed at the end. Callie returned her attention to the screen where the light was getting brighter, bigger – but still spinning crazily about.

"Oh my God," Minus said. And then there were more footsteps. And more. Within a minute, there were fifteen more people crowding into the theater. They all remained quiet though.

Minus turned to look toward the door, seeming not to notice the crowd that had formed. He looked through them. "Someone get the crane crew up. Get them on deck!" he shouted, pointing toward the door. The last person to come through the door, a man with a thick beard and thicker spectacles, stopped in his tracks. He smartly turned and left the room with a quickness.

"They're coming," Callie said softly. Her heart was pounding in her chest. It felt like a sledgehammer against a hollow box. She could see the blood distorting her vision as it flowed through her eyes. The light was big enough now to identify. If one could not identify the light directly, one could now definitely recognize the shape of the silhouette in the middle of it. And there was no doubt what was about to happen. Callie gripped the seat in front of her with white knuckles, anticipation and fear closing in quickly.

Minus reached back awkwardly and put his left hand on Callie's shoulder, squeezing. Callie didn't think he was even aware of what he was doing. It was just a natural preparation for something about to happen. The light flipped another time and there was a terrible, tremendous bang somewhere behind them. It sounded like someone had dropped a safe in a warehouse. It shook the boat. Everyone screamed out and involuntarily took a step forward. Callie, who had been holding tightly to the seat back in front of her, rocked forward but quickly caught her balance. The ship was now rocking crazily like they were in the midst of a summer storm on the waves.

The chill of fear and the resounding echo of that horrific crash reverberated through her body. She could feel its chills run up her legs, over her pelvis, through her crotch and up her belly, up her spine and into her neck. It was a crazy sensation. The chills burned in the crown of her head as she watched the screen resolve. The light was no longer spinning. It was, however, moving. Rolling off to one side now. And then she was screaming, "Get out of my way! Move!" as she fumbled down the aisle between the seats. Minus was hot on her tail.

"Make a hole, people!" he shouted. They did. Fifty people cleared a path to let the two MVPs through. Callie ran up the ramp and through the door that someone had mercifully propped open. She felt Minus right on her back. She whipped around the corner, slipped on the wood of the hall and felt his hands in her armpits, helping her back up. On she ran. The door at the far end of the long corridor grew larger in her vision. She ran all out with everything she had. Down the slight slant of the hall, to where it reached its trough, then back up the slight slant of the other side. They were halfway to the door. People stood on the sides of the hall, backs against the wall, trying to stay out of the way for them. She passed an open door where someone was blasting music, obviously completely unaware of what was going on around them. The song, however, seemed a little too appropriate. She would have to think back later about what song it was. But she knew the band. It was One Last Orbit.

She slammed through the door and onto a rainy wooden deck. The night was black but bright. The deck lights illuminated a messy annoying mist falling from the moonless sky. The white rails of the ship stood out against the absolute blackness of the sea beyond. She ran straight up to the rail, no intention of slowing. She let the rails be her brakes. She slammed into the bar, letting the force of her run bend her over it to look below. She almost went over the damn thing.

Below, she could see the lower deck of the ship. Minus had turned left instead of slamming into the railing, and she noticed he was now halfway down the stairs. Clearly, he was more familiar with the layout of the ship, so now she chased him. She slipped on the deck again, but didn't fall, and was halfway down the stairs before her feet hit anything solid. Whipping around the rail at the end of the landing, she jumped down half the next flight, letting her hands slide along the cold wetness of the metal. She landed at the bottom, slipped again, and this time went down. Her knees cracked against the wooden deck and she cried out in sharp pain. But she got back up, and limp-ran after Minus, who was approaching the railing on the port side of the ship, where the crane crew all had spotlights and were looking down into the water. Again, she slammed into the rail, almost going over, but Minus was there this time with his hand on her butt, to keep her from completing the flip. There, below, in the cold dark water, was the scout. It bobbed like a lifeless depth charge, rolling on the slight motion of the water, giving no indication of what was going on inside. There were no windows. Callie had won that stupid battle, and now regretted it. Two men were already suited up, full wet suits, and were checking each other's tanks. One turned to face the other and secured his mask in place, popping his octopus into his mouth, and Callie's heart flooded with love. These were the men who would jump down there and attach the hook to the sub, bringing her Jack back to her. At least this time she would have someone to bury. Unless, of course, luck was finally on her side. If just this once, the God she had not prayed to in too long would have a bit of mercy on her, maybe, just maybe… She did not allow the thought to prosper in her mind. She looked up at the sky instead. There were no stars out. Too many clouds. The misty rain wet her face, her eyelashes, and she prayed. "God, please. God, please. Just this once, answer my prayer," she whispered. Minus was running to the end of the rail, saying something frantically to the men, and then they were taking long strides off the edge of the deck. One at a time, they dropped into the water and popped back up, like fishing corks, giving Minus the OK sign. He put his hand atop his head, returning the gesture, and running comically down the plank never letting go of the rail. He was shouting down at them. The crane swung into motion and the cable started dropping. A spotlight burst into life, swinging wide and dropping its light down onto the water below. Suddenly, the submersible was washed in bright white light. The dark gray metal of its hull was covered with some sort of film. It looked like glue or something. Though it seemed to be transparent, she noticed the way the water stuck to it, not pouring off like a typical object in the ocean would. The men swam to opposite sides of the craft and tried to hold on, looking up at the hook as it lowered to the water. When it clanged against the solid steel of the sub, one of them lifted a hand and gave the OK sign again. And then they were pulling against the small seams and affordances where steel came together, spinning the sphere in search of the gudgeon loop. They found it finally and clipped the hook through it easily. And it was then that Callie finally noticed that the propulsion cage was missing. Completely gone. How had a solid steel framework that wrapped the sub entirely just disappeared? The diver gave yet another OK sign, and then they were backing off, swimming away from the craft as the crane started pulling in cable. The clank and whine of the chain as it went over the pulley was like sweet music to Callie's ears. And within five minutes, the sphere hung, slowly swinging, at eye level. A crew of men in yellow jumpsuits was guiding it back in over the launchway, pulling it slowly to its resting cradle. Callie clasped her hands in front of her face, standing in place, bouncing softly with anticipation and hope. Hope. And prayer in her heart. She was mouthing the words of prayer constantly, but no sounds formed in her throat. She stood with mist turning to water on her face, her hair. It was running down her back, inside her clothes. She was already soaked. The bright lights shut off with a loud clack, and she had to let her eyes adjust as flashlights took over. They were at work on the portal. It took a special tool that had to be connected from the outside. And then there was a hiss she wasn't entirely sure she actually heard. She just knew to expect it. And the portal was open. It dropped to the floor of the ship with a crack against the wood, and settled into place like a coin at the end of its spin. Steam escaped from the darkness of the interior of the sub. One of the men with a head lamp stepped up and put his hands on the edge of the opening, standing on his toes to peer into the sub. Then he turned to face the crowd that had gathered there on the launch deck of the ship. It was two in the morning. The only light in the world came from the deck of that ship. The mist continued to drizzle down out of a detached and uncaring sky. Callie looked up at that sky again, hands clasped in front of her face, wondering, silently, if the God behind those clouds could see through them. If he could hear through them. And if he had heard her silent prayers.

Callie sat by the window, staring at the slow-moving tiles and patchwork of earth from thirty thousand feet above. The hum and shush sound of the engines lulled her into a sleepy haze. Thoughts of the previous weeks flowed by like silent moving pictures in her mind, ghosts of a time out of reach. A soft tap on the shoulder and a soft voice requested her attention from the aisle.

"Can I get you another bloody mary?" Callie looked down at her plastic cup, still full of stained ice and shook her head. She tried to smile, but didn't feel like it came out as intended. She was still lost in thought, dangling on the edge of sobriety. Drinking at altitude never made her feel like she wanted; never made her feel like it did on the ground. But somehow she always gave it another chance. The thoughts of yesterdays and previous weeks kept bubbling back to the surface of her thoughts. Perfect clarity into a world she had no power over. Walter had gone to the pen. When would she get to talk to him again? To see him again? Her heart ached for him. For Thevi, as well. She could not help but blame herself for his going away. Her ridiculous outburst in the courtroom had no doubt swayed the judge to move for a trial. She could not, of course, be held responsible for the opinions of the jurors. But what if the only reason he had to face that jury was because of her crazy episode in front of the judge? And what if something happened and she never made it back from Fiji? What if something happened to *him* before she made it back? What if that stupid exchange they halfway shared in the courtroom that day was the last she ever spoke to him? These and other morbid thoughts were cheap this morning. She couldn't get away from them.

Callie was also very aware that she was running on less than three hours of sleep. Gravity itself seemed to be evident in her belly this morning. All the important things in her life seemed to be flying off in every direction, like toys set on a merry-go-round. Someone had flung the bars, set it to spinning and sent her life into chaos. She had to remind herself that these things were only temporary though. Mr. Lancey had told her that her job was completely secure; to take as much time as she needed before coming back. She felt the undertone in that statement, in that when she did come back, he wanted her fully back. Fresh and ready to get back to it with full strength. But lately she had not felt the drive she had once felt. Was it her career path that constantly put her and her loved ones – well, specifically her loved ones – in danger? In death's way? She had lost Chris because of her stupid desire to sign on to that idiotic chase-the-big-sea-monster project. What had they been thinking? So they had found the monster, but didn't know what to do with it when they made contact. Someone had seriously dropped the ball there, and she was fearful that it might have been her. How do you go after something and not plan for the inevitable contingency you'll face when you catch it? Ridiculous. In reality, she had probably written it off to that disconnected skepticism wherein she didn't seriously believe they would ever find the Bloop. Or that it even existed. She was just playing Minus's little game. For the glory of creating, inventing, designing – and for the money. She had accepted the check. But she had also made herself a pact: she would use that to fund her investigation of the Atlas catastrophe. Use Royal's own money to bring them down. If it cost every penny of that million dollars, she would spend it. And gladly.

Maybe when she finished that, she would take a vacation for a while. Take Mr. Lancey at his word, and just sail the globe for a year to come back down. To reconnect to earth. Well, she reconsidered, maybe she wouldn't do much sailing at all. Maybe she would never set foot on a boat again. Though in hindsight that hadn't ever been the problem at all, had it? It was when she tried her hand at going under – or sending her loved ones under – that things went sideways. Jack was alive, thank God. So was Codi. They had lost Richard Baltey, but Callie didn't really know him. A little too close to home for comfort, it was, and indeed, Jack and Codi had almost been lost. When they had cracked open the submersible, the two were beat up pretty badly. Still strapped in their seats, unconscious and starving, running very low on oxygen, they were alive. Maybe barely, but they were alive. It became obvious pretty quickly that they had not run out of oxygen because there were only two of them left breathing it. Callie was just thankful for being heard.

Codi was a mess. She was unlikely to ever again go into a confined space. That whole debacle had ruined a part of her that most people never had. Most people, Callie included, were born with the fear of close spaces. Being closed in one – locked in one – was a quick way to send her packing, leaving the city limits of sanityville. Codi had been one of the odd ones; to be born without that switch, only to find it later in life due to a traumatic experience… Callie shivered. Poor girl might be scarred for life. She couldn't imagine what it had been like for Codi. Not only was she trapped in a sub she couldn't get out of, but everything had gone wrong, they had been attacked by some otherworldly squid-like thing and held underwater. On top of all that, she was seeing-impaired. *Jeez.* Callie couldn't imagine the fear she had gone through, but was – all the same – secretly thankful it had not been her.

Jack and Codi were both on bed rest. They had both spent several days in the hospital. Jack had some broken ribs, for which, the doctor had said, there was nothing they could do. It would just take time and rest. Codi had broken her arm and a collarbone. Callie was so happy to have them back. Especially Jack. It had taken everything in her power not to just jump on him, smothering him with hugs and kisses in the light mist of that cold night on the ship. Elation, excitement, dizzying fear... They had all been present and close that night. It had been hard to leave his bedside at the hospital. To take this trip, where anything could happen. And she didn't even know how long she would be gone. But it was something she felt called to do.

She had an internal obligation to find out what had happened on the Atlas, and why Brian Bradley had gotten away. Why had he left the others to die? She had seen the video a hundred times now, watching it over and over on her phone – studying it. She always saw the same things though. Which was to say nothing. Nothing stuck out at her. Why had someone chosen to send her that one particular clip? Why that one? Why show her the crash into the planet? She knew Discovery Channel had put many cameras on board the ship. They had tasked the late little girl, Shanna King, with operating and managing the inventory. So surely there must be hundreds of hours of video from that ship. And someone had gotten some of it back – maybe all of it. How had they gotten the videos? It was obviously someone who knew Callie's email address, too. Someone who, therefore, potentially knew Callie. Callie could not place who that could be though. Just about everyone from the Oliver Company was dead now.

Callie took a deep breath and looked out the window again. They were no longer over land. She was finally out over the great ocean. She stretched her legs and pulled her blanket up close to her chin. Closed her eyes. Thought of where she was going. Why she felt everything was spinning out of control. She was pretty good, usually, at holding things together. Why though, was every project she touched doomed to some kind of failure? Maybe she wasn't as good as she had thought she was. She knew she had been a good scientist, at least at one point in her career. But maybe her ideas were too far-fetched. Maybe she was too out-of-the-box for anything to ever realistically stand a chance at working. Maybe she was in the wrong field.

She was paid very well, and she sure had fun doing what she did. Who got a check for a million dollars? *That never happens to anyone!* But at the end of the day, where did that leave her? If she had all the money she could ever need, but no one to spend it on, no kids to spoil with huge gifts, no husband to pamper and spoil with random acts of love: a new wrench with a bow left on the kitchen table; a new hammer or power drill left by his sink; a new sports car in the garage... She suddenly realized the startling dichotomy that if she had the other but not the one, she would have neither. The pampering only existed with the high-paying job. The love and family time only existed without it. What was she missing? She reckoned she had better get busy if any of that was ever to happen. Was Jack the right one? She didn't want to rush anything with him. Or anyone, for that matter. Didn't want to force something just to get busy making a family. It had to be right. He sure seemed right. Time would tell. There was that word again. Time.

As almost a physical shock, she realized with startling clarity that she did want children. She wanted a bunch of them! She wanted to be a mommy. To get up in the night and pick her little bundle of warmth up out of a crib and hold him 'til he stopped crying. To soothe him and sing to him and smother him with kisses and love. She wanted to pop open the buttons on her flannel pajamas and hold him to her breast, to give him life, to provide something no one else on the planet could provide, at a moment's notice. Now, at almost forty years old, she felt like she was probably too late for the party. Her prude and delicate sensibility had kept her on the bench, and she had most likely missed out on all the fun.

She felt her stomach tremble as she sat against the window, chin resting on closed knuckles. The tears were stinging her eyes, threatening to break through. She worried though, that once they started, she would not be able to stop until the cry was ready to stop. She would not be in control of that. But she couldn't stop the train of thoughts that steamed through her mind like an angry, sad and lonely locomotive. She had been through so much emotional trauma in the last few months. On top of a childhood she had never quite found a reckoning for, she was like an emotional time bomb. Callie had lost her mother when she was young, and her father had never really been in the picture at all. A failed attempt at a relationship at twenty-two had been her only real connection to him. She had managed to find him, contact him and even hear back. But it became quickly evident that nothing had changed. He had no more desire to be a part of her life now than he did when she was born. Was it her fault? Was she not good enough for her daddy to love her? She didn't think that was supposed to be how it played out, but she was still living on the thoughts and reasoning of a child in that department. As a child she had believed that he would come back if she acted a certain way. If she were just a good enough girl, he would be forced to reassess the scenario and he would have no choice but to love her. To want her. How could a man not love his little girl when she was so good? She followed all the rules, and always brushed her teeth, even though her mom didn't watch her to make sure. She always put her dishes away and made her own lunches and helped with the laundry. She even fed the dog, proudly putting on the shoes of an adult when mommy couldn't be bothered to remember. And many were the time she sat waiting on the front steps of the porch for daddy to come pick her up for the movie. She never even knew what movie they were supposed to be seeing. She trusted daddy would take care of the hard decisions. She just wanted him to take her. To pick her up and kiss her chin and hold her hand while they walked into the theater together. She wanted to snuggle against his warm shoulder while the movie played, and show off while she walked through the mall with him. This is *my* daddy! See what a great daddy I have? But he never showed. In all the years and all the times he promised this would be the day he would come... this would be the evening it would all change... he never did. She wasn't good enough.

She took a deep breath, stuttered and riddled with the pressure of holding back the cry, and wiped her eyes. She needed to get herself out of this funk. To stop thinking about the negatives and start appreciating how far she had made it *without* the support of her parents. So what, daddy had abandoned her. How could she really miss and love someone she didn't know? Oh, but she did. Her heart felt heavy like the weight of a safe sat upon it. And the combined weight of an empty childhood with the last several months of chaotic ramblings, she could not push it away. It was just too heavy. It was coming. She realized it was now inevitable. The cry was coming, and she would not be able to stop it. The best she could do was hope to make it to the lavatory before it could explode.

Callie popped the buckle on her seat belt and stood, sliding out into the first-class aisle and moved forward, hand on her forehead, trying to shield her eyes from the other passengers. Thankfully, most of them were asleep or simply paying her no attention. She made it to the small accordion door and pushed into the tiny cramped compartment, sliding the latch, and then it was here. The cry arrived with the force of a tractor truck, slamming her full in the chest, causing her wracking pain and tightness in her chest. And as she bent toward the sink, eyes overwhelmingly heavy with pain, the sobs came forward. They took over completely. She let the grief break through, and spilled her tears full force into the compact sink, covering her mouth to stifle the wails. And for a long time, nothing else mattered.

The rest of the flight was spent in misery. Callie sat staring out the window, trying to keep the tears from resurfacing. She had cried hard and long and loudly in the bathroom, thinking she had gotten it all out. But it kept threatening to rise back to the surface. She practiced long-forgotten relaxation techniques she had learned from a yoga class many years before. Yoga seemed to her to be one of those practices that if you fell out of it, you were likely to look back on it with skepticism and wonder as to why you had wasted your time with it to begin with.

Callie tossed the rest of her bloody mary when the attendant came by with a bag. She had spared herself future headache by cutting herself off after that first cocktail, opting instead for a Coke, but it stood sweating and untouched in the little indention on the seat back tray in front of her. And they were now well out over the ocean. The ocean sparkled and sang like bright blue crystals, though it seemed to move in slow motion from this height. None of the waves looked to be in any serious hurry. Why did she feel so rushed?

They would be flying into Nadi, on the western side of the largest Fijian island. From there, she would be taking a taxi to Suva, where she would await a helicopter to come fly her into the Royal outpost. The outpost itself was about twenty kilometers north of Suva, surrounded by dense forest, and nearly invisible from above. There was simply no way in or out but by helicopter. And only then by strict invitation. The Fiji office, it was said, was the highest security Royal complex in the world, and mostly because of its remote location. It took an act of will so strong just to get to the island, that anyone serious enough to even try it would have to be nothing short of professional, and professionally funded. Callie had worked for Royal for about eight years of her adult life, but had only just become aware the Fiji outpost was even a reality. It was one of those nighttime fairy tales that seemed more rumor and hearsay than anything else. No one was ever quite sure if it was all just a joke – the supposed 'Fiji Location' that people got sent to occasionally. Like the upper levels of a secret society, only a select few ever really found out about it. Well, unless Royal was playing an incredibly expensive card just to keep the joke alive, Callie was going to find out.

After years of unrest and unsure about what had happened to the Atlas Crew, Callie felt like she was perhaps on the verge of discovery. She was near the turning of that all-important page that would show the true faces of the enemy and give her the final say in their fate. She felt empowered. Here stood a five-foot-five waif of a woman, barely over 115 pounds, arms as skinny as walking sticks, and not an ounce of physical fight in her. But she was empowered. This was her Hail Mary. If she failed here, she would likely never go at it again. This was it. Her swan song. Her last-ditch effort to connect the final two dots of a mysterious puzzle in which the shape only comes clear at completion. And beyond that, she was out of options.

Taking a deep breath, she pushed her seat back a few inches and tried to close her eyes. The rushing sound of the air outside the cabin was peaceful and consistent, and her ears had built up some pressure that she had not yet relieved by yawning or swallowing. It provided a padded buffer of silence within which she could find some peace. And after a few minutes, she was out.

A loud *Ding!* woke her with a start, and Callie realized she had been sleeping so hard she was snoring. Her chin was wet with drool and her neck was cranked around so her face was pressed against the back of the seat, her legs curled up beneath her and arms covered in goose flesh. She looked around cautiously but no one was paying her any mind. Everything was still very muted. She swallowed several hard gulps of her soda and heard her ears pop; a world of noise washed back into her senses. She was back among the living.

Callie sat up and dug through her purse and found a compact, then snapped it open to have a glance at her face. *Oh, brother.* It was a sad sight. Her eyes and face were red and puffy, and her cheek was creased with leather stitching from the seat. Her hair was a wreck, too. Leaving her shoes beneath the forward seat, she sneaked to the bathroom one more time to freshen up and run some mouthwash through her teeth.

When she returned to her seat, Callie found a tray awaiting there with a hot plate with a plastic cover holding a hot, damp rag. She slipped into her seat belt and put the rag against her face. It felt wonderful and helped revive her spirits more than the water in the lav had done. Looking out the window, she could still see nothing but the sea, and it was growing dark. She could already see evidence of a few hundred million stars and had to take a deep breath. It was spectacular. She pushed her face up against the plastic window, feeling its cold, but could not see far enough forward to see the island yet, and reckoned she might not ever see it at all from the air. The airport was pretty close to the water, according to the moving map in the small computer screen on the seat back in front of her.

The crew came on saying they would be on the ground shortly, and to please return seat backs to their upright position. She did so and trembled with anxiety and excitement for the days to come. Hopefully, she thought, they would be short days, and not very many of them. She was already ready to get back to Jack and find out what that path in her future held. She wasn't sure where she would go. But she did know one thing. She would be staying far away from the oceans. If this thing with Jack turned into something major, something big, this ocean avoidance policy might become permanent. She swallowed as the plane rumbled, the landing gear extending. The sound of the new drag filled the cabin. The air rushing by her window now was Fijian air. The mythical place where the legends ended up. She was close. She felt close. Her next breaths of non-circulated air would be on that little island of so many dreams. What would she find waiting for her there? If not glory, then at least a reckoning? An answer? Or would that page she turned just be a flyleaf? A blank page left to confuse her, to add to the riddle? Whatever the answer was, she was determined now to find it. Callie Simmons was on a mission now. And hellbent to finish it.

As the plane touched down, she stretched, then looked around the cabin. It was darker outside; by the time she got her bags and found a taxi, the darkness would be complete. All alone on a foreign island with nothing but an idea and a desire to spend it. She trembled with anxiety. And then she got up. Her purse, beneath the seat in front of her, sat against the foot rail. As she scooted out into the aisle, she had no more thought of it than she did the weather in Phoenix. She shouldered her carry-on and made her way up the aisle, past the flight attendants, and into the jetway. A new breath of determination in her lungs and a new gait in her step, she walked boldly up the carpeted mobile hall, chin up and hands in her pockets. Callie Simmons was done with failure. Done with falling short. She was unstoppable now. For the short foreseeable future, she was on her own. No one else to bring down but the bad guys. And she had all the time in the world. She smiled at that, and marched into the murky, shadowed face of her next big mystery.